FLOODTIDE

ASH FITZSIMMONS

FLOODTIDE

HALL OF THORNS, BOOK FOUR

Print Edition ISBN: 978-1-949861-49-5

Cover design by MiblArt.

www.ashfitzsimmons.com

CHAPTER 1

I held it together on the drive out to my great-aunt's house on Christmas Day. Even though my heart was breaking, even though I kept my thoughts focused on the driving beat of Metallica and Guns N' Roses coming from the radio so as to ignore my rising panic that I'd never see the man I loved again, I clutched at my composure like a rope chucked over a quicksand pit and told myself that everything would be fine.

This was just a nasty little blip. Pateme ti'Tam would relent in time. I'd be allowed back into the Pactlands—or Yven would be allowed out, either way. If I never saw Pateme again, I wouldn't exactly weep bitter tears after this stunt he'd pulled. The important thing was that I'd be reunited with Yven, and then we'd find a way to work past the fact that I hadn't been acknowledged into one of the elven Halls. Neither of my great-grandfathers seemed eager to claim me, a tricky problem to negotiate, but I drove right over that roadblock in my mental effort to prevent myself from making a scene on the side of the Interstate. True, there wasn't much traffic between Richmond and Briardale on Christmas morning, but I didn't want some well-meaning state trooper pulling over and catching me in the middle of a crying jag.

So I sucked it up all the way to Aunt Lily's tiny mountain town, which still bore refrozen piles of gray snow from the recent blizzard. I told myself I was a strong, independent woman as I slowed on the winding road up to her house, trying not to think of the escape I'd made just six days before in a convoy of Pact law enforcement, plowing through the night as the nymph in the lead simply lifted the thick snow off the road to give us passage. I reminded myself that Aunt Lily had made a lovely meal for us as I turned up the steep gravel driveway toward her nursery, saw the shop—finally still after the holiday rush—and imagined Yven behind the counter, wrapping poinsettias as I badly belted Christmas carols. I took a deep breath as I parked, then put on a smile as Aunt Lily emerged from her cottage in her old pink polka dot apron and waved at me.

"Hello, darling! Come on in, it's freezing," she called, then paused, the wrinkled brow of her magical mask furrowing. "Where's Yven? Did something come up?"

I looked back at her for a moment, my dear great-aunt, who'd surely set the table for three and had probably already prepared mugs for mulled wine, and that's when my brittle composure crumbled into angry, hitching sobs.

Bless her, Aunt Lily was the closest thing to a grandmother I'd ever known and the only family I had left, and she swooped into action. She hustled me into the house, and before I knew it, my coat was thrown onto the couch, my head was bent over the kitchen sink, and she'd draped a cool rag on the back of my neck. She kept me standing there like a little kid—in fairness, I *was* more than three hundred years her junior—until I could breathe well enough that I wasn't at risk of making myself vomit, and then she pulled me into her arms and shushed me while my fit ran its course. Once I'd calmed, she murmured, "Next time Agent ti'Ansha comes out here for my inspection, I'll let Sally kill that son of a bitch. Occupational hazard."

I pulled away from her and wiped my eyes on my sleeve. "Yven won't be doing your inspections anymore. This is all Pateme's fault."

"Pateme?" she echoed, her brown eyes narrowing. "What's my dear uncle done now? Wait, drink this first," she ordered, pressing a mug of wine into my hands as my lip began to tremble again. "Come on, Rosie, sit down. Talk to me."

Though there was no one around but the two of us, I appreciated that Aunt Lily kept her mask on. Until the previous spring, I'd thought that was her natural appearance: five-foot-two, sinewy from years of work in the garden nursery, white-haired, gnarled-knuckled, and creased with age. She was blonde, in truth, with a complexion as smooth as mine, but her cheekbones were higher, her teeth sharper, and her ears rose to points. Aunt Lily was fully elven beneath the mask, after all. As for me, while I might have inherited talent from her brother and my other grandfather, my looks were decidedly human. Now that I'd known Aunt Lily's secret for a few months, I didn't find it disturbing when she unmasked, but I took comfort that day in the familiarity of the face I'd always known as I stumbled through recent events.

I'd awakened Yven from a siren's hypnotic spell. That meant he loved me, and I loved him—it wouldn't have worked any other way. True, the siren had been trying to kill us, and I'd done at least two Pact agencies a solid by helping to bring him down, but the disastrous secret was out. Once Pateme learned of it and I was out of the Pactlands, he'd revoked my portal credentials and Yven's, then turned off the function of Yven's DPP-assigned phone that allowed him to make calls to numbers like mine. While Yven's phone could register calls from outside the Pactlands, he could no longer answer them, and text messages were similarly one-way. If Yven tried to get around the director's new rules by quitting his job, then Pateme would tell Yven's family that he was contemplating taking the death draught for me, and that would land Yven in whatever passed for psychiatric care among the magical set. Never mind the fact that I'd told him numerous times not to even consider the draught—I'd be damned if he condemned himself to a premature grave to spend a measly couple decades with me. Unfortunately for us, Pateme had sat back and let Aunt Lily's brother take the draught in order to be with my grandmother, and so, determined not to lose another lovelorn agent to a slow suicide, he was taking no chances. Yven's best friend, Pars Mera, had broken into my house like a deranged Santa in tactical black that morning to deliver a Christmas gift from Yven and the news that left me weeping on Aunt Lily's old couch.

She listened without interruption, merely nodding as I spoke. "Did you know?" I finally asked, sniffling over my half-emptied mug. "That he loves me?"

"Oh, darling," she murmured, reaching out to tuck a strand of hair behind my ear. "I'm not *blind*. And I'm going to fix this," she added, rising from the couch. "Now, where did I leave that darn phone?"

"You can't."

She turned and regarded me quizzically. "I most certainly can call my uncle and chew him out. It's Christmas here, but it's just another Wednesday in the Pactlands. He'll be in the office."

"No—he doesn't know that I know what's going on," I explained. "Gentle Breeze made up a bullshit assignment to send Pars to Richmond so he could tell me why Yven hasn't been answering my calls. I don't want to get them in trouble."

"*Ah.*" She folded her arms and pursed her lips. "I knew I liked that woman," she said, but she scowled into space.

I was grateful to Pars and Gentle Breeze alike. The formidable Interdiction chief had been a friend of my grandfather's, and she'd almost taken me under her wing of late. If the troll in charge said I was all right, then the rest of Interdiction went along with it. Unfortunately, she answered to Pateme, and so she'd done what she could for me on the sly.

"Well, this is bullshit," Aunt Lily finally declared. "*How* many agents' lives did you save last week? Four?"

"Plus the two detectives, if we're counting," I muttered. "I mean…I get where Pateme is coming from, and I know Yven and I can't be together as long as I'm unacknowledged, but—"

"But after Friday, you should damn well be acknowledged," she interrupted. "Three times, now, you've come through for DPP and Laws. Father is…probably not an option," she admitted, "but if Diriem ti'Dana won't step up and acknowledge another farseer into that Hall, let alone his great-granddaughter, then surely someone on the Forum could find a workaround. Pateme has connections—he could make a case for you."

"He won't. I even asked about getting acknowledged into ti'Tam through your mother, right, but he doesn't think she would want to upset Inade." Pateme's mother was the lady of Hall ti'Tam, but her son-in-law—Inade ti'Cren, Aunt Lily's father and my other great-grandfather—outranked her.

"He's probably not wrong, but there has to be an option out there," Aunt Lily mused. "Diriem married a ti'On girl, as I recall—you'd have just as much claim to her Hall as you would to ti'Tam." Resuming her seat beside me, she took my hands and gave them a firm squeeze. "As soon as I can tell Pateme what a cruel idiot he is without blowing your friends' cover, I will. Mark my words, darling." She paused, then asked, "Are you hungry? Or do you want to do presents?"

Aunt Lily tried so hard to keep the holidays special for me after my parents' deaths, and I didn't want to ruin everything by blubbering all day, so I pulled myself together and told her that lunch sounded nice. As usual, she'd spared no expense, and she was a fantastic cook when she set her mind to it. While lunch that day tasted like sawdust in my mouth, I ate every bite and tried to smile for her.

Though I hadn't brought so much as a toothbrush with me to Briardale, I spent the night with Aunt Lily, as she wouldn't hear of me going home to my empty house on Christmas. We curled up in her cozy den by the fireplace and watched movies for much of the day—she was partial to comedies and had a fat stack of DVDs and VHS tapes to choose from—and by midafternoon, I told her I wouldn't mind if she dropped the mask. She made a gesture in front of her face, and suddenly, there she was, still sporting one of the worn denim work shirts she favored but physically my peer. Losing her wrinkles didn't end her no-nonsense mothering, however, and I let her bring me mugs of warm wine and afghans against the chill as the sun went down in the mountains.

I slept the sleep of the depressed and slightly overserved that night, and when I woke in the darkness in the guest bedroom, I briefly panicked when I couldn't find Gentle Breeze and Enva Orafer on the floor. That was last week, I told myself as I reoriented. The Interdiction chief and the DOL detective were back in the Pactlands, presumably tucked in their own beds instead of making the best of air mattresses in the cottage. Liogh Birrid, Enva's third, wasn't snoring like a chainsaw in the den, Emarae ti'Mal and Pars weren't camped by the fireplace, and Yven—

In my mind's eye, I saw him standing in the kitchen in Aunt Lily's pink apron, grinning at me as he pulled his perfect biscuits from the oven, and bit my knuckle to keep from crying again.

Alone behind closed doors, I admitted to myself what I'd tried so hard in recent months to deny: I loved him. I loved his smile, his gentleness, his ridiculous knowledge of plants. I loved how his idea of casual attire involved collared shirts at his most reckless. I loved that he made vanilla extract from an orchid he grew in his *apartment*, in the freaking Pactlands, where almost nothing grew without significant magical assistance, and yet he treated his accomplishment like it wasn't anything special. I loved how he'd sneaked over to spend the weekend with me and teach me the rudiments of magic for months, using painting lessons as his cover story—and then he'd worked so diligently to actually learn to paint. I loved how he'd blushed to the tips of his ears the first time I kissed his cheek.

I loved the way he looked at me when he didn't think I was watching him.

And unless someone acknowledged me, I'd lost him forever.

I understood why the peoples of the Pact didn't want humans around. You don't pick up and move into your own homemade pocket world without *really* good cause, and to be fair, humans have a long history of not even getting along with each other. But I wasn't just human—both of my grandfathers had been elves from high-ranking Halls. My paternal grandfather, Fradin ti'Cren, had been a DPP agent like Yven before abandoning his life—and apparently, incurring his father's unending ire—to be with the redheaded schoolteacher who'd captured his heart. My maternal grandfather, Caradin ti'Dana, had been a farseer for the Division of Intelligence—an impressive résumé before factoring in his pedigree. His father, Diriem, had surrendered his throne and brought his people into the Pactlands to save them from extinction, making Caradin, if not precisely royalty, quite close. I knew a bit about Fradin from Aunt Lily, who had fiercely loved her little brother, but Caradin remained largely a cipher. The only person I'd met who'd discussed him was Liogh, and the detective hadn't gone into any detail.

Neither of my parents had ever told me much about their extended families. Dad had lost his father at eight and his mother at twenty-three, and according to Aunt Lily, he hadn't known that his father wasn't human until he was twenty-one, when she unmasked to prove that his mother hadn't been pulling his leg. His mother's parents had died young, leaving Dad alone with only Aunt Lily for family. She said that the silence from her family wounded him, but she always insisted that he was safer if no one else in Hall ti'Cren knew of his existence. Like Dad, Mom had lost her parents early—her father at fourteen, and her mother a few months before my birth—but she had no other family. She kept a few pictures of her parents in albums and told me about growing up on a tiny farm outside of Charlottesville, but she never dwelled on her childhood. More importantly, neither of my parents ever mentioned to me that they were half elven, though untalented and mortal, thanks to the continuing effects of the death draught their fathers had taken. Still, I'd have been interested in learning *that* fun factoid before Yven stumbled into my life and discovered that the potion that had killed my grandfathers and stunted my parents hadn't affected me in the slightest. I might have looked human, but I could manipulate magic just like any other elf.

Unfortunately, my genes alone didn't cut it. Unless one of my great-grandfathers accepted me into his Hall—or the lord or lady of any other Hall I might conceivably claim took pity on me—then I would remain legally human. If Yven wanted me, his only option would be the draught, which would rob him of his talent and, all too soon, his life.

I could understand why Pateme didn't want me around—hell, I didn't want Yven in the same room as the draught. But comprehension of the problem didn't stop my heart from aching in the darkness.

Aunt Lily invited me to stay longer—as an independent artist, I didn't have to open my studio the day after Christmas—but I needed the normalcy. Returning to Richmond midmorning, I unlocked the door, put on a massive pot of coffee, and picked up where I'd left off on my latest commission. My December schedule had been wrecked by my unplanned field excursion, and I owed my clients a finished canvas. I didn't mind working while the rest of Carytown either slept in or exchanged unwanted sweaters from well-meaning relatives. Frankly, concentrating on getting the shading of the rosy-cheeked toddlers' dewy baby skin *just* right kept my mind off both Yven and the previous week. I supposed the detectives and the Interdiction agents were accustomed to being shot at while on the job, but that had been a new experience for me, and one I hoped not to repeat any time soon. My unconscious mind wouldn't let it go, however, and over the last days, I'd caught flashes of guns and flying bullets in my dreams. I needed the distraction of my oils and of the laughing Paulson twins.

But on Friday morning, after another rough night, I decided to give myself a day at home in sweatpants. I took down my Christmas tree and packed the ornaments away, put up the few holiday knickknacks I'd pulled from storage, and dusted, swept, and polished until the house smelled like lemons. Feeling productive with a clean home under my belt, I thought about the basement and my annual effort to work through the debris. Ordinarily, I made it my New Year's resolution to sort the boxes and bags of junk my parents had squirreled away over the years, but I had yet to make it past my record of six boxes before getting bogged down by sentimentality and a crippling inability to throw away anything Mom and Dad had touched. To that point, my resolution had been abandoned by February, and it was rapidly becoming tradition.

This year would be different, I told myself as I descended to the basement. I was a whole year older now. Tougher. *Way* more magically talented. If I could hold together a shield while a siren shot at my face, then surely I could throw away my parents' old copies of *National Geographic*.

My resolve began to falter as I stepped onto the

concrete floor. I seldom came down to the basement—I wasn't afraid of it, but the place was poorly lit and smelled of must and damp, and the boxes spilled forth memories like ghosts. I just had to find a good beginning point. Not my parents' record collection, not my baby clothes—been there, failed at that—not the plastic bins of their old college T-shirts…

I decided to work from the back and move forward, saving the stuff I knew to be problematic for me until last. If my parents had buried boxes in the far corners of the basement, then maybe I wouldn't find anything quite so sentimentally triggering in there. Armed with a can of Raid and a broom to defend myself against cobwebs, I cleared a path through the dusty cardboard and black lawn bags to the other side of the basement, steeling myself to be merciless. Mom and Dad weren't hiding somewhere down here, and surely they wouldn't look down on me from the Great Beyond in disappointment if I threw away a rusty card table or a bunch of paperbacks they'd meant to donate and forgotten.

The first box I tackled was surprisingly easy: old Tupperware and what appeared to be plastic Jell-O molds, discolored with use and gross from their time underground. I carried the lot to the steps, dusted my hands off, and returned to work, already proud of myself. Below that was a box of computer supplies that I vaguely recognized as having belonged to my dad's first IBM PC, dirty gray cords, moisture-warped instruction booklets, and floppy diskettes almost the size of sandwich bread. Nope, nothing I needed in there, I told myself, and carried that box to the stairs to join its condemned comrade.

The third box, however, stopped me in my tracks.

It was large, about four feet long and maybe three feet wide and deep, and the cardboard clearly had some age on it. There were no identifying markings on the visible front of the box. Only after I'd moved Dad's computer junk was the label on the sealed top revealed: a single word, *Rose*.

That there was a box in my parents' basement with my name on it was hardly a shock. I was their only kid, and they'd hoarded all my childhood toys and art projects like relics.

No, the curious thing about *this* box was that my name was written in the Elvish script—not the word for "rose," but rather my name, phonetically rendered into neat loops and swirls.

CHAPTER 2

I stared at the box, trying to make the markings make sense.

Oh, I could *understand* the writing. Thanks to the language potion that had knocked me out for two days the previous May, I could read and speak Pactish and Low Elvish, the languages Yven had been able to offer me. (High Elvish, he'd later explained, was archaic, the sort of thing one briefly studied and deployed at the odd ceremony but never used in conversation.) But why was there a box in my parents' basement labeled with Elvish characters? Had one of my parents been taught their fathers' first language and neglected to mention it? Had Aunt Lily marked a box of my old things while distracted and used the wrong script?

I ripped off the disintegrating packing tape and found the box filled with sealed garbage bags. Opening the one on top, I discovered a weird, heavy piece of machinery. It wasn't until I dug around in the bag and saw the numbered hard cases of reel-to-reel audio tape that I understood what I'd found.

I was never an A/V geek in school, and soundboards were a mystery best left to someone who didn't approach them like a kindergartener offered shiny objects. The closest I'd ever been to an old reel-to-reel player like the one in the box was a photograph. Still, I had to know what was on the tapes, and so I lugged the player upstairs and got online to dig up directions. A few minutes later, having loaded the first tape and somewhat familiarized myself with the controls, I settled in at the kitchen table, quieted the butterflies in my stomach, and started the playback.

The tape popped and hissed briefly, and I heard a throat clear and a chair creak.

"Uh…" a voice began—male, I noticed, and fairly young—and then the speaker broke into a nervous chuckle. "Sorry, this is, uh…well, a little awkward," he said.

I didn't know the voice, but he was speaking Low Elvish.

"Hello, Rosie," he continued. "Um…if you're hearing this, then I'm dead…which is a strange and sobering thought," he added with soft laughter. "I mean, it's inevitable—you and I are…what's the saying? Ships in the night?"

I caught myself nodding at the player.

"And I hate that. Truly, I do. I'd love to meet you in the flesh, little one, but that's never been an option." The recording picked up a quiet sigh. "And here's the really awkward part. I feel like I know you, Rosie—I've known you for so many years, now—and yet, I'm a complete stranger to you."

He sounded kind, I thought—unsure of himself, but kind.

"I suppose an introduction is in order, eh?" he said. "I'm Caradin ti'Dana. Or Caleb Storm, if you prefer. One name's as good as the other. I'm your granddad…well, one of them."

I stopped the tape and stared at the silenced player, stunned.

Caradin. My mother's father had made a giant box of recordings…for *me?*

And he'd called himself my granddad. That was how my brain translated the word, anyway—a much less formal term than *grandfather.*

"Oh, my God," I whispered to the empty kitchen, then got up and rummaged through my mediocre liquor cabinet until I found a bottle of halfway decent rum. Sure, it was barely nine a.m., but my hand shook as I poured, and I clutched the counter as I focused on the burn running down my throat. I desperately wanted to hear what Caradin had to say, but I needed a moment first.

Duly fortified, I returned to the table, glass in hand, and pushed the button to restart the tape.

"It's 1956 here," he resumed. "Thirteenth of January, to be exact, eleven p.m., and Grace just got your mother down to sleep about half an hour ago. She's a good baby, and we love her to pieces, but her sleep schedule could be better. Grace has been amazing, and Jocelyn…I wish you could see her. She's tiny and so beautiful, Rosie. Absolutely perfect. I can honestly say I've never been happier than I am these days, and considering how little sleep we've had of late, that's saying a lot."

Mom would have been about three months old, I thought. I'd never seen her baby pictures, but she said that we'd looked much alike, both redheaded and gray-eyed—ti'Dana in coloration, if not in any other feature.

Caradin paused and cleared his throat again. "By now, since you're listening to this, you know something about farsight. I'm a farseer, too—or rather, I was," he amended. "Future oriented. I lost the talent when I took the draught four years ago. That's not altogether a terrible thing. We tend to be a lonely bunch because others often look at us either like all-knowing oracles or nosy meddlers. Neither characterization is entirely true. I mean, I do—I *did*," he caught himself—"see future events. I've known since I was twenty-two that I would marry your grandmother and that we'd have your mom, and that I'll die when Jocelyn is a teenager."

He said that far too matter-of-factly, but I supposed he'd been living with the knowledge for a long time.

"I can't tell you the moment of my death—I never saw that with any specificity. But I've extrapolated from other visions, many of which just *came*. It's not as though I ever wanted to see my daughter die," he murmured.

I took another shot of rum.

"And I've seen that, over and over. Not every vision we receive comes to pass—the backward-looking farseers are much more reliable there—but I'm usually right. Unfortunately, I can't warn her. I can't leave her a cryptic note telling her to stay home with Henry on Valentine's Day. I can't *intervene*," he said, strain creeping into his voice, "because I've seen time and again that doing so would end in worse consequences. Oh, no one minds if DOI is able to stop a bomb before it goes off or track down a murderer—with enough farseers on hand to examine the possibilities, you can choose the path of least destruction. But try to save your own child and…well."

His chair squeaked, and I heard the slosh of liquid in a glass.

"The nice part about farsight is that I've seen so much of Jocelyn's life that I'll never live to witness," said Caradin. "The good parts. I know how happy Henry will make her, and I've watched their wedding. I've seen her holding you. Farsight does tend to dim the further one looks into the future, but I watched you grow up so many years before you were born…or will be born. And since this is as close as we'll come to a first meeting, I just want to tell you how proud I am of you, Rosie. You're a remarkable young woman, and I'm *so* very sorry about everything you've struggled through on your own in the last years. If I could be there to hold your hand, I would," he said. "Not possible, of course. But I want you to know that I love you very much…"

Caradin paused to cough.

"I said losing farsight wasn't a terrible thing, didn't I? That's true, but there are drawbacks as well. One of them is that I can't see you anymore. I've known you, in this strange sense, for so much of my life, and now you're…*gone*. You don't exist yet outside of my memory— that, and whatever my dad might see. I don't ask too many questions about that these days. But I do miss you, Rosie. I think of you often. And I hope, whenever you find this, that you understand how loved you were."

I drained my rum and focused on the alcohol, staunchly ignoring the pricking in my eyes.

"Anyway," he said, his voice momentarily husky, "I'm not sure of the particulars of your life right now—in your present, I mean—but I know there will come a time when you'll be cut off from the Pactlands, and you'll need help with your talent. I've actually seen this moment, you know. If I remember correctly, you're sitting alone in a kitchen with this tape recorder in front of you, and you're *drinking*," he added with a hint of disapproval. "Rather early in the morning for that, I'd think."

"Yeah, well, you're not the one on this side of the conversation," I muttered.

"I'm not judging, just trying to prove that I'm not completely insane," said Caradin. "But more to the point, you need a teacher. I'm not the best man for the job—I can't even answer your questions," he said apologetically— "but I'll do what I can to help you along, little one. All right? Maybe we can muddle through this together. I don't have formal lessons planned, but I'll try to teach you what you need to know now."

A faint wailing began in the background of the recording, and Caradin sighed. "And *that* would be your mother. I'd better go. Until we meet again, Rosie, whatever's happened, don't despair. You'll get through this. I love you."

The recording gave way to static again, and I stopped the playback a few seconds before I burst into tears.

There were so many reels of tape in that big box. Caradin would never meet me, but he'd taken the time in the last fourteen years of his life to leave me a record. Even if I didn't learn a damn thing from him, he'd reached out over the uncrossable gulf between us.

I cried to hear my granddad's voice. I cried to hear my

infant mother, alive and possessed of healthy lungs as she demanded attention. And I cried at the knowledge that they were gone now, and all that remained was the tapes.

Those *precious* tapes.

I pushed the play button again, and soon, Caradin's voice returned.

"Hi, Rosie," he said quietly, and yawned. "Sorry. It's, uh…about three in the morning. I'm sitting here with a certain someone who much prefers to sleep in arms than she does in her crib, and all I'll say to that is that she'll get her turn at this soon enough."

I *had* been a rather colicky baby.

"Listen, I'll keep this brief for tonight, but there's something important I forgot to mention. You're a farseer, my darling. Indisputably a farseer, and if I'm correct, your talent is unlike any other farseer's because of its orientation. You have an incredible gift, Rosie." He paused, then said, "At this point, were I a wise tutor, I'd warn you to be responsible with your abilities and not use them to unnecessarily spy on people. Instead, I'm going to remind you that even if you can't get into the Pactlands, that doesn't mean you can't see what's happening over there."

An idea struck me, and my jaw dropped.

"I think you know what to do," said Caradin. "Good night for now."

Too anxious to listen to more of the tapes—and too paranoid of whatever else might be lurking in the basement—I gave up on both for the day and headed to the studio, where at least I could distract myself with the familiar rhythms of work. I turned on my music, alternated between the Paulsons' painting and a landscape in progress, reminded myself to hydrate, and took a long lunch, desperate to make the hours speed by. I had to time my plan just right, but even with distractions, the wait was killing me.

Finally, I let myself drive home around four, then headed straight to my bedroom and made myself comfortable. Keeping my phone close, I concentrated on my breathing until my inner eyes opened…

…and there was Yven.

He'd worn his new robe to work again, the dark gray one with a blue pinstripe. Pateme and the other executives favored heavily embroidered sleeveless robes that looked more like couture than business wear, but Yven was still a young agent, and his taste in professional robes leaned conservative. He sat hunched over his computer in his small, perfectly organized cubicle, typing away. He was probably still chiseling down the pile of work he'd left unattended after being drafted into the search for DPP's missing double agent, I thought.

Stepping into his cube, invisible, inaudible, and insubstantial as a ghost, I glanced at the inner wall by the door and saw that he'd left my little mountain landscape hanging there, hidden from anyone who might walk by and casually peek in. Maybe he just liked the piece, or maybe holding some part of me there in his workspace was a quiet act of rebellion.

I heard footsteps on the thin carpet and looked up to see Pars's hulking form approaching down the line. Unlike the Regulatory agents, Interdiction tended to eschew formal robes for black shirts and trousers, easy to move in and augment with body armor as required. The sorcerer cut a striking figure: seven feet tall and probably three hundred pounds of muscle, with a brown crewcut, mustache, and chinstrap beard, a heavy brow, a twisted nose—casualty of a childhood accident—a deep tan, and an even deeper voice. I could imagine Pars walking out of the office and singlehandedly storming a small fortress. Yven seemed like an utter bureaucrat by comparison—a foot shorter, far slighter in build, with neat, pale blond hair, turquoise eyes, and dimples that made him look a good twenty years younger—but the two had been best friends since they were ten, an odd couple bound by mutual respect.

"Working overtime again?" Pars asked, and belatedly announced his arrival with a rap on the thin wooden wall of the cube.

"Just a little longer," said Yven, spinning a quarter-turn in his chair. "Finishing this report."

He sounded exhausted, I thought, and the shadows under his eyes told me I wasn't too far off.

"It can wait until Monday, can't it? You've been here late every night this week," Pars chided. "Canna took the afternoon off and made a roast. Come join us, eh?"

Yven's smile was brief and polite. "Thanks, but I—"

"But what? Your orchids won't mind if you're out for a while. And you can help distract the girls before they decide I need another manicure," he added, waggling his fingers.

"I appreciate it—"

"You need to be with people," said Pars, looming over the cubicle and lowering his voice. "And not just in the breakroom. We're worried about you, brother."

The smile Yven produced that time offered slightly more warmth. "Really, I'm not on the edge of the cliff."

The sorcerer shrugged. "Never said *that*. I've seen my share of depression, that's all. Seriously, we'd love to have you. Tonight, later this weekend...we're taking the kids hiking at Green Lake tomorrow morning, but there's plenty of room on the trail for you."

"I'll be fine," said Yven, and reached up to grip Pars's arm. "But thank you, I mean it. I just...I need some time, yeah?"

Though Pars seemed unconvinced, he let it go. "You'll call me if you want to talk, right? Or if something comes up? With the twins, there's no telling when I'll be awake, so you can call me whenever you like."

"Thanks."

The two said their goodnights, and I lingered while the other agents headed for the elevators and Yven finished his work. No one else stopped by to chat, and I wondered what rumors had entered circulation in the last week.

Finally, Yven turned off his computer and gathered his things, and I followed him down to the parking garage. His red Mustang stuck out among the rows of utilitarian sedans and SUVs, and my heart clenched as he settled behind the wheel and stared into space.

Not yet. Not there.

I rode along with him, barely tiring as I gave my farsight a workout. His apartment wasn't far from the office, and soon enough, he let himself in, walking right past the glowing blue mail indicator. He flipped on the overhead lights, locked the door, and sank into a chair at his dining room table, which bore a single placemat.

Quickly, I pulled myself back into my body, scrolled to the right spot in my phone's contacts, and dialed. Yven's phone always went through six rings before the voicemail triggered, and I'd returned to his apartment by the fifth trill. He was still sitting, but he'd pulled his phone from within his robe and placed it on the table—and there was my name, in Pactish characters, on the caller ID. Unable to answer my call, he instead tapped the button that would play the voicemail message live and leaned toward the phone to better hear it.

"Hey, you," I said, concentrating to prevent my voice from sounding like I was talking in my sleep. "I hope you're keeping that station wagon of yours in good order."

He didn't laugh at my weak attempt at a joke, but the corners of his mouth twitched.

"I miss you, Yven," I said. "And I'm worried about you. Canna is a great cook, and you should have gone over tonight."

He jumped like he'd been goosed, then glanced around the apartment as if expecting to spy a hidden camera. "*Rosie?*"

"You look nice, by the way. That robe suits you well. Brings out your eyes."

Snatching up his phone, Yven held it close and whispered, "Where are you?"

"Richmond. I'm in my room…I put the phone on speaker…relaxed…"

He gasped as the answer hit him. "You're watching me right now?"

"Creepy, isn't it? And how long can this message go before it hangs up on me?"

"I don't know, but call me back. Rosie—"

"You don't have to talk in the phone. It's not transmitting, remember?"

"Of course," he muttered, and put it down. "Rosie, I am *so* sorry about Christmas. I would have called you—"

"I understand. Pars told me everything. Did he mention that I thought he was a burglar and pulled a gun on him?"

Yven sat back in his chair and laughed aloud, his expression vacillating between joy and giddiness. "No! He didn't tell me that!"

"Yeah, well, that's what he gets for breaking into my house," I replied. "But he makes a decent Santa. I love the necklace—thank you."

"I'm sorry it's not more."

"*I'm* sorry that I forgot to send your gifts back with Pars—"

"You got me something?"

"It was Christmas! I wasn't going to have you sitting there at Aunt Lily's empty-handed."

"That's kind of you, but you needn't have gone to the trouble."

"Says the guy who surprised me with jewelry," I pointed out. "Listen, Yven—"

The beep of the message ending cut me off, and he grabbed the phone and called my name as if I'd just hit a dead patch. I shifted my focus to my fingers long enough to hit the redial button, and by the time I was back with Yven, the voicemail was about to click on.

"Guess we've got a sense of message time now," I said as soon as his recorded greeting ended. "Yven, I…I can't tell you how sorry I am for putting you in this position."

"You did nothing wrong," he insisted. "It's the director being unreasonable, not you!"

"Technically, *yes*, but if I'd known six months ago you'd end up stuck at your desk and in forced therapy…"

He listened until my voice trailed off, then said, "I love you, and I wouldn't do a damn thing differently."

"I love you, too," I murmured. "And therein lies the problem."

He chuckled weakly. "Worst-case scenario, there's always the draught—"

"Don't even *kid* about that, ti'Ansha," I snapped. "Promise me you'll forget that shit exists."

"Rosie, I—"

"Promise me."

"I promise, okay?" he soothed. "It's just, you know…I wish we had a solution."

"I haven't given up on acknowledgement yet," I replied. "And Pateme won't keep me out forever. Eventually, he'll want a farseer to find a drug dealer or whatever, and he'll come calling—and when he does, I'll have leverage. Until then…I know this is weird and stalkerish, but if you're all right with the long-distance thing, I swear I'm not watching you sleep."

"I don't mind in the slightest," said Yven. "I'm grateful to hear your voice, even more so to be able to carry on a conversation with you. Stalk at your leisure. Perhaps you could refrain from critiquing my abs, but…"

I laughed as the message ended, then sighed in frustration and called him again.

"Any chance that you could get a burner phone?" I asked.

"Not one equipped to call outside the Pactlands.

They're regulated. Well, I mean," he amended, "all things are possible on the black market for the right price—"

"Don't worry about it—this isn't hurting me. Just remember to delete these messages once we hang up."

He whistled low. "Good point. And where are my manners? How are you?"

"Much better now. Oh! You'll never guess what I found this morning."

"Forgotten paintings?"

"Better. My grandfather left a huge box of recordings for me. Said he'd try to coach me along while I'm stuck outside the Pactlands."

Bemused silence greeted that announcement, and then Yven said, "Sorry…your *grandfather*?"

"Caradin ti'Dana, the farseeing one. He left me *dozens* of reels to go through. Apparently, he saw this coming."

"Did he see a way out of this mess, then?"

I sucked my teeth. "Don't know yet—I've only just started to listen. But if he gave me a solution, you'll be my first call. And speaking of calls…we'd better wrap this up, just in case Pateme reviews your phone records."

Yven seemed to deflate in front of me. "So soon?"

"I'll call again tomorrow, okay? Go hang out with Pars and Canna—it would do you good."

He sighed. "Yes, ma'am."

"Play along with Pateme for now. Our time will come," I told him with what I hoped passed for confidence. "I love you, Yven, and I'm not going anywhere."

Once I hung up, I lingered in the apartment, watching as Yven deleted the recordings of my one-sided conversation. He tucked the phone back into his robe, then stood and headed for the kitchen with a faint smile on his face. Unable to be heard there, I retreated to my room and stared up at the ceiling, reacclimating to physicality and thinking about Caradin's tapes.

Had he offered us a solution?

There was only one way to find out.

CHAPTER 3

I turned into a hermit that winter. Every morning, I got up, made breakfast, and listened to one of Caradin's recordings. If he offered some new technique to make my casting faster or more efficient, I'd spend an hour or two trying it out in the den. My parents' furniture and the poor paint suffered the most from my experimentation—thankfully, I had a fire extinguisher—but by late January, I had to admit that I was improving. After my morning session, I'd go to the studio and work through the afternoon, completing the paintings I'd promised and selling a few I'd already finished, and then I'd race home in time to be ready when Yven could sneak away.

He, too, had little social life at the beginning of the year. Aside from the occasional visit with Pars's family, he kept to himself, tending his orchids and reading. He dutifully went to his therapy appointments and lied as necessity dictated. I never sat in on them—therapy was meant to be private, after all—but Yven spoke of the DPP therapist often, and usually with frustration. "His specialty is workplace dynamics," he groused during one of our calls. "My situation is so far outside the normal bounds of his practice that he doesn't know what to do with me. He actually suggested that I ask a female agent out for dinner as a way to get past my 'infatuation,' and I laughed in his face."

If Yven ever took someone on a date during that period, I had no knowledge of it. He started leaving work promptly and went straight back to his apartment so as not to keep me waiting. Those illicit calls were a lifeline for us both, a chance for us to talk to the one other person in our lives who understood what we were going through. When Yven was forced to stay late or made sudden plans, he'd write a note on a small pad he kept beside his computer. Notes to me were always scrawled in red and in Low Elvish, protecting them from at least some of his colleagues' prying eyes.

I reassured myself that this was temporary, that lots of couples made the long-distance thing work, that Pateme would come to his senses soon, but I caught myself wondering if I'd ever be allowed in the same room with Yven again. Still, as the last of the holiday glow fizzled into the bleakness of January and the icy sludge of February, Yven's feelings for me didn't falter, and longing only made mine burn hotter. If Pateme's goal had been to break us up, his plan was a colossal failure.

Unfortunately, Caradin wasn't forthcoming with any immediate solutions to our enforced separation. At first, I'd been frustrated—he was a future-oriented farseer, for crying out loud, so shouldn't he have seen how this played out? Couldn't he have dropped a large hint? But the more that he told me about farsight and its complications, the better I understood his predicament.

As soon as their talent manifested, future farseers had drilled into them one simple truth: the future they saw wasn't guaranteed, and trying to change it would *always* lead to unintended consequences. This was why DOI worked with a team of farseers, who could all focus on a single event and try to play with the variables. Most might observe the same outcome, but one or two could see a different future. Older farseers like Caradin's father were skilled enough to see multiple possibilities, if they put their minds to it. And since DOI concerned itself largely with threats to the stability of the Pactlands, the ability to compare futures and choose the one with the fewest negative consequences—short-term *and* long-term—was key.

Almost always, they allowed the future that most of them first saw to go forward. "Majority" scenarios were hypothesized to be the way time wanted to flow; any meddling on their part would be tantamount to diverting a river. Recommending action that would change the future—or taking it, depending on how strongly DOI felt about the plan—was a decision reached only after great consideration and deliberation.

"In many ways, it's a curse, farsight," Caradin mused on one recording. "If you have any skill with it and you're future-oriented, you see flashes of how *horrible* the future could be—and then you realize that's the best option. It's knowing that the crash is coming and being powerless to stop it, not because you can't do anything to prevent catastrophe, but because you know you *shouldn't.* And that's just considering the parts of the future you attempt to view. Farseers get flashes of insight all their lives—you can tamp them down with training and practice, but even the week before I took the draught, I was still getting flashes. Some are great, now. I first saw your birth in a flash, for example, and if your parents never told you, they both cried with happiness. I've seen a few moments of you listening to these tapes. And then there are the awful flashes."

He sighed, and I heard the clink of ice against glass. Something told me he hadn't been drinking a Coke that night.

"I know how Joss will die," he murmured into the microphone. "I've seen it play out more times than I'd like to count. I know what she'll wear to dinner that night, and I know where Henry will make the reservation, and I know they'll be laughing when he hits black ice and spins out of control. I know that she'll be dead less than a minute after the car slams into that telephone pole, and Henry will never regain consciousness. He won't make it to the hospital, though the paramedics will try to save him. And I will *never* say a word of this to my daughter," he continued, his voice tightening, "because I've looked at other possibilities. Of course I don't want anything to happen to her—I want her to live a long, wonderful life. But if they don't have that accident…excuse me."

Judging by the background noise, he drank again.

"She's not even three yet," he said, audibly on the edge of tears. "She's this wonderful, curious, funny little creature, and I would die for her today if I could save her from that wreck. But when all the scenarios play out, the wreck does the least harm. I *know* that, Rosie. I know it because it's what I spent so many damn years doing at Intelligence. But that doesn't mean it kills me any less, and I can't tell a soul except Dad…and you, but you haven't even been born."

I bit my lip and leaned closer to the player.

"I wonder if you think I'm a monster," Caradin said. "I've wondered that myself, you know? Because I'm not infallible. People like me aren't meant to play at being gods. I have a duty, I *see* that, but at the end of it all, I have to look in Joss's eyes and live with the knowledge that I could save her, and I'm not, even as I tell her I love her. And I do—*please* believe that, I love her so much," he begged. "Joss and Grace are my world. But this miserable curse has saddled me with a responsibility to do the least harm, even if the people I love the most become collateral."

He took a deep, unsteady breath.

"I'm really sorry, little one," he said, his voice cracking. "I don't want to take your parents away from you. You don't deserve that. Maybe someday, Dad will sit down with you and tell you why it has to be this way, but I don't blame you if you hate me now. Sometimes, I hate myself, too."

The recording had ended on that bitter note, but before

I could get up from my chair, I heard a young woman's voice on the tape—in English, for a change, and with a noticeable drawl. "Hi, sweetie," she said. "This is your grandma, Grace. Caradin's gone to bed, and he's in a funk. I don't know exactly what he was telling you, but let's just keep it between us girls that I know more Elvish than he realizes. I haven't taken any potion, but Diriem's a good tutor," she said with what sounded like a hint of a smirk. "Listen…I don't know what it's like to be a farseer. I can't imagine what you three can do," she said, softly chuckling. "But I do know that Caradin takes it *personally*. There's plenty he won't tell me…but I'm not a fool, and sometimes, he talks in his sleep." She paused, then said, "Whatever he told you tonight, whatever you think of him right now, your granddad is a good man. An *honorable* man," she insisted. "And I want you to remember that, Rosie, okay? Whatever happens between now and the time you hear this, remember that he did his best."

As much as I valued the lessons Caradin offered on those tapes, I prized the glimpses he gave me of the family. Mom had spoken little of her youth beyond the generalities— she'd grown up on a farm until her father died, and then she and her mother had sold the place and moved to a small house in Charlottesville, where Grace worked as a nurse. Mom had been an only child; she'd told me that her father had no siblings, while her mother's only brother had died during World War II. Her mother's parents passed before Mom hit kindergarten, so she had no memory of them outside of photographs. I'd asked about her father's parents once, but all she'd told me was that they hadn't been in the picture.

To my surprise, I heard Caradin make frequent references to his own father—usually with the informal familial term, what my mind translated as "Dad"—but as the years passed, sometimes Diriem's presence registered as "Pop." *That* came through in English, and I gathered that was what Mom had called him. I heard snippets about his visits, about Diriem taking Mom to the circus and for hikes on the trails around town, about her baby ballerina phase and how she'd tried to teach her grandfather to plié. He came to her elementary school's open house the year that she won her first art contest and took her for ice cream afterward, insisting that he'd have her painting framed.

Diriem had been there, and all signs suggested he adored his granddaughter—so why had Mom never mentioned him to me?

Given what I'd heard about the dishonor the draught brought upon a family, I was initially stunned that Diriem had come around Virginia at all. Then again, I thought, he had nothing to prove...and as I pieced together the facts Caradin dropped and realized how close father and son had been, I began to understand.

Diriem ti'Dana was the eldest of three, with Miral, a sister sixty years his junior, and their baby brother, Jixan, rounding out the pack. Presumably, his parents would have had more children—kings usually had large families—but assassins from a rival southern Hall had murdered them in 1453. Thus, at the relatively tender age of one hundred twenty-seven, Diriem inherited the Hall and the throne. While Miral had married and started her own family by then—Jixan, only thirty-four, could be forgiven for not having settled down—Diriem remained stubbornly single, which caused no end of consternation in the more prominent Halls with available daughters. To most of his would-be in-laws, he politely expressed that his thoughts hadn't yet turned to marriage. To his siblings, however, who understood his farsight, he confessed the truth: he'd seen his wife in his future, and he would settle for nothing less while he waited for them to cross paths.

Of course, he had larger political considerations than marriage. Yven had mentioned to me the increasing danger to the magical factions from human encroachment, and Caradin's commentary echoed his account. In 1525, Diriem gave shelter to a group of sorcerers who'd proposed the radical idea of creating a world of their own as a way to avoid persecution. Protected and free to work in peace—and having been granted access to the vast ti'Dana library—they designed and built the Pactlands and opened their pocket world in 1538, then invited everyone in…but on equal footing. The Pactlands' architects could have tried to rule it as monarchs, but they proposed a representative government, the Forum, to give all races equal standing.

Many balked at the notion. Sorcerers who'd not been involved in the project recoiled at the idea of treating, say, *trolls* as equals, while across the board, those of the more magically gifted species, who had long maintained dominance through their talent, were loath to surrender power to people who couldn't so much as change their appearance on a whim. Among the elves, the long-ruling southern king rejected the offer of the Pactlands, declaring that *he* would not be ruled. But Diriem was a farseer, and he knew that his choice for his people was between their cooperation and their annihilation.

He chose the former. Eighty-five years into his reign, Diriem signed the Pact, surrendered his throne, and led the northern Halls—and a few of the wiser southern Halls—into the Pactlands. Suddenly reduced to the first among equals, Diriem served as his people's representative to the nascent Forum, then stepped aside to give a turn to another Hall. While he occasionally returned to the Forum in the following centuries, anyone who understood Pact politics knew that his public forays were merely an outing for him. Diriem's true usefulness was in the committee that grew into the Division of Intelligence, which relied upon farseers and less gifted agents and analysts to protect and guide the Pactlands.

"I think it suits him to be the power behind the throne instead of the one on it," Caradin explained. "Dad's not a hermit, but I've never seen him swept up in the Halls' social seasons. Farsight can be an incredibly isolating talent," he added more softly. "It's difficult to watch the sort of things we sought out at DOI, then plaster on a smile and go mingle with a crowd of people whose greatest concern is making themselves appear better than their supposed friends. Difficult for me, I mean. I can't speak for Dad in all respects, but…" He sighed. "He's seen *much*."

One of the subjects to which his visions frequently returned was his wife, but as the years passed, Diriem began to despair that he'd never meet her. He seldom pushed his farsight to look for details—prying too closely into one's own future was an unwise practice at best—but every time he attended a party or a banquet, he kept a close watch, hoping for a glimpse of the laughing blonde beauty in his memory.

Not until a late spring evening's ball in 1660, when he was a bachelor of more than three hundred, did he catch a glimpse of her. Spring was the perfect time for the presentation into society of young elves who'd come of age, and such balls usually included the announcement of at least a few men and women making their awkward entrée. That night, the honorees included Learil ti'On. Shorter than the other girls standing with her on the staircase and birdlike in structure, she wore her fair hair partially pinned up, partially draped across her shoulders and curtaining down her back. Her deep blue gown rose to the base of her neck, as was the fashion that year, and trailed ever so slightly behind her dainty embroidered shoes. Her smile seemed nervous, and her eyes, barely a shade lighter than her dress, darted over the crowd as if seeking an absent friend while the host recited her name and youthful accomplishments. She needed no necklace, but she had tucked a few sapphire-tipped pins into her coiffure, and they twinkled as her head dipped in acknowledgement of her introduction.

She was the most beautiful creature Diriem had ever seen…and only forty years old.

Though he was smitten at first sight, he made no move to corner her while her escort brought her around the ballroom and out through the gardens. To a race of immortals, age matters little, but still, Diriem thought it would be unseemly for him to pounce upon a woman who surely would have preferred the company of the young men cavorting on the dance floor. Tempted but resolute, he kept to himself for the first hour of the party, but when he caught Learil sitting alone against the wall, he could bear it no longer and joined her on the couch, asking if she was tired already.

Learil, who had spent much of her time with her nose in a book, had no idea who the redheaded man with the charming smile might be, but she laughed and blushed as she admitted the truth: she was a terrible dancer. Her parents had hired the finest tutors to fix her deficiency, but none had ever overcome her clumsy footwork. He said that he, too, was a poor dancer and offered to try with her—surely she would look poised by comparison.

Caradin reported that by all accounts, his parents were equally terrible that night.

Diriem left Learil just before the late meal, as the honorees were seated together in the banqueting hall. He promised he would meet up with her after they ate, but the arrival of a messenger from DOI cut short his evening. Poor Learil had barely noticed he was missing before the girls beside her demanded to know her secret—Lord ti'Dana *never* danced with anyone.

Ti'On was but a middling Hall, and Learil merely the seventh child of parents who were no better than second cousins to a ruling lord, but she refused to stay in the shadows when Diriem was around. While he continued to approach her with caution that year, she grew bolder, and soon, she was as besotted with him as he was with her.

After four years, frustrated that Diriem had yet to make his interest clear, Learil took matters into her own hands. Visiting a friend whose familial estate was within reasonable distance of Diriem's manor, she set off riding one afternoon, removed a shoe from her horse when she was within a few minutes of her destination, then walked up to the front door and played dumb while asking for help with her unshod mount. Diriem, who had foreseen this encounter for years, played along perfectly and insisted she stay for dinner while a groom examined her horse—she shouldn't ride off if the beast were lame.

When the two of them were alone, Diriem asked her for a truthful answer: exactly how far away had she been when she pried that horseshoe off?

Blushing, Learil confessed, then asked for the truth in turn. When Diriem promised to answer a question, she asked why he had never so much as courted a woman.

Carefully and with much hesitation, he explained how his farsight worked and revealed that it had long ago shown him the woman he would marry. He hadn't seen the point in pursuing another while he waited for her.

At that, Learil asked for a second truth—she was a guest, she reminded him, so surely he would grant her the courtesy. Diriem agreed, and with a nervous little smile, Learil asked if she was the woman he'd seen.

To Diriem's delight, Learil was overjoyed when he admitted she was the one he'd been waiting for.

Given the age difference, Learil's parents weren't entirely thrilled when Diriem proposed marriage, but a proposal from Hall ti'Dana—let alone the former king— would have been difficult to reject. The two were married in 1668, and neither could have been happier.

During their courtship, when the matter of children had

arisen, both had expressed eagerness—Learil to become a mother, and Diriem to make up for lost time. But shortly after the wedding, Diriem began to withdraw from his new bride. He remained as affectionate as ever, doting on Learil and even hosting parties to make her smile, but to her consternation, he seemed to take pains to avoid a pregnancy. She pressed him, insisting that he would make a wonderful father and had nothing to fear, but Diriem continued to find excuses to postpone a family.

At first, Learil wondered if his feelings toward her had changed. Perhaps, she worried, she had only been desirable before he'd won her hand. Perhaps there was another woman on Diriem's mind. But as the months passed, she began to suspect that something else was at work in their marriage—there *had* to be a logical explanation as to why Diriem kept his distance from his willing wife.

Finally, she confronted him as gently as she could and asked for the truth of the matter. When Diriem realized she wouldn't drop it, he shared with her his secret. The night after their wedding, he'd had a flash that had brought certain of his vaguer visions into terrible focus: Learil would die young, shortly after the birth of their only child, and someday, that child would take the draught and predecease his father.

Though shaken, Learil tried to reassure Diriem. The future wasn't set, and events glimpsed by farseers weren't guaranteed to come true. He'd only seen *one* possible future, not the unchangeable course of time. But knowing how distraught her husband was over his vision, Learil agreed that they would postpone having the children they both dearly desired.

For fifty-four years, they took careful precautions, both doing their part to ensure that they remained childfree. One January night in 1723, however, they sat at home all day while a rare deep snow blanketed their corner of the Pactlands. Having had too much to drink and a long evening in each other's company to set the mood, the couple threw caution aside in the warm glow of their bedroom fireplace.

"And that," Caradin relayed, understandably skimping on the details of the event, "is where *I* came in."

There are, he informed me, potions available to end a pregnancy—*old* potions, easily available. But once Learil realized she was carrying, she made up her mind to have the child despite Diriem's portentous visions. While Diriem also wanted a child, he feared for his wife's safety, but she was firm in her decision. As a compromise, she made regular visits to a healer who specialized in midwifery and avoided activities with even the slightest risk for months. Her much-loved horses remained in the pasture unridden, and she never walked more than a few feet beyond the door of the manor without an escort, just in case. The midwife tried to reassure Diriem that the pregnancy was proceeding beautifully, but while he smiled for Learil and allowed himself to imagine what their child would be like, unwanted flashes of farsight kept him awake with their warnings of doom.

When the day arrived, Learil's labor began normally, but it soon stalled. After a full day and night with no progress, the midwife could no longer hide her concern. After two days, with Learil exhausted and barely able to stomach water, the midwife took drastic action. Giving Learil a potion to make her insensate, she performed a C-section...or she tried to, at least.

"We had better medical outcomes in the Pactlands than in this world for a *long* time," Caradin explained, "but only because there was magic in the mix. I mean, surgery could still kill you. It's come a long way—healers have been poaching techniques from human doctors for centuries, and healing potions have only really become useful in my lifetime—but the midwife wasn't trained to do what she did, and she botched it."

Caradin survived the ordeal with only a little bruising, but Learil wasn't so fortunate. She bled badly, and though the midwife did her best to put her to rights, she was plagued by pain and weakness in the days following. Diriem called in another healer, who started Learil on a new and promising potion intended to dull the pain and invigorate her. And it might have done so, had it been properly brewed. The healer's brewer was old and forgetful, and the new potion was toxic if not assembled with precision. Thus, while Learil showed improvement at first, she was quickly poisoning herself. By the time the healer recognized the danger, it was too late to do more than make her comfortable.

Try as she did to fight her fate, Learil died one January night in 1726 with her husband by her side. Diriem awoke from bad dreams to find her lying cold in the bed and their young son crying inconsolably in his sleep.

CHAPTER 4

"I barely remember my mother," Caradin confided to me in one of his tapes, which he'd recorded after celebrating Mother's Day with Mom and Grace. Though by then it had been more than two centuries since her death, he sounded wistful on the recording, saddened by the loss he couldn't fix. "Impressions more than true memories. Dad kept her portraits hanging in the house, and that's how I see her face, in oils instead of flesh." He paused, then said, "You're named for her, did you know that? Her friends called her Lea. I've told Joss a bit about her—not everything, of course, not yet," he hastily added—"and she likes Mom's name."

That solved one mystery. I'd long wondered where my middle name came from, and though my parents had insisted it wasn't a misspelled homage to *Star Wars*, I hadn't entirely believed them.

But if Caradin had been denied a long relationship with his mother, Diriem had apparently stepped up to the plate. My granddad spoke lovingly of his father, of growing up as a doted-upon only child kept in check by his older cousins. He'd been a good student, eager to make Diriem proud, and by his early twenties, several of the Pact's agencies had taken note of him among the crop of likely future candidates. He spoke to his friends about pursuing a career in the Division of Laws, perhaps eventually overseeing tribunals.

Everything changed, however, when his farsight triggered at twenty-two. Practice and testing revealed that

Caradin had inherited his father's gift, which narrowed his career options. "I favored Laws," he told me, "but if you're a strong future farseer, duty dictates that you join Intelligence. My talent made the choice for me. Besides," he added with a chuckle, "Dad was the director. How the hell could I have said no?"

At least he had an expert on hand to mentor him. While Caradin began to explore his talent, his visions went in a surprising direction: a young, pretty brunette with crinkling green eyes, sporting a pale blue cotton dress with a hem just below her knees. The dress was curious on its own, far different than any style he'd seen in the Pactlands, but more puzzling still were the woman's features. She looked like a sorcerer, Caradin thought, and put the matter aside as a problem for another day.

But the woman kept plaguing his thoughts, and so he pushed his farsight for details. Within a month of his first glimpse of her, he knew that her name was Grace Marks, that she worked as a healer of some capacity (a nurse, he later learned), and that she was *human*, of all things. Why his visions had focused on her was a mystery until he closed his eyes in practice one afternoon, let his mind wander to Grace, and saw himself kissing her.

"I didn't know what to do," he murmured in one recording. "I was a kid, I had my life unfolding ahead of me…and suddenly, I was having visions of this strange woman in my arms. I couldn't see everything clearly yet, but even then, I knew that my future self was deeply in love—and Rosie, if you've grown up in the Pactlands, that is a *terrifying* thought."

I understood his fear. To be with Grace, he'd have to take the draught. There was no alternative.

At first, he told himself there had to be a mistake—he refused to accept that he'd condemn himself for some human girl, no matter how pretty her smile might be. But curiosity drew him ever more frequently to seek her out as he gained control over his farsight, and the longer he observed his future with her, the more he realized what he stood to gain. By then, Caradin had worked at DOI for a few years, and while duty kept him there, he knew he wasn't cut out for a life of choosing among tragedies to select the path of least harm. In his ever-stronger visions of Grace, his future self was *happy*—doomed, yes, and cut off from the world he knew, but so very happy.

"I saw myself with her," he told me, "and I watched our daughter grow up. I saw how deeply in love she'll be with Henry—I don't suppose I'll ever meet him, but I do like him. And I saw you, Rosie." He hesitated, then said, "As I've mentioned, with future farsight, visions get fuzzy the further out you try to see. I can't tell you exactly how your life will go, nor would I if I had that knowledge. But I have some idea of what's brought you to this point and hints of what lies ahead. I hope you understand if I don't share them with you. In our experience, those who know their future sometimes go to drastic lengths to change it, and if they succeed, it often ends badly for them."

Caradin knew the way his future wanted to go, and having seen what his life would become, he decided that his wife and daughter would make the sacrifice worthwhile. Still, he waited until he was fifty to tell his father what he'd been seeing. He braced himself for pushback, but to his surprise, Diriem, having seen this future long before, just sadly smiled and nodded.

"We were close, Rosie," Caradin said. "Still are, even with the physical distance. And I know Dad would have insisted I fight against this path if he saw a better future for me. Neither of us ever did, and you know, I'm glad of it. I gave most of my life to DOI, I lived with the worst side of farsight for more than two hundred years…and it's gone now. I wish I could see you again, and I'd give anything for more time with my family here, but I don't regret my choice. Pursuing Grace is the best decision I've ever made."

But before he could woo her, he had to *find* her.

From Mom, I knew the rough contours of my grandma's background. Grace was born in Charlottesville in 1924, the second child of a successful attorney and his loving wife. Her brother, Tommy, was two years her senior, and she'd trailed behind him as long as he'd allowed it. Tommy had enrolled at UVA, but two days after Pearl Harbor, he'd put his studies on hold and enlisted, just as his father had during the previous global conflict. Unlike his father, however, Tommy never came home.

Grace threw herself into her studies as a distraction and graduated at the top of her high school class. Her parents supported her decision to pursue nursing school, and in the late summer of 1946, she landed her first job at a small doctor's office in her hometown.

"By 1930, I knew I'd meet her somewhere around Charlottesville," Caradin explained. "I'd been seeing the Rotunda at the university for ages, and though I didn't recognize the place, I sketched it for reference. I'm not a terrible artist—not in your league, Rosie, but passable—and over the years, I made excuses to show it to some of the agents who left the Pactlands more frequently than I did and ask if they'd ever seen it. Do you know who finally gave me the answer?" he asked with a smile in his voice. "Fradin ti'Cren. He monitored several growers in Virginia, and he'd been through Charlottesville a hundred times."

I shouldn't have been surprised that my grandfathers had crossed paths. Socially, they were peers, the sons of high-ranking lords, and Fradin was only about forty-five years older than Caradin—a negligible difference in elven terms. Still, the fact that Fradin had guided Caradin to Grace left me inordinately pleased.

Once Caradin had an idea of where Grace would reveal herself, he found reasons to visit—masked, naturally, so as not to cause a panic. Most DOI agents had portal credentials, and Diriem turned a blind eye to his son's trips and their flimsy pretenses. But though Caradin scoured the little city, searching for a hint of Grace, she remained an enigma.

Chance brought him to the public library one sticky Saturday morning in August 1946. He'd planned to take a walk around downtown, but the dark clouds portended an imminent storm, and so he ducked into the nearest convenient facility minutes before the heavens opened. While thunder rumbled overhead, he wandered to the stacks, deciding to distract himself with a book until the rain slacked off...and as he rounded a corner, there she was.

Grace. The blue dress, the neatly tied-back brown hair, and all.

For a moment, Caradin stared at her as she stood on tiptoe atop a stool, trying to reach a book. Seizing the opportunity, he hurried over and offered to assist her, and she made self-deprecating jokes about her short stature while he plucked *Murder on the Orient Express* off the top shelf for her. Having read a few Agatha Christie mysteries himself, Caradin managed to strike up a conversation, and to his great relief, Grace seemed more eager for companionship than for a quiet morning with her book. He introduced himself as Caleb Storm, a graduate student sneaking a few hours away from his studies, and Grace told him about her new nursing job. By lunchtime, they were laughing like old friends over hamburgers in a small restaurant crowded with college students, boys who talked too loudly and smoked cheap cigarettes and cast interested glances at the pretty young brunette in the booth with the redheaded man.

Caradin took a leave of absence from the office and rented a small house near the university to keep up the ruse. He spent hours sitting in front of his new television, parroting lines as he worked to minimize his accent. On the weekends, he drove to Grace's tidy apartment to pick her up and take her out to dinner or for long drives in the hills. She never requested a chaperone, and he remained a gentleman, occasionally holding her hand or pecking her cheek in parting.

"I couldn't rush it," he said, "and frankly, I felt guilty for not being honest with her. I knew I had to tell her the truth eventually, but nothing in my visions ever showed me how I should go about dropping *that* bomb."

And then he saw the fire.

The flash first came upon Caradin about six weeks after meeting Grace: her office being swallowed by flames while a fire engine pulled up, too late to do more than soak the ashes. He tried not to panic, but as the days passed, the vision returned with increasing frequency, and his gut told him he couldn't afford to ignore it. The fifth time he returned to the fire, he ran down the street until he found a small law office, then slipped inside to look at the date on the newspaper in the lobby.

When he pulled himself back to his body, Caradin knew his options as surely as he knew his own name. If he did nothing, Grace would perish in the fire, and the future he had seen would die with her. While he'd lose Grace, he'd save himself. If he warned her, however, he would be sealing his own fate.

A week later, on a breezy Tuesday morning in mid-October, Grace was surprised to find Caradin on her doorstep before she'd even had time to fix her hair. He asked her not to go to work that day—to fake an illness, come up with a family emergency, *anything* to avoid the office. Bemused, Grace initially brushed him off, but when Caradin dropped to his knees and begged her to stay home, she relented. Satisfied that she'd keep her word, he left her to her breakfast, and Grace called her employer with imaginary "women's troubles."

Caradin was watching a Western in his rented house that night when Grace pounded on the door and demanded to know how he'd anticipated the fire. The building had been a total loss, and while the doctor and the patients had escaped, the other nurse had died in the blaze.

"Grace was so shaken," he recounted. "She stood there in my living room, hugging herself in her coat, yelling at me to give her an answer that made sense. Poor girl thought I might be an arsonist."

With a little cajoling, Caradin convinced Grace to take a seat on his secondhand couch and poured her a stiff drink of brandy, then pulled up a chair a few feet away and asked her if she really wanted the truth. He swore that he hadn't set the fire, but if that weren't good enough for her, he'd explain everything.

"Your grandma has never lacked for curiosity," he said to me, "and she told me to spill every detail." He paused and chuckled weakly. "So I did. I told her my true name, where I'd come from, what I did for a living, and all about my farsight. I said I couldn't sit back and let her die. She didn't believe me at first, not that I blame her, and so I took my mask off."

In the silence that followed on the recording, I realized I was holding my breath.

"She stared at me for a long, *long* minute, not saying a word," said Caradin, "and then she drained her glass and walked out. I sat there while she drove away, wondering if I'd ruined everything."

He didn't see her for the next two weeks, nor did he try to call, assuming that Grace had enough to worry about with her job. But one night, she returned to his house in the late evening and looked up at him from the welcome mat as he prayed to any available kind god and waited for her to speak.

"She asked me point-blank if I'd seen her with farsight prior to the fire," he recalled. "I admitted it. Then she asked me how long I'd been seeing her, and I told her the better part of two centuries. She wanted to know why. I said it was because I knew I'd fall in love with her. Well, Grace stood there with her arms folded, considering that—your grandma's stubborn, and she's got a steel spine," he added—"and then she asked if I was going to keep any more secrets from her. I was honest. Told her she could know whatever she wanted about me, but that the simple act of sharing information about the future could jeopardize it, and as a farseer, I had to keep many of my visions to myself. She considered that, too, then got right up on my toes and said, 'If there's something you *can't* tell me, then I'll accept that, but you'd better never lie to me.' I told her I wouldn't, and she asked if I was going to invite her in, or if we were going to talk over the threshold all evening."

Despite Grace's concern that word might get back to her parents about her car being found parked beside a strange man's house, they stayed up late into the night, and Caradin came as clean as he could with her. As Grace finally headed for the door, she paused and asked if he could tell her one thing about her future. He made no promise of an answer, fearing she would want to know about the stock market or her own death, but all she asked was, "Will we be happy together?"

"I told her my visions had a high accuracy rating," Caradin recalled, "and while no future was ever set in stone until it came to pass, the odds were good for us."

And that was good enough for Grace. They dated all through the fall and winter, growing ever more attached. Caradin managed to spend the holidays with Grace's parents without raising suspicion, and in January, he finally invited Diriem over to meet her.

"Dad's very fond of her, thank goodness," he told me. "About five minutes after he arrived, they warmed up to each other. Not that there weren't moments," he added, chuckling. "He'd aged his mask to human fifties or thereabout, and when she asked him to remove it, his true appearance took her aback. To human eyes, we look far too close in age to be father and son. Disconcerting for Grace, but she moved past it. These days, Dad normally keeps the mask on for safety reasons when he comes over, but I don't think it bothers her much anymore."

But Caradin didn't rush matters. Appreciating that he was the one coming to the relationship with a head start, he let Grace set the tempo and tried to give her space. Grace remained somewhat cautious—to be fair, nothing in her experience would have prepared her for an amorous elf—but she never broke off the relationship, and as the months passed, the two drew closer.

"Ours was a slow courtship," Caradin remarked, which, when I compiled a timeline, looked like a gross understatement.

My grandparents began seeing each other in the fall of 1946, but not until 1951 did they begin to seriously consider marriage. Caradin wasn't in a hurry, and he did have to return to his job and keep up appearances. As much as he'd have liked to live in Virginia full-time, that simply wasn't an option, and Diriem nagged him whenever his disappearances reached the limit of explainable absences. As for Grace, she was only twenty-two when they met, and while many women her age were married by that point, she was invested in her career. My grandma enjoyed nursing—Mom had shown me pictures of her in her old-fashioned uniforms, smiling with her perfectly coiffed hair and pristine hose—and she wasn't the sort to toss aside everything she'd worked for in college just because a handsome stranger waltzed into her life. Caradin appreciated that, and though Grace's parents dropped increasingly stronger hints that the two of them should fish or cut bait, they progressed at their own steady pace.

In the summer of 1951, Caradin used his savings to purchase a small farm outside of Charlottesville. Fortunately for him, gold held its value on both sides of the portals, and transforming his wages into useable cash was doable as long as he didn't sell too much gold in any one town. When the ink was dry on his deed—thanks to

Diriem's string-pulling, Caleb Storm's documentary credentials were impeccable—he drove Grace out to see the place. She liked it as much as he did, to his relief, and that night, back at Caradin's house in town, she finally broached the idea of marriage.

"I took the draught in 1952. March," said Caradin. "Dad got his hands on a vial and brought it to me. I did it at his place, just the two of us, and he fixed my face the next morning, once I'd slept off the aftereffects. The draught is miserable, Rosie—I hope you never consider it. But it did its job, and Grace and I were married that June."

He made no mention of how he'd told her about the draught—how it would leave him powerless and on the path to an early grave—and as I listened to the tapes, I wondered if that was one of the secrets he couldn't bring himself to reveal.

My mother was born in October 1955, and from everything I could deduce from the recordings, her father thought she'd hung the moon. I heard snippets about life on the farm as a family of three. Grace had stopped working once the baby came along, and though Diriem kept sneaking them money, Caradin put in long hours in the fields, breaking his back to make it on his own. They must have lived fairly frugally—I never heard him talk about exotic vacations or big shopping trips—and for years, he complained about his farm truck, old at the time of purchase, which spent about as much time at the mechanic's as it did in service.

But despite Caradin's choice to leave, Diriem continued to stop by. He never appeared on the recordings himself, but Caradin told me about his visits for Mom's birthday or at the holidays, or just on a random Tuesday night with cake and new art supplies for his only granddaughter. As I dug deeper into the box, it was almost as if I was hearing my mother grow up—her first steps, her first day of school, her first heartbreak when a boy in her fourth-grade class kissed another girl on the playground. Through it all, Caradin sounded so proud of her.

And then, when Mom was ten, he sat her down and told her the truth about himself.

"Dad tried to help," he recounted on the tape that night, his voice low and almost monotonic, a far cry from his usual mellow tone. "I don't have any talent to demonstrate these days, so he showed her—I mean, I'd have sounded like a lunatic without proof."

Mom wasn't scared, as Caradin had anticipated—surprised, but not afraid. Rather, once she understood that he'd given up his power, home, and family to be with Grace—and, moreover, that the draught would keep her powerless, too—she was *furious*.

"I didn't expect that much anger," he said. "Not at her mom and me, but at Dad. You know, 'How could you let this happen?' and all that." He paused for a moment, then murmured, "Dad hasn't liked the idea of the draught for a long time. He understands the rationale, and I think he was even able to rationalize the situation with me because I'm grown, and it was my choice. But tonight, he had to look Joss in the eye while we explained that she has a family she'll never know, and...I mean, he finally faced the fact that by Pact law, there's something intrinsically wrong with his granddaughter. No child deserves to hear that she's someone's dirty little secret. We didn't say that," he hastily added, "not in those words, but your mom's a smart kid. She understood what we weren't saying. I can't go home again, and since Joss is functionally human, she wouldn't be welcome there, even if Dad publicly acknowledged her. *That* would be a massive scandal." He sighed, then said, "Frankly, I don't think she's ever going to look at Dad the same way, and he's gutted. Maybe he'll push for change. Won't save me, won't save Fradin, won't save your parents, but maybe it'll be enough to help some other lovestruck fool."

I listened to Caradin's final recordings at the end of February. While he sounded healthy to me, he knew his time was winding down, and his lessons took on a new urgency. "I can't teach you everything," he apologized. "I'm sorry, Rosie, I'm doing my best, but there is *so* much that goes into a proper education. Even if I had my old books, I wouldn't have the years I needed to share it all with you, and you certainly wouldn't have time to listen to me ramble."

He made his last tape on March 1, 1970. "Dad and I have talked," he said, the only other sound in the room the clinking of ice against his glass. "Once my time comes, Dad will need to stop visiting. I can't tell you why, sweetheart—this is one of those secrets I have to keep close—but know that it's nothing we want. Dad's upset, and I know this will hurt Joss, but it's the only way to keep her safe. Please don't hold this entirely against him," he told me. "No one wants this, and whatever Joss may think after I'm gone, her Pop loves her very much. This is the best of the bad options."

I could hear Caradin drinking.

"Rosie, I hope you understand someday why we made these decisions," he continued. "I get the sense that your parents will never tell you the family secret, and I can't blame them. Hell, I chose to leave—Joss never got that option. Henry lost his father years ago, I think, and I can't imagine that he's had an easy childhood. I don't want to leave Grace and Joss," he said sadly. "I'd give *anything* for a few more years. But the best I can do is trust that our savings will keep them comfortable for a while."

He hesitated so long that I almost stopped the tape, then whispered, "I'm scared. I don't know what happens next, and I'm so scared. But I want you to know that I wouldn't change anything. I don't regret my life."

"I love you," I whispered, hoping he'd seen that moment, then sat there at the kitchen table as the tape unwound and hissed, hoping for another entry in his log.

Instead, the next voice I heard was Grace's.

"Hello, Rose," she said softly. "It's March 5, 1970. Caradin died three days ago. Heart attack. I don't think he suffered long..."

She cracked, then took a few deep breaths before she continued.

"The memorial's tomorrow morning. It's small—a few of our friends, Joss, and me. And his dad came over tonight. If you ever listen to these tapes and wonder why there's no gravestone, it's because he's been cremated, and I'm sending him home with Diriem. He should get to go home...I'm sorry..."

I waited, clutching my coffee mug, while she composed herself.

"Caradin said you would know a lot by the time you found these," said my grandma, who sounded like she was barely holding her tears at bay. "If you know about that stuff he took before we got married, I...I didn't know it'd be that bad," she continued, the words tumbling out as she broke. "He said it'd give him a normal lifetime, and I didn't want that for him, but he *insisted*, and I loved him, and I shouldn't have agreed, but...I didn't know. Diriem told me today. I didn't know it would kill him that quickly. God is my witness, *I didn't know.*"

That explained *that*.

"And now Diriem's saying he's got to cut ties," she managed through her sniffles. "Says if he doesn't, the wrong people are going to find Joss and hurt her, and..." She released a long, shuddering breath. "I don't even know what to think. Maybe you've got some insight, maybe this makes sense, but I don't know anymore. He's grieving, I get it, but Joss just lost her daddy, my parents are gone, and Diriem is the only other bit of her family in her life. He says he can't come back after he leaves tomorrow. No calls, no letters, nothing. Just going to pretend we don't exist, I guess," she said bitterly.

"Welcome to the club," I muttered.

"He brought money. For Joss's schooling, he said, and to keep us on our feet for a while. I yelled at him tonight—I told him I didn't want a damn thing of his if he's really about to cut off his granddaughter—but he'll probably find a way to leave it behind. He always does. Magic, huh?"

Her brief laugh sounded more like a sob.

"I don't know what we're going to do," Grace murmured. "But we'll get by. And, uh...I think this is going to be the end of these tapes. Probably not healthy for me to sit here and talk to ghosts. Caradin was sure you'll be born someday, and I'll keep these safe for you. He wanted you to have them." She hesitated, then said, "I hope I meet you someday, Rose. I hope I'm there to give these to you when the time comes. But for now...you take care of yourself, honey, okay?"

I listened to the tape until the reel ran out, but she never spoke to me again.

From my mom's stories, I knew what happened next. Mom was only fourteen when her father died. Her mother sold the farm and moved them to a house closer to Charlottesville, and she returned to work as a nurse. Grace went on dates with a few men over the years, but she never remarried. As for Mom, she graduated high school and put off college for a few years while she apprenticed with a handful of local artists. When she eventually got her degree, it was in graphic design—maybe not the most practical of programs, but Mom said that her folks' savings paid her way.

My parents met in 1989, and they married a year and a half later. Grace lived only about a year past that, dying of cancer six months before I was born. "She insisted you'd be a girl," Mom used to tell me, "and she was right."

CHAPTER 5

My granddad tried to teach me many things in his years of recordings. Some of the lessons stuck easily, while others I struggled to master during that cold, gray winter. When I practiced, I hesitated to unleash too much force, as I had no one on hand to step in if I set the house on fire. By the first of March, the couch had acquired a scorch mark that would never come out, and I'd explained the series of broken windows to the repairmen as the result of confused birds. I tried to blame the death of the big oak behind the house on snow, but the arborist, who must have thought I was nuts, insisted that even a blizzard wouldn't snap a tree in half with a clean *horizontal* cut through the trunk.

Sure, my aim needed work, but Caradin had proven to be a decent teacher.

Unfortunately, he never brought up the one lesson I wanted most: how to fix the mess in which Yven and I found ourselves. On an intellectual level, I understood that the future was malleable and could skew in suboptimal conditions if meddled with, but damn it, would it have killed Caradin to give me a hint about the problems with my love life?

Still, at least we had our short-term solution. Every day that Yven was available, I'd open my inner eyes and call him at home, where we could have a few minutes of stolen privacy. Yven continued to have little social life that winter beyond his mandated trips to his therapist, but I knew that Pars was keeping an eye on him, for which I was grateful. As far as I could tell, neither Pars nor Canna knew that

Yven and I had found a way around his phone restrictions, which was for the best. The fewer people who were in on our secret, the safer it was. I didn't even tell Aunt Lily that I'd discovered a line of communication for fear that word would somehow leak back to her uncle. Pateme wasn't DOI, but he had a building full of agents at his disposal, and I was positive that he wasn't above sending one to stake out my place if he thought I was acting up. Surely he thought he could keep me in line—after all, as far as he knew, I was just an artist with the bare rudiments of a magical education.

But Pateme had overlooked one *tiny* variable: espionage ran in my family. Maybe I couldn't see the future, but if he thought he was protected from nosy farseers, his confidence was sorely misplaced.

Back in the fall, someone—presumably a farseer, or at least a person with an understanding of the talent and a connection to DOI—had taken to writing me letters. My anonymous pen pal had only written twice, first to lead me to try a potion known as Awakening when I was fumbling through my early attempt at controlled farsight, and then to warn me of the blinding potion that DPP's missing agent and his criminal colleagues used to protect themselves from detection. The blinding potion, I'd learned, was expensive and difficult to brew, and its effects were only good for a few months. Moreover, the potion alone wasn't enough to grant protection—the drinker also needed to be the target of a spell performed by an elf and a sorcerer working together. Needless to say, most people couldn't afford the blinding potion, but those who could get their hands on it rendered themselves nearly invisible to farseers. For me, focusing on a protected target resulted in a frustrating whiteout. When I finally found an unprotected target, the protected people around them appeared as white blotches, their shapes and words indistinguishable.

My pen pal had explained that the higher-ups in the Pactlands' government were regularly dosed with the stuff. About half of DOI was allegedly screened from view, as were the Forum representatives, which seemed wise. Unfortunately for me, the heads of most of the Pact agencies were *also* shielded because of their sensitive work...including Pateme.

Oh, I tried. The day after I made contact with Yven, once I'd listened to more of Caradin's recordings, I focused for hours in an attempt to spy on the director. All I got for my pains was a blinding headache, however, and I decided my time would be better spent trying to learn from my grandfather than futilely searching for Pateme. But about two weeks later, when I checked on Yven at work, I saw that he'd left me a note: *Late meeting with director.* He'd scrawled that so I would understand why he wasn't home on time, but as I stood there unseen in his cubicle, I decided to tag along. Maybe I couldn't see or hear Pateme, but at least I'd get Yven's half of the conversation.

Around five, as much of the office was packing up for the evening, I followed Yven to the elevators and rode up to the executive suite. Darkness had fallen over the capital, and as Pateme's assistant showed Yven into the director's office, I headed for the tall windows to take in the view of the lights below. Glancing back at Yven, I found him hunched and tense in one of Pateme's visitors' chairs, evidently nervous but perhaps mentally preparing himself for the meeting.

Pateme marched into the room a moment later—or I assumed it was Pateme, as all I could see was an ambulatory white patch heading for the desk. It moved over the chair, and a spreading rectangle of red light swept across the ceiling and down the walls before contracting in the middle of Pateme's rug. Having been in that office before, I knew the light was the visual manifestation of a privacy spell, but I had no idea how Pateme designed it.

More importantly, while it might have prevented eavesdroppers from the hallway, it did nothing to keep me out.

Yven sat up straighter, and I assumed Pateme was speaking to him. "I've attended my appointments, sir," he said after a few seconds. "All of them. Ask my counselor if you need proof."

When Pateme spoke again, Yven's jaw clenched. "I think we both know the answer to *that*, sir."

"Answer to *what*?" I muttered, annoyed at Pateme's blinding protection. I flopped into the empty chair beside Yven and stared at the white splotch, wishing that it weren't completely futile for me to try to see him.

When the outline of a body appeared at the heart of the blankness, I jerked with surprise. Yven was growing more agitated as the conversation progressed, but I tuned him out and focused on the shadowy form within the space. Could Pateme have allowed his protection to degrade, I wondered, barely believing my luck. Was I witnessing it fall apart in real time?

I heard him before I clearly saw him, his voice low and controlled: "I'm not putting that sort of temptation in front of you."

"But *sir*," Yven protested, "you know she needs training. What if she loses her temper and lets a spell fly in downtown Richmond?"

"I trust she has more sense than that," Pateme replied, sharpening before my eyes. My great-great-uncle, a slender man with neat brown hair, appeared barely older than Yven, though he sported a crimson robe with rich gold embroidery on the collar that spoke of power and the sort of fortune a junior agent would never dream of wasting on a wardrobe. "She's young, but she's no fool."

"She needs training," Yven insisted. "I'll stay out of it. Let her come to Agent ti'Mal for lessons again—I won't go near the gym. She could stay with Agent Mera—"

Pateme interrupted him with a snort. "I wasn't born yesterday, boy."

"And I'm not so selfish that I would jeopardize his job by trying to sneak over to see her," Yven retorted. "All I'm suggesting is that Rose has stayed there before, they're aware of her situation, and it would be a safe place for her to camp while she works with Agent ti'Mal." As Pateme's mouth began to open, Yven hastily added, "Or send someone to her. *Please*, sir. Don't cut her off because of me."

The director, now fully visible, folded his arms and stared at Yven until the younger agent squirmed. "I understand what you're saying," he told Yven, "and I do wish the situation with Rose were different. But you're looking at this only from one angle, ti'Ansha. From *this* angle, it's a question of life and death, and acceptable risk. I cannot, in good conscience, put you in a position in which you were forced to confront temptation on that scale every few days. It would be irresponsible of me."

"She's your blood," Yven murmured.

"I'm very much aware of that fact," said Pateme, cool as ever. "As I said, I wish matters were different. Rose's circumstances are...regrettable," he allowed. "But if I brought her to this building now or, heavens forbid, allowed her to spend the night in the residence of your *close* friend—again, I'm not stupid," he said, arching an eyebrow—"then I might as well put the draught in your hand. I won't do that. I *can't*."

The meeting ended soon thereafter, and I rode back to Yven's apartment with him as he whipped the Mustang around corners and glowered at the night. Considering his mood, I decided it best to give him a little space and not let on that I'd been watching him try to negotiate my return to the Pactlands. Returning to my body, I typed a quick message to his phone: *Still at the studio. Got to finish this portrait. Talk tomorrow.*

As I drifted off to sleep later that night, I reflected on

how lucky I was to have caught Pateme with his protection failing. Maybe he'd catch on soon—maybe I'd only have a day or two to look in on him before he underwent the blinding procedure again—but for the moment, I had an in. Perhaps, I thought, snuggling into my pillow, I'd find a chink in his armor, a way to convince him that I wasn't walking poison for Yven.

Caradin had lost his farsight long before he sat down to make recordings for me, but his lessons often seemed oddly prescient, and the next morning's tape was no different.

"I think you've encountered the blinding potion by now," he said shortly after greeting me, "but just to be sure, let me go through the process and the effects."

I ate my oatmeal while he went over the spell and gave me a quick rundown of the ingredients that went into the potion itself. We both knew there was no point in trying to teach me how to brew it. I'd yet to reach that point of competence, and even if I'd had my own brewing equipment and access to the pricy ingredients, I'd never have attempted it alone. According to Yven, a misstep in brewing the stuff would result in an impressive fireball, and I didn't need firsthand proof—not with the fire department already suspicious of the teensy little blaze I'd accidentally started in the front yard the week before.

As I scraped the bottom of the bowl, Caradin said, "Now, the blinding potion is a pain in the ass. If someone's protected, it's nearly impossible for a farseer to get through his defenses."

"Unless they're wearing off," I muttered as I reached for my coffee mug.

"There *is* one weakness that isn't often discussed because it so infrequently applies," he continued. "Blood."

"His or someone else's?" I asked, awkwardly turning the recording into a quasi-conversation, as usual. My parents' house was too quiet.

"We're not sure of the precise mechanism. This is the case with far too many potions, to be frank with you—we know they work, but we're not always certain of *how*, and the brewers who could be researching answers for us prefer to spend their time working on new potions. But what we do know is that on a magical level, blood is powerful stuff. Even humans recognize that."

"Again," I said between sips, "whose blood do we need for this?"

"You're probably worried that I'm going to suggest slicing your palm open and doing something disgusting," said Caradin. "First, *no*. If you ever need to use your own blood, either ask a healer to draw it from a vein or else cut yourself in a less painful spot. Hands and fingers are highly enervated, so no matter how impressive you may think it looks to draw a dagger across your hand or whatever other nonsense you've absorbed, don't do it. It'll hurt like hell, and if you cut too deeply, you'll mess up your hand."

"Noted."

"Second, relax. No one needs to bleed for this to work. The weakness in the blinding potion runs up and down bloodlines. A farseer who truly focuses can break through the whiteout if the person protected is blood kin—not a family member by marriage, not a friend, only blood. It has nothing to do with how emotionally close you are to the target. Again, we don't know exactly how it works, but it *does*. You know, I've spent most of my life protected because of my work with Intelligence—not currently, but I was for a couple hundred years. Dad was able to see me during that period, and I could see him. I couldn't see anyone else on our team, but the blood exception is legitimate."

I almost dropped my coffee. Pateme's protection wasn't degrading…

"And it doesn't need to be as close a relationship as parent to child," he continued. "Theoretically, it would work for any two people who share kinship, though I believe it grows more difficult with distance. If I had a third cousin who were protected, it would be harder for me to see him than it would be to see Dad. That is, uh...if I were still a farseer, I mean."

Pausing the tape, I leaned back in my chair and stared at the pale yellow wall while I considered Caradin's lesson. After a moment, I realized I was smiling.

It wasn't a *nice* smile, but then I didn't hold any warm feelings for my great-great uncle those days.

In the weeks that followed, when I wasn't listening to Caradin, I trailed Pateme around Beukal like a shadow whenever I could steal the time. I don't know quite what I expected to find, but I held out hope for some tidbit so compromising that if I sent it to the director's office via Yven, Pateme would allow me to return in order to buy my silence.

Unfortunately for my half-cocked dreams of espionage, Pateme proved to be as boring as a choirboy. His daytime meetings seemed to be all agency business, totally above-board. He wasn't carrying on an affair with an underling. He packed a lunch most days—a salad with a rotating selection of protein and a dinner roll—and at least three days per week, he headed for the DPP gym in the evening. At home, he usually settled in with a book to wind down. In truth, his only vice appeared to be his caffeine consumption, judging by the number of times per day he made a pit stop at his office tea bar, but I certainly wasn't one to criticize on that front.

A squeaky-clean bureaucrat with a monastic home life wasn't helping my grand plan of muscling my way back into the Pactlands. I'd almost given up on Pateme as a waste of my time by late February, but when I checked in on him on the evening of March 2, I overheard more than I'd bargained for.

I needed a distraction that night. All day, I'd caught myself musing about the fact that it was the fiftieth anniversary of Caradin's death. Part of me thought I should acknowledge the occasion in some way—heck, after two months with his recordings, I almost felt like I knew the man. Grace was buried in Charlottesville, but there wasn't even a marker for my granddad. I couldn't have left him flowers if I'd tried. Nagged by guilt, I stretched out and turned my attention to Pateme, whom I found working late, alone in the executive suite, tea close at hand beside his computer. As he frowned at the screen, his phone began to chime, and he absently hit the button to take the call. "Yes?"

"Pateme?" came a woman's voice through the speaker. "Is that you?"

His demeanor changed in an instant. Straightening in his chair, he closed his document and leaned toward the phone. "Liventi? What's the occasion? And a premature happy birthday to you—tomorrow's six hundred eighteen, is it not?"

Liventi. Pateme's older sister, and Fradin and Aunt Lily's mother. That was my great-grandmother on the line, I realized, and I moved closer to the desk to listen in.

She didn't seem to be in a festive mood. "Is this private?"

He triggered the protections around his office with a quick gesture. "It is now. You sound troubled."

Liventi sighed. "Mafora."

"What about her?"

"She's missing," she said, lowering her voice to a near whisper. "I need your help, little brother."

Pateme rested his chin on his fist and studied the phone. "Missing *how*, exactly? Has she run off? You don't think she was kidnapped, do you?"

"I…" She hesitated, then said, "Inade thinks she was abducted."

Even I could hear the caution in that remark.

"And what do you think?" Pateme asked.

"I don't know. But I would sleep better if I knew my daughter was safe. You have connections," she continued. "Couldn't you spare an investigator or two to check on your little niece?"

Pateme chuckled. "You mistake me for a man with a private army, Liv—"

"*Please,*" she interrupted. "Inade hasn't gone public yet, and he's hoping to keep this quiet, but he's furious. If I could just have some reassurance that she's safe…"

Liventi's voice died away, but Pateme took his time before answering her. "I can't instruct my people to go on a manhunt for Mafora, but I…might have an idea for you," he said slowly. "Fradin's granddaughter."

I heard Liventi's sharp intake of breath. "A *granddaughter?* Already?"

"She's in her mid-twenties, I think. Maybe late twenties. Hasn't seen thirty yet, so she's still—"

"A baby. My goodness. I didn't even know he had children…"

She left the question unspoken and hanging, and Pateme volunteered an answer, albeit with apparent reluctance. "Just one, a son. Henry."

"Henry," she repeated with a smile in her voice. "Curious name. Have you met him?"

"No."

"Oh. Do you plan to? I don't know how often you leave the Pactlands these days…"

Pateme closed his eyes and rubbed his forehead. "I'm sorry to tell you like this, but he died a few years ago."

"*Died?*"

"A car crash. He and his wife both. They left a daughter, but that's all."

"A tragedy," she murmured. "And after Fradin, I know tragedy…"

Pateme sat motionless at his desk, glowering at the phone.

"Teme?" Liventi asked. "Are you there?"

"I am."

"Oh, good, I thought we'd been disconnected." She huffed in frustration. "You know, Liliol didn't even tell me of her brother's passing until five years after the fact. My children never make life easy for me."

His expression remained inscrutable—not sad, empathetic, or even bored, but simply neutral. Whatever his feelings, he kept them locked carefully away.

"Do you think Fradin could have been saved?" she asked. "If she'd told me in time."

"No," he said, an edge creeping into his voice. "No, I do not. And don't you dare blame Liliol for his death."

"All I'm saying is that if someone had brought him to a healer, then surely—"

"He contracted a bad cold that turned into pneumonia," Pateme interrupted. "And his body wasn't strong enough to fight it. Miranda did what she could. I know he died in a hospital—"

Liventi snorted dismissively. "Human healers are useless. Might as well entrust your health to a child."

"You...couldn't be more wrong, actually. And I doubt that our most talented healers would have been able to save Fradin. That's what the draught does to you. It weakens, and then it kills. *Quickly*. He knew what he was doing when he took it. But you didn't call me for an argument," he said, resuming his forehead massage. "As I was trying to tell you, Fradin left a granddaughter. The draught doesn't seem to have affected her."

"At all?" Liventi asked.

"I mean, she's three-quarters human—she certainly looks the part."

I frowned at Pateme. He knew damn well I was half-blooded, so why had he lied to his sister?

"But she's a farseer," he continued. "I'm sure of it. Not fully in control yet, but she's got the ability."

"More in control than you think, bub," I muttered.

"A farseer?" Liventi echoed. "How is she possibly a *farseer?*"

"It's a wild talent. They pop up, you know that," he said, smoothly avoiding the pertinent fact he wasn't sharing with her. "I've seen the girl. She has an odd orientation—she sees current events, not the future or past. If there's another like her at DOI, they aren't telling me. Anyway, if you're sufficiently worried about Mafora to come to me but not so desperate that you'd seek out assistance through the proper channels"—he raised his voice as Liventi sputtered—"you might consider asking her for help."

"You know how Inade is," she protested. "If word spread that another of our children had shamed the family—"

"Be honest with me: is there any chance that Mafora is considering the draught? Because if she is, then I *will* take this to Laws and have a proper missing person investigation opened, Inade's pride be damned."

Liventi paused, then mumbled, "No. None at all."

"You're positive?"

"I'd tell you if I thought she was after the draught. I can't lose another child like that, Teme…"

I caught him as he rolled his eyes at the phone, but he remained professional. "If this is a matter less serious than the draught, then I would seek out Rose."

"Rose…"

"Thorn. Fradin's granddaughter," he said with a hint of impatience. "She's an artist who lives in Richmond. Within an hour's drive of the Oilville portal," he added before Liventi could ask. "If you and Inade want to pursue that avenue, let me know, and I can tell you how to contact her."

"Thank you," she said. "I'll be in touch."

"You know how to reach me, sister."

Before he could cut the connection, she asked, "Why didn't you tell me about Fradin's son sooner?"

"Because you didn't ask," he replied, and hung up.

Pateme sat there for a moment longer, staring into space and keeping his thoughts to himself, then pushed himself up from his desk, turned off the soundproofing, and stalked toward the elevators.

Releasing my hold on the vision, I opened my true eyes to the blackness of my bedroom and replayed what I had witnessed in my mind, trying to make sense of Pateme's actions. Aunt Lily had always shielded me from her family, and Pateme certainly hadn't suggested that I look them up during my trips to the Pactlands. Had something changed?

And if so, why wasn't he being honest with Liventi?

CHAPTER 6

Eight days later, on a wet Tuesday night, I stayed late at the studio to catch up on the commissions I'd pushed to the back burner between my lessons with Caradin and my amateur sleuthing. Yven had already told me he'd be out of pocket—he'd mentioned the previous evening that Pars and Canna had invited him over for dinner—and as he'd barely been cooking for himself in recent weeks, I encouraged him to take them up on the offer of companionship and a hot meal. Unable to steal a long chat with Yven, I grabbed takeout in Carytown and ate in my studio, the back half of my building. With the gallery lights dimmed and my playlist shuffling through pop piano covers, I perched on my padded stool and clutched a takeout box of fried rice, contemplating an unfinished canvas while my chopsticks poked around for shrimp. The client wanted an Appalachian sunrise rendered in oils, and I kept cutting my eyes from my reference photos to the painting, considering the mix of colors in the clouds and the gradations of the mountains' shadows. It wasn't *bad*—I was close—but the painting wasn't yet near enough to perfect to satisfy my inner critic.

Only when the bell over the gallery door jingled did I realize I'd forgotten to lock up when I'd dashed in from the storm. Kicking myself, I put my dinner aside, wiped my mouth, and pushed back the curtain that separated the halves of my professional space. "Hi, there," I said, tucking my hands into my old purple hoodie's front pocket. "I'm so sorry, but I'm closed. Is there something you need help with?" Glancing out the wide front window at the pouring rain in the streetlights' glow, I added, "Need to call an Uber? I don't mind if you want to wait here until your car arrives."

That spiel should have been enough to garner a rushed apology from the average shopper, but the man in the gallery just stared at me, brow slightly puckered, as if trying to make sense of my damp slouchwear. I studied him in turn: he looked a few years older than me and maybe three inches taller, slim-built but not scrawny, and winter-pale like so many of us after the long cold. His hair was an unremarkable medium brown, and he wore it pulled back in a low ponytail—far too close to Founding Father cosplay to be stylish. His eyes, too, were brown, and what he lacked in eyelashes he more than made up for with his thick eyebrows. He carried no umbrella against the storm, instead opting for a long black coat with a high collar and hood that dripped on my vinyl floor. He didn't smile, but then again, considering the deluge on the other side of the door, I couldn't really blame him.

"Look around, if you like," I offered, hoping I sounded sufficiently confident that he wouldn't try to rob me. "I'm just grabbing a bite back here. If you see something you can't live without, let me know—I've got some heavy-duty plastic wrap that'll keep the rain off." With that, I turned and headed for the safety of my studio and my fully charged phone, craving its reassurance in case the evening's browser got any dangerous ideas.

Before I could take three steps, however, I heard his clipped voice behind me: "Are you Rose Thorn?"

That wasn't an odd question—as the gallery's owner, artist, and sole employee, I got it all the time—but the fact that it was posed in Low Elvish made me stop in my tracks. Turning back to the man, I eyed him more carefully, as if that would do me any good. If he'd come out of the Pactlands, he was either a sorcerer or masked. "I am," I replied in kind. "Who wants to know?"

He flicked his hand toward the windows behind him, and the glass instantly darkened toward opacity. With another quick gesture in front of his face, his mask fell away. He hadn't deviated far in designing his disguise—same hair, same eyes, same narrow lips—but his cheeks had risen and his ears elongated, and when he opened his mouth, I caught a glimpse of his suddenly sharper teeth. The man was unmistakably elven.

"Do you know who I am?" he asked.

I shook my head and folded my arms, willing my nervous stomach to settle. "Can't say that I do."

He sized me up for a few seconds longer, then said, "I am Inade ti'Cren."

It took every ounce of my willpower to keep my expression neutral as my mind whirled.

Inade. My dad's grandfather, Aunt Lily's father. He'd disowned his son for daring to love my grandmother. From the little I'd gleaned, he was one of the wealthiest men in the Pactlands, the head of one of the most prominent Halls. Aunt Lily had mentioned that he was a floramancer like her—that wild talent ran in Hall ti'Cren—but she'd also insisted that I was safer if Inade didn't know of my existence.

On the other hand, he could be my ticket to acknowledgement. If one of the Halls acknowledged me, then it wouldn't matter who else was hiding in my family tree—Yven and I could be together without the specter of the draught hanging over our relationship. Diriem surely knew about me but had never said a word, so I didn't hold out much hope for Hall ti'Dana. If I played my cards right and impressed Inade, however, maybe I'd find a way out of my predicament and into Hall ti'Cren.

His body language dampened my enthusiasm, however. Ramrod straight and unsmiling, Inade gave off an air that was anything but familial, and I saw little of Aunt Lily or of Fradin—the sunburned, laughing blond with his arm around my redheaded grandmother—in his face. In truth, the way he looked at me suggested he'd befouled himself by coming through my door.

And how *had* he found me, anyway? Pateme had offered Liventi my contact information, but I'd have expected a phone call, not a visit. Sure, there couldn't be many artists with my name in the Richmond area—and I *did* have a website for the gallery—but why had he looked me up instead of just calling? More importantly, how did he have credentials out of the Pactlands? I didn't know much about him, but no one had ever suggested that he was an agent. Then again, maybe Inade was wealthy enough that the folks in charge of granting portal access didn't mind if he took the occasional field trip.

Though hopeful, I proceeded with caution and played dumb.

"Lord ti'Cren," I replied, keeping my distance. "What can I do for you?"

His head cocked ever so slightly. "I'm surprised you speak this language. Did Liliol instruct you?"

"No, sir. I got it by potion."

He grunted. "Explains the accent, I suppose. So," he continued, his eyes narrowing, "'Thorn,' is it?"

"Yes, sir."

"He had the gall to give you that name?"

I wasn't sure which *he* Inade was referring to, but the tone of his voice suggested his indignation was directed at Fradin instead of my dad. Both of my grandfathers had adopted new surnames as part of their aliases, but they hadn't strayed far from the originals. Ti'Dana—"of storms"—had become simply "Storm" for Caradin, and Fradin had done much the same for ti'Cren, which, translated from the Elvish, came out as "of thorns."

"Most people around here get their father's name," I replied. "It's not like my folks gave me a choice. I went through school dealing with floral jokes."

"Well, then, Ms. Thorn," he said with distaste, "I've come to retain your services."

"You…want a portrait painted?" I guessed.

Inade folded his arms. "I have it on good authority that you're a farseer."

It sounded like Liventi had spilled the dirt from Pateme. Still, I tried not to admit too much. "I have the talent, yes, but I've known about it for less than a year. If you really need a farseer, I'm not the best for the job. Still figuring it out, you know?"

"I accept your limitations," he replied, "but procuring assistance through a more public route is not an option. Besides, I hear that you can see events as they happen, not the past or future."

"Yes, sir," I allowed. "And I'm happy to try. All I'm saying is that I can't guarantee results."

As I stood there, my dinner growing cold in the studio behind me, Inade began to pace the gallery floor. "What I tell you now is to be held in the *strictest* confidence, girl. Is that understood?"

"Yes, sir…"

"My daughter has been kidnapped," he said, barely looking at me. "My youngest. She's been missing for ten days."

"And you haven't gone to Laws?"

His head jerked toward me, annoyance tightening his features. "The last thing the Hall needs is another scandal. Surely you can appreciate that."

Though I inwardly bristled, I tried to maintain my polite façade. "What's her name?"

"Mafora."

"Any idea who might have taken her, or why? Have you received a ransom note?"

"Nothing. She's simply vanished, and I need you to tell me where she is."

A ghost of an idea that had been brewing ever since Inade announced himself suddenly began to take on form and detail. Judging by Liventi's conversation with her brother, Mafora wasn't in immediate danger—hell, maybe she hadn't been kidnapped at all. Her father seemed more concerned about shame than about her safety, which suggested that Liventi was on to something. If there was no true emergency, then maybe I could work this to my advantage.

"I can't just give you an answer," I said to Inade. "That's not how my talent works." Stretching the truth, I explained, "In the best of circumstances, it takes time and luck for me to find anything useful. And my farsight is most reliable when I have a connection to the target—when I'm trying to see someone I know."

"What do you need for this to work?"

"I need to get to know your daughter or know enough *about* her that I can find her. That's not an overnight process." I hesitated, then asked, "Do you think she's still in the Pactlands?"

"I have no reason to believe she's fled," he replied, marching down the gallery.

"Well, in my limited experience, I've found that my farsight works best when I'm close to the target. Get me into the Pactlands, and I'll have better luck finding her."

He stopped in his tracks, then wheeled on me. "You want *me* to bring *you* into the Pactlands?"

"You want me to find Mafora?" I countered.

For a moment, I thought I might have pushed him too far, but Inade seemed to concoct a plan as he glanced at the paintings hanging around the room. "I suppose I could get you in," he said. "Hide you in my home for the duration. Mafora mostly lives with me—would that give you enough information?"

"I mean, it would help if I could ask questions about her…"

He huffed an impatient sigh, then pointed to my work. "You painted these?"

"Yes, sir. I do landscapes and portraiture—"

"Then that's your cover story," he interrupted, heading for me so quickly that I stepped back toward the curtain in alarm. "You're a sorcerer I've hired to do a family portrait. That would give you a reason to be in my house and to talk to my other children. I trust you can be tactful in how you ask for information about their sister…and that you can maintain your cover."

Inade's plan stung. Sure, I hadn't been expecting a grand homecoming from him, but if I agreed to his ruse, the rest of his kids wouldn't know that I was family. Clearly, he was in no hurry to acknowledge me into the Hall.

But if I found Mafora—if I played along and did him an undeniable favor—then maybe he'd think better of me. A farseer had to bring something of value to the family, right? Maybe even something sufficiently valuable to balance out Fradin's sin.

If nothing else, I'd be back in the Pactlands, and *not* under Pateme's watch. Plus, I couldn't deny that I was curious to at least meet Aunt Lily's siblings, even if I couldn't introduce myself.

"Works for me," I said. "If you can wait an hour, I just need to pack—"

"I need to make the arrangements first," he said, and started for the door as he masked up again. Returning the windows to transparency, he ordered, "Be ready to leave this time tomorrow. I'll meet you here."

I watched from inside the gallery as he hurried through the rain to a black sedan and sped off into the night. "Nice to meet you, too," I muttered.

I had little appetite for the rest of my fried rice, and I soon abandoned my work for home. After checking to see that Yven was still at dinner—and being fussed over by Pars and Canna's elder daughters, who came armed with sparkly nail polish—I put together a few halfway professional outfits and threw a smock into my weekender duffel, wondering what I'd just gotten myself into.

How the hell was I supposed to pass myself off as a sorcerer? Whether I attempted Pactish or Low Elvish, my

Virginian drawl asserted itself, and I hadn't been around native speakers long enough to address my pronunciation quirks. Okay, so I'd just say that I wasn't from Beukal—maybe there were weird accents out in the Pactlands' version of the sticks. I'd let Inade take the lead there. And I did look the part of a sorcerer, as long as no one asked me to do anything with magic. Sorcerers tended to cast by using verbal triggers, while elves relied on gestures. Inade's kids wouldn't ask me for a demonstration, would they?

And then there was the issue of clothing. I certainly didn't own a formal robe, the Pactlands' alternative to a suit, but hell, I was an artist. Perhaps that fact would be enough to explain away my fashion choices, especially if I kept my wardrobe basic and left my earrings at home. The sorcerers I'd met didn't go for piercings, and I decided that I could pass off my holes as youthful folly if pressed.

I kept looking in on Yven, and around eight, I finally caught him in his car, headed home. As soon as he walked through the door, his phone beeped with my incoming message: *Need to talk. Okay?*

"Of course," he said to the empty apartment, and I gave him time enough only to glance at his indoor orchid garden before his phone rang.

Once it went to voicemail and he triggered the speaker, I said, "Long story short, I'm coming over tomorrow."

"*What?*" He stared at the phone as if I'd suggested a refreshing picnic on Mars. "How? Your credentials won't work—"

"Inade ti'Cren came to see me tonight. I'm going over to help him find a missing person, and you don't know *anything* about that. Got it?"

"I know nothing about nothing," he assured me, sinking onto his couch. "But...your great-grandfather? Truly?"

"I think he only found out I existed in the last week," I replied. "Doesn't seem too keen on me. But look, if I can get in his good graces and get acknowledged..."

Yven smiled to himself. "Do you think he would?"

"If all goes according to plan, he's going to owe me."

"Obviously, but how much?"

"I can't go into detail, but I think acknowledgement would be fair for what he's asking."

He whistled softly. "Are you in danger, Rosie? Do you need help? I know where the ti'Cren mansion is, I could sneak out there…"

"Thanks, but I've got to fly under the radar for now," I told him. "Anyway, don't worry if I don't call in the next few days. I may have my hands full. But Yven…*this* could be the answer we've been looking for."

"That would be wonderful, but worry about keeping yourself safe for now. If you need me, just call. Night or day, I'll drop everything."

"I know," I murmured, and smiled even though he couldn't see me. "Thank you. Wish me luck," I added as the recording beeped its ending.

"I'll be waiting," he said to the silent room. "Love you, Rosie."

When Inade swept into the gallery the following evening to collect me, he frowned bemusedly at the baggage waiting by the door. "Just how long do you anticipate this taking?" he asked.

"Probably not more than a few days, hence the weekender," I replied, pointing to my luggage. "Clothes, toiletries, battery packs for my phone. I should warn you that I don't trust myself to magically dry my hair yet, so I hope no one's offended by ponytails."

He gestured to the pile beside it. "And the rest?"

"Travel easel," I explained, starting with the cylindrical black carrying case. "Couple of canvases. Oils and brushes in the padded bag. Drop cloths. Sketchpads and pencils. Normally, I'd work with a camera, too, but I don't want to have to explain my tech." As Inade still seemed displeased,

I said, "You've never been in an artist's studio before, have you?"

"Can't say that I have."

"Well, if this is the cover story we're working with, then I want to make it convincing."

His expression softened fractionally. "You're taking this seriously."

"You sound surprised." Hoisting my duffel onto my shoulder, I asked, "Are you out front? Could you hold the door, please?"

Inade popped the trunk of his sedan, a sleek Mercedes—no shock there—and waited as I schlepped my gear outside. He made no move to assist me as I played Trunk Tetris, and by the time I'd wrangled all of my bags into position, he was behind the steering wheel.

I posted a sign informing passersby that I was on vacation, locked up, and slid into the seat beside Inade. "At least it's not pouring tonight, eh?"

He grunted and headed toward the Interstate.

The drive to the Oilville portal didn't take much longer than half an hour, even in the dark, but the time stretched painfully as I alternated between staring out the window and trying to make awkward conversation with my taciturn companion. I could imagine why Inade wasn't doing much in the way of small talk—having to deal with me due to his missing kid couldn't have left him in the most genial of moods—but without even the radio to cover the uncomfortable silence, I did my best to drag a semblance of civility from him. "Tell me about Mafora," I said as we passed a milk hauler.

Inade stared out at the light traffic. "What about her?"

Everything, I wanted to snap, but I bit my tongue. "Uh…start with basics. How old is she?"

"Forty-two."

Younger than Yven—in elven terms, barely more than a kid. "Is she still in school? Working?"

"What sort of question is *that*?" he said icily.

"Just trying to get a sense of her. I heard that school normally goes to thirty-five—"

"Then why would you ask whether she's still a student?"

"Because I don't know much about how things work in the Pactlands," I replied, choosing my words carefully, "and I'm trying not to make assumptions. Didn't know if she was going for a graduate degree or something—I wasn't implying that she's stupid."

His hackles seemed to settle. "She and two of her classmates opened a bespoke tailoring business several years ago. They're hoping to eventually make a name for themselves as designers."

"Nice. I tried to sew a dress once back in college, and it was a *hot* mess. Fine art major," I offered. "My emphasis was in painting, but the degree required classes in a few other media, and I stupidly took an elective in fashion design. *Barely* passed that one."

Inade made no effort to continue the conversation, and silence descended upon the car once more.

"You said Mafora mostly lives with you. Where else does she go?" I asked.

"She has an apartment in Beukal when needed."

"Ah. Roommates? Boyfriend, girlfriend?"

"No."

"All right. Her business partners, have they said anything about her, uh…abduction?"

"They said only that she claimed she was going on vacation out of the city for a few days. She never mentioned where."

Something told me that Mafora's friends knew more than they were letting on, but I didn't press the issue with Inade. "What does she look like? It'd be helpful to have a picture of her to focus on, but can you give me a description?"

He shrugged. "Approximately your size, perhaps a little thinner. Brown hair, brown eyes. Freckles, but she keeps those masked. Favors my family. I can give you her picture once we arrive."

Inade made no attempt at conversation until we pulled off the Interstate in Oilville and turned toward the country road that led to the portal. The way into the Pactlands was well hidden at the end of a wooded track. A thick, fallen oak seemingly blocked the road to discourage exploration, and the portal itself wouldn't open until the attendants on the other end had verified credentials and ascertained that the coast was clear. Fortunately, there was almost no traffic around us, as I couldn't imagine what other drivers would think about a Mercedes turning off the paved road. Inade had sense enough to idle on the shoulder for a minute, waiting for a farm truck to disappear before driving into the woods, and he sped through the ensorcelled tree barrier without hesitation.

"So, uh," I said, holding on to the door as the car bumped along, "how were you planning to get me through the portal, again?"

"You're going masked."

When we pulled into the clearing at the end of the trail, Inade turned on the dome light, dropped his mask, then made a quick gesture in front of my face. I felt the slight pins-and-needles sensation of the mask forming—odd but painless—and slid open the visor mirror to see the result.

The woman who looked back at me strongly resembled my dad, a brown-eyed blonde who seemed about thirty. My cheekbones had risen, and when I opened my mouth, I saw sharper teeth in my reflection. Tucking my hair behind my ears, I found that they now came to points, and my piercings had vanished.

But more than that, I was *stunning*. Had my features been slightly more human, I could have fronted a makeup campaign.

"Mind telling me who I'm supposed to be?" I asked.

He reached into the back and handed me a silky purple shawl. "Put this on and say nothing," he replied, then opened the glove compartment and handed me a slim black wallet. I opened it to see the woman whose face I was wearing looking back at me, then read her name: Liventi ti'Tam.

"Simpler to procure a pass for my wife than for a random sorcerer," Inade explained. "And don't be alarmed, I'll take the mask off you once we're through. It's not a difficult spell, but it might be unduly challenging for a quarter-blood."

"Thank you," I replied, deciding not to correct him. Yven had taught me how to mask—I could do it with ease—but I was suddenly grateful that I'd been too preoccupied about the trip to have masked my own pierced earlobes. After all, there was no reason for Inade to know just yet that I was more elven than he thought.

As Inade called the portal attendant, I thought of Yven, alone in his apartment with his flowers. Knowing him, he'd be worried—not only because I was running around with the ti'Crens, but because I was returning to the Pactlands by decidedly illegal means. But although Yven was a narc, he was *my* narc, and I trusted that he wouldn't be the one to sound the alarm.

After a few minutes, the trees in front of the car began to flash with rainbow colors as the portal opened—a pinprick of light in the skin of reality that rapidly widened into a hole about six feet in diameter. Inade drove through into Beukal's external portal building and proceeded to the checkpoint, where the attendant on duty, a centaur who sported a dark green uniform only on his top half, waved us through with little fuss. Credentials back in hand, Inade sped out of the building and headed toward a part of the capital that I didn't recognize.

"Where are we going?" I asked, looking for landmarks outside the windows.

"Internal portal. Not a word, now."

I obliged, riding in silence until we reached the portal building that connected Beukal to other cities in the

Pactlands. The external portal building reminded me of an oversized version of the domes that dotted the sides of the road back home, where sand was stored until needed by the road crews. The building that housed the internal portals, however, looked more like a ten-lane toll booth— that is, if toll booths came equipped with psychedelic light shows. On the far side of each booth, past the protective barrier arm, was an open portal, which flashed and sparked with no discernable rhythm. Above the booths hung lit signs indicating the portals' destinations, places I'd never heard of and couldn't have plotted on a map if my life depended on it. As we joined the line of vehicles headed toward the portals, I was relieved that Yven knew of my whereabouts, as heading off to points unknown with a stranger is seldom the wisest course of action.

Inade veered toward the right, and after the bored attendant waved us on, we drove through the portal marked for Kelomb. As soon as we were clear of the smaller portal building on the far side, Inade removed my mask with a grunt.

Folding my borrowed shawl, I asked, "How far are we from Beukal?"

He shrugged. "Doesn't really matter. I wouldn't make the trip without the portal, if that's what you're asking."

"Like, physically…fifty miles? Five hundred?"

"You do realize that we don't employ human systems of measurement here, correct?"

"I'm sorry, I'm just trying to get my bearings."

After a moment, he said, "New Orleans."

"Pardon me?"

"I was told once that Kelomb is virtually atop New Orleans. You know the place?"

"Yes, sir," I replied, marveling at the distance we'd covered. "I visited once in college. The food's great, and the party scene is fun if you're not in the middle of a hurricane."

He briefly chuckled. "You needn't worry about such

here. There is no true ocean in the Pactlands."

"No?"

"No. The architects ringed it with water, but that may have been more for their own sense of aesthetics. I can't say that the design displeases me, though."

"Do you not like the sea?" I asked.

"When I'm on shore, admiring the view, and not troubled by a storm rolling in...I like it very much." Shifting in his seat as he turned onto a smaller road that passed through a stand of the Pactlands' oddly stunted trees, he said, "Before we arrive...while you are here, your name is Rose Anomi. Is that clear?"

"Yes, sir," I murmured.

"Don't forget it. Now, many of my children still reside with us. If you wish to ask them about Mafora, you may do so, but I trust you can manage this with discretion. None of them know she's been taken, and I intend to keep it that way. Understood?"

"Sure."

"The servants will assist you if you need anything. Three meals will be set out, but if you can't wait for some reason, simply ask. The staff has been informed of the purpose of your visit and will accommodate you. When you locate Mafora, come to me *immediately*. Otherwise, if I have need of you, I will seek you out."

There would be no bonding on this trip, *that* was for sure. "I'll stay out of your way."

"See that you do. I'm a busy man. And one other matter: my wife is not to be disturbed."

"Does she know who I am?" I asked, feigning ignorance.

"She does, but she's a fragile creature, and she seldom ventures out of her suite these days. Leave her in peace."

Though disappointed, I agreed and watched the road for signs of habitation.

When I was ten, my parents decided that I needed some culture over my spring break and took a road trip to Asheville to see the Biltmore Estate. The place was, to my child's eye, a palace—a grand château of a mansion set with the Blue Ridge as a backdrop. I wasn't all that thrilled to be dragged along on a tour, being ten and all, but I returned during college after taking a survey lecture in the architecture department and found a greater appreciation for the site. The house had nearly four *acres* of floor space—my parents' home could fit comfortably within it about fifty times over—and boasted over two hundred rooms. I remember wandering through the banquet hall with its seventy-foot ceilings, tapestries, and pipe organ, wondering what poor soul was tasked with cleaning the high windows.

Hall ti'Cren made the Biltmore look modest.

Outside of the few nature parks and the agricultural zones in the Pactlands, which were anchored to the outside world, few plants grew well in the soil of that artificial space. The land between the portal and the estate was thus largely a rolling prairie, which made me feel like we were plowing through a formless sea as we drove in the darkness. Without trees to block the view, the mansion rose like a shining beacon, an irregular shape of glowing windows and pitched roofs against the night sky. I couldn't make out many details as we approached—it wasn't as if Inade kept spotlights on the place—but the house seemed to loom over us as we neared on the winding drive.

Almost as soon as Inade parked the car in front of the main doors, a set that wouldn't have seemed out of place on a medieval cathedral, four servants dressed all in black hurried out to greet him. "Leave your belongings," he told me as he slid out of the car. "The staff will see to them."

I murmured my thanks to the servants as they opened the trunk and began to unpack my gear, then jogged after Inade as he marched into the house.

Examining the vaulted wooden ceiling of the foyer

required me to crane my neck. A massive staircase rose ahead of us, but it only went up to the next level. Smaller staircases on that floor led to the others, balconied corridors that ringed the foyer before disappearing toward the more distant ends of the mansion. Fortunately, someone had thought to install an elevator behind the main stairs, a decorated brass and glass tube that rose at least a hundred feet. I barely had time to admire the polished oak floor, the sumptuous carpets, and the delicate crystal chandeliers before Inade hustled me into the elevator and hit the button for the fifth floor.

"Your guest room is in the east wing," he said as the car smoothly ascended. "I trust you'll have what you need for the night. Breakfast should be laid around dawn, and that will be in the dining room in the south wing."

"Is there a *map*, by chance?" I asked.

He smirked. "There is a telephone in the room that will connect you to the chief steward. Call him if you need directions."

Once we reached the fifth floor, Inade led me through a maze of well-appointed corridors, the carved stonework of their walls almost blending into the wooden ceilings like the shore abutting a river. The rich tones and thick pile of the runners suggested they'd cost far more than my Subaru, and even the brass sconces seemed to gleam.

Pars and Yven had warned me that Hall ti'Cren was image-conscious, and I could see where they'd gotten that impression. The mansion might as well have been wallpapered with money.

At the end of a hallway, Inade opened a beautifully arched wooden doorway, revealing a suite that would have set most people back a mortgage payment at a five-star hotel. The bed, covered in blue and gold brocade, could have slept three with room to spare. The posts had been carved in the likeness of young trees—the sort that would never naturally grow in the Pactlands—and their boughs entangled above the center of the bed, forming a canopy of painted wooden leaves. More thick rugs covered the slate floor, leading to a sitting area with a couch and a pair of chairs covered in the same brocade as the bedspread. Far across the room was a wide, arched window with a simple wooden table and chair beneath it—a desk, I gathered, though out of place with the rest of the opulent furnishings.

"I didn't know what you would require for your painting," said Inade, catching the direction of my gaze. "I had that brought in for your use. Should you stain it, it would be no real loss."

"Thank you. I brought drop cloths, so I'll do my best not to make any permanent messes."

He grunted. "The window has eastern exposure. I trust that you won't mind morning light."

"Not at all. This...this should work nicely," I said, noting a door that had to lead to the bathroom. "Thanks. I'll get my mind straight tonight and see what I can come up with in the morning."

"See that you do. And your name was..."

"Rose Anomi."

"Good. The servants should be here with your belongings presently, Ms. Anomi. Inform them if you need anything further."

Inade was three paces down the hallway when I called after him, "One more question for you, sir."

Though visibly irked, he returned to my room. "*Yes?*"

I lowered my voice in case of the servants' sudden arrival. "Has Mafora ever taken the blinding potion?"

His brow furrowed. "Why would you ask that?"

"Well...I've been told about it," I replied, which wasn't untrue, "and I've heard that some of the more prominent people around here use it for privacy. Given what I've heard about your Hall, I didn't know if your family would want that sort of protection."

"And what *have* you heard, then?"

I didn't rise to the challenge in his tone. "That Hall

ti'Cren is one of the most prominent Halls in the Pactlands. That your philanthropy is widely recognized. All things considered, I wouldn't be surprised if your family used the blinding potion as a precaution. If that's the case, then it may take longer for me to locate Mafora, and I might need to try other avenues."

My flattery cooled Inade's temper. "Mafora has not been given the blinding potion, so put that thought from your mind." He turned to leave again, then glanced back at me. "Time is of the essence. Do not fail me."

I closed the door once he'd rounded the corner, then carefully sat on the couch, hoping not to rip the fine fabric. While I waited for my luggage to arrive, I pulled out my phone and sent a quick message to Yven: *Getting settled. All is well.*

He couldn't answer me, of course, but I hoped that would put his worries to rest for the night.

CHAPTER 7

The house phone was a simple black number, a handset atop a base with a keypad and a few preprogrammed options, but it came equipped with a ringer loud enough to wake the dead.

I bolted upright, disoriented and swimming in the bedding until I remembered where I was and located the source of the sonic attack. Fumbling for the handset, I stopped myself in the nick of time from muttering a groggy, "Hello?" and switched to Pactish. "Yes?"

"Good morning, Ms. Anomi," said a pleasant female voice. "Lord ti'Cren said you wanted an early wakeup today."

"Uh…yes, thank you," I lied. "Um…"

She chuckled as I tried to form coherent sentences. "Breakfast will be served in an hour. Would you like an escort?"

"That would be fantastic."

"Coffee as well?"

"If you could just have it waiting…"

"An incentive. I understand," she said. "Do let me know if you need anything before then."

The sky out my eastern window was just beginning to pinken, and so, quietly cursing Inade, I flipped on the lamps and took stock of my room. I'd set up my easel before going to bed, and I'd spread my paints and other supplies across the tarp-covered desk. That the labels on the paints were in English was an unavoidable hitch in my cover story, but I figured I could explain the situation away as a special order from someone with connections. I'd hung my nicer clothes in the heavy wooden wardrobe and pre-stocked the bathroom with my toiletry kit, though I realized as I considered the phone that I'd neglected to charge my own overnight. Rummaging in the wardrobe for my duffel bag, I found one of the battery packs and plugged up my phone, then hid it away in case of snoops.

At least the shower was hot and the water pressure strong. I stood under the stream, letting it knead my back as I tried to wake up, then dried off and made myself decent. I opted for a simple black tank top and sweater over black leggings that morning, throwing on a chunky green necklace to offset the monochrome palette, and clipped my damp hair back in a bun. A little makeup hid the shadows under my eyes.

"Hi. Rose Anomi," I said, introducing myself to my steam-shrouded reflection in the bathroom. I tried for a confident smile, which came out as slightly pained, and hoped that caffeine would improve my social skills.

Right on schedule, a servant knocked to show me to the dining room, and I grabbed a small sketchpad, just in case. He was quiet and polite as we wound through the house, slowing as needed when I dawdled to look at an ornate carving or admire a burst of stained glass, and he offered me a brief history of the building. "Lady ti'Cren commissioned the main part of the house a year after the Pactlands opened," he explained as I peeked out at the ribbon of sea gleaming in the dawn light, a shining expanse lapping against the stone wall at the end of the long, manicured lawn that marked the edge of the estate. "It took five years to complete to her satisfaction. Shortly after Lord ti'Cren inherited the Hall, he began construction on the north wing, and the others have followed."

"Forgive my ignorance," I replied, "but what happened to…Lady ti'Cren?"

"His mother," my escort murmured. "Drowned,

unfortunately. His Lordship has ruled the Hall since 1674."

While I knew that elves could live a very long time, actually being confronted with proof of it still left me reeling. "That's quite a tenure."

He grinned. "We've been fortunate to see older heads of Halls since we joined the Pact—and your people have enjoyed longer lives with the peace, have you not?"

"Uh…sure," I said, quickly reminding myself that for the moment, I was meant to be a sorcerer. "No complaints."

After a few more stops for me to check out the artwork and surreptitiously try to map my mental trail of breadcrumbs, we reached the south wing's dining room, a space half the size of a basketball court with glass walls on three sides, giving diners a comfortable view of the sea. Ferns and small palms grew in pots scattered around the room, strangely healthy plants for the Pactlands—but then again, Inade *was* a floramancer.

"Please help yourself," the servant murmured, gesturing toward the laden sideboard. "If there's anything else you'd like, you need only ask."

He slipped away while I was still goggling at the beautiful room. Left alone, I studied the spread, tried to figure out what was in the pastries, and decided that my powers of deduction would improve with coffee. The urn at the end of the sideboard yielded a dark brew, and I tasted it before adding sugar. The coffee was rich and almost chocolaty, and while I was no expert, something told me that it wasn't Maxwell House.

When the door opened, I spun around, victim of a sudden, irrational fear that I was about to be caught intruding, but the short man who'd come in smiled as he noticed me. "Ah—sorry, I didn't intend to scare you. You're the painter, right?"

"Rose Anomi," I offered, my heart slowing. "Good morning."

"Likewise. Teolm," he said, and held up his hands,

which were stained with bright green streaks. "I'm not being antisocial, just giving you fair warning that I've been at work *all* night, and you don't want this gunk on you. Trust me. This is after five washings."

A curious smell had begun to waft in my direction, a stench like a pond bottom left to dry out in the summer sun, musky, pungent, and suggestive of decay. "No problem," I replied, and hurriedly carried my coffee to the table. "What do you, uh…do?"

"Are you familiar with Dashom Brothers?"

"No, sorry…"

He waved it off and began loading a plate. "Experimental greenhouses are much of the business. Three sorcerers, they were *brilliant* fellows, spent most of their careers trying to improve the agricultural situation here. It's so labor-intensive to keep our farming districts anchored, you know? Life would be much easier if we weren't so dependent upon the outside world to keep us fed. Anyway, some of the side projects have grown more prominent since the original Dashoms died, and our experimentals are *really* coming along." Glancing back at me from the buffet, he grinned with the manic happiness of a little kid expounding upon his favorite dinosaurs. "I head up the unit that deals with produce for potions. Floramancer, so…" He shrugged. "It was inevitable. And are you not hungry?"

"Working up to it," I replied, and sipped my coffee as he came to the table. Teolm seated himself several chairs away from me—considerate, if not ideal for conversation.

I studied him as he settled in. He was brown-haired like Inade, but his dark eyes reminded me of Aunt Lily's in their shape and the way they crinkled when he smiled. He favored his sister in his size, too—Aunt Lily was five-foot-two on a good day, and Teolm was probably no more than three inches taller.

"Dare I ask what's all over your hands?" I ventured.

He grimaced. "Not dead fish, contrary to what your

nose might be telling you. Ever seen where anophala extract comes from?"

"Can't say that I have…"

Teolm winked. "There's a reason for that. The extract is taken from the fruit, right?" he said, spreading his hands apart as if he were holding a beachball. "Inoffensive stuff. Tastes sweet, actually—I'm sure your potions teachers told you not to try it, but it's harmless in the long run. Just makes your mouth numb for a few days, and for about a week afterward, everything tastes *off*. Professional hazing," he added, spearing a piece of sausage on his fork. "Anyway, to get the fruit, you've got to pollenate the flower, and that's where the goop comes in. They're as tall as I am, narrow, and deep, and they're very temperamental, so the best way to make sure everything takes is to hang upside-down and do the pollination by hand."

"Oh, wow. That's…intense," I said, grateful that Yven preferred orchids.

"Not even the best part! They only flower for about a twelve-hour period, so between collecting pollen and passing it around, we scramble. And because I have *terrible* luck, six of our anophalas bloomed just after dinner last night. We're all on standby right now as it is, but still, there's nothing like hanging by your ankles at midnight, trying to fertilize a flower that smells like rotting corpses, to make you question your career trajectory." Coming up for air, he grinned and returned to his food. "I'm sorry, anyone who's around me after a long night gets the decompression rundown."

"Go right ahead," I replied, and stood. "Think I might have an appetite. Want some coffee?"

"Ooh, yes, please."

As I fixed my plate, I said, "I've got a friend at DPP who'd probably love to see your problem children."

Teolm brightened. "Yeah? Is your friend in the greenhouse? There's a bit of flow back and forth between the government and private facilities."

"No, he's a Regulatory agent, but he grows orchids recreationally. Makes his own vanilla, too, and it's pretty damn good."

"Floramancer?"

"He says no."

"Wow." Teolm seemed genuinely impressed. "Well, tell him we could make arrangements if he wanted to see the anophalas. Professional courtesy and all."

He thanked me when I brought him a hot mug and watched while I resettled myself at the table. "Father's thrilled that you agreed to do the portrait."

"Oh?" I asked, brightening.

"Absolutely. He told a few of us yesterday that you'd be coming out to do some preliminary work, and to spread the word. Said he saw some of your paintings in a gallery about a month ago and couldn't resist hiring someone with your talent."

My warm fuzzies cooled when I heard Inade's lie, but I tried not to let on. "He's too kind."

"My father's not exactly effusive with praise, so I'd take that seriously." Taking a test sip of his coffee, he smiled and seemed to sag in his chair. "How did you plan to go about this, if I may ask? Do you want all of us in a room together, or do you plan to work with us individually? The latter would be much simpler, given our schedules."

"Individual sittings would be just fine," I replied. "I thought I'd do sketches and produce a family composite from those. But I do have one question."

"Ask away."

"How many of you *are* there? Lord ti'Cren never gave me a roster..."

My voice faded as Teolm choked on his drink, but his coughing resolved into laughter. "And that's Father for you," he said once he could breathe again. "Gives orders and lets someone else figure out the details. I can help you there, and with the planning."

"I don't want to impose," I protested. "You're tired—"

He waved my concern aside. "Meh. I'll be running for at least another hour or two before I collapse, so let's do it. I see you brought paper," he added, glancing at the sketchpad by my plate.

I shoveled down a bite of biscuit—passable, but nowhere near as good as Yven's baking—and flipped to a clean page.

"So, Father and Mother, of course," he said. "Let's start at the top. Grabbing Father long enough for a full sitting might be a challenge, and Mother isn't the most social of creatures, I'm afraid. Can you work from photographs?"

"I have, and if that's what the client requires, then I can do it. Sketching, I feel, leads to better portraits because I'm generally able to get a sense of the subject's personality."

"Understandable, and I'm sure most of us can work with you. The painting is to be us and our spouses, correct?"

"That was my impression," I replied, not wanting to contradict Inade.

"An undertaking, that. There are nine of us, six married. How big is your canvas?" he joked.

"If all else fails, I can make it a diptych," I teased back.

Teolm's head tilted. "A what?"

"Oh, uh…a pair of pictures designed to be displayed together," I explained, kicking myself. The term had come out in English—I couldn't think of an equivalent in either of the languages I'd learned via potion—and I hoped Teolm would chalk it up to an artistic technicality.

To my relief, he let it go. "Maybe it won't come to that," he said, and took another bracing sip of coffee. "Right, then, the sibling list. I'm the eldest, never married." He waited while I made notes—I took care to do so in Pactish—then continued. "After me is my brother Jomin, married to Dania. They live here, but he works with Father, so good luck catching him. Liliol is after us, and she's going to be another problem."

"How so?" I asked, feigning ignorance.

"Lives outside the Pactlands," he replied, grimacing. "She's a licensed grower, and from what she tells me, she's doing well for herself, but we seldom see her around here. Liliol has always lived her own life, know what I mean?"

My petite great-aunt was a force of nature, but I couldn't agree with Teolm as heartily as I'd have liked. "Understood. I'm sure I can get by with photographs."

"That's the spirit." He paused, letting me jot down her name and the details, then said, "After Liliol is Otun. She and her husband also live here—Kelar, nice guy. She works for Father, but he's a writer, so he's often around. Then there's Nalani and her husband, Invaton, but they live in Beukal. Healers, both of them. Kilch is next—he works for Father, and his wife, Meala, is a teacher, so you'll have that schedule to contend with."

"Do they live here?" I asked as I scribbled notes.

"Yes, but Tranar and Varil don't. The youngest two boys," he explained. "They married siblings ten years ago, Ovir and Ameru, and they share an apartment in Beukal."

"What do they do?"

Teolm laughed. "Good question. They *claim* they're looking for investors for a film project, but I think that our parents' money keeps them under a roof."

"Artist here. I get it."

"You're working with parental funding, too?" he inquired.

I focused on the paper to avoid looking at him. "Actually, no. My parents died four years ago. Accident."

He hissed and straightened in his chair. "I...I'm so sorry, I meant no—"

"It's all right," I assured him, putting on a small smile. "I don't exactly go around announcing that, so you couldn't have known."

"Still, I do apologize," he mumbled.

I tried to steer the conversation back on track. "Any other siblings?"

"Just one," he replied, following my lead. "Mafora, our baby. She's trying to become a fashion designer in the capital."

"So...she doesn't live here?"

"Only part of the time, and I hear she's gone on a trip. Looking for inspiration or some such—I don't know. We don't have much in common, you understand."

Either Teolm was a decent liar or he had no idea that Mafora was missing, which concerned me. If Inade was so worried about his daughter's safety, then why hadn't he told the rest of his children? Most of them seemed to be successful adults, so couldn't they have tried to quietly help? Of course, Liventi hadn't seemed to think that Mafora was in grave danger. Maybe Inade knew something he wasn't telling me.

I let it be for the moment. "That's it, then?" I asked, counting up the names. "Nine of you, six with spouses?"

He drank his coffee for a moment, contemplating the view out the glass walls, then murmured, "You've heard about our *other* brother, I take it."

My grandfather. "Bits and pieces. I know there's a song..."

"How old are you?"

"Forty," I lied. While Pactlands citizens could marry, rent their own places, and take part-time jobs at twenty-five, mandatory education didn't end until thirty-five, and I didn't want some well-meaning bystander to haul me in for truancy. As sorcerers aged slowly, the fib was plausible.

"Mm. The worst of the scandal was before your time, then." He sipped again, thinking, then quietly said, "This stays between us, yes?"

I nodded.

Tapping the column of names I'd made on my sketchpad, he said, "We had a brother between Liliol and Otun, Fradin." The name came out barely above a whisper. "DPP. He spent too much time outside the Pactlands. About...oh, seventy years ago, he ran off with a human. Father has never forgiven him, so unless he tells you otherwise, I would plan for the nine of us siblings written there."

"I'm sorry."

"It is what it is," he replied with a brief shrug. "And Fradin made his choice. Honestly, I worry about Liliol, all alone out there…"

He needn't have bothered. Aunt Lily was stubbornly independent, and the closest thing she had to a gentleman caller was Jack Carpenter, an octogenarian with macular degeneration who tried to woo her in an old green Cadillac he had no business driving. I couldn't imagine her taking the draught for her widower friend.

"It's none of my business," I said, "but does Liliol keep up with Fradin? Just in case Lord ti'Cren changes his mind," I hastily explained.

Teolm didn't seem offended by the question. "She did, but he didn't live long after taking the draught. He's been gone for a while. Never even met Mafora." After a brief pause, he said, "Again, between us, if you don't see my mother wandering the house, she's been somewhat, uh…*fragile*, shall we say, since his departure. Otun and Kelar practically raised Mafora—they have a daughter about her age. If Mafora is still traveling when you finish your work here, you might ask them for recent pictures of her."

"Thanks," I said, and lowered my voice as I leaned closer. "And I'll keep the rest in confidence. I appreciate the help."

"Oh, certainly," he replied, and returned to his neglected plate. "Any other questions?"

"Well, since I've already been told there isn't a map of the house for guests"—he chortled into his eggs—"just one."

"What's that?"

I slapped on a winning grin. "When do you want to sit for me?"

Perhaps Teolm was just too tired to think straight, but he agreed to serve as my first victim. Fortified by coffee and breakfast, he took me into a lovely old living room, a space of dark wooden paneling, burgundy furniture, and an iron-grated fireplace—an aggressively masculine sort of parlor—and plopped into a leather chair by a window. I sat on an ottoman nearby, sketchpad propped in my lap, and chatted with him while I tried to capture the planes and curves and points of his face.

Of all the people I'd ever drawn, he was one of the most pleasant by far. Teolm understood the assignment—sit relatively still and let me sketch—but he wasn't rigid in his chair. Sometimes, I had to work to make my subject comfortable, but he followed along when I tried to make conversation, and within a minute or two, he was happily telling me about the perils of breeding anophalas. By the time I'd finished the first drawing, I knew far more than I should have about Teolm's most problematic charge, and he'd moved on to war stories concerning the exotic plants in his care. Having spent a little time in Aunt Lily's nursery, I had an idea of what he was up against…and I definitely saw the resemblance. Beyond their eyes and short stature, the two shared mannerisms—their tilt of the head, their dimpled smile, and even the cadence of their laughter told me they were siblings.

I liked him. I could see myself listening to his stories over the dinner table, could imagine him and Aunt Lily picking back and forth and trying to one-up each other with floral hazards. As I drew, I wondered what he'd say if I told him the truth—would he be pleased, or would he cut his sitting short so as to avoid the reminder of his brother?

When I showed Teolm the results, he beamed and declared the drawings far too flattering, then yawned and staggered out of the room. "Come along, Rose, before I drop," he ordered. "Let's find another face for you."

As it turned out, Jomin, Otun, and Kilch were tied up

in an all-morning meeting with their father elsewhere in the mansion, but Teolm was able to snag Kelar, Otun's husband, for me before he wandered off to bed.

Kelar ti'Har was a poet and balladeer who had enjoyed modest success on the stage before deciding that he much preferred to hold a pen. As someone who'd married into the ti'Cren orbit, he didn't know much about Mafora, but he proved more than willing to answer my dumb questions as I drew him. While I made no progress on getting to know my missing great-aunt, I picked up a few tidbits: Teolm was four hundred sixty years old and had spent two months with the healers after inhaling the wrong pollen, Tranar took Varil on as a partner in his film project after Varil's insane dream of running a greenhouse on the estate's property failed spectacularly, and the more responsible members of the family—like Kelar's wife—worked for Inade. "Lord ti'Cren is a jeweler," Kelar explained as I shaded his dark eyes. "Makes some of the finest masking pieces in the Pactlands. Have you never seen his work? I'm surprised you aren't familiar with it."

"Sorcerer," I lied with a shrug.

"Well, yes, I don't suppose you'd need assistance with masking," he allowed. "But he doesn't just make utilitarian pieces—his designs are *exquisite*. Otun's as well," he added, chuckling. "I don't dare to attempt to surprise her with jewelry."

Once I finished with Kelar, he passed me on to Dania ti'Lir, Jomin's wife, who was then occupied with their two-year-old son. The kid was a rambunctious, towheaded ball of perpetual motion—and my first cousin once removed, I calculated—and his mother kept rising from her chair to attend to him while I drew her. She hadn't worked outside the home for some time, instead devoting herself to raising their children, now seven with the youngest. "I look after my grandchildren sometimes, too," she said, proudly pointing to a wall of framed photographs. "And their children. My eldest great-great-grandson will only be twenty-two this year, and he used to spend a month here in the summer."

Dania looked barely old enough to have a kid in middle school, but I tried to accept the weirdness of someone apparently close to my age cheerfully bouncing her baby boy on one knee while telling me about her granddaughter's grandson's scholastic awards. Fortunately for me, she'd lived in the mansion since her wedding in the 1690s, and with only her little boy around the apartment for conversation, she was *delighted* to talk to me about the other ti'Cren siblings.

Teolm, she said, was an odd one. As the eldest, he should have taken an interest in the family business, but he'd followed his passion into experimental botany instead. "Don't get me wrong, he's a *talented* floramancer," she added, "but then so is his father, and you don't see Lord ti'Cren coming home covered in muck." Odder still, as far as she was concerned, Teolm had never taken an interest in romance. "His sister is like that, too," she said, pursing her lips in disapproval. "But so is their mother's younger brother. None of my children seem affected in that regard, fortunately, but as the presumptive heir to the Hall, Teolm should do his duty."

"But wouldn't that leave your husband as Teolm's heir, as it stands?" I pointed out.

"Well, *yes*, but it's the principle of the thing," she replied primly. "Unnatural, you know."

I wasn't surprised when Dania spoke glowingly of Jomin—"Lord ti'Cren's right hand in the business, such a gifted artist"—or of Otun and Kilch, the other jewelers in the family, though she had nothing but disdain for Aunt Lily. "Can you *imagine*?" she asked, leaning toward me and lowering her voice as if fearful that her son would overhear and run away to join his aunt. "If she wants to work in the dirt so badly, she could always join Teolm. But no, she had to register a greenhouse out *there*." From the way Dania spoke of the world beyond the Pactlands, one might think it a radioactive waste. "Why she would leave her family and run away like that after—"

She caught herself with a cough and quickly changed the subject, but I knew damn well which ti'Cren child's transgressions were on her mind.

Dania had nothing but respect for Nalani and Invaton, the healer couple of the group, and Meala, Kilch's wife, earned her praise for being able to manage a classroom of small children. As for the youngest brothers, Tranar and Varil, she offered only rolled eyes. "They want to make *movies*," she said, and sighed. "Children, honestly. And it's all Tranar's fault—Varil's a decent floramancer, but instead of pursuing it in a legitimate fashion, he had this wild idea of trying to run a greenhouse *on the estate* while he lounged about the house all day. No imported soil, none of the measures the actual growers take to make plants flourish here—he just thought he'd put up a building, fill pots with dirt from down the beach, and actually grow something. It was a *miserable* failure, and then he slunk off to play with Tranar and the ti'Pons."

"The ti'Pons?" I asked, trying to get Dania's blonde updo just right.

"Their spouses, I mean. The ti'Pon siblings. I don't know *why* Lord ti'Cren ever agreed to the double marriage. Hall ti'Pon is old, but it hasn't been prominent in four hundred years."

"Love matches?"

She shrugged. "Perhaps. Their father is a business associate, though, which I suspect is the primary cause. Anyway," she added, lowering her voice, "it would never have been allowed if both ti'Pons were female. Varil married a man, and in any case, I understand that he's medically unlikely to sire children, even if he *had* married a woman. Can't risk too much intermarriage, you know."

I attempted to be casual as I shifted the topic. "What about…Mafora, is it? That's the youngest daughter, right? Teolm mentioned she was trying to be a fashion designer…"

Dania chuckled. "She's *young*. Her work isn't bad, and she's pretty enough to model her own pieces, but it's difficult to stand out in that field, and…well."

"Well what?"

She gave me a look that would have given the disapproving biddies of my youth a run for their money. "It's a low-class profession. I'm glad we have designers and tailors and such, but one from *this* Hall? I'm sure her parents are hoping she'll grow out of it."

Fighting back the urge to retort that at least Mafora was doing something more than enjoying her husband's family home, I smiled politely and finished my sketches. Dania practically purred when I showed her the results—a good trick to portraiture is knowing which clients want a more realistic look and which just want to be flattered, and I'd been generous. As I packed my pencils away, she said, "Unfortunately, you'll need to wait until evening to catch my husband or any of his other siblings. Or you could go to Beukal—I have the addresses…"

"I'll just do some preliminary work until everyone returns," I replied. "Thank you anyway—and do tell your husband that I'd like to draw him."

"He won't be thrilled," she said, and rose to escort me to the door. "You must understand that Jomin works all day—sitting for a portrait would be *quite* an inconvenience."

With time to kill before the rest of the available siblings came home, I retraced my steps to my room, then used the house phone to call the chief steward. He was pleasant and professional, and immediately asked if I was in need of a morning snack.

"Not just yet," I told him. "Is there any chance that someone could show me to Mafora's room?"

He hesitated. "May I ask why?"

"Lord ti'Cren said that she had recent photographs in there," I replied, concocting an excuse on the fly. "Since she's apparently out of town, I'd like to see what I can of her."

"*Ah*. That makes sense," he said, and my stomach unclenched. "Yes, I'll send you an escort momentarily."

The promised escort gave me no trouble, and soon, I found myself alone in Mafora's well-appointed suite. Taking my time, I searched the room for pictures and found four tucked into the corners of the silk-covered tackboard hanging by her desk. Two showed the same three women in matching formal robes—Mafora and her business partners, I assumed—but the other pair were of a single subject, a thin brunette with large, dark eyes and a suggestive pout, sporting extravagant gowns. Either a party or a fashion show, I mused. Mafora was objectively pretty, though I saw little of Aunt Lily or Fradin in her.

Taking one of the solo photos as a focusing tool, I locked the door and stretched out across Mafora's wide bed, then stared at the picture until my arm grew tired and flopped to the purple brocade. "Where are you?" I whispered, then closed my eyes and let my farsight engage.

After about a minute of fumbling in the darkness, my inner eyes opened to show me Mafora's face. She sat cross-legged in a wicker chair, beaming and slightly flushed, as if she'd just come off a good, long bout of laughter. Her dark hair was pulled back in a messy bun, the sort of hairdo that takes effort to make it look casually perfect, and she wore a chunky gray sweater over blue leggings. I'd have thought her emerald and diamond necklace to be costume jewelry if not for the family business.

Okay, that answered one question: wherever Mafora might be, she was alive and seemingly happy. While that didn't entirely rule out kidnapping, I doubted she was being held against her will.

Expanding my focus, I briefly studied the room—a

cabin, perhaps, with whitewashed walls and rustic, unfinished pieces of pine framing the door and windows. The cabin held four narrow wooden beds, which had been squashed together to Frankenstein a bed fit for guests. Having lived in a dorm, I had my doubts as to the mattress situation, but at least there was room to sprawl. Brass lamps hung on the walls at regular intervals—unnecessary with the daylight streaming in—and the soot-blackened fireplace would probably be a welcome feature at night.

Was she camping? A glance out the window revealed nothing but a flat expanse of trees, which seemed to rule out the mountain cabin where Aunt Lily had hidden the summer before…but what about the recreational area near Beukal, Green Lake? Weren't there cabins there, too?

Before I could better inspect the view, an interior door opened, showing me a glimpse of a tiny kitchen before a man walked through, carrying a laden tea tray. Mafora grinned at him and patted the low table beside her, and he carefully slid his burden into place. Two plates filled with eggs and diced potatoes, thick slices of warm bread, a pot of a fragrant brew that smelled of peaches and jasmine…

Brunch?

If Mafora had been kidnapped, then she sure as hell wouldn't be *brunching* with her captor unless Stockholm syndrome had hit her hard.

The apparent chef pulled up a matching chair to join her as she poured the tea. He was obviously an elf, though as usual, I couldn't peg his age. His hair was brown and tightly curled, sufficiently close-cropped to keep it manageable, and his eyes, large and blue as an autumn sky, turned up at the corners when he flashed his slightly crooked smile. While Inade had told me that Mafora masked her freckles, the man with her apparently didn't care about his own facial imperfections, a few small acne scars around his chin and a birthmark the size of a quarter descending from his hairline above his left eyebrow. His hands and forearms were lined with faded red welts—not claw marks, I thought, given their irregularity, but I couldn't name the source.

"This smells amazing," said Mafora as he settled in. "Thank you."

"My pleasure. The finest takeout in the region…"

She chuckled. "You plated it—that counts." Cradling her steaming teacup, she said, "I miss you. Must you go in today?"

He nodded sadly. "Afraid so. I was only able to clear the morning, and if I'm not back by lunch, my chief will have my head. But just today and tomorrow, eh?" he added, reaching for her hand. "We'll have the weekend to ourselves, and then I'm on vacation after that. I'll be here so much, you'll be sick of me."

"Impossible," she replied, shifting her grip on the cup to clasp his fingers in hers. "I could never—"

A pounding on Mafora's bedroom door yanked me back to my body in a hurry, and I hastily unlatched it to find a concerned servant on the threshold. "Excuse me, Ms. Anomi, but I was sent to inform you that lunch is served."

"Thank you." I smiled and tried to look collected, though the transition between farsight and my true vision always left me slightly discombobulated for a minute or two. "I'll be down in a bit. Just sketching Mafora's pictures," I explained, holding up my target photo as evidence.

The servant was gracious enough to leave me with directions back to the dining room, and I hastily drew what I'd seen from my vision: Mafora, the young man, and the cabin in the trees.

The trees.

That should narrow it down, I thought—few places in the Pactlands had trees larger than four or five feet tall, but the ones I'd seen through the cabin window looked full-sized. I'd just need to do some digging.

But I'd do it without Inade's help. I didn't know what,

exactly, was going on with Mafora, but it was clear to me that she wasn't a prisoner. Wherever she was holed up, she was there of her own volition—and until I knew more, that would remain our secret.

CHAPTER 8

Hoping to snag the other ti'Cren siblings who lived in the mansion that evening, I made myself comfortable in the dining room as soon as the food went out and waited for them to come home. They arrived about an hour later, talking among themselves, though the conversation came to a screeching halt as soon as they noticed me at the far end of the table. "Hello," I said, raising a hand in greeting. "I'm Rose Anomi."

A dark-haired man—unquestionably Teolm's brother, though which, I couldn't as yet have said—sighed and folded his arms. "Did you need something?"

"Actually," I replied, holding up my list from that morning, "I was hoping to meet and sketch a few more of the siblings. Uh…which are you?"

"Busy," he snapped, then filled a plate and left without another word to me.

The blonde in the trio did likewise, barely acknowledging my presence with a nod. This left only the other man, brown-haired like his brother, who sloughed off his elaborate robe and draped it over the back of a chair before heading for the buffet. "Let me apologize for my brother and sister," he said as he lifted the lid of an ornate silver chafing dish. "Ball season is almost upon us, everyone wants new baubles, and we have a *particularly* demanding slate of customers this year. If you want time with Jomin and Otun, you'd best make an appointment, and you might want to ask Father to put a little pressure on them to show up and smile."

"*Ah*. Kilch, I take it?"

"The same." He turned from the food and grinned, though his smile seemed weary. "Is my presence required for this project of Father's?"

"I could work from photographs," I replied, "but I find the result is always better if I spend time with the subject. Do you have dinner plans? Your wife—"

"On an overnight trip with her students, and I don't know how she does it. How are the potatoes?"

"Sorry, haven't tried them yet. Mind if I sketch while you eat?"

He was amenable to that, and so I made light conversation and tried to catch his facial quirks in pencils while he inhaled a heaping plate of food. I took care to ask him several questions about his work as a jeweler and about his wife before steering the topic toward his other siblings. Kilch chuckled when I told him about Teolm's miserable night with his anophalas, volunteered that Jomin was a workaholic and that Otun disliked unnecessary socialization, and was only slightly more optimistic than the rest of his family had seemed about his younger brothers' chances of success in film.

"What about Mafora?" I asked. "I heard she was into fashion…"

"Very much so," he replied around a hunk of bread. "Always has been. She's talented, and I'm not saying that as her brother."

"Should I expect to see her around here, or does she stay in Beukal these days?"

"Mostly the city. She and her partners have a shop downtown, what was it called…" He snapped his fingers as it came to him. "House of Wonder. Don't ask me how they came up with the name. Personally, I've always thought it sounded like a brothel"—he smiled as I laughed behind my sketchpad—"but that's their business, not mine."

Unable to pry more details from Kilch about his sister

without revealing that she'd gone missing, I finished drawing, thanked him for his time, and made up a plate to go. I ate my lonely dinner in my room, wishing I could call Yven, then spread out my sketches to look over what I'd done that day. Four live subjects wasn't a bad beginning, though if Inade wanted to keep my cover story strong, I'd need a field trip to Beukal to hunt down his absent children. Aunt Lily I could draw in my sleep. And then there was my sketch of Mafora and the mystery man— rushed and hardly my best work, but a beginning. I wanted another look at his face, but more than that, I wanted a name.

Left with more questions than answers, I went to bed early, hoping my unconscious mind would sort things out for me.

Unfortunately, sleep didn't bring me a flash of brilliance, but the next morning, I figured that I could at least draw. I'd unknowingly painted a mural of Yven's parents' home in my friend Maya's restaurant, and I'd drawn Aunt Lily and the men who'd sent her on the run before I knew how to access my farsight. Surely I could put pencil to paper and come up with *something* useful—if not Mafora's whereabouts, then preliminary work for my alleged commission.

I grabbed an early breakfast, said good morning to the few servants I passed on the way to and from the dining room, and settled in with my door locked for privacy. Fed and caffeinated, I stretched out on the unmade bed and closed my eyes, willing myself back to Mafora.

Soon, my inner eyes opened in the cabin once more. There she was, reading a book by the cold fireplace, her feet propped on a spare chair and a cup of tea waiting on a table beside her. Of the man, there was no sign. Frustrated, I searched around the place for a hint as to his identity, but I found nothing—and even when my formless body slipped through the closed door of the closet to snoop around, all I discovered was a folded pair of pajamas and a drawstring bag of laundry. Mafora seemed perfectly at ease, and judging by the half-naked sorcerer embracing a scantily clad woman on the cover of her paperback, she was having a bit of fun while she waited for the man's return.

The locked front door was no impediment to me, and I passed through it to check out the exterior of the cabin. It was a simple building, barely more than a concrete foundation below weather-warped planks patched with a putty-like sealant in the cracks. Two steps down, I landed in a clearing and noted tire tracks in the dirt. The man had an escape vehicle, but trying to follow him up the rutted gravel track would have been futile. Practice had shown me that I was tied to my subject by a roughly two-hundred-foot tether, able to leave their immediate vicinity but not wander indefinitely. I wondered if there was a sign at the end of the road, some clue as to the cabin's location, but Mafora seemed unlikely to get up and take a stroll that morning.

With a sigh, I opened my true eyes and blinked a few times, readjusting to the guest room. Mafora was alive and well—that much was evident—and as far as I was concerned, that was the most important fact. I considered trying to focus on the man, but my drawing had been skimpy on the details, and I wasn't sure if I could find him without a better picture.

But maybe farsight would show me what I needed to know.

I slid off the bed and stood before my easel. The blank canvas stared back at me, waiting to be given life. I thought about how I'd need to fit all the figures into the painting: Inade and Liventi, their nine living children, the six spouses. I could try to transfer the sketches I'd made the previous day, leaving room for the missing...but that wasn't why I'd been summoned into the Pactlands.

As a young artist, I'd developed a sort of meditative drawing technique, blanking my mind as I allowed my hand to render on paper what my eyes were seeing. The previous June, I'd put myself into that sort of Zen place and accidentally tapped into my nascent farsight. Now that I'd had a few months of practice and a basic understanding of my talent, maybe I could do it again.

I drew the curtains over the window and dimmed the room's lamps to a twilight glow, then connected my phone to one of my battery packs and called up a playlist of tranquil piano music. Making myself comfortable before the canvas, I arranged three sharpened pencils within easy reach, then chose one and closed my eyes.

Show me the family, I asked whatever force powered my visions. *Show me how they're meant to be.*

My inner eyes didn't fully open, but I was still vaguely aware that my deeper senses were awakening. With a few deep breaths, I'd returned to the familiar place in which my brain was nothing but the organ that powered my heart and lungs and moved my hand—only this time, the vision was internal, piecemeal but coming into focus.

I readied my pencil, waited until the flow seemed to move through me, then began to draw.

Under ordinary circumstances, I *enjoy* eating. Irregular feeding leaves me hangry and liable to scarf down whole bags of anything salty and crunchy within reach. But sometimes, when I sit down to create and get into that perfect zone, my stomach goes quiet. It doesn't happen often, and my appetite returns with a vengeance as soon as I'm finished, but I can go uninterrupted by little nuisances like hunger or exhaustion for hours if left to work with a glass of water at hand.

I can't say what happened outside of my suite from roughly nine o'clock Friday morning until dawn Saturday. My cell phone never so much as beeped, the house phone remained silent, and my piano playlist kept cycling until the battery pack was drained. I'm sure I stepped aside once or twice to run to the bathroom and refill my cup at the tap, but I lost myself in that euphoric stream until the shrill chiming of the phone by my bed ripped me out of the flow.

Blinking as if I'd emerged from a cave into full sunlight, I staggered to the phone and croaked, "Hello?"

"Ms. Anomi?" said a voice I recognized as the chief steward's—still polite, but with an edge of concern. "Breakfast will be available soon. Are you feeling well?"

Was I? Starving and gradually becoming cognizant of a caffeine withdrawal headache, yes, but otherwise intact. "Uh…fine, thank you."

"I don't mean to pry, but no one saw you after breakfast yesterday, and we didn't know if you required a healer."

At least the staff gave enough of a damn to check on me. "No, no," I reassured him, "I just started working and lost track of time. But thank you."

"Of course." He sounded relieved. "Would you like an escort downstairs, or have you learned your way by now?"

I told him I could manage and hung up, deciding that manners dictated I shower off the funk before emerging to eat. But first, and not without a flash of trepidation, I needed to see what I'd come up with…

Wait, *overnight*? There was definitely a nap in my future.

Twisting my stiff back, I turned to the canvas and froze.

I recalled starting with pencil, and I had a vague recollection of opening my paints at some point, but I was unprepared for the extent of the work before me, especially as I had no conscious memory of planning most of it.

Inade sat in an elaborately carved wooden chair at the center of the painting, more complete than any other figure. I'd painted all of the faces, but he was detailed down to the ornamental stitching of his robe. His unsmiling eyes stared straight ahead, and his hands clutched an offshoot of the thorny gray vine that framed the scene. Behind him and slightly to his left stood Liventi—I recognized her well enough from my drive into the Pactlands—still mostly a pencil outline below the neck except for the hand resting on Inade's chair. She looked down and seemed to stare into the distance in contemplation.

To Inade's right stood Jomin, with Dania seated before him, then Otun and Kelar behind her right shoulder. Kilch and a woman I assumed to be his wife, Meala, continued the line. Otun held one of Jomin's hands, while Jomin's other clutched the back of their father's chair. Kilch, separated from his elder siblings, instead held a dark blue jeweler's loupe, which he was lifting to his eye as if he'd just noticed Meala's necklace and wanted a better look.

I ascertained the identities of some of the faces I'd painted only through deduction. The couple in matching purple lab coats and gray scrubs had to be Nalani and her husband, Invaton, and the other two couples I pegged as Tranar, Varil, and their ti'Pon spouses.

Teolm's posture was curious, I thought: I'd drawn him squatting in the far right corner of the painting, grinning at the viewer. Like his father, he held the decorative thorny vine, but the portion he touched was green and pliable, its tendrils budding with tender leaves as they encircled his wrists. Behind him, holding his shoulder and sporting a denim work shirt and flowers in her golden-blonde braid, stood Aunt Lily. Part of me wished I'd put her in the other corner, balancing the painting with the active growers instead of clustering them, but I didn't hate the arrangement enough to redo it.

Besides, the painting had a bigger issue.

Moving behind Aunt Lily, reaching for someone out of the frame, was my grandfather. Precisely *why* I'd added him was a fact known only to my subconscious, which wasn't in a chatty mood that morning. Yes, it rubbed me the wrong way that of the ti'Crens and their spouses whom I'd met, only Teolm had mentioned his missing brother. Fradin didn't deserve to have his existence erased. Still, I knew that Inade would lose his shit if he saw what I'd done.

And then there was Mafora, another figure in motion. Like Fradin, she was heading out of the painting, albeit in the opposite direction, reaching for something hidden from view.

The man from the cabin?

Was *that* the truth?

I mulled over what Liventi had told Pateme on the phone. Inade thought Mafora had been abducted, but Liventi hadn't believed she was in danger. Had she eloped? Was that what this was about? Like her older brother, had Mafora chosen a partner unacceptable to the family? Her companion had definitely been an elf...but maybe he wasn't the right kind of elf, I mused. Hall ti'Cren was old and among the most prominent. Maybe he came from a lesser Hall, something that would cast shame upon the family.

Again, I considered Inade, who held fast to the thorny branches and grimly stared back at me.

Control. He was the lord of the Hall, and he needed to maintain control over his family. Fradin had disgraced him, and if Mafora was about to do likewise...

"Shit," I muttered, and carefully threw a sheet over the canvas to protect it from prying eyes.

Hungry though I was, sleep won out over my appetite. After a quick shower, I took breakfast to go, shoveled down a plate of bacon and eggs in my room, and collapsed into bed to make up for the all-nighter.

When I awoke, my dying phone said it was a little past noon, and I wasn't sure what planet I was on. Once I remembered who and where I was, I hastily dug a fresh battery pack out of my bag for my phone, then propped up my pillows, made myself comfortable with my sketchpad, and closed my eyes. I was hungry again but far from starving, and if I spied with farsight, maybe I could catch Mafora and the man together.

Luck was with me that day. I found the two of them sitting across from each other at a wooden picnic table beneath the spreading boughs of a pine tree, chatting as they ate some sort of chicken dish with a fruity sauce. Judging by the containers, the man had sprung for takeout again, and the smell made my stomach rumble back in my body.

Trying not to get distracted by my physical needs, I focused on the man's face, memorizing its shapes and colors. His hair would give me fits, were I trying to paint his portrait—curls had been my nemesis in college—but I took careful notes about the rest of him, vaguely aware of my distant wrist's motion as I drew his crooked grin. The scratches on his arms and hands still bothered me, but given the way that Mafora was looking at him, I doubted that she'd been his assailant.

Suddenly, the ringing of the house phone drew me out of the vision, and I groaned as I reached for the receiver. It was no emergency, merely the chief steward checking to see whether I wanted lunch delivered. I couldn't be angry with him for the interruption, which he meant only as a kindness, though I was disappointed to have learned nothing new about where Mafora was or who her companion might be. Still, once I was back to physicality, my stomach protested to be remembered, and I decided that lunch wasn't a terrible idea.

I wound my way downstairs to the empty dining room and made a plate from the buffet, looking for familiarity among the dishes on offer and settling for whatever smelled the best. Slumping into a chair, I tried a bite of what turned out to be roast pork and groaned happily as I tucked in.

I hadn't been there ten minutes before I heard a

woman's voice coming from the direction of the door: "And who might you be?"

Swallowing quickly, I patted my lips with my napkin and turned to find the speaker. "Rose Anomi...ma'am," I squeaked.

Liventi stood in the opening, clad in an elaborate day dress, her blonde hair loose over her shoulders but softly waved. She stared at me as I rose from my chair, and one delicate hand reached up to cover her sternum.

"Lord ti'Cren hired me to do a family portrait...my lady," I said, unsure of the proper form of address. Courtesy titles hadn't been included in my limited Pactlands education. "I'm sorry to intrude. Just came down to grab a bite—"

"He didn't mention anything about you."

I chose my words carefully. "He told me you weren't to be disturbed. Maybe he intended to make this a gift."

"Is that what he said?" she murmured, and quickly swept down the length of the dining room table toward me. She studied me for a moment in silence, only breaking away when a servant popped her head into the room to inspect the situation. "Make a plate for me," she told the other woman. "I'll take lunch in my room. Ms. Anomi will be joining me."

Though I wasn't keen on directly disobeying Inade, I saw no other good option, and so I left my plate where it was and followed Liventi upstairs to her spacious suite. She bolted the door behind us and drew the curtains, then gestured, casting a privacy spell very much like the one Pateme used at work. Once the room was secure, she folded her arms and frowned at me in the lamplight. "Rose Thorn."

"Yes, ma'am."

"Had I seen you in public, I'd never have suspected." Her head tilted as she considered me in my best leggings and slouchy sweater. "You do look rather human, don't you?"

"Uh…yes, ma'am."

"Rather like *her*," she said, her lips tightening in disapproval. "Your hair, at least."

Fradin had famously married a redhead, and I gave silent thanks for Miranda's coloration, which made mine instantly plausible. "I think so," I said cautiously. "I never met my grandmother, if that's who you're talking about."

"Not ever?"

I shook my head. "She died before my parents even met."

"*Good*," Liventi muttered. "She killed my boy. That creature doesn't deserve to live…" Her voice trailed off as she remembered her audience. "You understand, yes?"

"Like I said, I never met her. Never met any of my grandparents, actually. Aunt Lily's been great, but that's as close as I've come."

Leaving me standing there, she sank into an overstuffed armchair and rested her head on two fingertips. "Why did Inade bring you here?"

"To look for your daughter," I replied. "He's worried."

"I told him how to contact you—my brother gave me that information," she explained—"but Inade never told me he'd be bringing you into the *house*."

"Under a pseudonym, obviously. I'm here as a portrait painter who just happens to be farsighted in her free time."

"Mm." She nodded. "My other children, do they know about you?"

"Lord ti'Cren asked me not to tell them," I murmured, and stepped closer to her chair. "Look, I don't expect you to trust me right away, but I really am trying to locate Mafora—"

Liventi's eyes lit up. "Have you seen her?"

"Yes," I admitted after a moment's hesitation. "She's unhurt. Lord ti'Cren thinks she was abducted, but given what I've seen, I don't think she went wherever she is unwillingly."

Her mother smirked. "Oh, *no*, she went of her own

volition. Do you know where she is?"

"Not yet, and what do you know about all of this?"

"Slightly more than Inade does, and that information doesn't leave this room, understood?"

"Uh…all right, sure…"

With a small smile playing on her lips, Liventi said, "My daughter has eloped. The boy is from ti'Gata. Her father knows only that she's eloped with someone, and he's furious."

I kept my face blank and hurriedly tried to remember the Halls that I'd heard mentioned. "Ti'Gata is…a low-ranking Hall?" I guessed.

"A *new* Hall," she replied.

That was where I'd heard of it before—ti'Gata and ti'Van were the two largest of the new Halls, the conglomerations of families that had coalesced within the Pactlands once everyone started over on slightly more equal footing. Hall ti'Cren was an old and high-ranking noble line. Hall ti'Gata was, by their estimation, a mob of upstart commoners.

"They ran off to be married thirteen days ago," Liventi continued. "I have to assume it's been completed by now, but Inade is trying to nullify it."

That put the marriage at March 1, by my count—the day before Liventi had called Pateme for help. "If they've been married for almost two weeks, and they're both adults, then—"

"An old rule applies. Any *inappropriate* marriage can be annulled within a month if the lord or lady of one of the Halls involved objects to it. But there's a catch, you see: the objecting party must physically bring at least one of the couple before a tribunal and make the objection public."

"So," I said as the pieces fell into place, "if Mafora and her guy can stay hidden until…what, April 1? Then the marriage would be unbreakable?"

"Twenty-eight days by law, but yes, that would make them absolutely safe."

I stared down at Liventi, trying to make sense of her role in this mess. "Why drag me into this? You must have known I'm farsighted before you told your husband how to find me. Are you *that* opposed to the marriage? If you break this up, do you honestly think Mafora will forgive you?"

"It's not the marriage I would choose for her," she replied, "but I would never try to ruin my daughter's happiness. I'm just concerned for her safety while she's in hiding. If I knew where she was and that she was relatively comfortable, that would be enough. That's all I want. And that's why I mentioned you to Inade," she continued, picking up speed. "*You* can find her, can't you? Give me that reassurance, Rose."

"I'm still looking," I said, "but Lord ti'Cren also wants to know—"

"You *cannot* tell him. Promise me," she interjected, going to her feet. Before I could move back, she was gripping my arms. "Stall, lie to him, I don't care. But don't ruin this for Mafora, *please*. I don't know the boy, but I do know she loves him, and she trusted me enough to warn me this was coming. Her father can't find out. Two more weeks, I beg you..."

I froze, my mind whirling. If I could do this for Inade—find his wayward daughter, lead him to her, let him end her marriage before it brought shame to the Hall—then he would owe me. Surely I could leverage that into acknowledgement, couldn't I? I'd have helped the Hall's reputation, maybe even taken steps to undo the damage my grandfather had done...

But there was no guarantee. Inade hadn't said a word about compensation, and without any sort of contract, what recourse would I have if he dropped me back in Richmond and told me to have a nice life? Hell, I wasn't even legally allowed in the Pactlands, so how could I force him to take me in?

And Mafora...

Damn it.

She'd looked happy with her new husband. Content. If she loved him enough to elope, then how could I break up her marriage? I *couldn't* tell Inade. And it's not like he would disown her, would he? Hell, I was living proof that Mafora's wasn't the worst marriage a ti'Cren sibling had ever made.

But if I failed Inade, there went my shot at my own happiness.

Maybe not. Liventi was set to inherit Hall ti'Tam, wasn't she? Maybe someday, once she had power of her own, she'd pull a string for me if I did her this favor now. I had no idea when that day might come—after all, Inade had ruled his Hall for more than three centuries—but perhaps she'd think of me then.

Assuming Yven would wait that long.

I closed my eyes. Possibilities and probabilities aside, I couldn't ruin Mafora's marriage just because her father was a classist dick.

"I won't spoil it for her," I murmured to Liventi. "If Lord ti'Cren finds her, he won't have heard it from me."

"Thank you," Liventi murmured. "On your way out, would you see if our plates have been delivered? I assume you'd prefer to finish your lunch in private."

"Sure," I said, smarting at the dismissal, but I paused and turned back to her before I reached the door. "You know, my dad never told me anything about his paternal grandparents. He always said you were estranged, and that was it. I mean...Lord ti'Cren has portal credentials, so did you ever even *try* to visit?"

"No," she said softly.

I crossed my arms, my face beginning to flush with my controlled anger. "Why were you so embarrassed of Fradin that you cut off your own child? He left here, and you really never spoke to him again? Never tried to see your grandson?"

Liventi, who had been holding my gaze, looked away.

"Inade insisted…"

"And?" I retorted when her voice petered out. "So what? You've got your own Hall, right? Isn't your mother the lady? You're not some helpless waif caught at his mercy."

"It's not that simple."

I waited, but even as the silence stretched between us, Liventi refused to meet my stare.

"My dad's parents were never well off," I finally said. "Fradin worked hard to keep food on the table, but the best he could do was maintenance for the city. Didn't have the education or the credentials to get a better-paying job, and he couldn't afford life insurance. Dad said he was outside every day, rain or shine, even shoveling snow when he got bad colds every winter. That's what killed him, you know. A cold turned into pneumonia."

She made no reply.

"So," I continued, "that was Fradin. He died when Dad was eight. My grandmother had to go back to work to support them—she was a schoolteacher, so she could keep them off the streets, but she scrimped for every penny. Never remarried. She didn't have any family left, so the only person in the world they could count on was Aunt Lily. Dad said she used to take him shopping because they all knew his mother couldn't afford to clothe him."

Liventi still held her tongue.

"Dad kept his grades up, and he put himself through college with a partial academic scholarship. Wasn't good enough at basketball to get the rest of his way paid," I said, shrugging. "Became an accountant. He wasn't in love with it, but he was so afraid of ending up in poverty that he chose a career he knew would give him steady work. You know what he really loved doing when he had the chance? He'd work on busted old pocket watches. Find them at estate sales or junk shops, clean them up, fix the gears. He even had a little kit for engraving, and he'd put initials or flourishes or whatever on the cases. Told me that he'd have wanted to be a watchmaker if money were no obstacle. That or a jeweler. Guess he came by it honestly, huh?"

When Liventi continued to avert her eyes, I said, "He looked a lot like Fradin, and he was the best dad I could have asked for. But I guess you don't care, do you?"

That seemed to pierce her armor. "I *do* care," Liventi insisted, lifting her eyes. "But you cannot know what it's like to lose a child—"

"You could have had longer with him! Or hell, you could have had a grandson. Forget me," I muttered. "Dad refused to talk about his extended family. *Always*. The only person he'd ever tell me about was Aunt Lily, and she certainly never mentioned you. Someone else told me the truth. And it wasn't until a few months ago that Aunt Lily told me how much it hurt Dad that no one here ever cared."

"Fradin should have explained—"

"*Fradin* didn't tell him anything. Miranda and Aunt Lily did, but not until he was twenty-one."

I didn't mention to Liventi what else Aunt Lily said she'd told Dad: that he was safer as long as no one in the Pactlands knew of his existence. I didn't know about *safer*, but considering the way Fradin's parents had treated me to that point, I imagined that any effort Aunt Lily could have made to integrate Dad into the fold would have been deeply wounding for him.

"Dad's mom died two years after that," I continued, "so Aunt Lily was the only family he had until he met my mom, and they had me. All of you over here, hiding out in your mansion, and *no one* but Aunt Lily could be bothered with an orphan fresh out of college."

That the same was true for me only made my temper rise, and I struggled to keep my tone civil.

"I didn't know he existed," Liventi protested.

"Did you ever ask your daughter?" I snapped back. "And would it have made a difference if you'd known?"

She had no answer to that, and though part of me itched to stay and berate her, I knew it wouldn't accomplish anything. "Well, you don't have to worry," I said. "I told Lord ti'Cren I'd keep up this cover story, and I will. I'm not going to go running through the hallways, shouting at your kids that I'm their long-lost great-niece from Richmond. But it would be nice to know that someone besides Aunt Lily gives a damn whether I live or die."

I turned toward the door, only to hear Liventi say, "Please try to understand—"

"*Understand?*" I echoed, wheeling around again as my fists clenched.

I thought of all the things I wanted to shout at her— that I'd heard Caradin's recordings, that even Diriem ti'Dana had deigned to meet and provide for his half-blooded granddaughter—but I suppressed the urge. Pateme hadn't told his sister about that side of my family, so I decided to let her continue in ignorance.

"Justify this however you want," I said. "I don't care. The fact remains that none of you except Aunt Lily wanted anything to do with me until you realized I might be useful to you, and even now, I have to pretend to be a stranger passing through. I don't care," I muttered, repeating the lie as if I could make it the truth through force of will, and slammed the door as I departed. My half-eaten lunch was waiting for me on a tray against the wall, and I left it where it sat.

Ordering myself not to get weepy in public, I locked the guest room door and flopped onto the bed in hopes that I could find Mafora's hiding place and be done with the whole mess. I didn't want to give her up to Inade—not after what Liventi had confessed—but I could either spy or cry, and the former sounded more appealing.

With a little concentration, I found myself back in the

cabin with Mafora and the man—her new husband, rather. He was sitting on the edge of the bathtub while she fussed over the welts on his arms, dabbing them with a burgundy liquid I recognized as an expensive but highly effective healing potion.

"You needn't use so much," he told her as she poured more onto a beige washrag. "They don't even hurt anymore."

"But I'd still rather you not end up scarred," she replied, and pressed the cloth onto the red scratches covering the back of his hand. "Glad you found one of these."

"Field kit at the back of the storeroom. Hopefully, no one will know I went digging."

"Do you not get a kit, too?"

"Not for another year or so. Trainee," he explained, and winced as the potion hit a sore spot. "And *this* is why I'm staying out of the greenhouse."

Mafora *tsk*ed. "You shouldn't hug the prickly ones."

"I fell into a bush! This wasn't on purpose—"

"I'm just teasing," she said gently, and kissed his forehead before going back for more potion. "My poor darling. Is there anything that would make you feel better?"

He looked up at her and flashed a sly grin, and she laughed and swatted his shoulder. "Only if you're a good boy and let me take care of these nasty welts."

"I'll be *very* good," he insisted with mock solemnity.

"Mm. We'll see about that, won't we?"

Fearing that I was poised to intrude upon an impromptu bathroom romp, I retreated to the main room and looked around. There was Mafora's book on the table, there a pair of used tea mugs, there a lone shoe peeking out from beneath the bed, and on the dresser…

A wallet. A thin wallet made of black leather, tossed onto the counter and left open to reveal the badge inside. The silver eight-pointed shape had by then become familiar to me, and I knew that the red border around the central circle denoted a DPP badge. Peering closer, I found the man's name engraved in the middle in Pactish characters: *Deono ti'Gata*.

"Gotcha," I whispered, and withdrew before the newlyweds could get down to business.

After a brief reorientation on my bed, I found my cell phone and scrolled through the contacts. I didn't dare try to use the house phone to call out, but as far as I knew, only Yven's phone had been blocked against me.

The phone on the other end rang twice before I heard a woman answer in Pactish. "Hello?"

"Canna, it's Rose. Please don't hang up."

I caught her short, quiet inhalation, but the line didn't go dead. "I can't let Yven talk to you on our phones. You know that. Pars would lose his job."

"I'm not asking you to," I replied, cupping my hand around the end of the phone as I dropped my voice to a whisper. "But I'm in Kelomb, and I need help."

CHAPTER 9

When I reached the foyer that afternoon with my loaded overnight bag, I thought I'd timed my escape perfectly. I was about a minute too quick, however, and I hadn't anticipated bumping into Teolm.

"Hi, Rose," he said, walking through on his way from the kitchen. Noticing my luggage, he stopped and frowned. "Leaving so soon? I thought you'd be here for a few days longer."

Having psyched myself up as well as I could, I sniffled and dabbed at my smeared mascara with a tissue. "Family emergency. My cousin called—our great-grandmother probably won't make it through the night. I need to see her—"

His face fell. "Oh, of course. I'm so sorry." He paused, then asked, "Is there anything I can do to help? Do you need a ride?"

I thought of the half-finished painting I'd left covered in my room, along with most of my supplies, which I'd probably have to write off as a loss. The longer I spent around Teolm, the better I understood why I'd put him next to Aunt Lily in the family portrait.

"That's so kind of you," I replied, "but my cousin is on her way to pick me up...and there she is," I said as a gray sedan stopped in front of the mansion. "If you would, please give my apologies to your father. I'll return as soon as I can."

"I'll explain. Take your time," he said, and held the door for me as I hurried out into the sunlight.

The trunk popped, and I hastily stowed my gear—my weekender, my purse, and the tote bag in which I'd packed my sketchpads and pencils—before sliding into the front seat. "I owe you," I said to Canna Nerin, who'd hit the accelerator as soon as my door closed.

"You're insane," the sorcerer replied. "This whole business is crazy. But then again…" She reached over and patted my leg. "Welcome back, Rose. It's good to see you."

"I don't know if the mansion has security cameras or anything—"

"I'm sure it does, which is why I'm not driving my own car." Cutting her eyes to me, she flashed a wicked grin. "This old girl belongs to my great-great-aunt's neighbor, who's two hundred seventy years old and only takes it out once a week to do her shopping."

"She *loaned* it to you?"

"I run errands for her on occasion, and when I said I needed the car to help a couple of kids in love, she didn't ask questions." Pulling a potion vial from within the armrest, she added, "Have I ever mentioned how convenient it can be to find yourself married to an Interdiction agent?"

"Is that the stuff that DPP uses on their license plates?" A few drops would make the tag temporarily impossible to remember—useful when working outside the Pactlands.

"Exactly."

"I didn't see a plate on your car…"

Canna thumbed one hand toward the rear as we sped through the stunted trees. "See the sticker with the red dot in the window? That can be scanned."

"Oh," I mumbled, feeling stupid for never asking Yven about his matching decal. Of course it was no big deal that he drove around Beukal in a Mustang with Virginia plates when the tag that mattered was located elsewhere on the vehicle. "The potion works on that, too?"

"*Beautifully*. We're using her pass through the portal as well, so there'll be no record that I was ever out here. I mean, it wouldn't take a great detective to make the connection," she admitted, "but I think we can have you on your way before anyone comes knocking." Glancing my way again, she said, "You know Lord ti'Cren is going to be livid, don't you?"

"Yeah."

"And you're still going through with this?"

Slumping in my seat, I stared out the windshield, noting the glint of water in the distance. "I think it's what my grandparents would have wanted me to do. I've seen the newlyweds—they're *happy*. What right does Inade have to break them up?"

She grimaced. "Technically?"

"Morally. They're not hurting anyone. And they only have two weeks to go until they're safe, so if I can make that happen…"

Canna quietly considered that for a moment, then nodded. "Fair enough. But I still have a question."

"Shoot."

"Assuming you can find them, how do you plan to get out of the Pactlands?"

"One problem at a time," I muttered as Hall ti'Cren shrank behind us.

Canna and Pars lived in a charming two-story home in a quiet neighborhood on the outskirts of Beukal. But as we turned onto their street, Canna said, "I'm dropping you at the driveway. Get your gear and hurry inside."

"You're not coming?" I asked, preemptively unbuckling.

"Returning this car first. Sneaky, see?"

As soon as the vehicle slowed to a stop, I jumped out, grabbed my bags from the trunk, and barely had time to adjust my things on my shoulder before Canna had sped off. She disappeared around a bend, and I climbed the front steps and rang the bell.

When the door opened, there stood Pars Mera: seven feet of muscle, brown crewcut and chinstrap beard, dark eyes, twisted nose, and hot pink feather boa.

"Am I interrupting?" I asked.

He grinned and tossed the boa's trailing length over his broad shoulder. "Get in here, Red," he ordered, and pulled me into a rib-crushing hug as soon as the door had latched behind us. "Good to see you, you little maniac," he declared, thumping my back hard enough to leave bruises. "How the hell are you?"

"Need air," I wheezed, and Pars relaxed his grip with a mumbled apology.

Stepping away from the windows, I dropped my bags in a pile and smiled up at him. "I'm fine. Better now. But I need your help—"

"Yeah, Canna mentioned there's a *situation*," he said, beckoning me deeper into the house. "Come on, let's sit down. Thirsty?"

Before I could answer him, a pair of dark-haired little girls peeked out from around the corner, both wearing boas very much like their father's. "Daddy," the elder protested, "you're not supposed to leave the party!"

"I know," he replied, "but look who's here! Can you say hello to Rose?"

Dieta and Maliul might have invited their father to their imaginary soiree, but they seemed eager enough to extend him a plus-one. "You come, too," little Maliul insisted. "You and Daddy come back to the party."

"I'm afraid Rose and I have to do grownup stuff for now," Pars told his daughters, though he made no move to divest himself of his feathery finery. "But I'll play later, all right? And to make it up to you," he smoothly continued before they could object, "how about some cookies?"

Thus mollified, the girls scampered back to the den with their bribe, and Pars and I continued on to the relative peace of the kitchen. "The twins are napping," he said, pouring me a glass of water. "And let's hope they keep it up until their mother returns. Now, Canna gave me the broad picture, but *what* is going on?"

Quickly, I told him what I'd been up to in the last few days, beginning with Inade's unexpected visit to my studio. "So, just to wrap this up," I concluded, "I'm here super-illegally, Inade's going to lose his shit—"

Pars pointedly cleared his throat and glanced toward the other room.

"Lose his *mind*," I amended, "when he finds out I've run off, and he's hunting for his daughter and her new husband, who's DPP."

"Any idea where they are?"

"I drew it, but I didn't recognize it. Want to look at my work?"

"Sure," he replied, and I hurried back to the foyer to retrieve my sketchpads. "This guy, do you have a name?" he called after me.

"Yeah, hold on, I wrote it down…"

A minute later, I returned to the kitchen, flipping through the pages for my notes and drawings. "Deono ti'Gata. Sound familiar?"

Pars's heavy brow knit. "Maybe…"

Turning the pad around, I showed him my rendering of Deono's face. "Him. I think he said he's a trainee—"

"Oh, *him*!" Pars exclaimed. "The kid who tripped over his own feet and fell in the greenhouse on Tuesday—"

"Welts on his arms, yeah?"

"Rule number one of the greenhouse is 'touch nothing' for a very good reason. But yeah, I know his face. He's an Interdiction trainee in Veona's group. Haven't worked with him yet—the newbies don't do cross-group outings until they learn the basics—but I've seen him around. Got himself a ti'Cren, huh?"

"Looks like it."

He whistled. "Talk about marrying well. So, now, what

about their hiding place?"

"Start here," I said, going back a few pages in the sketchpad. "It's a cabin in the woods, but, like, *real* woods, not your weird little trees—"

"Oh, pardon me for having poor growing conditions in this world we literally *built*," he began, then looked at my drawing of the cabin interior and did a double take. "What the…" he mumbled, leaning closer to the paper.

"You recognize it?"

"Uh, *yeah*. That's our offsite."

"Come again?"

"DPP has an offsite camp adjacent to Green Lake. That's where the trees come from. It's a training facility," he explained. "Groups go out, spend a few days beating each other up, bond. You know, teambuilding stuff." Turning to the next page, which showed the picnic table beneath the pines, he nodded. "Yeah, that's our place. Absolutely. I've eaten in that spot. There's a pond on the other side of the cabin, down a little hill…"

"I didn't look over there," I admitted. "But from what I've seen of Mafora and Deono, they've been hiding at this camp of yours all along. Mafora hangs out all day, and Deono joins her at night with food. He said he's on vacation as of Monday."

"Easy to check." Pulling out his phone, Pars poked at the screen for a moment before grunting and showing it to me. "There he is, see? Two weeks' vacation."

"And their marriage will be final after that. Is the camp far? If it's possible, I'd like to go out there and tell them that Inade is searching. If he was desperate enough to come to me, he's probably willing to take drastic measures."

"Don't worry. We're *absolutely* going out there," he replied, "because Loverboy's an idiot."

I frowned. "What do you mean?"

Pars pulled up another document on his phone for my inspection—his calendar. "See that lovely four-day block next week?"

"Yeah…"

He smirked. "Well, that would be when Emarae is taking us camping. We've got to get those two out of there."

Of course, with four small children to consider, we couldn't exactly leap into action.

Once Canna returned and heard the new wrinkle, she agreed that a visit was in order—"Under cover of darkness, naturally," she said, fixing her husband with a warning stare. "Because just in case a certain someone is trying to find Rose now, too, shouldn't she stay out of sight?"

Chastised, he returned to entertaining the girls, and I gave Canna a hand with the twins once they woke. She set up a playpen in the kitchen so that she could make dinner, and I tried to keep the two of them entertained while their father rampaged around the den as the monster chasing the happily squealing older kids.

"They'll be two in two months," Canna said as she popped an enormous casserole dish into the oven. "I can't believe it. My *babies*," she added, beaming down at the twins.

"Birthday plans?"

"There's a pool for the little ones at Green Lake. They have a few…I won't call them 'friends,' exactly, but other kids in their age range that they don't seem to loathe. Coincidentally, Pars and I are friends with the parents," she confessed with a wink, "so we'll make an afternoon of it." After a moment's hesitation, she said, "I'm sure you don't know what your situation will be in May, but if you're around and don't mind overexcited toddlers, you're welcome to join us."

"You're sweet, but I wouldn't want to intrude—"

Canna bent close to me and lowered her voice. "You

brought my husband home alive. No more need be said." She patted my shoulder, then turned her attention to the stove, where the following day's dinner was simmering in a fragrant stockpot. "Speaking of birthdays, have we missed yours? It's been a few months…"

"Monday."

"*Monday*! Well, premature congratulations, and which will this one be?"

"The big twenty-seven."

She groaned and shook her head. "I forget how young you are…"

"We do things at an accelerated rate," I replied with a shrug, giving the twins gentle high-fives. "My friends back in Richmond tend to freak out that they're on the downward slide once they hit thirty."

"Be that as it may," she said, stirring the chicken soup, "you should be in school. An untrained talent is a dangerous thing."

"I've, uh…been doing a sort of self-study since I got sent home."

Canna glanced over her shoulder, one eyebrow lifted. "*Oh?*"

In response, I made a quick gesture, and the pitcher of juice she'd left on the counter flew across the room and refilled my glass. "My grandfather made some recordings for me before he died. Tips, techniques, exercises, stuff like that. The crash course in 'weaving the subtle energies,'" I said, grinning.

"Spell casting? That's the translation from the Elvish?"

"As far as I can tell."

"Unduly poetic, but who am I to judge? And if you've got your 'subtle energies' under control, mind setting the table?"

Taking care with my hand motions, I willed the cabinets open and began floating a stack of plates toward me. "Do you have something less breakable for the twins?" I asked.

Before she could answer, the doorbell rang.

I ducked behind the kitchen wall, irrationally sure that Inade had tracked me down, but Canna seemed unruffled. "Get that, dear, won't you?" she called into the next room.

As I stayed out of sight, I listened to Pars cross the den and crack open the front door. "Hi, brother," he said bemusedly. "What brings you out here?"

A voice I would have known anywhere answered him, sounding just as perplexed as he did. "Uh…well, Canna called and said you were feeling terrible, and she was taking the kids to her parents' house, and she asked if I could come over and keep you company…but you seem healthy enough…"

I'd emerged from my hiding place before Yven finished his explanation, and when he saw me in the kitchen doorway, he fell into shocked silence.

"Why don't you come in?" said Pars, almost dragging him into the house.

I don't know how long Yven and I stared at each other—it was probably only a second or two. But there he stood in neatly pressed chinos and a blue rugby shirt that brought out his eyes, looking back at me like he wasn't quite sure how to process what he was seeing.

"Hey, stranger," I managed.

"*Rosie*," he whispered, and the paralysis that had overcome us broke.

In the next moment, I found myself in his arms, holding on for dear life as I breathed in the scent of his woodsy cologne. A part of me that I'd tried to silence had believed I'd never smell it again, and never had I been so happy to be wrong. I pulled back just enough to see his face—his eyes were still shocked, but his dimples were on full display—then told prudence to go screw itself and kissed him.

Yven returned the gesture with gusto, and I might have stood in the den for the rest of the night, content to be caught up in the sight and smell and taste of him, had

Canna not said, "Let's not do that in front of the windows, please."

We hastily mumbled apologies and broke apart while Pars took the more practical step of drawing the shades.

"Sorry for the subterfuge," Canna continued from the kitchen. "We're trying to be cautious."

"Inade let you leave?" Yven asked me.

Pars chuckled and slung his meaty arm over his smaller friend's shoulders, and Yven grunted with the impact. "No, he most certainly did not. Come on, I'll tell you at the table."

"*Daddy*," Dieta whined, "you're supposed to be chasing us!"

"Daddy needs to talk to Uncle Yven, darling," he replied, ruffling her hair, then tossed the end of his feather boa over his shoulder and propelled Yven into the kitchen for the update.

Two hours after sundown, fortified by Canna's turkey casserole, Yven and I climbed into Pars's brown Jeep and buckled up. "You know," he said, sliding behind the wheel, "one of you is welcome to join me up here."

Having already taken my hand in the darkness of the back seat, Yven replied, "We'll let you chauffeur, thanks."

"*Right*. Just remember that I can see you miscreants, eh?"

"Best behavior," I promised.

"Says the illegal visitor."

I slid forward and punched his shoulder, and he swatted good-naturedly back at me.

Pars's original plan hadn't included Yven—he and I were going to drive out alone and inform the newlyweds that their hiding place would be exposed by the start of the work week at the latest. But we both knew that Yven wasn't leaving my side as long as I was in the Pactlands— not after almost three months' forced separation.

"Besides," Canna told us as Pars brought out dessert, "it looks far less suspicious for two agents to go out to the camp than it does for one to roll up by himself."

She had a point. Canna was a healer by training, but her years with Laws had paid off.

I'd been the first to broach the idea of getting Mafora and Deono out of the Pactlands. "Inade is on the hunt, and they still need to hide for two weeks," I said over strong coffee while the kids played in the next room. "Ti'Cren is *loaded*—have you been inside the mansion?"

The others regarded me as if I'd asked them whether they regularly overnighted at Buckingham Palace.

"We don't rate invitations, remember?" said Yven.

"Fine, then take it from me. If Inade was worried enough to sneak me in, then I bet he's got a backup plan, and I'm sure money is no object. So let's make this harder for him."

"You want to hide them in Richmond?" Pars asked incredulously.

"No—Richmond's been burned. If Inade could track me to my store, then he probably has my home address, too. But I've got a college friend, Toni, who keeps a rental house in Charlottesville. It's nothing fancy, just an old cottage she rents to weekend tourists. I bet I could get a deal on the place."

"For the rest of the *month*?"

I shrugged. "Painted her bridal portrait as a surprise gift, and she *bawled*. I think she'll do me a favor."

To my relief, Toni came through. She was a textile artist by trade, and I caught her out at a relative's cabin in Colorado. "Jack's dealing with the bridezilla from hell," she explained as I flopped onto the guest bed farthest from the children's play area, "but she's flown him down to the Bahamas for their destination wedding, and I said I wasn't sitting around the house for the next week while he takes pretty pictures and self-medicates with rum."

I pitied her husband—I knew enough professional

photographers to feel for anyone who took on a wedding—but I used their circumstances to my advantage. "Speaking of weddings," I said, "I've got a slight situation."

Toni gasped. "Oh, my God," she said in an excited rush, "you didn't tell me you were seeing someone—"

"Not me," I clarified. "One of my friends here is a real sweetheart, but her parents are the *worst*. They tried to get her to break up with her boyfriend for ages, then tried to make her call off the engagement, and when that didn't work, they decided to micromanage the wedding. She finally said to hell with them, and they eloped today."

"Oh, wow, that's tough…"

"Yeah. I snapped some pictures at the courthouse—nothing nearly as good as Jack's work, but when you're doing it at the last minute…"

"Yikes. Have they told her folks yet?"

"No, and that's why I'm calling. They're currently at my place, but I'd love to give them a honeymoon out of town, someplace nearby where they can hang out and breathe with their phones off. Considering how many wineries are around Charlottesville…"

"I'm sure they could use a tasting or seven," said Toni. "You're calling about the rental house?"

"If it's open. I'd like to book it through the end of the month."

She whistled. "Let me check my calendar…yeah, it's open. Tell you what: give it a good cleaning before you leave, and I'll do it for fifty a night."

That figure was grossly below market rate, and we both knew it. "That's so nice of you, but I don't want to rip you off—"

"Don't worry about it. What can I say, I'm a sucker for happy endings."

She gave me the key codes for the door and the alarm system, I sent her the cash, and then I rejoined the others in triumph. "House is a go," I announced. "Now we just need to get them and get the hell out of the Pactlands."

Which, I mused as Pars drove us through the dark streets heading past the city limits, might be easier said than done. Assuming we could convince the couple to come with us, we still had to find credentials that would get us through the portal home.

One problem at a time, I reminded myself, still clasping Yven's hand.

Green Lake, I learned, was accessed via the portal for Tanaar, which, as far as the guys could estimate, was Nashville-ish in terms of our overlapping geography. Their parents' homes were about fifty miles away, an easy drive when the boys had needed to blow off steam in the lake and on the wooded trails. But while the recreational area was a public space managed and maintained by a government committee, DPP's adjoining camp was clearly marked as private property. A tall wooden fence blocked the view from the road, and posted signage informed trespassers that unauthorized visitors would be subject to prosecution.

Judging by the empty guard post at the gate, the threat rang hollow. Still, I ducked to the floor mats in case of hidden camera surveillance.

Pars slowly drove down the one-lane road through the camp, which gave way to gravel before long. Peering into the distance, I picked out the shapes of cabins in his high beams...including one cabin with lights glowing inside. "Is that the place?" I asked.

"That's it," Pars confirmed. "Let's hope they don't run."

We pulled up in the dirt parking area beside Deono's unassuming blue sedan and slid out. "Let me do that talking," Pars murmured as we started toward the cabin. "The kid should recognize me."

He pounded twice on the door, then waited through

thirty seconds of silence and knocked again. "Ti'Gata," he called through the thin wood, "it's Pars Mera. Let me in, *now.*"

No answer came from within the cabin.

"I *will* take down the door," Pars continued, "and then you can explain what happened when Emarae brings my group out here on Monday."

When the door finally cracked open, I was struck yet again by just how small most people looked beside Pars. Deono was maybe an inch or two shorter than Yven, but he seemed positively dwarfed as he stared up at the black-clad sorcerer. "I'm sorry, sir," he said in a rush, "I wanted to do a little fishing, and I'd heard the camp wasn't in use—"

"Where is she?"

I couldn't make out the details of his face, backlit as he was in the doorway, but Deono sounded like a terrible liar. "I…I'm sorry? Who? It's just me and my bait bucket—"

"Allow me," I interrupted, and Pars made room on the stairs. "Hi, it's Deono, right?"

He nodded cautiously.

"Nice to meet you. I'm Rose, and Inade ti'Cren hired me to find Mafora." As he started to stammer, I held up a hand. "Your cover's about to be blown, and frankly, I don't think you're safe in the Pactlands. Inade's *pissed.* I've got a place you can hide in Virginia for the rest of the month, if you want it."

Deono retreated a step, frowning. "If he hired you—"

"Her mother told me what's really going on. Also, I'm a farseer—I've been watching you two for the last couple of days, so I tend to believe Liventi. If you want to stay married, then let me help you."

"Just a minute," he replied, and closed the door.

I glanced at Pars and Yven, who shrugged. "These cabins only have one exit," said Yven, "unless they try to escape through a window. Should we spread out, just to be sure?"

But there was no need. When the door opened again, Deono stood beside Mafora, who regarded us with wide, frightened eyes. "He hired a *farseer*?" she demanded, turning to me.

"Yeah. Your dad's not happy, your mom's worried about you, and this place is going to be swarming with agents in less than two days. If word were to get back to, say, the *director* that you were hiding out here…"

She swore in Low Elvish—colorfully—then folded her arms. "How do I know I can trust you?"

"I can't exactly give you ironclad proof. This is one of those 'take it on faith' situations," I replied. "But I *can* tell you that I just left an expensive chunk of my painting supplies at your parents' house, and I've probably made an enemy of your father, so…" I spread my hands. "Stay here and try to avoid DPP, or come with me and try to break out of the Pactlands. Your choice."

"Not to seem suspicious, but why would you possibly help us?"

"Because I think you two are in love," I said quietly. "And if Inade is so set on breaking you up that he would come to me, then he's not going to stop until he gets what he's after."

Her eyes narrowed. "What does Father have against you?"

"Other than this? Let's just say I'm an inconvenience and leave it at that for now. But look, he tracked me down *in Virginia*, sneaked me back here, and has been housing me at the mansion since Wednesday."

"Virginia?"

"Outside," Deono murmured to her, then considered me. "So…you're *human*?"

"Yeah," I said, which seemed easier in the moment than the truth. "Inade's on a mission."

"I didn't know your father had portal credentials," he said to Mafora, who could only shrug. Turning back to me, he said, "I can get through the portal, but Mafora can't.

And how were you planning to leave, anyway? Ask Laws for a ride?"

"We've got a source," Pars interjected. "And if that fails, as a last resort, I'll try to smuggle you out. Now, are you two coming, or are we going to stand here and argue all night?"

They remained unconvinced. "What's in this for you?" Deono asked him. "If the director learns that you're sneaking people out of the Pactlands—"

"Rose saved my life last year," he interrupted, then pointed to Yven. "And his. And the lives of several other agents. So if Rose wants me to help her hide Mafora until her parents calm down, then that's what we're going to do. *Understood*, ti'Gata?"

Deono studied him for a long, silent moment, then murmured, "Sir."

"Good boy. Get your things," he said, and headed for the Jeep. "I'll follow you home, and then both of you will come with us."

Back in the privacy of Pars's vehicle, I told him, "I really appreciate this, but if it's too much—"

He turned in his seat and lifted a finger to cut me off. "Listen to me, Red. I've sat back and watched for three months, and the director hasn't come to his senses yet. You're owed more than a few favors."

"I don't want to jeopardize your job."

Pars flashed a smile that would make strong men think twice. "If I'm fired for this, my first stop is any reporter who'll listen to me. I'll tell them *all* about how I learned that Lord ti'Cren had illegally brought a human into the Pactlands, and how I lost my job after I removed the danger so that Pateme ti'Tam could help his sister's husband avoid a tribunal. And if it should come out that said human is, well, slightly more elven than she appears…that would be too bad, wouldn't it?"

I smirked back at him. "Your backup plan is to blackmail Pateme?"

"You're damn right it is," he replied, and started the engine.

CHAPTER 10

The newlywed fugitives didn't try to run from us. Having received the directions from Deono, Pars tailed them back to his downtown apartment, and once Deono's car was safely in the garage, Yven took the front seat so the two of them could join me in the back. We returned to Pars's house without incident and hustled inside, where Canna was waiting with tea. "The kids are asleep," she said as we trooped in. "What's the plan?"

"Just need to pull an address," said Pars, kissing the top of her head as he breezed past, and we loitered awkwardly in the den until he returned with a torn slip of paper. "If she kills me, tell my children I died in battle," he told his wife.

She crossed her arms. "And who should I say did the foul deed?"

"Chief. Back as soon as we can. Deono?"

"Sir?" the nervous elf replied.

"Stay here and guard my house. Got it?"

"But—" Mafora began.

"No buts," he said, shepherding her toward the door. "The fewer witnesses, the better."

Once we were back in the Jeep and on the road, I asked, "Mind telling me where we're going?"

"Just the other side of the neighborhood. She lives pretty close."

"*She?*" Mafora interjected.

"My boss."

Old Farm was a large area—having been Beukal's

breadbasket, it had to cover significant acreage—but traffic was light that night, and Pars didn't seem to put much stock in speed limits. After a ten-minute meander through the winding streets, we reached a well-lit powder-blue bungalow with a tidy front yard and even a pair of small hedges separating it from its neighbors, an achievement for Pactlands landscaping. The house wouldn't have been out of place in Richmond but for the fact that it seemed about fifty percent too tall for a one-story home.

"Here we are," Pars announced as he turned onto the driveway. "If this goes poorly, it's been fun knowing you all."

The agents led the way up the wide walk, and I coaxed unsettled Mafora to follow them. By the time we climbed the extra-high steps to the porch, Pars was ringing the bell. I barely had time to register that I'd finally seen a residential doorway tall enough to give him passage without stooping when the door opened to reveal a mottled green face with a sandy blonde mohawk...and dark, suspicious eyes beneath a heavy brow. The Interdiction chief's lower lip jutted around her tusks as she frowned and tightened the sash of her soft pink bathrobe with taloned hands.

"*Mera?*" she demanded. "What the..."

Her voice faded as I stepped out from behind him and waved. "Hi, Gentle Breeze. May we come in?"

She goggled for a few seconds, then stepped back and motioned us inside.

Once the door was locked, she wheeled on me and gripped my shoulders—not a painful gesture, but still, staring down more than eight feet of agitated troll is never a comfortable place to be. "How the hell did you get here?" she asked. "Are you hurt?"

"I'm fine, and Inade ti'Cren sneaked me in."

"I'm sorry, *what?* And don't just stand there, ti'Ansha, close the shutters," she snapped.

As Yven jumped to work, I gave Gentle Breeze the

short explanation. "I don't know why, but Pateme told Liventi how to find me. Inade showed up at my studio earlier this week. This is their youngest, Mafora," I said, pointing to my silent companion. "She eloped with a guy her father doesn't like, so now he's hunting them."

"And he... *brought* you here?"

"He wanted a farseer on the job, and I told him that my talent would work better in the Pactlands."

The chief snorted. "*Really*, Rose."

"Can't blame a girl, can you? Anyway, once I realized Mafora hadn't been kidnapped and had just run off with her boyfriend, I got a ride away from Kelomb, and now I'm trying to help them hide from Inade until the end of the month."

Her thick eyebrows furrowed. "What happens then?"

"Inade won't be able to annul the marriage."

"It's an old rule," Yven offered. "The head of an involved Hall can intervene if he or she has a problem with it."

"*Elves*," she muttered, then surprised me with a brief, strangulatory hug. "Welcome back, I suppose," she said as I gasped for air, then effortlessly switched to English. "Does your little friend understand this?"

I cut my eyes to Mafora, who regarded us blankly. "Don't think so."

"Does she know who you are?"

"Not yet. She thinks I'm just a weird human. I told her parents I'd keep my connection under wraps."

Though Gentle Breeze snorted her disapproval, she said, "I won't spoil it, then. But why are you in my house?" she asked, segueing back to Pactish.

"Because we need an exit plan," Pars replied. "I can get through the portal, and the groom's got credentials—"

"Who is he?"

"Deono ti'Gata. He's one of our trainees."

She grumbled unintelligibly. "Which leaves Rose and the ti'Cren girl—"

"And me," Yven interjected.

The rest of us turned to him as one. "Absolutely not," I said. "Pateme would have your hide."

"I don't care," he murmured. "I'm not going to stand back and let you run off with Hall ti'Cren in pursuit. Forget it."

"Yven—"

"*No*, Rosie," he insisted, then stared up at Gentle Breeze. "Can you fix my credentials in the system? The director has me locked down, but if there's a way to undo that…"

She grimaced. "Unfortunately, no. I don't have access to those permissions, and even if I did, something tells me he has a notification on you in case you try to use the external portals." She scowled at the ceiling as she contemplated the matter, then pointed to Pars. "This might work."

"What's that, ma'am?"

"You're not going. Your records will be the first checked once Pateme notices that ti'Ansha's missing. This ti'Gata kid can drive, yes?"

"Sure," said Mafora, "as can I—"

"*You* aren't going to be anywhere near a vehicle window until you're out. Where is he, anyway?"

"My place," said Pars.

"All right." She ran one hand over her short hair as she mentally finalized the plan. "I don't have access to the portal permissions, but I *can* give ti'Gata access to our field vehicles. That'll take me a few minutes, and I'll call you when I'm finished," she told Pars. "Take him to the deck and get him in number fourteen. There's a *substantial* secure cargo area in that one, and it's got proper safety restraints. If I were you, I'd drop him off outside the building, away from the security cameras. Understood?"

"Perfectly, Chief."

"Tell him to drive *away* from this neighborhood until he's also clear of the cameras," she continued. "I suppose your departure point will be your house?"

"That's logical," he replied.

"Fine. Stay the hell away from here, and get them on their way as soon as you can. Rose…" She turned to me and offered a small smile. "I'm sorry, kid. I really am."

I smiled back at her. "Hey, you sent Pars at Christmas. I appreciate it."

"That hardly makes us even. And as for you, ti'Ansha," she continued, looking Yven up and down, "well…you know what you're getting yourself into, right?"

He nodded. "Yes, ma'am."

"I'll play dumb if Syvin or Pateme ask me, but I won't be able to cover for your absence."

"I understand."

She paused, then thrust out her hand, which looked like a green catcher's mitt beside his when he shook it. "Be careful," she said as she released him. "Now get out of here. I've got work to do."

The others trooped to the door, but I lingered where I stood. "Gentle Breeze?"

She'd already turned on her computer and was logging in. "Mm?"

"Thank you."

Glancing up, she nodded and shooed me on my way.

We were loaded within the hour.

While Pars drove Deono to the office to pick up our escape vehicle, Yven rushed home to pack a bag, and Mafora and I hung out in the kitchen with Canna and a steady supply of hot tea. "I'm sorry we can't give you the language potion now," Canna told Mafora. "You might have an easy time of it, but we can't be certain—"

"Knocked me out for two days," I offered. "We need you conscious."

Mafora nodded, though she slumped over her tea, and her face seemed drawn. "How did a *human* get that potion, anyway?"

"Long story," I replied. "Tell you when we're not breaking the law, all right?"

She had little more to say, and Canna and I made quiet conversation, trying not to disturb the children sleeping upstairs. Soon enough, Pars returned, having waited two blocks away from Yven's apartment to give him a lift, and Deono followed in short order, driving a black luxury Jeep that looked like it had just rolled off the assembly line. With the neighbors in for the night, Pars and Canna hustled us out to the Jeep, and Pars popped open the rear door. Lifting the trunk carpet out of the way, he revealed a hatch in the floor, which led down a six-rung ladder into a space that couldn't possibly have existed without the copious use of magic. The storage area beneath the Jeep was invisible from the outside and should have hoisted the vehicle off its wheels—the ceiling had to be eight feet high—and the walls were lined with padded benches fitted with four-point harnesses. A pair of collapsible cots had been strapped to the ceiling in case of medical need.

Pars helped Mafora down, and Yven followed on her heels. I stood outside for a moment longer with Deono and Pars, going through the directions until all three of us felt confident, and then I hugged our hosts goodbye.

"Thank you again," I told Canna.

"Take care of yourself out there," she whispered as she patted my back. "And remember, Yven's a big boy—he can look after himself."

"Unless the situation calls for defensive magic," Pars added. "This place you're going—will there be weapons available?"

I grimaced. "Probably not, and I'd like to avoid a firefight, all things considered." I slid into the trunk, then turned and started down the ladder. "See you around, eh?"

"We'll see you, Red," he replied, though his certainty sounded forced.

A light in the ceiling of the compartment showed me

an empty seat beside Yven, and once I was buckled in, Yven flipped it off. With a last wave, Pars closed the hatch, leaving us in the darkness.

"Don't forget to mask," I murmured as I found Yven's hand.

"Ooh. *Yeah*," he mumbled. I couldn't see him, but a few seconds later, he assured me, "All better. Mafora, do you know how to mask?"

"Of course I know how to do that," she snapped from the other bench.

"She does," I added. "Inade says she keeps her freckles hidden."

"He *told* you that?" she asked, aghast. "Did he tell you that he hides a hairy birthmark on his arm, too? I mean, while we're sharing our least favorite features..." Her voice trailed off as the Jeep began to move.

"It's all right," said Yven. "We needn't worry about noise until we reach the portal. And I wasn't implying that you don't know how to *mask*—have you ever put one together to go outside the Pactlands?"

"Never had the need," she replied, sounding somewhat placated.

"Then we'll help you with the details once we get there."

"Deono knows how?"

"It's part of our training. Anyone with portal credentials learns how to pass for human."

"Kind of," I muttered, and he jabbed me in the side.

When Mafora went quiet, I tried to reassure her. "You're going to be fine. Your father knows where I work, and he presumably knows where I live, so we're going to a town an hour away. A small city, really. Lots of places to hide—I can't imagine that he knows the area well. My friend's house isn't huge, but it's comfortable, and it's in a pretty quiet neighborhood. There are a few shops in walking distance, but it's far enough from the college that it doesn't get foot traffic beyond the local joggers."

"College?" she asked.

There wasn't a good Pactish equivalent for the term. "Uh…assuming you don't skip any grades, our education's required until you're eighteen. College is optional, usually a four-year degree after that."

"You can leave school at *eighteen*?"

"Sure, plenty of people do."

"But—"

"Consider the human lifespan," I said. "Most people get married in their twenties and thirties. Having a spouse and kids while still being in school, not bringing in an income…that's tough."

"So…wait, how old are you?"

"Twenty-seven on Monday."

"That's *all*?"

"You really don't know much about the outside world, do you?" I replied.

"What's worth knowing out there?" she retorted. "We left."

Telling myself that she was stressed and in a bad place, I bit my tongue.

I knew when we'd reached the portal because the Jeep stopped moving for a few minutes. Yven squeezed my hand, and I held on tightly, praying that the attendant on duty that night wouldn't look askance at a DPP agent leaving long after dark. But soon, the vehicle slowly drove forward, and then I felt the rocking motion of uneven terrain. "We're out," I whispered.

"I think you're right," Yven whispered back.

Deono didn't immediately stop, however. On my trips back and forth to Beukal, I'd noticed an abandoned gas station near the portal, barely a shack with a pair of inoperable pumps out front and a much newer charity drop box off to the side. I'd given Deono directions to the place and told him to drive around back, out of sight of the road, so that we could emerge from our hiding spot without attracting attention. He'd paid attention: the Jeep parked a few minutes later, and when Deono lifted the hatch, I looked up to see a burned-out security light above us. Yven and I climbed free with the luggage, and Deono helped his bride out of the hold.

"Mask," I reminded the others, and pulled out my phone as a flashlight.

Quickly, the agents guided Mafora through the necessary facial modifications, and I signed off on the result. While she looked no happier, she seemed convincingly human, and that was good enough for the night.

Yven took the wheel, and I slid in beside him, leaving the back for the anxious couple. As he pulled onto the quiet road, I turned around and smiled. "That was the hard part. Now all you have to do is hang out in a rental house for two weeks."

"And what of you?" Deono asked. "If Lord ti'Cren finds you—"

"He won't. I'll be staying with you, and Yven—"

"Will be staying as well," he interjected in a tone that firmly discouraged argument.

"I've been around Charlottesville enough to find my way," I continued, "and if someone brought a language potion, we could get Mafora fixed up. There are some decent wineries in the area, and I can think of worse ways to spend a couple weeks in hiding…"

I could just make out Deono's grin in the dark.

"Maybe not right away," said Yven as light rain began to fall on us. "Have you checked the weather lately, Rosie?"

"No…" Glancing at my phone, I saw a week of storms in the forecast and groaned. "Well, we could always drink at home instead."

The rain only worsened as we drove west, turning into a steady downpour that slicked the roads and twinkled in our headlights. It was later than I'd realized when we reached Oilville, and our best snack option had been an all-night convenience store just off the Interstate. Fueled by caffeine and chips, I navigated us into Charlottesville and through the downtown Belmont neighborhood just after midnight Sunday. The midcentury homes and narrow streets were dark with the hour—any carousing undergrads were blocks away, thankfully—and no one was parked on the street in front of Toni's place, which faced the back of a vacant dry cleaner. Telling the others to wait, I jumped out and ran up to the porch to punch the door code, then propped the front door open with an iron umbrella stand and started turning on lamps.

The house, which sat on a small corner lot at the top of the road, was best described as "cute," a postwar cottage that had been heavily renovated but could comfortably house perhaps a young couple and a baby or two. The main room was divided between a sitting area with a TV hung on the wall over the fireplace and a dinette for four—and as Toni considered thrifting an art form, none of the furniture matched in color or time period. Doors led to a pair of bedrooms, which flanked a small bath. At the back of the house was a tiny kitchen, and while Toni had done her best with cheery yellow paint and modern appliances, I couldn't envision doing much more than nuking soup in those cramped quarters. The fridge was empty but for a box of baking soda and a few bottles of water, but I found ground coffee, sugar, and powdered creamer in a cabinet. Toni didn't have much on hand, but she wasn't an *inconsiderate* host.

While I finished my sweep, the others came in with the bags. Mafora stood by the door, surveying the cottage with weary dismay, and I opened the door to the nearer bedroom. "Why don't you two take this one?" I offered, beckoning for her to follow me. "I think it's a little bigger."

Deono coaxed her into the room and murmured his

thanks, leaving Yven and me alone for the first time all night. He held me by the dining table, both of us damp from the rain and exhausted by the night's work, and I leaned into his chest as he rubbed my back.

"You think the car's safe on the street?" I mumbled.

"I don't think we have an option tonight," he replied. "It's locked."

I grunted.

"Go to bed, Rosie."

"You take the bed," I suggested. "I'll camp on the couch. That way, in case Pateme tracks us down and breaks in, you can sneak out the window."

"Or not." Before I could protest, he scooped me off my feet and awkwardly carried me into the bedroom, then put me down again to turn back the thick duvet. "Shoes off, in with you."

"Yven—"

"You've spent enough nights on my couch—it's your turn for a real bed." He waited until I kicked aside my flats and laid down, then gave me a tired smile and started for the door. "Sleep well."

"Don't leave."

He looked back at me, brows rising. "Really, the couch seems comfortable—"

"It's been three months. Please don't leave."

Yven poked his head into the den, but Deono and Mafora had gone quiet. Satisfied, he shut the door and slipped off his loafers, and I made room. When he cut the bedside lamp, I closed my eyes and snuggled into him, still almost fully clothed but too tired to care.

"I've missed you," he whispered, brushing my hair from my face in the darkness.

"I've missed you, too," I said, but my throat began to tighten.

He ran his hand up and down over my arm as I sniffled beside him. "It's okay," he soothed, "we're here, we're safe…"

"I'm sorry I blew it."

"Blew what?"

"*Everything*. For us. I'm so sorry, I just...I didn't want Inade to ruin their lives..."

He shifted closer until our foreheads were touching. "Do you *really* think he would have acknowledged you?" he said gently. "Even if you'd led him to the cabin tonight? If he's willing to break up *that* marriage to avoid the perceived shame, then do you honestly believe he'd acknowledge the product of a relationship that he must think is a hundred times worse?"

"But if I'd helped him—"

"Rosie, he's wealthy and powerful. You wouldn't have any leverage. He'd probably have taken you home, thanked you, and never spoken of it again."

"I'm sorry."

"Don't be." His lips found mine, and I kissed him until some of the constriction in my chest relaxed and my eyes didn't prick quite as badly. As Yven held me, he said, "I don't give a damn about acknowledgement. If it happens, great, but I don't care. I love you, Rose Thorn, and I want you just as you are."

"And I love you," I replied, "which is why you're not going anywhere *near* the draught."

"Rosie—"

"You promised me."

"I did," he said after a moment's hesitation, "but if it's the only way..."

"No."

Yven sighed, but he let the matter go as sleep took us.

Dawn hid itself in the gray drizzle, which suited me nicely. Toni's curtains were lovely, flowing panels only marginally more effective than sheers, and I didn't need a face full of sunlight that morning. Barely conscious, I shifted in the sheets, warm and comfortable beside Yven and buried beneath the duvet.

A sudden sharp knocking snapped me closer to awareness, but I hardly had time to recall where I was when the door opened and Mafora poked her head inside. "Hello?" she rasped. "Is anyone...*oh*."

The last syllable emerged as an appalled croak, and I threw back the covers to show that Yven and I were both decent, if rumpled. "Only two beds here," I said as he sat up and rubbed his eyes. "Do you need something?"

But she wasn't buying it. "Are you two..." she began, aghast, then stuttered briefly before managing, "Don't tell me you're—"

"What?" Yven snapped. "Don't tell you I have feelings for your great-niece?"

"Yven," I started, but he shook his head.

"No, Rosie. You put yourself out for her. This ends *now*." He stood and folded his arms, staring Mafora down as she regarded us with a mixture of distaste and bewilderment. "We didn't have time for proper introductions last night," he told her. "Rose is your brother's granddaughter."

She backed away a pace. "My..."

"Fradin," said Yven. "Calling Rose human isn't entirely accurate, but you know, the priority yesterday was escape." As Mafora's expression shifted toward horrified, he pressed on. "We met last year at Liliol's nursery, and Rose's farsight helped us find her when she went on the run. I suppose you and your sister don't talk much, do you? Anyway, that's how the director learned of Rose. Why he felt compelled to drag her into this mess between you and your father is beyond my comprehension, but here we are."

"I'm sorry for the shock," I offered. "Your father asked me not to tell any of you who I am, so I didn't bring it up, but..." I shrugged and tried to smile. "Hi, I, uh...I realize I don't exactly look the part, but I *am* talented. I mean, who's ever heard of a human farseer, right?" I added, hoping to lighten the mood.

It didn't work. Mafora stiffened and drew herself up to her full height, though her evident attempt to convey a sense of authority was hampered somewhat by her mussed hair and baby blue pajamas. "I would like you to leave," she announced.

I crawled off the bed and tugged down my sweater. "*Excuse* me?"

"I...would prefer it if you stayed elsewhere. Not here."

Her blatant rejection stung, but I tried not to let on. "That isn't an option. This is my friend's house, and—"

"Who the *hell* do you think you are?" Yven spat.

Mafora wheeled on him as if he'd slapped her. "Who are you," she retorted, slipping into Low Elvish, "to tell me that I have to share space with *that* creature?"

"That *creature*," he replied in a voice like ice, "is the only reason you're not locked in your room in your parents' house right now. *She* took pity on you, and all of the favors that got you here were done on *her* behalf. And do you know what's worse?" he pressed, glowering at her. "She agreed to help your father find you because she was hoping he might acknowledge her, and she tossed that aside to protect you instead—"

Mafora's incredulous laughter cut him short. "Acknowledge *her*? My father would never debase the Hall like that! Are you insane?"

"No," he said, "but she was hopeful."

"Then she's an idiot. Who would ever acknowledge a human? Ti'Cren certainly wouldn't."

"Ti'Cren wouldn't what?" asked Deono from the other room. Finding the three of us in a standoff, he frowned and looked to his wife for an explanation. "What's going on?"

"*That*," muttered Mafora, pointing to me, "is Fradin's blood."

He winced, but I saw pity instead of disgust in his reaction. "And she helped us. From one of ti'Cren's unauthorized marriages to another—"

She spun toward him, eyes blazing. "Do *not* compare me to Fradin! We are nothing like him and that whore—"

"I never met my grandfather," I interrupted, and the newlyweds looked at me in shock. "He died years before I was born. But I do know that he loved my grandmother very much. Also…yeah, I speak Elvish. Got it by potion at the same time I got Pactish," I said, thumbing one hand toward Yven, "so you'll have to forgive my accent. I'm doing my best, but the drawl comes through. Anyway," I continued while Mafora was still caught between fury and embarrassment, "sorry, no, I'm not leaving. I'm responsible for this house, and I've paid for it. I'm guessing you haven't been here much," I said, pointing to Deono, "and I *know* you don't have the first clue what you're doing, Mafora, so maybe we could all act like adults for two damn weeks."

Yven, who by then had flushed with anger, started to interrupt, but I grabbed his arm to stop him. "This is just me wondering," I said to the couple, "but did either of you bother to bring any money? Any of the local currency?"

Mafora said nothing, though Deono looked like he just remembered he'd left the stove on.

I folded my arms. "Didn't think so. Guess that means I'll be housing *and* feeding you for the duration. Incidentally, is either of you a farseer?"

"No," Deono mumbled.

"Uh-huh. So that means I'm housing, feeding, *and* keeping watch on Inade to make sure nothing's gone wrong. Have I forgotten anything?"

While Mafora continued to glare at me sullenly, her husband seemed well and truly abashed. "Thank you, Rose," he said, his shoulders hunching. "We're sorry for the trouble."

"I don't mind," I muttered, then locked eyes with Mafora. "And before you get the brilliant idea to call your sister and complain about the injustice of having to share space with me, you should be aware that Lily has no idea what's going on. If I tell her how you and your parents have treated me, then I *guarantee* that she will drive you back to Inade herself. Is that perfectly clear, Mafora? Or is my accent too much for you?"

"Fine," she grunted, knocking Deono in the shoulder as she swept back to their room and slammed the door.

Left alone to face us, Deono took the path of appeasement. "I'm sorry, this has been hard on her—"

"Whatever. I'm going to go buy bagels," I said, jamming my feet into my shoes. "Need a brush. Yven, is my junk still out there?"

"Mine, too," he said, and Deono moved aside as he headed out to retrieve our bags. Before he could clear the area, Yven gripped his shoulder and stared the younger agent down. "Keep her out of my sight," he said, and stormed off.

When Deono looked my way, I smirked and straightened the bedding. "I'd welcome you to the family, but as you may have noticed, I don't exactly qualify."

"I'm truly sorry about, uh…"

"Save it," I said, retrieving the throw pillows with a quick gesture toward the floor, and smiled to myself to see his unease. "Oh, I *am* talented. Don't let the ears fool you."

Deono made ample room as Yven returned with the luggage. "Not that it's any of my business," he ventured while I dug through my suitcase for my hairbrush, "but are you two—"

"It's none of your business," I replied, and with another gesture, I closed the door in his face.

CHAPTER 11

While I might not have been authorized to drive DPP's loaded Jeep, no one stopped me when I grabbed the keys.

As I followed my phone's directions toward bagels and blessed caffeine, Yven, who'd been quiet for the first mile, murmured, "I'm sorry."

"Not your fault," I said, slowing as I approached a yellow light.

"No, it is. I had no right to spill the family secret, and I should have let you handle that, and…you know, I'm sorry."

I leaned over the center console to kiss his stubbled cheek. "Thanks anyway for trying to defend me."

He chuckled weakly. "It wasn't even all that. I…" After a brief struggle, he said, "Between the director and my therapist, I've spent the last three months being told that I'm some kind of deviant who would bring down the very pillars of society if given the opportunity to do so, and when Mafora came in and started running her mouth—"

"You saw red."

"Yeah. But that's no excuse."

The light changed, and I drove on through the rain. "Need you to be honest, okay?"

"Sure."

"I've never seen anyone over there act like she did about me. Have I just been lucky to this point, or if I go public, are people going to treat me like I'm carrying a plague?"

Yven propped his arm on the door. "Some will, I

imagine. We don't see many crosses, and there's a certain segment of the population that thinks pursing someone outside your people, let alone making a family with them, is on par with murder. Most of the rest are at least polite about it, even if they disapprove."

"So Mafora's reaction could just be a ti'Cren thing? Fradin's the skeleton in the closet, and here I come, tapdancing out?"

He cracked a small smile but quickly sobered. "Fradin's departure isn't exactly a shining moment in the ti'Cren legacy. That could have a lot to do with it."

I hesitated, trying to decide whether I honestly wanted an answer, then asked, "How would your parents take it?"

"You mean—"

"If you brought me home today and acknowledgement wasn't an issue, what would they say?"

He thought about the question for the space of a couple blocks. "I don't know," he finally muttered. "They've never made a big deal about it around me, but none of my siblings have brought home anyone...*interesting*, so I'm not sure. Wouldn't matter to me."

"No?"

"They have fifteen children, and they've shown no indication of stopping. Let them think what they like about me—they'll have other chances if I disappoint them."

"But I probably still shouldn't hold my breath for an invitation to Thanksgiving dinner?" I said.

"Well, seeing as we don't celebrate Thanksgiving—"

"You know what I mean."

He sighed. "I can't say. Would that be a dealbreaker for you?"

"No," I replied, and smiled at him as we stopped at another light. "You'd be enough. You, me...seventeen thousand orchids..."

"I'm not *quite* there yet."

"Closer by the day. And if it matters," I added, "Aunt

Lily likes you. That's literally the only family I have to impress, so congrats, you're in."

He smiled back at me, though I caught the wistfulness in it before I headed through the intersection. "There's just the tiny matter of the legal complication to work through."

"Minor hitch."

"Barely a speed bump."

"You know," I said as we pulled up at the bagel shop, "I used to think you were *so* straitlaced. I'm beginning to wonder if I haven't been a bad influence."

Once I turned into a space and parked, he leaned over to kiss me properly. "Nonsense. You bring out the best in me."

We returned to Toni's house in short order with a sack full of bagels, a couple varieties of cream cheese, and coffee for four. Even if Mafora had acted like a raging bitch, hospitality dictated that I not leave them to starve. Mafora refused to emerge from her room for breakfast, but Deono appreciated the carbs. He apologized again for his bride's behavior, but I waved it off, trying not to make an uncomfortable situation worse.

Once we'd eaten, Yven suggested grocery shopping, but I gave him my credit card and passed on the trip. "I want to look in on the situation in Kelomb," I explained as I stretched. "Deono, don't knock unless there's an emergency."

With Yven back on the road, Deono watching TV, and Mafora still sulking, I lay in my room with the lights off and the minimal curtains drawn, psyching myself up for the task ahead. That Inade took the blinding potion was no secret, but if I'd been able to break through Pateme's protection, then surely, I told myself, I could spy on him. I just needed to clear my mind and concentrate.

As I sank into the proper headspace and opened my inner eyes, at first, all I saw was a whiteout. That was no shock—Pateme had taken a little effort to bring into view—and I focused on Inade, calling to mind his dark eyes, his narrow, unsmiling lips, his boring brown ponytail…

…and suddenly, I found myself in the dining room, standing between the buffet and the table. Morning sunlight poured through the three glass walls, illuminating Inade, who stood at the head of the table in an ornate robe, staring down at Teolm. His son appeared to be halfway through his breakfast and still wearing a grungy T-shirt and stained khakis, presumably evidence of another long night at the greenhouse.

"What do you mean, she's *not back*?" Inade asked. Though he kept his voice level, almost conversational, I could see the tension in his face and the vein beginning to bulge at his temple. "Where did she go?"

"The capital, probably," said Teolm. "Her great-grandmother was on her deathbed yesterday."

"What?"

He nodded. "Poor girl. Her cousin came to collect her yesterday afternoon. She said she'd return as soon as possible, but you might want to give her some space, Father—I think she'd been crying."

"Of course," Inade stiffly replied. "This cousin—did you get a name?"

Teolm bit into his toast. "No. All I saw was a gray car out the window, and before you ask, I wasn't about to pry," he added with a look of reproval. "'Oh, sorry your beloved family member is dying,'" he minced. "'Aren't you going to introduce me to your cousin before you hurry to her bedside?'"

For a man who had to be infuriated, Inade kept remarkably cool. "Thank you for letting me know," he told Teolm. "Were you planning to bathe today?"

"I'm not staining your chair," his son retorted, waving him away with his half-eaten toast. "Are you joining me, or did you just come in to critique my hygiene?"

"I'll eat later," he replied, and left the room.

I followed at a jog as Inade swept through the corridors toward the elevator, and then I realized his destination as he hurried into the east wing. But when he reached my guest room, I saw that he hadn't been the only one to come exploring.

Liventi looked up from my uncovered, half-finished painting as Inade stormed in and slammed the door. "She's quite an artist," she said with casual indifference. "Good with faces, though I think she rather flattered Dania."

"What have you done?" Inade demanded.

"*Me*? Nothing. I'm not the one who sneaked a human into the Pactlands—"

"You told me about her!"

"I didn't intend for you to *bring* her here," Liventi retorted. "And now I hear she's gone missing. A sick great-grandmother, was it?"

"Damn it, woman, *where is she*?" he yelled, grabbing her by the shoulders.

"How should I know?" she replied, wresting herself from his grip. "I wasn't aware she'd left until Teolm mentioned it this morning! And I didn't know she was here at all until I *chanced* upon her yesterday. Honestly, Inade, what were you thinking?"

He lowered his voice almost to a growl. "I'm going to ask you one more time: where is Mafora, and with whom?"

"And I'll give you the same answer as always: I don't know."

Leaving Liventi, Inade studied my painting in silence for a moment before he punched a hole through the canvas and sent the easel clattering to the stone. "I am trying to save this Hall," he murmured, turning back to his wife.

If Liventi feared his reaction, she showed no sign.

"I know Mafora has eloped," he continued. "A friend at the Tribunal building saw her in there with a young man, but he couldn't name the boy. Her marriage record won't be posted until next month. So why don't you do the sensible thing and tell me with whom my daughter is sullying the reputation of this family?"

I caught a faint flicker of unease in Liventi's mask of calm. "She could have been at the Tribunal building for any number of reasons—"

"Do *not* take me for a fool." Glowering at his wife, Inade demanded, "Name. *Now.*"

Liventi breathed deeply, staring him down, but after a brief period of indecision, she cracked. "I don't know his full name," she said. "Mafora wouldn't tell me. She knew you wouldn't give him a chance, and that's why she ran off. But I do believe she's in love," she pressed, picking up speed, "and it's not like she's eloped with a troll—"

"Name."

She huffed. "Couldn't tell you his personal name, but…she mentioned that he's a ti'Gata."

"*Ti'Gata?*" Inade bellowed, purpling in his fury. Had my painting not been on the floor already, it would have made an ideal target as he looked around for an outlet and settled for sweeping my paints and brushes off their table. "You allowed her to run away with a ti'Gata?"

"She says he's a respectable young man—"

"She might as well have taken up with a troll!" He marched across the room, and Liventi backed away from his advance until her legs hit the bed. "Now there's a human on the loose," he said, trapping her where she stood. "And if she's caught, what do you suppose she'll say, hmm? That she just happened to wander in by herself, or that I brought her over to hunt down my daughter, who's tied herself to a damn ti'Gata? What do you think?"

"I think you were a fool to bring Rose here," Liventi replied, "and you need to let Mafora go."

"I will *not* endure the bards' taunting for another decade," he snapped. "And what does it say about this Hall if I can't maintain the slightest semblance of discipline? I can gild all the monuments and patronize all the theater companies I like, and they *still* laugh about your son. Now they'll laugh about your daughter, too. Congratulations on ruining the reputation I've worked so hard to build."

As he headed for the door, Liventi called after him, "You brought this on yourself."

Wheeling around, he snapped, "Say that again, I dare you."

She rolled her eyes. "Enough with the dramatics, Inade. You were foolish enough to bring Rose here without consulting me. Frankly, I'm not surprised she's run off," she continued, crossing her arms over her delicate silk morning dress. "You've hurt her feelings."

He scowled. "How so? I brought her here, gave her whatever she needed—"

"Idiot boy," she interrupted, and sighed. "She's a young orphan with no one but *Liliol* to look after her, and what did you do? Brought her into the mansion and showed her a family she can't have. She told me she'd agreed to keep her identity secret—how do you *think* that made her feel? A touch on the unwanted side, perhaps? Once she learned that Mafora had eloped, perhaps she thought her a kindred spirit to Fradin. I certainly don't know, but—"

"What would you have had me do, then? Introduce her to the children? Acknowledge her?"

"Don't be stupid. All you would have needed to do was dangle the possibility before her. If she thought she could win your approval, imagine what she might have done for you." Shrugging, Liventi said, "But you didn't consider all the variables, and now your largely human great-granddaughter is somewhere in the Pactlands. Moreover, if you don't leave your daughter alone and let this marriage stand, you *will* lose her," she warned. "Is that what you want? Another child we pretend was never born? Wasn't one enough?"

"You coddle them," Inade replied. "That's your failing. So now, if you'll excuse me, my dear," he muttered, "I need to find Mafora *and* the damn human."

As he stalked off, I pulled myself back to my body and stared at the ceiling until I felt grounded once again.

They didn't want me. They would never want me.

But I didn't have time for self-pity. Steeling myself once again, I went in search of Inade.

By eleven, I was long overdue for a break.

Squinting at the light outside my room and shuffling—I fully trusted neither my feet nor the floor—I made it to the kitchen and grabbed a Coke. The evidence of Yven's shopping covered the counter and filled the fridge, and when I opened the cabinets, I found them stocked with bags of rice and pasta, dried goods that would easily last for the duration of our stay. After leaning on the counter for a moment and letting the sugar hit my bloodstream, I felt sufficiently recovered to step into the den and be social.

But the house was too quiet, and the only person I found was Mafora, who'd curled up in an oversized chair near the fireplace and regarded me with wet, red eyes as I emerged. "Uh...hi," I said, glancing around the cottage for less hostile signs of life. "Where are the guys?"

"Gone," she said. "Deono wanted to see the area by day in case we need to flee, and what's-his-name took him for a drive."

"Yven." I settled onto the couch and looked out the window at the downpour. "You didn't want to go with them?"

She sniffed and pulled her knees closer to her chest, and I suspected that she hadn't been invited.

"What's wrong?" I asked, kicking myself as the words came out.

"What *isn't?*" She moped for a moment, but when the silence grew too uncomfortable between us, she mumbled, "It wasn't supposed to be like this."

"Your elopement hideaway? Sorry, I don't have a spare cabin on hand—"

"Deono had it worked out! He said no one would find us there, and I didn't think Father would *still* be angry. He was supposed to be over it by now…"

My laughter cut her off. "Oh, trust me, he's *pissed*. I've been watching him all morning."

"How? He protects himself from farseers. Mother used to, but she says it's just paranoia…though I suppose that's been disproven," she allowed, eyeing me.

"I have my ways," I replied, disinclined to go into the details of farsight with my sullen great-aunt. "But yeah, he's furious. Teolm let slip that I left yesterday, so now he's worried that I'm going to find an authority figure and blab that he sneaked me over the border to begin with."

"Does Teolm know—"

"About me? No, I'm just the random sorcerer Inade hired to do a family portrait. Speaking of which, he punched a hole through my painting when your mother wouldn't tell him where you were."

Mafora barely smiled. "She told me she'd keep my confidence—"

"Wouldn't count on that. Someone at the Tribunal building mentioned to Inade that he'd seen you and a mystery man over there, so Inade's figured out that you've eloped. Once he told Liventi, she admitted that your husband's a ti'Gata."

Wide-eyed with indignation, Mafora uncurled as if poised to leap from her chair. "Why would she…Mother *promised*—"

"I did mention the painting-punching, right? He threw a tantrum and intimidated her. Anyway, he's put calls in for help to a few people. I don't know who—he didn't make the calls on speaker," I explained, "and he didn't give me any clues to work with. But trust me that Inade's asking for favors, and now he's hunting all of us."

She stared at the rug, then murmured, "He'll accept us.

If he doesn't find us in time, then he'll have to accept us."

Clearly, her version of *us* didn't include me. "I mean, considering that he compared marrying a ti'Gata to running off with a troll…"

"He said *what?*" she snapped.

"Uh-huh. And seeing as Liventi only learned of my dad's existence a few weeks ago, I really wouldn't assume that this is going to blow over and Inade will have his new son-in-law around to the mansion for bonding time. He seems to hold grudges when his children don't marry properly."

She regarded me carefully, as if looking for signs of deception. "Fradin had a son, then?"

I nodded. "Just one kid, and then my parents just had me. Only child of only children."

"Do you think Father will try to use your parents to find us?"

"I mean, first, you're assuming that he knows you and I are together, and I don't think he's reached that conclusion yet. Second, not unless he's got some wild talent that lets him talk to the dead."

"Oh," she mumbled.

"Yeah. I'm more concerned that he'll lean on Aunt Lily, which is why we're *not* contacting her. Got it?"

"Understood." Growing pensive again, Mafora readjusted herself to stare out the window at the dreary morning, then sighed. "What if Father cuts me off?"

"You think he'd disown you?" I asked.

"No, he can't do that," she replied, her tone suggesting that the answer should have been obvious. "But my allowance keeps my business afloat. If he stops supporting me…"

"Look," I said after a moment, "I get it. I'm an artist and a small business owner, too. But if you're more concerned about your allowance being stopped than you are about your marriage being annulled, then you might as well run home to Daddy right now and beg forgiveness."

She glared at me, but I pressed on. "My grandfather gave up his home, his family, and his job to be with my grandmother. He drank freaking *poison*. A little extreme, sure, but if you don't love Deono enough to give up your spending money—"

"I never said that. It's...fashion is all I've ever wanted to do, and without Father's support, either our business will fail or I'll have to take on more tailoring work, and I won't have time for my designs—"

"And that would be a shame," I interrupted, "but you'd be with someone you love, right?"

She turned away again. "You couldn't understand."

"No? Maybe I'm mistaken, but I see a spoiled little princess who's realized for the first time in her life that her actions might have consequences."

Huffing, she said, "I'm not—"

"How far are you willing to go for Deono? What's your limit? Who would you rather have in your life, him or your parents? Or are you just worried that if you're cut off, you won't get invited to the nice parties anymore?"

Her cheeks flared with her indignation. "I *love* Deono, and don't you dare insinuate otherwise. But there are complications in my life—"

"Oh, go cry me a river," I snapped. "If you can hang out here until the end of the month, you'll get to live the rest of your life with the man you love. At least one of us is so lucky."

"You're being dramatic," she countered with a knowing air. "You've got an infatuation, nothing worse. It'll pass."

My eyebrows rose. "I love Yven, and he loves me."

Her tone shifted toward pitying. "I don't mean to be cold, but he doesn't *love* you. He's working something out of his system, I suppose, but what you're seeing here isn't love."

I stared back at her, my arms quivering with my anger, but I forced myself not to jump off the couch and throttle her. "You can't imagine him loving me, can you?" I managed.

"It's nothing personal—"

"It is! Because you think I'm somehow *less* than you," I said, gathering steam. "Well, I reject that. Think what you like, but I am *not* your inferior."

"You *reject* facts?" she scoffed. "What's next, you reject gravity? I'm sorry if the truth is uncomfortable, but—"

"I woke Yven from a siren," I said. "Think you could do the same for Deono?"

Mafora's mouth snapped closed, and I pushed myself to my feet to go make a sandwich. "Deono seems like a nice guy," I told her, walking away. "The least you can do is be grateful for what you have."

I couldn't be sure of what was keeping Yven and Deono out on such a miserable day, but frankly, I didn't blame them for exploring more than our immediate surroundings. Mafora, who seemed by turns aggrieved with the world and melancholy, refused when I offered to throw together lunch for her as well, and so I ate alone in my room with the door closed, watching videos on my phone to pass the time.

I'd just finished and was about to attempt an afternoon session of espionage when my phone rang. Assuming it was Yven, I hurried to grab it, only to see Aunt Lily's name on the screen.

Shit.

Putting on the most nonchalant voice I could muster, I answered the call. "Hi, there!" I said, aiming for breezy but falling short. "How's it going? Resting up for Monday?"

"Not exactly," she replied. "Where are you, darling?"

"Working."

That wasn't *entirely* untrue, but Aunt Lily had a keen ear for my fibs. "Mm-hmm. This work wouldn't have anything to do with my little sister, would it?"

"What do you mean?" I asked, willing my racing heart

to slow.

"Well," said Aunt Lily, who sounded far too calm for our conversation, "I just had a call from my mother, of all people. Said Father had smuggled you over to find Mafora, and now you were on the run somewhere in the Pactlands. I assured her I hadn't heard from you, but now that I've got you on the line, mind telling me what the hell is going on, Rosie?"

I hesitated, trying to decide how much trouble I'd be in if I hung up on her. "Uh...probably best if I don't."

"Shocking," she said dryly. "Mother mentioned that Mafora has run off with a ti'Gata boy. Know where she might be hiding?"

"Not specifically." She could have migrated to her room by then, for all I knew.

Aunt Lily let the silence spin out for a moment, then said, "Charlottesville's a lovely town. If you need restaurant recommendations, I have a few."

"Why would I need recs for Charlottesville?" I replied as my stomach knotted.

"No reason. Nothing that I'd mention to Mother, anyway. But it's odd, you know—do you recall that anonymous letter you received back in November? The one that suggested I make a batch of Awakening for you?"

"Yes, ma'am..."

"I might be mistaken," she continued, "but I think your pen pal just sent me one, too. Looks rather like your letter."

I swallowed hard. If my unknown correspondent wasn't a farseer, then he or she was intimately acquainted with one. "What did it say?"

"Not much. It was brief. Warned me that Mother would be in touch, suggested I play dumb with her, and told me to be in Charlottesville next Sunday evening. Got an address, too." She paused, then said, "I won't ask you to confirm it. But whatever you're doing, darling, I want you to promise me that you'll be careful. Okay?"

"Okay," I whispered. "Thank you."

"Of course. How *is* Mafora, anyway? I haven't seen her in years."

"I'm sure I couldn't say," I replied. "But since your dad seems to be looking for her, I'd imagine that she's worried, maybe homesick…kind of bitchy," I added, grateful that Mafora couldn't understand me if she were eavesdropping.

"That so?" I could practically hear the smirk in Aunt Lily's voice. "If you should see her, then, keep her in line for me. Until next week," she said. "I love you, darling. Don't do anything stupid. And if we don't speak tomorrow, happy birthday."

"Thanks. Love you, too," I said, and held the phone long after we hung up.

One week.

I lay back on the bed and closed my eyes. Time to get to work.

CHAPTER 12

Monday morning, I woke to an empty bed and the smell of Yven's biscuits. Staggering into the kitchen, I found him opening a package of bacon while the main event—at least for me—cooled on top of the stove. Seeing me, he grunted in frustration. "This was meant to be a surprise," he griped.

"You can't bake in the room next to me and expect me to pretend nothing is happening," I replied, and kissed him. "Thank you. After three months of biscuits from a tube…"

He looked pained at the thought. "Happy birthday, Rosie. Go back to bed—I'll bring it to you in a few minutes, and you can pretend to be shocked."

"Or I can keep you company," I said, trying to find an out-of-the-way spot in the tiny kitchen.

Yven started laying strips of bacon in the hot pan, and by the time he'd finished the pack, the coffee's brew cycle was gurgling to an end, and I'd scrounged up a pair of mismatched plates in one of the cabinets. When Deono poked his head into the room and smiled hopefully, I pulled out a third.

That Mafora would decline to join us was understood. Yven and Deono had stayed out for much of the afternoon the previous day, driving around the city and avoiding a fight back at the house. "He hides it better than she does, but he's stressed," Yven had told me that night, once we were alone in the darkness of our room. "All month, he's been trying to keep up appearances at work while sneaking off to that cabin to take care of her. She'd assured him that her parents would get over it quickly, but he sees now that this is obviously not the case. Assuming that the director doesn't fire him for the unauthorized trip out, he's worried that he might lose his job because Inade will lean on his brother-in-law, and with an inauspicious career record like that…"

"Mafora's freaking out about her finances, too," I'd told him. "It's hitting her that she might lose Daddy's money over this stunt."

Stress and the interruption to their honeymoon had left Mafora and Deono on edge and testy, and the two had said little to each other before Mafora called it a night…and locked the door behind her. We'd helped Deono make up a bed on the couch while he waited for the storm to blow over.

He seemed no worse for wear after the night in quasi-exile, and if Mafora was still displeased with my proximity, Deono was more than civil. Over breakfast, I finally learned how the two of them had crossed paths: his sister's wedding two years before. "I needed a new robe," he explained, topping up his coffee. "Something nice but not too expensive—I'd blown most of my savings during the gap between graduation and starting at DPP. One of my friends suggested House of Wonder for formalwear at a decent price, and when I stopped in, I met Mafora." He smiled at the memory. "She didn't tell me who she was. I just saw this gorgeous brunette who laughed at my dumb jokes, and I took a chance and invited her out. We started seeing each other, and she assured me that the ti'Cren thing was no problem…and then, a few months in, she confessed that she wasn't just a cousin. And there I was, a mere agent—a *trainee* agent. My parents make furniture," he added with a chuckle. "I couldn't compete with *ti'Cren*. But she said it didn't matter and everything would work out."

"So you opted for asking forgiveness over permission,

huh?" I said.

He nodded. "Mafora thought her father would try to break us up if we did things properly, so that's why we decided to elope. She insists that he'll come around once he gets to know me, but..." He grimaced and reached for another biscuit. "Doesn't look too promising, does it?"

"Maybe he'll feel differently in a few months," I suggested, though given what I'd seen, I didn't hold out much hope.

"Perhaps. But if she ends up estranged from her family because of me...I don't want that for her. I love her," he murmured. "I want her to be happy. And now, with all of this..." Sighing, he said, "I don't want her to *resent* me. If we went back now, let the marriage be undone, and then tried to work on her parents to get their approval—"

"You won't," Yven interrupted. "Not from Lord ti'Cren. Trust me."

Deono's forehead furrowed. "Have you pursued someone in that Hall? That is, uh," he stammered, glancing at me, "someone...I mean..."

"I'm not in ti'Cren," I told him. "Your father-in-law has made that quite clear. Relax."

Still, he flushed as Yven said, "No, but I know how Halls like ti'Cren work. I'd make a poor match."

"But you're—"

"Ti'Ansha doesn't look that high for marriages. We *might* be acceptable to someone beyond the ti'Cren main line, but barely."

Deono hunched his shoulders and scowled into his coffee. "The Hall system is antiquated. We're all citizens, you know. I have just as many rights as any of you—"

"I know," said Yven, cutting him off as he ramped up, "and I agree. If you and Mafora chose each other, then there's no reason that you two should be denied. But practically speaking, how many centuries do you think it'll take before the old attitudes fade? Some of the current ladies and lords held their Halls before the Pact—you think they're going to change their minds overnight?"

"We're closing on five hundred years. That's hardly *overnight*," Deono grumbled. "So what do I do, then? If we go back now, he'll break the marriage. But if we make it the month and her father cuts her off, she—"

"She's got two weeks to decide what's important to her," I said, glancing at her closed bedroom door. "Until then, from where I'm sitting, you've tried." Pushing back from the dinette, I quickly drained my mug and headed for the kitchen. "And now it's time to get to spying."

"You could take a day off," Yven suggested.

I turned and gave him a tight smile. "We've got a pissed-off lord to consider, and I'm the early warning system. But thank you for breakfast."

I didn't limit myself to Inade and Liventi. After all, we had a DPP vehicle parked outside our hideout, and I had to assume that someone would ask about the missing Jeep eventually.

I just hadn't expected the reckoning to come so quickly.

Habit led me to check up on Pateme, whom I located in his office, brewing a mug of tea at his office bar. He glanced up from the steeping tea at a sharp double rap at the door, then called, "Come in."

Gentle Breeze, now sporting the tactical black shirt and pants favored by Interdiction over the rest of the building's robes, poked her head into the room. "You wanted to see me, sir?"

"I did," he replied, his tone pleasant. "Have a seat. Something to drink?"

"Thank you, no." She closed the door and perched on one of his chairs, which seemed dangerously undersized beneath her.

Pateme locked the door with a casual gesture, then engaged the soundproofing spell around his office. The chief watched as the red light swept down the walls, her expression far more placid than mine would have been, though I supposed that private meetings between the director and his top lieutenants weren't an odd occurrence.

Tea in hand, he sat behind his desk and took a bracing sip, then faintly smiled. "*Ah.* The greenhouses here do fine work, but there's nothing quite like proper Assam."

She grinned back at him. "My bribery list lengthens."

"You can try anything once. Speaking of which," he said, putting the mug aside and folding his hands, "I'd like to know why you changed a trainee agent's permissions without consulting me."

Gentle Breeze didn't flinch. "Could you elaborate?"

"Certainly." Glancing at a piece of paper on his desk, he said, "Deono ti'Gata. I don't see any disciplinary notices in his record, but he's not yet qualified to have access to our fleet. And yet, on Saturday night, you overrode the trainee block and authorized him to check out..." He made a show of squinting at his notes. "Number *fourteen*. That's a considerable rig."

"Yes, sir."

"Portal records show that he took it out that evening, bound for Oilville. No passengers."

She nodded.

"And he has yet to return." Pateme sat back and folded his arms. "I'm not here to micromanage your section, and I think you'd agree that I seldom second-guess you. But would you care to explain to me why you sent a trainee to Virginia in a high-capacity vehicle, much less for an unplanned, unlogged trip over the weekend?"

Gentle Breeze remained silent.

"He's not the only one missing," Pateme continued. "I had the attendance logs pulled a few minutes ago. Agent Mera is here—that was something of a surprise—but I see that Agent ti'Ansha has yet to appear. Now, perhaps I'm growing suspicious with age, but I can't help thinking that ti'Gata's weekend trip and ti'Ansha's absence are somehow related. Ti'Ansha hasn't tried to use his portal credentials, I'm told, but then again, were he to stow away in the vehicle you authorized ti'Gata to borrow, I doubt anyone at the portal would have been the wiser. Saturday night isn't a shift given to the best attendants, I fear."

For a time, the two considered each other across the expanse of Pateme's desk, neither flinching. But after a long, uncomfortable moment, Gentle Breeze broke the standoff: "If you want my badge, sir, just say so."

"I don't," he replied. "Just give me the truth."

"You're not going to like it."

He shrugged. "Try me."

"Fine. Inade ti'Cren sneaked Rose across the border to look for his missing kid when she eloped with ti'Gata. The happy couple needed a place to hide, and so I loaned ti'Gata a vehicle capable of getting the three of them out."

Pateme's face remained impassive. "And ti'Ansha?"

"Mera probably tipped him off that Rose was here, and he wouldn't let her go on the run without him." When the director didn't immediately respond, she asked, "Is this the part where you call Laws and I leave with an escort, or what?"

Instead of answering her, he opened a locked drawer in his desk, flipped through his files, and extracted a slim envelope...

No. *Not* an envelope. A piece of thick, cream-colored paper folded and formerly sealed with a blob of gray wax, which still clung to one flap. I knew that sort of correspondence, and even without looking too closely, I knew that the seal would have no identifying marks and there would be no return address.

My pen pal preferred privacy.

"Do you know what this is?" Pateme asked Gentle Breeze.

She stood and took the letter from him, giving me a chance to note the pair of circular stamps and the address:

Pateme ti'Tam
Division of Plants and Potions
Beukal, District 3

"Rose received one like this when she was looking for Kritsa last winter," said Gentle Breeze, who kept Pateme's letter folded shut. "Where did it come from?"

"Good question. I haven't tried to bribe Parcels and Letters yet." He motioned toward her and leaned back in his chair. "Read it."

Frowning, she sat again and opened the letter, and I read over her shoulder:

Pateme,

Calling you an idiotic asshole would be an insult to fine, hardworking anuses. What were you thinking in sending Rose away? You know as well as anyone that she's a farseer, and you should know by now that farseers are almost always well gifted. Rose is no exception. She is very talented and very much under-trained—a perfect combination for producing accidental craters but less than ideal for anything else. She's a danger to herself and everyone around her.

You could have mitigated that risk by continuing her training. We both know that she has been useful to you. How many cases has she solved for DPP, three in the span of six months? How many lives did she save on her last jaunt for you? You remember, the one in which your people allowed an untrained woman too young to even apply for a position at your agency to confront a siren? And as soon as you had your answers, you banished her. You could have kept her safe here.

The ti'Ansha boy is no fool, Pateme, unlike yourself. He could have tolerated Rose's presence here without guzzling the draught. What you have done to the two of them is needlessly cruel, and whatever guilt you may still carry over your nephew doesn't excuse your behavior now.

With all of that said, listen closely and try to follow along.

In two weeks, Liventi will call you here in the early evening. Don't be surprised. Her youngest will have, by then, run off with her paramour, and it goes without saying that Inade will be displeased. Liventi will ask for your help. Tell her about Rose, but let her assume that Rose is quarterblooded. You need to trust me.

Inade will find a way to return Rose to the Pactlands. She will leave of her own volition, and she will go to ground in Charlottesville, west of the Oilville portal. The address is as follows:

That my pen pal had at least a connection to a farseer wasn't news to me, but he or she had never been quite so explicit in the letters I'd received. While Pateme's letter explained where he'd gotten the idea to reveal my existence to Liventi, I didn't know why Pateme had trusted his anonymous correspondent—or, more annoyingly, why my pen pal had given away our hiding place. True enough, that was Toni's address on the page, and I skimmed past the directions from Oilville to see what else had been divulged.

You need to be in Charlottesville on the evening of March 22. Do not go alone. What transpires at that time will be crucial to Floodtide.

Do not fail, Pateme.

My stomach began to knot. Sunday. Pateme was supposed to come to me on Sunday, just like Aunt Lily. That my unknown correspondent was calling in backup seemed obvious.

"Any idea who wrote that?" Pateme asked as Gentle Breeze finished reading.

She shook her head. "No, but as I mentioned, Rose has received a letter like this. More than one, actually—she said she got another when we were dealing with the Roulette situation." Handing the letter back to Pateme, she asked, "What's Floodtide?"

He put the note away and locked the drawer again, then took a sip of tea. "Project Floodtide," he murmured, "is a joint initiative among DPP, Laws, and Intelligence to bring down Silver."

That got my attention. The biggest drug kingpin in the Pactlands was just as slippery as he was deadly.

Gentle Breeze whistled softly. "Why am *I* just now hearing of this?"

"Because Floodtide is one of those projects discussed only on a need-to-know basis. It's been around for more than a century, though we haven't had much luck—"

"So why not bring us in to assist?" she protested. "Interdiction's file on Silver probably weighs more than your desk."

"I wouldn't doubt it," said Pateme. "The reason we limit participation to select personnel is because there are obvious leaks within our agencies. You saw what happened to that boy last fall when he offered to talk about Silver, yes?"

He didn't need to spell it out. I'd heard about how Goobers had met his fate: poisoned while he slept in a DPP lockup.

"And I needn't bring up Kritsa and his friends," Pateme continued, breezing past the recent murders and maiming within DOL's secure area. "As one of our goals is for Silver to remain ignorant of the initiative and its reach, we keep it very quiet." He paused to drink again, letting that sink in, then said, "I trust you, Gentle Breeze, and I trust your judgment. What you did over the weekend will not appear in your file."

"If you trust me, then let me help you," she pressed. "I want Silver as badly as anyone, and if he's more than a ghost, I want him hauled in and tried."

"You'll get your chance. For now, I need you to swear to me that nothing said in this room today leaves. No word to your second, nothing to Syvin, not even to your therapist."

"I don't have a therapist, sir."

"Good. Less temptation, then. Any questions?"

She stared back at him incredulously.

"Any questions that I can answer?" he amended.

"Maybe," she said, going to her feet. "Who do *you* think wrote the letter? Do you know?" When Pateme hesitated, she continued, "I'm asking because this person has been making contact with Rose, and I don't want that kid being hurt. So who's the author?"

"I...have my suspicions," Pateme admitted. "Several possible candidates. But that's not information that needs to be shared at this time."

Gentle Breeze grunted her dissatisfaction. "Answer me this, then: how much danger is Rose in? I've been through Charlottesville—it's not a warzone. If your anonymous friend wants you at her location six days from now, then what *else* is going to be there? You haven't told ti'Cren about this, have you?"

"Of course not. And I don't know why I was told to go to her. But what I can tell you," he said quietly, "is that if she's been swept up in Floodtide, then she's in plenty of danger."

The chief pulled her phone from her pocket. "I've got her number. We should tell—"

"No." He raised a hand as she sputtered. "There's no need."

"That girl is your *blood*," she snapped. "You're not even going to warn her that she's not safe?"

Smirking, Pateme reached into his robe pocket and passed Gentle Breeze a folded slip of paper. "This came inside that letter."

I slid as close to her as I could to read the short message: *Rose is watching you.*

"How?" Gentle Breeze asked. "I thought you were protected."

Pateme shrugged. "I am, but they have their ways. And

Rose," he added, folding his arms, "if you're hearing this, I'll be there."

Gentle Breeze glanced around uncomfortably, but I remained as invisible as always. "That's it? That's all you've got to say to her?"

"For now."

She rolled her eyes. "May I get back to work, sir?"

He turned off the protective spell and gestured the door open. "Thank you for coming up. Your discretion is appreciated."

A meaty thump from the other bedroom yanked me back to my body, and I opened my eyes as Yven let himself into our room. "Good thing your friend didn't leave breakables near Mafora," he muttered. "She's raging."

"What *now*?" I asked.

"I don't know, but if I were Deono, I might slip back to the Pactlands and turn myself in." He winced at the sound of muffled shouting. "So…you mentioned wineries nearby, didn't you?"

"That I did."

"Any interest in a field trip, birthday girl?"

Mafora's screams shifted toward sobs, and I slid off the bed. "Get the keys. We're sneaking off."

As Yven drove us out of town through a popcorn shower, I relayed what I'd seen that morning. "Which brings me to the big question," I concluded. "Do we run, or do we stay here and see what's coming our way?"

"I…don't see how that's a question," he replied, glancing at me as if wondering whether I'd suffered a secret concussion. "Your letter-writing friend—*if* it's a friend at all, and I'm still not convinced of that—has made it clear that something's coming for us on Sunday. Why tell you if not to warn you to get away?"

"Because the person writing the letters is a farseer," I

replied. "Or taking cues from one."

"*Exactly*. So since they see this coming, why shouldn't we avoid it? There is *no* reason," he said, taking my hand, "for you to wind up in any more danger because of DPP. None. You've done more than your share."

To be frank, I didn't exactly disagree. "But what about Silver?" I countered. "If the fact that I'm there when…whatever this is…goes down brings him to justice, then don't I have a responsibility—"

"To whom? You don't owe us anything!"

"I don't know…a responsibility as a decent person, I guess. You saw what happened to Goobers and Kritsa."

"And I can't say I feel entirely sorry for them."

"I mean…*fair*," I allowed, "but if Silver is willing to kill his own people, then you can't say he isn't a danger to the public at large."

"I never did," said Yven. "What I'm telling you is that putting a target on yourself in the hopes of getting him off the streets is more than DPP or Laws or anyone has a right to ask. Your pen pal warned you—let's get out of the city before the weekend. We could leave Mafora if she's still being obnoxious," he suggested. "Let the director and Lily deal with her."

Leaning back in my seat, I sighed as I put my thoughts in order. "I hear you," I finally replied, "and what you're saying is logical—"

"*Thank you.*"

"But."

"But?"

"But what if I'm supposed to stay?"

Yven pulled onto the edge of the road and parked the Jeep, then turned to me. "Tell me how that makes sense, Rosie. You've been warned. Why not do the smart thing?"

I hesitated, listening to the thumping wipers and looking over Yven's shoulder at the cars going by, and exhaled slowly. "In Caradin's recordings, he said that farseers sometimes see multiple versions of how events could go. When that happens, they try to direct the people involved onto the path of least harm."

"Okay…"

"Let's assume that the person behind the letters is a farseer. If I were supposed to run off, then wouldn't the letters have mentioned it? 'Hey, Lily, give Rose a call and warn her. Hey, Pateme, she needs to know this.' Something like that. Instead," I continued, raising my voice as Yven started to protest, "they called for backup. The writer knew that I'd find out about the letters. All I can deduce from this is that I'm meant to stay at Toni's and see what happens on Sunday."

Yven considered that in silence for a moment, then said, "If you really are being directed onto a timeline, then how do you know it's the best one for *you*? What if this one ends with you dead by Monday? Your buddy didn't give you any reassurance that you'll be fine, right?"

"No," I allowed, "but if it leads to Silver—"

"*Forget* Silver," he said, squeezing my hands. "Forget Mafora and Deono. I'm asking about you."

"Look at it another way," I tried. "Let's say I make it past Sunday. If I do something that helps bring Silver down, then maybe one of the agencies could help me in turn. Inade isn't going to acknowledge me, especially after this, and if Diriem's ever thought about it, he hasn't said a peep to me. Maybe there's a workaround, or the Forum could give me some sort of special dispensation. If I help—"

"There's no guarantee. The director should have helped you by now, and look where we are. Do you really want to risk yourself on a remote possibility?"

I tightened my grip on him until my knuckles whitened. "If it means us…*yeah*."

"Rosie—"

"I'll do it for us," I told him. "We'll find a way."

He raised our interlocked hands to his lips and kissed my fingers. "Or we could run," he murmured. "Go back to the house, get our things, and hit the road."

"Yven, we—"

"As long as no one finds us, we'll be safe. We can make a life together here," he said, speeding up. "I've thought about it. We could sell the Jeep, get a camper, and move around. You can paint anywhere, and I'll find odd jobs, and we'll make it work."

Reading his expression, a curious mixture of hope and desperation, I thought about Mouse and Daniot, the producers we'd captured in December. In exchange for information about Kritsa and the rest of their gang, Daniot had been given a vial of the draught, permanently masked, and sent off into the unknown with his human lover. The two had little more than their truck and overnight bags when they ran away to forge a new life together, and though Mouse was middle-aged, I suspected that she'd outlive her boyfriend.

Could I do something similar with Yven? Abandon my home, my studio, and everyone I knew to disappear with him and a stolen Jeep? The elements of that plan that struck me as romantic were grossly outweighed by the other consequences. We could never stay in one place for long in case someone from the Pactlands discovered us. We'd be sleeping with one eye open for the rest of our lives—and since ours could be long lives, we'd be forced to remake ourselves over and over. If we brought children into the mix, what sort of existence would we be able to offer them? A lifetime masked and in hiding? And if Yven were caught and brought home to be held accountable...

They'd leave him no choice but the draught, and I couldn't live with myself if that happened.

"I think we should at least wait through the weekend before we do anything hasty," I told him. "We have time. If we're going to make a break for it, then we have to plan and be smart about this."

"I'd agree," he replied, "except for the part about the problem coming our way in six days. If something happens to you…"

I smiled weakly and gestured, producing a flame the size of a matchhead on my index finger. "Been practicing, eh?"

"You know I'm not great at defensive magic. I can't speak for the others—"

Leaning across the center console, I closed my eyes and kissed him. "We'll make it," I murmured, praying I was right, as his hand gently gripped my neck to pull me closer. "We'll find a way."

CHAPTER 13

By Wednesday, though the weather remained miserably moist, Hurricane Mafora seemed to have blown over. Oh, she still wasn't happy with her situation. The house was cramped, the neighborhood dull, the food unappetizing, the television incomprehensible. She hated catching sight of herself in the mirror with her mask on and would have dropped it days before if the rest of us hadn't insisted on masking as a safety precaution. But though she griped and continued to fret about the future awaiting her once she was cleared to return to Beukal, she allowed Deono back into their bedroom and joined us for meals, going so far as to make civil conversation with me. On Wednesday night, I even pulled up my website on my phone, and she scrolled through my gallery's offerings with polite interest.

Yven and I still had no idea what to expect that weekend, and not wanting to further stress the newlyweds, we hadn't warned them that there might be trouble on the horizon. Instead, he and I made trips out of the house to the grocery and outdoors stores, burdening our already stuffed kitchen with shelf-stable food we could pack in a hurry and loading the Jeep's hidden compartment with basic camping equipment. If worst came to worst, I thought, we could quickly dump the food in our escape vehicle and head for a campground. The Appalachians were dense enough that we could find a place off the main trails and rough it for a bit.

Between trips, as Yven drove around the neighborhood on patrol and Deono tried to narrate TV programs for his wife, I spent most of my time in my room with the lights off, looking in on Pateme, Inade, and Liventi. Pateme remained as well behaved as ever, though if he tried to talk to me, I always missed it. His sister went about her business, as far as I could tell, generally staying in her suite and taking her meals alone. She read, shared breezy phone conversations with her friends, and occasionally opened one of the many scrapbooks she kept hidden in a deep drawer. Obviously, there were no photographs of my grandfather as a child, but I caught her studying several black and white pictures of him with his siblings, laughing with Lily or slinging an arm around Teolm's and Jomin's shoulders. Whether she spoke to Inade that week was beyond my knowing, as I never saw the two of them together.

As for Inade, I found him either in his home office or locked in the opulent office at his store, always in a foul mood and often yelling at someone. Time was running out, after all, and every day, his sources reported no sign of Mafora or of me in one district after another. That he was frustrated was no secret at all, though it irked me that he seemed not to care about his daughter's safety unless he was employing a sob story for a potential assistant in the search.

With my frequent spying, I slept reasonably well—even better once Yven and I worked out the spooning situation. After a trip to Target, I was able to surprise him one night with lacy pajamas, but while he'd been eager to look and touch, he didn't try to coax me out of my flirty shorts. Worry and stress aside, neither of us was eager to try to hide a night of passion from our housemates...but I didn't mind at all when we laid together in the darkness and he attempted to casually cop a feel.

On Friday afternoon, with a break in the weather, Yven took me out to lunch at a downtown restaurant. True, since I was the only one of our quartet with useable currency, I was doing the treating, but neither of us bothered with the semantics of the situation. I was just thrilled to be out in public again with the man I loved and unconcerned that someone might see us and draw the wrong conclusions. After the meal, we did a bit of window shopping, remarking on the mannequins in the window of a secondhand boutique and stopping for gelato—even in March, I wasn't about to turn *that* down—and around two, we headed back to the Jeep to return to Toni's.

When I unlocked the front door, I didn't see Deono lounging around, which was no surprise. He'd taken to going for runs around the neighborhood as a way to burn off nervous energy, and his shoes were missing from their usual spot by the rug. But the other bedroom door was open a crack, and I could hear Mafora carrying on a one-sided conversation in Low Elvish.

"I'm not starving," she said. "The food is…*odd*…but I'm not wasting away. I haven't been out yet to see the area, but Deono says it's nice enough. Far too many humans for comfort," she added with a weak chuckle, then paused. "Yes, Charlottesville is the city. I believe this area is called Belmont. The house where we're staying could be so much better, but I suppose it was all that was available on short—"

"Who are you talking to?" I interrupted, opening her door wider.

Mafora looked up at me like a frozen deer, clutching her phone. "I need to go," she mumbled, and ended the call.

"Who *was* that?" I demanded as Yven joined me. "What was that about?"

"Nothing to concern you," she began, but I cut her off.

"Uh, I'm *pretty* sure you were just telling someone from back home that you're in Charlottesville. Who? One of your business partners?"

She sat up straighter and glared at me. "My communications are none of your—*hey!*" she cried as Yven strode into the room and plucked the phone from her hand. "You have no right!"

The phone was still unlocked, and he tapped his way to her recent calls. "Your *mother*?" he asked, aghast. "What the hell, Mafora? Do you want out of your marriage that badly?"

I folded my arms and stared down at her. "You told Liventi where we are? What's wrong with you?"

"Let me explain! She's going to fix things," said Mafora. "In case Father tries to cut me off, she's taking measures to ensure that I'm not left destitute. All she wanted to know was where we are and whether we're safe. That's it."

"And you told her," I replied in disbelief.

"Mother swore she wouldn't say a word—"

"She's broken a promise to you once already, or did you forget that she told Inade your husband's Hall?"

"She apologized for that," Mafora insisted. "If you think Mother would lie about a matter like this, then—"

"I'm not going to stand here and pretend that I know the details of your parents' relationship," I snapped, "but I haven't seen them in the same room for *days*, and I've been spending a lot of time watching them. Maybe Liventi wants to get back in Inade's good graces. Have you thought of that possibility, genius? You told her where to go—did you give her the address, too?"

"No," she said, though she seemed to shrink from the force of my displeasure. "Just that we're in Belmont."

"You told her I'm with you?"

"She said Father was worried! He's been looking all over the Pactlands for you, and…" A dawning look of sick realization crossed her face, and she slumped back against the wall. "I…she's my mother, I've never kept secrets from her—"

"And now your father has a target," said Yven, his arms tense and slightly trembling with his anger. "Not just you, not you and Deono, but all four of us." He shook his head and turned away. "You stupid *brat*."

"How soon do you think Inade will find us?" I murmured to Yven. "Sunday night, maybe?"

"Right. We've got to get out of here," he said, marching past me into the den.

Mafora scrambled off the bed. "Where are we going?" she called after him.

He wheeled on her. "*You* aren't going anywhere. You'll stay here to wait for Daddy, and if Deono wants to wait with you, that's his prerogative. But Rose and I don't need to be a part of this mess you've made…"

The opening door cut him short, and I turned to see Deono, who regarded Yven and Mafora with a *what now* expression. "Everything all right?" he asked cautiously.

"Ask Mafora," said Yven. "She just told her mother where we are, but I'm sure that's not cause for alarm."

Deono's eyes widened. "What…why would you do that?" he sputtered as Mafora slunk against the wall. "Do you *want* them to find us?"

"Mother's worried about me," she replied in a rush. "She said that if I could tell her where I am, she'll make sure that we have the money we need—"

"We don't need their money!" he shouted, then turned away and pushed a hand through his sweaty curls in agitation. "We're supposed to be a team, and you unilaterally decided to give up our location."

"Mother won't tell Father," Mafora insisted, though not with much confidence.

"Whether she does or not, he'll find out," I said, and the others looked my way. "I've been warned that something will happen on Sunday night. I don't know what to expect, but the impression I've received from these warnings is to be prepared, not to flee. Now that Mafora has dropped this information into her parents' lap, I think it's fair to expect a visit from Inade."

Immediately, Mafora pooh-poohed my conclusion. "He can't find us! There are plenty of houses here, and I didn't bring my vehicle. If we stay inside and keep the windows covered, he'll never figure out where we're hiding. Or we could change our masks—"

"The Jeep can be tracked," Yven interrupted, and Deono nodded. "All agency vehicles have trackers installed in case they need to be recovered. Pay the right person enough money, and you can get a visualization spell cast to let you follow any of them. It's a known security hole," he told me, "and the team in charge comes up with fixes, but—"

"You're in an arms race with a magical hacker," I finished. "Right. Assuming Liventi spills the details, he'll know our general area, and that would let him narrow down the possible vehicles to ours."

"So we move the Jeep," said Mafora. "Problem solved."

"I...don't think you comprehend just how angry your father is," I replied. "But yeah, she's got a point. We could park it a few blocks away, make him work harder—"

"Or we could pack and leave now," Yven countered. "It's the sane thing to do."

I grimaced. "If he gets that tracking spell running and sees one Jeep driving hard away from Charlottesville...can we destroy the tracker?"

"Technically?" He hissed. "Yes. I know where it's installed. But I'd be in a world of trouble for destroying government property. We can find another car," he suggested. "Or we could go by train—"

"Mafora sure as hell doesn't have the right ID to go galivanting off. Did you bring yours? What about Deono?"

"Don't worry about me," said Deono. "I'm staying right here."

"That's not a good idea—" Yven began, but Deono held up both hands and shook his head.

"Lord ti'Cren may not like me for his daughter, but if I stay and talk to him, then maybe he'll at least respect me. If I don't keep running away, if I do him the courtesy of listening to his concerns..."

His optimistic spiel petered out as I chuckled. "I've met the man, remember," I told Deono, "and that plan has about as much chance of success as did my pipe dream that he'd acknowledge me. But I think you're right—running isn't the answer. Not yet."

Yven's face tightened. "Rose—"

"I know it doesn't make sense, but my gut's telling me to stay. If you want to take Mafora and find another safehouse—"

"Absolutely not. But..."

I crossed the room to him and rubbed his arms as he struggled for words. "Can you trust me?" I murmured. "Just this once. If I'm wrong about this, I'll own it."

Though he didn't look happy, he finally nodded and hugged me. As I leaned against his chest, I heard him tell Mafora, "Draw the curtains and turn out the lights. You're not setting foot outside."

We began our final preparations that evening. With about two days to go and no idea of when Liventi might give us away—*if* she was planning to do so—we couldn't afford to waste time.

When I left the house after dark Friday, I was masked as a deeply tanned brunette with the sort of assets I'd never otherwise possess without a push-up bra. Yven had made himself half a foot shorter, about fifty pounds more muscular, and bald. His new muscles, he explained ruefully, were just illusion—convincing illusion, but useless in a fight. I dressed him in one of the spare T-shirts we'd picked up over the last week, cut the sleeves off, and suggested a barbed wire tat around his bicep, and though he told me he felt ridiculous, he obliged.

The trick was leaving the Jeep somewhere that it wouldn't be noticed and towed. My phone suggested a Walmart a little ways away from the downtown area, and we parked at the edge of the lot near an overnighting RV.

After a brief perusal of the store for the sake of appearances, I got us an Uber back to Toni's house.

On Saturday, we hunkered down. The curtains remained drawn, the windows and doors locked, and the TV on low. We cooked and ate in, and though no one showed much of an appetite, Mafora was uncharacteristically complimentary of the food. During the daylight hours, we took turns peeping through the windows at the passing cars, being sure to mask up in advance. Having not paid much attention to the neighbors' vehicles, I studied each that drove by, wondering if some were slowing to look for us.

Sunday dawned with a low, slate-colored sky. By late morning, the drizzle and fog had rolled in, hampering our local spying but giving me an excuse to check on the developments in Kelomb. While Yven made lunch, I tried to relax—not an easy task—and focused on Liventi.

I caught her just in time. As I watched, she swept down a hallway I hadn't seen in person, then rapped on a wooden door. The muffled voice from inside barking for her to enter was undeniably Inade's, and I slipped in behind her as Liventi walked into his office.

He looked up from the papers spread across his desk, his face hard and stubbled despite the hour. "Yes?"

"I don't want to fight anymore," she murmured, almost hugging herself as she stood before him. "Not about Mafora, anyway."

He huffed and turned back to his reading. "Unless you've got her waiting outside for me—"

"I know where she is."

That got his attention, and his head shot up again. "Where?"

"Outside the Pactlands. Rose helped her flee, her and the boy."

Inade's eyes narrowed as he considered that information. "Why would you think that? Rose didn't take them home with her—I've already had her house and shop searched."

"Give the girl a *little* credit, Inade. She's smarter than that." After a final moment of hesitation, Liventi said, "Mafora told me everything. They're in a place called Charlottesville. I don't have an address, but I have a district."

Her husband moved with surprising speed as he jumped up from his desk, gripped Liventi by the arms, and kissed her. Without another word, he hurried from the room, dressing gown flapping, leaving her there to stare at his cold fireplace in silent contemplation.

I pulled myself away, quickly reoriented, and found Deono and Mafora sitting in the den with cups of microwaved soup. "Your mother just spilled everything to your father," I told her. "And I do mean *everything*."

Mafora's face blanched. "Are you certain?"

"Just watched it happen. It's not my business, but you might want to put Liventi on an information diet going forward." Hearing Yven emerge from the kitchen, I turned to him and nodded. "Looks like Inade is on the move."

Yven swore under his breath. "Any idea when he might arrive?"

"Too early yet, but I'll keep watching him."

"After lunch," he insisted. "And I'll cook dinner once we eat. No sense in getting caught with pots boiling over."

Inade didn't mess around. I scarfed my meal, but in the twenty minutes he was out of my sight, he started making arrangements to come over. I peeked in to find him pacing his bedroom, shirtless and still unshorn, his phone pressed to his ear as he gave orders. "Five of your best," he said. "And keep this *absolutely* quiet. Meet me in the city in two hours."

"The city," to my relief, meant Beukal instead of Charlottesville. I watched as Inade parked in front of his ornate storefront in an upscale shopping district—a jewelry showroom, really, with rows of pristine glass cases and carefully arranged lighting that cast miniature spotlights on the finest baubles resting atop the black velvet padding. I couldn't have begun to guess at the gender of the indigo-complexioned troll guarding the door, but they were a few inches taller than Gentle Breeze and seemed less inclined toward conversation. The troll nodded to Inade as he strolled in, and he returned the gesture with a dismissive flick of his chin. Before his few customers could notice him, he hurried through a locked door in the wooden paneling, which led upstairs to his spacious office area.

I quickly studied the men waiting in the vestibule for him. Three elves and two sorcerers, by my count, all male. None of them were anywhere near Pars's size, but then again, in a fight with magic, did physical size really matter?

"You understand the job?" he asked them without preamble.

They nodded, and their apparent leader, one of the elves, spoke up. "Any thoughts on casualties, sir?"

"I want my daughter unharmed," he replied. "As for the rest…what happens, happens."

Though my head began to throb with a coming headache, I followed Inade and his merry band out of the store—or rather, I followed Inade, who slid into his Mercedes and idled a few blocks away until a pair of black SUVs with deeply tinted glass pulled up behind him. Looking though Inade's back window, I tried to make a note of their license plates, but the SUVs carried no tags in the front. When one of them pulled ahead, I saw that it had a temporary paper tag as if it had been driven fresh from the dealer.

I wondered where Inade had found a security detail. That he could afford one didn't surprise me, but I had no idea how such an outfit might be acquired, let alone bodyguards with portal credentials.

None of the vehicles received more than a cursory

check from the portal attendants, and by two-thirty that afternoon, they were driving west from Oilville. The weather was with us—the rain had worsened, and I smiled to find Inade and his buddies caught in stop-and-go traffic behind a wreck on I-64—but all too soon, the little convoy pulled into Charlottesville.

As Inade left the Interstate, his phone beeped. "Sir?" came a female voice through the speaker. "I have the information you requested."

He slowed and pulled to the berm, and the SUVs parked a few yards away. "What have you found?" he asked the caller. "And why the delay?"

"Tracking agency vehicles outside the Pactlands isn't easy. We had to get a team through the portal and out, then find a quiet area in which to set up the spell," she replied. "But it shows three tagged vehicles currently within geographic proximity to Beukal."

"Likely suspects?"

"I'm sending you the map now, sir. It should orient to your current position…"

He took his phone from its cradle just as it dinged, and the screen flashed to a black field of pulsing red dots. The steady blue dot I took to be Inade's location. Frowning at the phone, he asked, "No road directions?"

"I'm afraid not, sir. The area outside isn't well mapped for our purposes. We can't show you the best route, but we can offer you—"

"This will do," he interrupted, and ended the call. Another tap of his phone brought two of the men in the other vehicles on the line. "We're close to an agency car," he told them. "The spell's only partially functional out here, but I think we can find the target. Follow me."

Invisibly riding shotgun, I stayed with Inade while he slowly made his way around town, noting his changing relation to the nearest red dot. After about an hour of careful searching, he discovered the Walmart and soon zeroed in on our abandoned Jeep, now bereft of its RV neighbor. Stepping out of his car with a golf umbrella, he approached and held his phone near the red dot on the window, then made a flicking gesture. The phone's screen changed in an instant to reveal the Jeep's registration.

That couldn't be a legal app.

"It's DPP," he announced as the other men climbed down from their vehicles. "I wonder if any of their fleet has gone missing in the last week."

One of the elves snickered but quickly sobered as Inade shot him a look.

"Obviously, they're trying to be clever," he continued. "Mafora said they're in a district called Belmont. Who has a map handy?"

A sorcerer turned on his phone, and I recognized my familiar mapping app. A few taps later, he said, "About a fifteen-minute drive, sir...well, longer today with the conditions," he muttered. Charlottesville's roads were no better than the Interstate had been, and several people seemed to have forgotten how to drive in the rain. "Do you know *where* in Belmont?"

"No. But we'll find them." Without another word, he returned to his car and dropped the wet umbrella beside me. Closing his eyes, he wrapped his left hand over the gold signet ring on his right, then whispered, "Mafora."

When he pulled his hand away, the surface of the ring, which had formerly been a flat piece with an engraved design, had turned smooth and dark as onyx. He lifted his hand as if trying to catch the play of light off the nonexistent faceting, and as he slowly turned his wrist, the ring began to change color. When the pure black had shifted toward deep violet, he considered the direction, then pulled up the directions to Belmont on his own phone.

I didn't need to look at his screen to know that a line in the purple direction would lead right to us.

Forcing myself back to my body, I staggered out of the room and found Mafora eating chips while Deono took a shift at the window. "How do your parents track you?" I demanded, pointing to her.

Mafora looked at me like I was spouting gibberish. "What are you talking about?"

"Inade's ring. He did something to it and said your name, and it changed color when he aimed it toward us. He's only a few miles away. So *how* is he tracking you?"

Her bemusement shifted toward panic as Yven joined us in the den. "I...I don't know! He's never tracked any of us! And besides, if he could find me with a ring, then what's taken him this long?"

"Maybe it only works within a certain radius," Deono suggested. "He must not have come close enough to the camp to find us—"

"And the camp has protections on it to stop that sort of spell," Yven interjected. "Unlike this house."

I turned to Yven, rubbing my aching head. "How do we block him?"

"A counter-spell, quickly. Deono—"

"On it," he said, heading for the door. "Could you help me?"

"Of course. Mafora," he added on his way out, "go through your belongings and figure out what he's tracking. It's probably an item, a piece of clothing, something like that."

The door slammed behind them, and I cocked my head toward the honeymoon suite. "You heard him. What did you bring that's trackable?"

"Nothing!" she cried, wrapping her arms around herself as if she feared I'd rip her shirt off where she stood. "Father doesn't track me! He *wouldn't!*"

"Well, then, for my peace of mind," I replied, planting my hands on my hips, "which of your things did you purchase yourself? Like...what do you have that's never been around your parents?"

Mafora looked at me like I was crazy, but when I didn't budge, she sighed and began to run through her clothing.

"I made or bought almost everything with me here. All of my shirts...all—no, *most* of my pants, both dresses, my shoes. I suppose you'll want to rummage through my underthings?"

"Not if I can avoid it. Come on, show me what you've got," I said, and marched toward her room.

"Hey, you can't just—"

I ignored her and flung the door open wide. Within, the bed was sloppily made, and Mafora had taken the folding luggage rack for her main bag, leaving Deono to stow his gear in a corner on the floor. As Mafora protested, I picked up her stuffed bag and dumped it on the duvet, the better to sort through her frocks, blouses, accessories, and cosmetics.

"Get away from my clothes!" she demanded, pushing me back before I could begin my search. "What's wrong with you? Have you no manners?"

"Not when your daddy and five of his buddies are on their way here. Show me what you *didn't* procure for yourself, and..."

The thought died as I glanced at the little pine dresser and attached mirror, a relic from Toni's childhood bedroom. Scattered across the wood were Mafora's brushes and hair pins...and there, on the right, was the necklace she'd been wearing when I first met her.

The exquisite emerald and diamond necklace.

"Where did you get that?" I asked, plucking it off the dresser. The faceted jewels glinted in the weak glow of the neighboring streetlight, which had come on early with the gloom.

Mafora snatched it from me and clutched it close. "It was a graduation gift from my parents. Quite normal."

"*Normal?*" I laughed. "My folks sure as hell didn't get me a necklace that cost as much as a freaking car!"

"I assure you," she said, her voice frosty, "that this isn't what you're looking for."

"Oh? You remember the part about how your father

makes magical jewelry for a living? Doesn't seem like much of a stretch to me."

We were still haggling over the necklace five minutes later when the guys returned. "The house is somewhat shielded," said Yven, popping his head into the bedroom, "but it won't hold until dawn. We'd need more people to cast a longer-lasting spell. Find anything?"

"Maybe," I replied before Mafora could deny it. "Any way to tell if a piece of jewelry has been ensorcelled?"

He glanced at the necklace, to which Mafora was clinging as if it were a golden teddy bear. "Sure. Let me get my field kit."

Yven disappeared into our room and returned with a vial of clear liquid. "What does that do?" I asked.

Uncorking the potion, he explained, "Reacts in the presence of magic constructions. It's an old test, but it's reliable." With that, he pulled an eyedropper from his pocket and sucked up a small amount of the potion, then turned to Mafora and said, "Give me the necklace." When she hesitated, he huffed impatiently. "I'm not going to hurt it, and this stuff washes off. Now give me the necklace."

She relented with much reluctance. Cupping the jewelry in one hand to prevent spills, he gently squeezed the dropper, dripping the potion onto the diamonds. Instantly, they turned bright yellow where they were splashed, and Yven grunted. "Well, *that's* obvious. So what does your gut say, Rose?" he asked. "Are we supposed to let Inade and his crew find us now, or do we get rid of the tracker?"

"You can't throw my necklace away!" Mafora protested, but I ignored her.

"Everything I've seen and heard over the last week suggests that our backup is coming tonight," I told Yven, glancing out the window, "but maybe that means full dark. I think we need to stall Inade. The defenses that you and Deono put up—"

"Might give us a few hours, but they'd work better if we got the thing he's homing in on away from here. As the spell degrades outside, the signal from the necklace will leak through."

"What if we put it on a bus?" I suggested.

"A *what?*" Mafora shrieked.

"A local bus," I continued. "We board, drop the package, and get off. Now Inade's on a wild goose chase around town."

"And how, exactly, would I get it back?"

I shrugged. "You probably wouldn't. Might be able to put in a claim once we're sure that your father's gone home, but I kind of doubt you'd be able to recover it."

She glared at me, flabbergasted. "*That* is my graduation present—"

"Do you care about it more than your marriage? Because that's where we are right now."

"I like the bus idea," Yven interjected, "but I'd prefer it if we could put the necklace on something headed out of town. What about the train station?"

"Trains aren't frequent. This isn't like a metro subway. We could pack it up and drive it to the Post Office, but assuming we could make the drop without Inade finding us, I don't know what we'd put for the address. My studio?"

He frowned. "It wouldn't move immediately, though...right? Your mail system isn't instantaneous—"

"No, but Inade would find himself outside a government building and realize we were on to him."

"Toss it in the river."

I turned to find Deono standing just outside the bedroom, watching us. "Throw it away," he continued, focusing on his wife. "We don't need it. Your parents are trying to control your life. Toss the necklace and be done with it."

"I..." she started, then faltered and tried again. "It's my necklace, I could never afford to replace it—"

"We're running out of time," I interrupted, and pulled out my phone. "I'm calling an Uber."

CHAPTER 14

Our driver was a laid-back recent graduate and avid backpacker who didn't mind waiting for a group of tourists who just wanted a peek at the Rivanna River, albeit in the damp gloaming. I sat up front with him and made conversation while Mafora and the guys took the cramped back seat. To explain their silence, I told him that my companions were visiting from Europe and spoke minimal English—the last thing I wanted while we sped toward the park was to field questions about the others' accents. When the driver asked which country, I randomly offered Lithuania and prayed, and he deemed the answer cool.

Outside of the protective spell on Toni's house, we needed to move quickly. Luckily for us, our driver was of the mindset that speed limits were more like suggestions, and soon enough, he parked and directed us toward a sandy canoe launch. Given the hour and the cold drizzle, the park wasn't crowded, and we had the area to ourselves as we hustled Mafora toward the little river.

"Go ahead," I coaxed. "Just toss it in the middle. If it sinks, fine, but even better if it drifts."

She clutched the necklace and gazed out at the water.

"It's leading him to us as we speak," Deono murmured. "We need to get back to the house. Now or never, darling."

Still, she hesitated for a long, tense moment, then reached a decision and shook her head. "No. *No.*"

"Please, Mafora," Deono tried, "we shouldn't make this easier for him—"

"I can't do this," she whispered.

He reached for her shoulder. "Sweetie, I know you don't want to lose it—"

"I can't *do* this," she said more firmly, pulling herself free of his grasp. "*This*. I…I can't lose my family, my life…"

Her poor husband looked as stunned as if he'd been hit in the head with a two-by-four. "What are you saying?"

"I want to go home." She stared at him as he reeled. "I'm sorry, but this was a mistake."

"You don't mean that," he pleaded. "We can make this work! Just another few days, and we *will* go home. Everything will be fine."

But her grip on the necklace only tightened. "Father won't forgive me if I stay with you. He never forgave Fradin. I was foolish to think he'd come around. And I…I can't *live* like this."

"I'm not asking you to! We won't be on the run forever, and there's no reason we can't go back to Beukal—"

"No," she said firmly. "I can't live like one of *you*. That's not who I am, and I can't give up my family, and…" She paused as his face fell. "You understand, don't you?"

"You told me that Halls didn't matter," he mumbled.

Mafora had the grace to look away as she replied, "Guess I was wrong."

I glanced back and forth between them, the one firm but slightly guilty, the other heartbroken. They needed time and a therapist, neither of which we had that evening.

"Here's the deal," I announced. "That necklace isn't coming back with us. Mafora, if it's worth more to you than Deono is, then stay here and wait for Inade." With that, I turned and started back to our waiting ride. Yven fell in beside me, walking as close as our umbrellas would allow. After a few yards, I looked back to see Deono still staring at Mafora, and I called, "We need to go!"

He turned away from her, huddled under his umbrella, and hurried to join us.

As we piled back into the car, our driver asked, "Is your friend *staying*? The rain's only supposed to get worse tonight, and it's getting dark…"

"She's waiting for someone," I explained, and smiled to sell the act. "He'll be here in a few minutes. Nothing to worry about."

Satisfied, he started to drive away, and I glanced behind his seat at Deono, who sat with his hands clasped in his lap and seemed unaware of the wet umbrella soaking the left leg of his pants.

While we still had about two hours until sunset, it barely mattered with the storm. I tipped our driver well and ran for the house as Yven coaxed Deono, who still seemed shell-shocked, out of the car and through the pounding rain. Lightning crackled overhead as I punched the door code and dripped my way inside, and Yven locked up behind them.

We had no booze in the house beyond the few bottles of wine that Yven and I had bought on my birthday outing, but I made Deono a cup of tea and brought it to him at the table, where he was silently processing what had just happened. "I'm so sorry," I murmured, taking the chair beside him as I nudged the warm mug his way, and tried to think of something useful to say. "Is there, uh…anything I can do?"

He shook his head and mumbled his thanks as he reached for the tea.

"Well," said Yven, who had taken the next logical step and gone for Toni's guest corkscrew, "the good news is that your pen pal's predictions of doom seem to have been overblown."

I frowned. "Inade is still in town—"

"Yeah, but all he needs to get the marriage annulled is

Mafora, *especially* if she's willing. He can take her to the Tribunal building in the morning, and everyone can go on with their lives." The cork came free with a soft pop, and he cocked the bottle my way in invitation.

"Better make it three," I said, cutting my eyes to our morose companion. "Deono, I'm not going to pretend to know what you're going through—I mean, I've had a bad breakup, but nothing like this. But, um…better to know now, right? Before kids and such?"

"I guess," he replied, his voice barely rising above a whisper.

Yven and I traded a look, and he filled Deono's wine stem a little fuller than manners would have dictated.

With no clue as to how we should begin to console a man whose bride of three weeks had walked out on him, we sat around and drank with Deono in quiet solidarity. Eventually, Yven warmed up the chicken casserole he'd made that afternoon, and we ate by candlelight near the covered windows while the rain hammered against the glass and sheeted over the asphalt. Deono never reached full inebriation, but the wine lowered his defenses to the point that the tears finally flowed. As I snagged the tissue box from the bathroom, Yven coaxed Deono onto the couch with another cup of tea and started asking him questions about his brief time at DPP. Two and a half years was still well within the probationary period by agency standards, but Deono had begun going out with Interdiction teams as the rookie, and Yven distracted him with queries about his cases and stories—almost certainly from Pars—about his older colleagues. I didn't have much to contribute to the conversation, but I didn't mind letting the guys chat in peace. Dinner was sitting uneasily with me due to my knotting guts, and I kept sneaking peeks out the windows at the miserable evening.

Around seven, as I was refilling the water heater in the kitchen, I heard a pair of car doors slam near the front of the house. The noise alone didn't worry me—slamming doors and running for shelter was the order of the day—but the *location* set off my internal alarms. Toni's house sat at the end of the residential portion of a quiet neighborhood, and the homes behind it and across the street were empty. The block beyond consisted of the vacant dry cleaner and a run-down parking lot, its opening blocked with heavy chains. In the last week, *no one* had parked in front of the house but us.

Fighting my flipflopping stomach, I hurried to the den and sneaked a look past a chink in the curtains. There, tucked up by the dry cleaner's loading dock, were a black SUV and a familiar black Mercedes. Even with the rain, I could make out the shapes of Inade and three of his men in the streetlight's glow as they climbed out of their vehicles and opened their utilitarian umbrellas.

Darting away from the window, I ran to the couch and whispered, "He's here."

"Inade?" Yven asked, leaping to his feet.

I nodded. "With three buddies. The other SUV isn't out there, so maybe Mafora's with them. How'd he find us?"

"Bet you a million that his brat daughter gave him directions," he muttered. "The better question is *why* he's here. He got what he came for, he doesn't need Deono to have the marriage annulled—"

The shout from across the street—in Low Elvish, no less—cut Yven's musings short. "Ti'Gata!" Inade bellowed over the percussion of the rain. "Face me! I want to meet the worm who thinks he's worthy of my daughter!"

A glance out the side window revealed no other vehicles. The cavalry hadn't arrived, and the three of us in the house—the agent with poor defensive talent, the distraught trainee, and I—were clearly outmatched by the four elves lurking outside.

"I'll just go talk to him," Deono mumbled, starting to rise, but Yven pushed him back to the couch.

"*Nothing* good will come of that," he said, and quickly

studied the cottage. "Rosie, take him out the back and run down the street. Surely there's a shed or a garage or something—"

"Hell, no," I replied as Inade continued to yell his challenge. "*You* take him and run. I'll stall the mob."

Yven looked at me like I'd suggested having them in for cocktails. "He could rip you apart—"

"Oh, and *you're* protected, are you?" I retorted. "Look, I said I would own the mess if I was wrong about us waiting here. You're right, we should have left. I'm sorry. I'll handle this."

"Rosie—"

I slipped past Yven as he reached for me and strode to the door. Flinging it open wide, I stood on the threshold and stared at Inade and his muscle waiting mere yards away. With the house nearly dark behind me, I hoped Yven and Deono could sneak out without being spotted, but I couldn't risk a backward glance to see what they were up to. "What do you want, Inade?" I called. "And why are you shouting, anyway? You're going to bother the neighbors!"

I couldn't see his face well beneath the umbrella, but I could hear the sneer in his voice. "Well, now, if it isn't the faithless creature herself! I brought you into my home, and *this* is how you repay me?"

"I'm not even going to dignify that bullshit with a response," I said, folding my arms. "And if you want to talk about *faithless*, start with yourself—Liventi gave me the whole story."

"I hired you—"

"You haven't paid me a dime, bub. I was helping you as a favor to the family, and then I helped Mafora when I realized you were trying to break up her marriage. Of course, I guess you did everyone a solid in the end," I continued with feigned nonchalance. "At least now Deono won't be stuck with someone like her. He deserves better."

"Bring him out here, *now!*"

"*No!* You won, asshole." I didn't know how well my profanity was translating, but I was too riled up to care about the linguistic nuances. "You got Mafora back, the marriage is over, end of the story. Go home. She broke the man's heart—have the decency to let him grieve in peace, why don't you?"

"Bring him out," said Inade, "or I'm coming in."

I heard the sound of an engine roaring up the road behind me and hoped it wasn't the local cops on a noise complaint.

"Haven't you ever heard of being a gracious winner?" I tried. "You got what you came for, and you don't need Deono. Just get out of here. I'm sure you and Mafora have plenty to catch up on…"

The nearing vehicle—two, actually—cut me off, and they squealed to a halt on the slick street. Before I could do more than register a pair of dark SUVs, the driver's door on the lead vehicle flew open, and out jumped Pateme. Eschewing an umbrella, he instead wore a gray trench coat with an upturned collar, and I assumed he'd left the formal robes at home. From the SUV behind him came a petite figure in a familiar green anorak, ignoring the rain that soaked her golden-blonde braid as she jogged toward her father.

"What are you doing here?" Pateme began, his voice snapping like a whip as he confronted Inade. "Go ahead, explain to me how *any* of this is authorized."

The thuds of closing doors briefly drew my attention back to the SUVs, and I saw three additional figures joining Pateme and Aunt Lily. With the weather, the twilight, and the presumed masking, I had no idea who they were, but none of them looked at all fazed to be facing down Inade and his backup trio.

"You four are to get back in your cars and proceed to the Oilville portal," Pateme continued. "*Now.*"

Inade stood up straighter beneath his umbrella. "And who are you to be giving *me* orders, little man?" he replied.

"You, who allowed one of the vermin in your employ to abscond with your niece—"

"I," said Pateme, pushing back the left side of his trench to reveal the badge on his belt, "am the law. Not you, Inade. Mind telling us just how you got a pass out of the Pactlands, hmm?"

"I don't answer to *you*."

"Really? Well, here's how this is going to work. Either you follow my orders and return to the portal at once, or *I* will return you to the Pactlands as a detainee. Your choice."

"You wouldn't dare," Inade shot back.

"Try me."

"*Stop* it, both of you," Aunt Lily interrupted, pushing past Pateme. "Father, be reasonable. Leave Mafora alone."

"She's already gone," I called from the porch. "Broke up with Deono this afternoon. We left her in the park for Inade to pick her up."

Aunt Lily seemed taken aback by the news. "Is that true?" she asked Inade.

"Yes," he admitted, "but the boy—"

"Is none of your concern!" Approaching Inade, she said, "You leave him alone, and you leave my Rosie alone, understand?"

"*Your* Rosie?" he spat.

"Mine," she almost growled. "Just like Fradin was my brother—"

With a flick of his hand, Inade sent a burst of force into Lily's midsection, knocking the air from her lungs and throwing her off her feet. She flew backward, plowing into the old oak on the neighbors' property with a sharp crack, and sank to the muddy lawn.

Seeing her fall, I was barely cognizant of something red and raw welling up within me, and I shouted wordlessly as I gestured in Inade's direction.

He never saw it coming—nor would he have worried about a threat from me, given what he knew of my background. The wave of energy I shot from my open palm was strengthened by my rage, and it bowled Inade over, sending him into an ungainly backflip that nearly took out his associates. While two of them quickly produced defensive constructions and the third helped Inade right himself, Pateme's team advanced and moved between Inade's group and me.

"You have one minute to depart," Pateme announced as Inade groped for his umbrella. "I love my sister, but that only goes so far."

To my surprise, Inade didn't fight him. Within seconds, he'd slunk back to his Mercedes, and the help piled in their SUV to follow him out of town. Pateme waited until they'd rounded the corner, then jogged over to Aunt Lily, who was sitting at the base of the tree, cradling her left arm against her chest. I ran out to join them, and by the time I arrived, one of the others in their crew had produced a glowing orb the size of a tennis ball to aid in the inspection.

"Are you okay?" I asked, slipping back into English out of habit as I crouched beside Aunt Lily. She appeared human enough that night, though she'd left the wrinkles and white hair out of her mask. I didn't see any blood, but I was more concerned about a concussion.

Groaning, she focused her dark eyes on my face. "Rosie…"

"Where are you hurt?"

"I…I'm not sure. Don't think I hit my head," she mumbled.

"Not hard enough to fracture your skull," one of the agents offered, "but I think you might have made impact. We'll need to have your ribs checked, too. And that arm—"

Aunt Lily cried out when the agent touched it. "*Don't*, please."

"Probably broken," said the agent. "We need to take you to a healer, Ms. ti'Cren."

"No…no, I'm—"

"You're coming home with me until you're medically cleared," Pateme interrupted. Turning to me, he asked, "Are you hurt, Rose?"

"Why the hell would you care?" I muttered, pushing myself off the ground. "Nice of you to swan in, Pateme."

The other agents watched us with interest, and their boss cleared his throat. "Might we take this inside for a moment?"

"Once Aunt Lily's safe."

"We've got this under control," the agent with the light offered. "Come on, Ms. ti'Cren, let's get out of the rain…"

As the team helped her stand and stagger toward a waiting vehicle, I marched up the porch and into the house, expecting to find the place abandoned. Instead, I discovered that Yven and Deono hadn't taken the opportunity to run—on the contrary, Yven was throwing himself against a translucent bubble, fighting to break free, while Deono shook with the strain of holding it together.

"What the hell?" I managed.

At the sound of my voice, Deono broke the spell, and Yven spared only an instant to punch him in the chest before running toward me. "Rosie! Are you hurt? What happened out there?" he demanded. "The little bastard—"

"I'm fine. Aunt Lily's hurt, but Inade's gone," I said, and slid aside as Pateme appeared in the doorway. "Come in, I guess," I told the director. "What do you want?"

He closed the door and stood dripping in the den, his features rendered slightly strange by the mask he'd assembled. "Rose, I…understand why you're upset," he began.

I cut him off. "Do you? *Really*? And don't give me some claptrap about how you're here because you care," I added as he tried to get a word in. "Your blinding spell can't stop me, and I know damn well that you're only here because of your precious Project…uh…"

"Floodtide," he murmured.

"*That*," I said, hiding my embarrassment with indignation. "You got a letter. Big of you to show up."

He sighed quietly and stuffed his hands in his trench coat's pockets. "I've been trying to protect you and ti'Ansha. Please understand—"

"With all due respect, sir," Yven interrupted, "you can go fuck yourself."

Deono froze like a possum staring down a semi, but whatever lightning storm he anticipated from Pateme failed to materialize. Instead, Pateme calmly turned to him and said, "Ti'Gata, you're coming home with us. Pack your things."

"Yes, sir," he mumbled, and scurried into his bedroom.

Pateme closed the door behind him and pointed to the far corner of the house, and I reluctantly followed him toward the dinette. "There are pieces in motion that you know nothing about, little one," he said softly, holding my angry stare.

"Like what?" I snapped.

"I can't tell you. It's for your own safety," he hastily explained. "If the wrong person gave you a potion to make you talk, I wouldn't want you to have that sort of knowledge in your memory."

"*That's* some mighty convenient bullshit."

"It's the truth. And I have a favor to ask of you."

I waited in silence, one eyebrow cocked.

"I want you to try to find the man called Silver," he said, his voice barely above a whisper. "We need a farseer, and you clearly have the talent. Your temporal orientation makes you invaluable in this endeavor. Now, I can't give you Silver's true name, his photograph, or anything useful, but I'm asking you to try. See what you come up with."

When he finished, I just folded my arms. "No."

Pateme straightened, taken aback. "No?"

"No," I repeated. "You were happy to have me around when I was useful to you, then you kicked me out of the Pactlands for three months, and now that it's convenient to remember me again, you expect me to do you *favors?*"

"I—"

"You cut me off from everyone who was helping me gain a measure of control over a talent I'm only just discovering," I continued over his protestation.

"You certainly exhibited control tonight!"

"Because *Caradin* left me tapes!" I shouted. "I found a box of recordings he'd made for me, so yeah, I've been learning magic from a dead man all winter. At least he gave a shit about me. It's nice to know that someone in my family beyond Aunt Lily considers me more than an embarrassing curiosity."

I didn't think I was imagining the flicker of guilt in Pateme's expression.

"Rose…" he began, then took a long breath and composed his thoughts. "I apologize. I could have handled things…differently."

I snorted. "You think?"

"And I will make it up to you, I swear. But this is important. I think you have what it takes to find Silver, and the longer we wait, the greater the ongoing harm."

I considered that as I traded glances with Yven, who stood by in silence while I had it out with his boss. Finally, I told Pateme, "If you want me to help you, then I want something first."

"I don't have the authority to acknowledge you—"

"Not that. You turn Yven's phone back on—*full* functionality. Restore our portal credentials."

He nodded. "That's doable."

"And you stay out of our love lives," I continued. "We'll keep things quiet and respectable in Beukal for now, but you're going to let us be."

Pateme hesitated, his face working, then said, "You understand that I'm bound to uphold the law, Rose."

"Sure. Why is why I *know* you're going back and arresting your brother-in-law for sneaking me in, your niece for sneaking out, and Deono for trafficking. Right?"

I asked sweetly.

He shot me a look of impatience. "This is a complicated situation—"

"No, it really isn't. You want my help, you agree to my terms."

"I won't be able to cover for the two of you forever."

"I'm not asking for forever," I replied. "Just for now. Do we have a deal?"

Though he seemed uneasy about the matter, he extended his hand, and I shook it.

As we concluded the negotiations, Deono emerged, having hastily packed both his bags and Mafora's. "I just need to get her things from the bathroom, sir," he told Pateme. "Another minute, if you will."

"Take your time," said Pateme, heading for the front door. Opening it, he waved to the second SUV, which started off without him. "Better for Liliol to be on her way to a proper healer. She'll be cranky tomorrow, but she'll thank me someday," he said as Deono grunted and softly swore at his luggage. "Ti'Gata, do you have anything clean to wear?"

"Not much, sir," he called.

"That's fine. Once we're back in the city, you can do a load at my place, and I'm shipping you off to a training facility *far* out of town for the rest of your vacation."

His head popped out of the bathroom. "Sir?"

"You're not going home just yet," said Pateme. "Not until I'm sure that the matter of the annulment is settled and Inade has calmed down. No need to press our luck...and I'm sure you wouldn't mind a diversion, would you?"

There wasn't much that Deono could do but agree.

"As for you, ti'Ansha," said Pateme, turning to Yven with a smirk, "am I to understand that your unexpected absence is to continue for the immediate future? Syvin is *not* pleased, if you were wondering."

Yven shrugged. "If you're asking Rose to hunt for

Silver, then someone needs to stay here and look after her."

"That's not unreasonable," the director replied. "Very well. You'll have your phone and your portal credentials restored by morning..." He paused as Deono hurried out, breathing heavily but packed. "You can take your things to the car, ti'Gata. I'll be along in a moment."

Deono and I shared a look as he shouldered his bags. "Thank you again," he murmured. "I mean it, I'm grateful—"

"And I'm so sorry about Mafora," I replied.

He smiled sadly and cocked his head. "Better to know now, I suppose," he said, then nodded to Yven. "I'm not sorry for holding you back tonight."

"I'm not sorry for punching you," Yven replied.

Deono rubbed his chest and winced. "Your technique's pretty good. Uh...guess I'll see you at work, then," he offered, and walked out.

I glanced at Pateme in time to catch him rolling his eyes, and then he reached into the inner pocket of his coat and handed me a sealed envelope. "Came for you this morning," he said. "I haven't peeked."

I would have recognized my anonymous pen pal's correspondence anywhere, but I suppressed my urge to rip into the letter until Pateme's vehicle had pulled out of sight. Yven offered to make fresh tea, leaving me alone in the den to read in peace. The letter was addressed to me, care of Pateme at his office, and as usual, there was no return address. As I opened the seal, I found a smaller sealed note tucked within the first and put it aside, then unfolded the letter to see what awaited:

Dear Rose Lea,

At the outset, I apologize for my silence over the last months—not because it was the wrong thing to do, but because I fear I have only added to your recent grief. It has never been my desire to cause you pain. Unfortunately, as

Pateme took somewhat drastic measures, the only mailbox through which these letters could have reached you was Liliol's, and I wish to involve her in this matter no more than is strictly necessary. My reasons, for now, must remain my own.

That you have hypotheses as to my identity is no secret, child. I will neither confirm nor deny anything at this time. My reticence is not intended to frustrate you, but rather out of concern for your safety.

You are in danger, Rose Lea.

"*Still?*" I muttered, peering at the neat script.

Much—but not all—of this danger stems from the agreement that you have, by now, struck with Pateme. I wish you good hunting, but I hope you heed my warning: <u>do not</u> let the sun rise on you in Charlottesville. Pack and leave <u>tonight</u>.

I wish you'd had more training. You are still learning to swim, and Silver is a large fish with sharp teeth who lurks in deep water. Should you give him cause to fear you, he will lash out with every weapon at his disposal. While I am impressed with the progress you've made on your own, your grandfather's recordings are no substitute for a proper education. Pateme should have been training you all this time. His behavior is somewhat understandable—he carries substantial guilt for allowing his nephew to take the draught, and regardless of your protestations to the contrary, your agent is heading toward that path—but Pateme allowed his emotions to cloud his judgment as to your safety. He knows how I feel about this, and he will <u>continue</u> to know of it for some time to come.

I chuckled to myself, thinking of the letter I'd read in Pateme's office with Gentle Breeze.

You have felt abandoned of late. In truth, this is not the case. When we next speak, I hope I can set your mind at ease.

For now, be careful. Your instincts are strong—trust them. I have included with this letter a guide to the portals along your eastern coast. Curiously, we seem to have hidden at least one in every state but Maine. Use this information as you see fit, and tell your agent to remove the tracker and the registration decal from your vehicle.

Be brave, Rose Lea. You are never alone.

Now go.

I read the letter twice, then unsealed the other document to find a hand-drawn map of the eastern seaboard. It wasn't an atlas-quality production, but the state borders were clear enough, and the margins were crowded with detailed notes about portal locations.

"Yven?" I called.

He poked his head out of the kitchen, where the water heater was coming to a boil. "Anything interesting?"

"Yeah. Apparently, we've got to get out of here tonight. My pen pal says we'll be in trouble if we stick around until morning."

Yven's jaw tightened. "You think Lord ti'Cren might come back?"

"I mean, I pissed him off pretty badly *before* I knocked him over in front of his buddies, Pateme, and a handful of agents, so…" I shrugged. "You tell me. And here, read for yourself," I offered, handing him the letter.

I took over the tea preparations while Yven read, and he joined me with the portal map while I stirred in sugar. "This could be useful," he said, smoothing it on the counter. "We drive to a hotel tonight, wait for the director to restore our credentials, then go back to Oilville and make a jump through Beukal to one of these other places."

But I shook my head. "I don't think we're supposed to use the portals. Inade's loaded, and I bet he could pay the right person for intel about our destination."

Yven's brow furrowed. "Then why give us a map?"

I grimly smiled at him and handed over a steaming mug. "Maybe those aren't places to visit. They're places to *avoid.*"

CHAPTER 15

The one bright spot of that Sunday night was the gradual shift in the weather. By eight, the rain had given way to a damp mist—still bothersome, but nothing a jacket couldn't fight. While Yven caught a ride to retrieve our Jeep from the Walmart parking lot, I hastily packed our belongings and tidied Toni's house, throwing the sheets in the washing machine, scrubbing the bathroom, and running the vacuum. I called her to let her know that the honeymooners had vacated early due to a work emergency and that I was doing the promised cleanup, and she was grateful for the condiments and paper plates left behind.

Once Yven returned with our ride, he stripped off the decal with its Pactlands registration information and removed the tracker, a little metal contraption the size of a matchbox that lived in the glove compartment. Borrowing Toni's hammer from the storage closet, he smashed it into pieces on the sidewalk and swept the leavings into a garbage bag with the perishable items I was dumping. Working together, we had the house clean, the beds remade, and the laundry folded by eleven, and we loaded up for the trip out of town.

We had no real plan, no set destination other than avoiding the portals, and by then, we were both coasting on adrenaline and caffeine—hardly conducive to a long haul through the night. But the letter had been clear that we needed to make tracks, and so Yven picked up I-64 west until we ran into I-81. I opted to go north, and we stayed with the Interstate until about three the next morning, when we found a Holiday Inn in southern Pennsylvania and stumbled into bed.

When I finally woke around ten Monday morning, I couldn't even remember the name of the town where we'd landed, but Yven had returned with takeout from the diner next door, informed the desk clerk that we'd be extending our stay, and hung the sign for privacy. I devoured the plate of pancakes and sausage he'd bought with my credit card, then sat by the window, sipping my cheap coffee and considering the gray parking lot. Spring had arrived, as far as the calendar was concerned, but word of its advent didn't seem to have crossed the Mason-Dixon line.

Somewhat refreshed, I tried to prioritize our problems. First, we needed a more permanent hideout. While the motel was clean and comfortable enough, it wasn't the most economical of solutions, especially since we couldn't cook there. An extended-stay facility could help on that front, but *where*? Were we safe with a couple hundred miles between us and Toni's house? Then there was the matter of my agreement with Pateme. I needed to get to work on finding Silver...on whom I had *nothing*. At least I'd had photos and hints about Mafora to guide me. Silver was a big, fat cypher, and unfortunately, my supply of Awakening, the LSD-like potion that had helped me focus my farsight, was hidden in the back of my liquor cabinet in Richmond.

But as I puzzled through our next steps, I realized how exhausted I was—and Yven looked no better. "You've been away from home for almost two weeks," he reminded me. "A solid week of that was dealing with Mafora, and yesterday was a disaster. *Rest*, Rosie. Nothing's on fire today."

He had a point, and so I snuggled back into bed while he drew the shades and cut the lights. Nothing in my life felt settled, but I was full and warm, and Yven held me as I drifted off to sleep.

By Tuesday morning, I felt close to human again…or whatever I was. Yven went ahead and paid for another two nights in our room, insisting that we deserved a little time to catch our breath. "Take it easy," he coaxed as we cleaned up from breakfast. "Have a nap, watch television. You don't need to rush into this business with Silver."

But I was rested enough to grow bored by basic cable, no matter how comfy the bed, and after lunch, I told Yven that I was ready to make an attempt. "You might want to take a walk," I suggested. "Or a drive, whatever you like. It's not like we have to worry about gas." Pactlands-modified vehicles retained their fuel gauges, but only for show.

Yven seemed uncertain about leaving me alone, but after we tested his phone and ascertained that he could answer calls from me once again, he agreed to take the Jeep for a spin and give me peace and quiet.

"There's probably a home center around here somewhere. Go treat yourself to an orchid," I teased as I saw him to the door.

He started to fire off a retort—I could see it in his eyes—but instead, he raised my chin and kissed me. I didn't mind in the slightest, but as we parted, I grinned and asked, "What was that for?"

"Lost time," he replied, and kissed me again before I shooed him out.

Alone with my thoughts and not much else to go on, I grabbed my notepad and colored pencils, then took a seat at the little table by the window. With no hints as to what Silver looked like or where I might find him, I closed my true eyes and awakened my inner sight, breathing slowly with a pencil poised above the page until I felt the familiar shift.

Show me Silver, I told the universe.

My vision remained black, and I fought the urge to panic. This wasn't a whiteout from a blinding spell, I reassured myself, just a lack of focus. I was trying to force it, and that wouldn't work. I had nothing to lock on to, no rope in the darkness to lead me into the light.

Okay.

I took a deep breath and recalled what it had felt like back at the mansion when I'd lost myself for hours and awakened to find a partly finished family portrait. I'd never seen half the people on the canvas, but they'd come to me when I allowed myself to open up.

Not the director of this show, but rather the conduit for information.

A few more deep breaths sent my mind toward that receptive state, and my hand began to move as an image came into view…

Inade. *Shit.*

I snapped out of it and dropped my pencil, kicking myself for the distraction. This was only going to work if I kept my mind clear, and that meant pulling my thoughts away from my obnoxious great-grandfather. Giving myself a moment to recenter, I took a sip of water, shook out my arms, and then tried to slide back into that open state…

"*Damn it,*" I muttered as Inade once again came to mind.

I rose and paced the room, wondering how I was supposed to work around this. I'd been focusing on the guy for a week, plus Pateme and Liventi—small wonder that my farsight was defaulting to the places I'd been sending it lately. Maybe, I mused, if I gave it a moment to run its usual check on Inade, I'd be sufficiently reassured that he wasn't lurking outside the motel to attempt the search for Silver.

Returning to the table, I found my black pencil, held it in position, and closed my eyes. "All right, then," I whispered, "what do you want to show me?"

Yven's hand on my shoulder pulled me from my trance with a cry, and he hastened to reassure me while I readjusted to full consciousness. "Are you okay?" he asked as I panted. "I'm sorry, I didn't mean to frighten you…"

"It's fine," I insisted, and rubbed my forehead as the internal pounding thundered along in time with my heartbeat. "What time is it?"

"About seven. I came back once, but you were drawing, and I didn't want to disturb you. Uh…any interest in dinner?"

"Just a minute, let me see if I came up with anything. And would you mind grabbing my Advil, please? It's in the bag in the bathroom."

By the time Yven returned with two capsules and a glass of water, I'd pulled the new drawings out of the pad and spread them on the table for closer study. "Any luck?" he asked.

I popped the pills and chased them with the cold tap water, then gestured to the sketches with my empty tumbler. "Not a damn thing. Inade's been on my mind all afternoon."

He peered at the first two drawings—one of Inade smiling at a customer in his shop, his dark hair pulled into its customary ponytail and falling over the back of his ornate robe, and the other of him bent over a worktable, loupe fitted to one eye, as he engraved delicate lines on a gold pendant. Judging by the robe, the sketches were snapshots from the same day—probably a live feed, considering my previous work.

The third sketch, however, was different. Once again, I'd drawn Inade as I'd depicted him in the family portrait: sitting in a fancy wooden chair, sporting a formal robe, and grasping a thorny gray vine as he almost glared outward. But in this second iteration, I'd added a few drops of blood to his hands, evidence of his wounds from the thorns.

"Is this one from today?" Yven asked, lifting the third drawing off the table.

"No. That's a copy of what I did back at the mansion.

Well, almost a copy," I amended, standing to point out the difference. "The blood is new. Symbolism has never been my gift."

"What do you mean?" he asked with a bemused frown.

"Just that the symbolism is *way* too obvious. He's holding a thorny plant, yeah? 'Hall of Thorns.' And he cares so much about those damn thorns that he's willing to hurt himself to protect them. He lost my grandfather, he almost lost Mafora, and I doubt that Aunt Lily has much use for him after Sunday night."

"Ah."

"This is only the partial picture," I continued. "See, Inade's holding an old section of the plant—maybe a dead section, I don't know. The vine framed the family portrait in the original, and it was green in one corner, over by Teolm and Aunt Lily."

"Strange," Yven mused. "Is the symbolism meant to show the Hall itself as a dead thing? If so, I think your vision's a little off—ti'Cren has been growing for centuries."

"Yeah," I said, studying my sketch. "I guess Inade's part should be green, too, since he's probably driving the Hall's growth. Gray wood like that would be…"

I froze as a flash went off inside my head. The conclusion was facially ludicrous, but my gut wasn't so sure.

"What is it?" Yven asked when I fell silent.

I licked my lips, hesitating to be certain that I wanted to give voice to the idea, then murmured, "The vine's not gray."

"No?"

"No," I said, shaking my head. "It's *silver*."

I sat on the edge of the nearer bed, my mind racing, and Yven dropped the drawing and joined me. "Rosie?" he said, wrapping an arm around my shoulders as if he feared I'd topple to the carpet. "Talk to me. What are you thinking?"

Even as the logical part of my brain laughed off the idea, as I considered the pieces of information before me, the puzzle began to take shape. "My pen pal's letter to Pateme said that what happened Sunday would be crucial to Project Floodtide, which exists to bring down Silver. That's the day that Pateme asked me to look for him. By then, he knew that I could control my farsight well enough to see through blinding potions…but only in my bloodline. That's the weakness in the defense," I continued, staring at the wall. "The letter told him that I was looking in on him. I wonder if he knew I'd been spying on Liventi and Inade, too."

"That would be logical," said Yven, "since we were trying to hide Mafora and Deono."

"Right. There isn't a farseer in ti'Cren—not one I've heard of, at least. If they had one, then surely Inade would have gone to that person instead of me. So he's never had to worry about the problem with the blinding potion—I'm the first farseer able to exploit that. And Pateme…he knows who Silver is," I realized. "He *has* to know."

"If Inade were really Silver, then wouldn't Pateme have arrested him on Sunday night?" Yven countered. "He had cause…"

"Unless he's playing a long game. Maybe Inade doesn't know what Pateme knows." I thought of the two men as they'd been in the rain, the wealthy lord sneering beneath his umbrella and the civil servant getting soaked in his trench coat. "Maybe I'm wrong, but I don't think Pateme is all too fond of his sister's husband."

"I doubt that, too, but do you honestly think—"

"Ti'Cren is *wealthy*," I interrupted. "Inade can afford the blinding potion, he's obviously bought himself portal credentials…he could be Silver."

"Silver is a ruthless, murderous drug baron, and Lord ti'Cren is an extremely prominent jeweler. I don't see them overlapping. And if the director really thought Lord ti'Cren was his man, then why wasn't he upfront with you on Sunday?"

"I'm not sure," I admitted. "All of this is just an idea. But…"

"But what?" he pressed.

I sighed. "But I need more information."

With the chaos of the last week and a half, Yven and I hadn't exactly had a talk about where *we* stood, but his working assumption appeared to be that he loved me, I loved him, and thus, it was his job to see to it that I ate at semiregular intervals while I stalked Inade. As unofficial boyfriends went, I couldn't have asked for a better one. On Tuesday night, he waited for me to clean up, then drove me to the finest restaurant in the area— Applebee's—and didn't bat an eye as I devoured a rack of ribs and downed a frozen daiquiri-adjacent cocktail. He coaxed me to bed around midnight, once my feverish drawing subsided, then brought me breakfast early the next morning and left me with several cups of coffee, a bottle of water, and strict instructions to call if I needed *anything*.

For hours, I focused on Inade and followed him like a shadow, trailing him through his mansion and back to Beukal to his store. I watched him approve paperwork that his children brought him and stood by in silence as he schmoozed with customers, never doing anything as degrading as making a sale but often around, lending his prestige to the showroom. I sat at the next table while he had a pleasant lunch with two sorcerers whose robes and rings suggested that they were his financial peers, if not social equals, and observed as he got into his Mercedes that evening, dropped the mask of geniality on the way home, and ate dinner alone in his office.

"I'm not there yet," I told Yven when he pulled me away to eat a hamburger and pop painkillers against my pounding headache, and so he told the desk clerk we'd need another night.

I woke early on Thursday morning and carefully slipped to the bathroom, trying not to disturb Yven beside me. He grunted in his sleep but didn't wake, even when I slid back into place, and I decided to follow Inade for a while before breakfast.

I'd expected to find him in the dining room, or maybe in his home office. Instead, I trailed Inade into a small, three-story brick building—probably somewhere in Beukal, I thought, though I didn't recognize any landmarks. Despite the early hour, he was dressed and seemed alert, and he walked into the unmarked establishment like he owned the place. For all I knew, perhaps he did.

The foyer reminded me of an old country club, heavy on the dark wood and polished brass. Landscapes of no particular merit, mostly of grasslands, hung around the room between sconces and doorways. An elf stationed behind a mahogany reception desk rose from her stool as she noticed Inade and nodded deeply in a near-bow. "Lord ti'Cren, good morning," she murmured. "Your room is ready, and your guest has been seated. Would you like an escort, sir?"

"That won't be necessary," he replied, and swept past her toward a staircase.

He saw himself up two flights and down a paneled corridor toward the door at the end of the hall, which had been left open a crack. The room beyond the door was intimate, perhaps the size of Yven's apartment's den, and furnished with a table for four. The man who'd been waiting—a sorcerer, blond, broad-shouldered, and quite tall—rose from his chair and waited until Inade had seated himself. "Good morning, sir," he said as Yven shook out his napkin. "I took the liberty of ordering your usual."

"And that's why I keep you around, Jona," he replied with a slight smile, then reached for his coffee. "You have the reports for me?"

Jona patted the leather satchel hanging from his chair. "As requested. I—"

A waiter opened the door, cutting their conversation short, and deposited two covered plates before them. "Lord ti'Cren," he said, removing the cloche from Inade's breakfast, then did the same for the sorcerer. "Mr. Kero. Enjoy, gentlemen."

They waited until he'd seen himself out and closed the door, and Inade studied Jona's plate. "You really must try the sausage sometime. The club's herb blend is perfection."

Jona smiled and tucked into a bowl of oatmeal. "I'll take your word for it, sir."

"This truly cannot tempt you?" he asked, cutting a patty in half.

"Alas, lifelong vegetarian," Jona replied with mock gravity. "And if I took you up on the offer, the resulting gastric distress would probably put you off your breakfast." He sipped his juice while Inade chuckled, then said, "I heard the news of your daughter's safe return."

"Oh?"

"Falli apprised me when I returned to the city yesterday."

Inade nodded. "Ah, good. If word came from Falli, I'm not concerned."

Jona paused briefly and cleared his throat. "I *have* been listening, sir. Word of Mafora's abduction has circulated below."

An eyebrow rose. "And?"

"And *only* word of her abduction."

He seemed to relax. "Good. *Very* good."

"The marriage has been corrected, then?"

"Monday morning," said Inade between bites. "I brought her into the Tribunal building by the back entrance—the girl didn't have the foresight to use it on her first trip," he muttered. "But yes, the matter's been resolved. Wiped clean."

"And I'm sure you're relieved to have her back within the bosom of the family," Jona replied.

Inade grunted. "She's in her mother's care for now. The girl knows it will be a long time before she regains my trust, but at least we can put the affair behind us."

"And the boy? What of him?"

"Unaccounted for." Attacking what appeared to be a pile of roasted purple carrots, Inade said, "He left their hiding place—I sent a team to pick him up on Monday, but he'd already run. Whether he's yet returned to the Pactlands remains an open question."

Jona considered that information while he took a swig of coffee. "He'll surface eventually, I have no doubt. Would you like for him to be removed, sir? We could make it look like an accident, or, uh…" A smirk played on his lips. "We could make it a more *memorable* experience for the lad. Whatever you think best."

In that moment, I was exceptionally grateful that the two men couldn't sense me watching them.

"My thanks," Inade replied, spearing a piece of carrot as calmly as if Jona had suggested taking a stroll on a sunny day, "but not at this time."

Jona's brow furrowed. "Not to be impertinent, sir, but may I ask why? What's one fewer DPP agent?"

"A good thing, I'm sure." He chewed and quickly washed the bite down. "But I promised Liventi I wouldn't hurt him," he muttered, rolling his eyes. "Mafora, apparently, remains somewhat tender toward the little worm. Her mother feels that his sudden death might unduly pain the child, and she nagged me until I agreed." He paused and smiled at Jona. "Give it a year, why don't you? Let your creativity blossom."

"As you like, sir. And, uh…" He paused, seemingly considering his words. "It's my understanding that there was another person assisting your daughter."

Inade eyed him over the low floral arrangement. "You've debriefed my security detail, I trust."

"That I have. Their silence will not be a problem for you."

He grunted and stabbed his carrots. "This remains between us, yes?"

"Of course, sir."

"The girl is Fradin's granddaughter," he murmured, holding Jona's stare. "*Talented*. She was there with another agent, Mafora says. They were also missing when the team came for the boy."

Jona considered this information as he lifted his glass. "Fradin's line should have ended with Fradin, I think. Tying your Hall to...*that*..."

"My thought as well. Can you take care of the matter for me?"

"The girl and the other agent?"

"Yes. However you find it convenient." He chewed briefly, then said, "Be discreet. Should Liventi learn of this, she would protest. She still has a soft spot for her son," he muttered.

Stirring the melted swirl of brown sugar atop his oatmeal, Jona said, "Again, if you'll forgive the impertinence..."

Inade waved him on.

"Just how long do you intend to put up with your wife? To be frank, she's seldom more than a hindrance."

"I'm well aware," Inade replied, sighing. "The children are reasonably fond of her—"

"An accident could be arranged."

He reached across the table and gripped Jona's wrist. "Your loyalty does not go unnoticed, my friend. Unfortunately, ridding myself of my wife would be more troublesome than keeping her alive."

Whatever love my great-grandparents had once shared had quite obviously cooled, at least where Inade was concerned.

"A divorce, perhaps?" Jona suggested. "Let her return to her mother's Hall and wait for her inheritance."

"Liventi would never consent to that—and before you ask," said Inade, lifting his delicate coffee cup, "she knows far too much to be removed by anything less than death. I can't afford to ruin her, no matter how much she vexes me. But if she were to meet an unexpected end, her idiot brother would come snooping around."

Jona shrugged. "I don't mind adding an idiot brother to the list, sir."

"Too risky. Pateme may be an idiot, but he's a *useful* idiot. His replacement might not be so blind, and there's no need to complicate business, is there?"

The sorcerer paused and squinted at his oatmeal in thought. "Do we not have sufficient influence within DPP to nudge an appropriate candidate into the director's office?"

"Not yet. And it's not DPP you need to worry about—directorships come from the Forum alone."

Smiling, Jona replied, "Surely you could secure the necessary votes there, sir. How many of the representatives are immune to contributions, eh? Why," he added, chuckling to himself, "if *you* wanted the directorship, I don't doubt that you could afford it."

"But why bother with bureaucracy?" Inade countered. "Especially when I already have people like you who manage my affairs so skillfully."

Jona's head dipped in acknowledgement. "I aim to please, sir."

"And you seldom miss the mark. Now, tell me about the latest run of Sweet Heat."

I was vaguely aware of my distant body's quick gasp.

The potion known as Sweet Heat was an incredibly dangerous drug, the combination of two nasty potions already on the market. Bottled Heat, a highly addictive potion brewed with a heroin base, could leave users in a coma. Sweet Bliss, another incredibly addictive potion, offered a ride like a remarkable acid trip, to the point that users could starve to death as they kept chasing the high.

Combining the two was risky—from what Pars had told me, it sounded more dangerous than cooking meth in an oil refinery—but the high was better, and the addiction rate was nearly one hundred percent. As could be expected, Sweet Heat was responsible for a growing number of deaths in the Pactlands. Gentle Breeze had lost a cousin to the stuff, and considering the strength of the troll constitution, that alone was testament to its danger. But users clamored for the drug, and while I wasn't anywhere close to an expert on the street value of illegal potions, even I understood how wealthy Sweet Heat could make the right brewer.

Reaching into his satchel, Jona extracted a sheaf of papers and passed them to Inade to peruse. "Numbers this month are down but recovering. We lost three brewers in explosions—"

"*Three?*" Inade's eyebrows rose. "What were those fools doing, working by candlelight?"

"Given the state of the debris left behind, we may never know. But as I said, sir, the numbers are climbing. I put another two brewers on it, and as the current crop seem to know how not to kill themselves, I predict steady growth into the summer."

"Excellent." He flipped through the report and slowly nodded. "You think you'll earn your bonus this time, then?"

Jona grinned. "With any luck, sir."

"I should really give you more challenging targets," Inade replied, and handed the papers back. "Let's talk about the new crew…"

I didn't stick around to listen. Pulling myself away from the club and back to my body, I lay on the bed until I regained my bearings, then rolled over and nudged Yven. "Babe?" I whispered.

"Nng."

"*Yven.*"

A brisk shake of his shoulder roused him, and he

yawned as consciousness returned. "Hi," he croaked. "Sleep well? Are you hungry? I'm starving, actually…"

The thought of Inade's breakfast meeting dampened my appetite. "Not yet. Quick question."

"Sure…"

"Do you have Pateme's phone number? I just watched Inade and his pal talk about Sweet Heat production figures and whacking his wife, and if I'm not crazy, he called in a hit on the two of us."

And with that, Yven was well and truly awake.

Unsurprisingly, Yven didn't have the director's personal phone number, and we decided that this wasn't the sort of matter to mention on his office voicemail. But I knew that Pars could contact Gentle Breeze, and since she was Pateme's third in command, I trusted that she could find him.

Despite the early hour, Gentle Breeze sounded unbothered by the interruption, and she gave us Pateme's number without hesitation. "He told me you might call," she explained as I wrote down the last digits on the bedside notepad. "Are you all right?"

"For now. Quick question?"

"Sure."

"Is Deono safe?"

She chuckled. "Can't say for sure, but Pateme has stashed him somewhere for the moment. My gut tells me this is one of those situations in which knowledge can be a dangerous thing, you know?" She paused, then asked, "Have you seen something?"

"Maybe," I said, reluctant to tell her more without talking to Pateme first. "Just, uh…if you see him, tell him hi for me, okay?"

"Will do," the chief replied. "Be careful, Rose."

With Yven sitting beside me on the unmade bed, I dialed Pateme's number and put the phone on speaker mode. It rang twice, and then I heard his cautious, "Good morning?"

"It's me," I said, using English in case he wasn't alone. "Can we talk?"

"Of course," he replied in kind. "One moment…"

The line went staticky for a few seconds, a sure sign that Pateme was using strong magic nearby. "Are you at work already?" I asked.

"Home, but I've assembled a privacy spell here as well. Are you alone?"

"It's just Yven and me. We're in a hotel in—"

"That's enough," he interrupted, switching to Low Elvish. "Tell me no details, understood? The name of the game is plausible deniability."

I followed his linguistic lead. "Uh…all right, fine. Sorry to bother you so early, but I've got the information you wanted."

"Mm. You have a name for me?"

Hesitating, I looked at Yven, who nodded encouragement. "Inade," I told Pateme, keeping my voice low.

To my surprise, he didn't immediately protest. "What's your basis for that conclusion?"

Quickly, I reported my findings over the last few days, culminating in a rundown of Inade's breakfast with Jona. "I'm *sure* they were talking about Sweet Heat," I concluded. "And your sister."

I held my breath, waiting for the explosion on the other end, but Pateme just sighed. Whether the sound was indicative of disappointment or relief, I couldn't say.

"It's possible that I'm wrong," I began. "I mean, you know my training hasn't been—"

"You're not wrong," he murmured. "You're not wrong at *all*."

"Huh?"

"Inade is Silver," he said, far too matter-of-factly. "I've known that since, oh…1907."

"But you told me you couldn't give me a name or a picture to go on—"

"I was testing you, and I wanted to be absolutely certain of my conclusion. Fradin agreed with me, incidentally, and those involved at our level share that suspicion, but I didn't want to taint your analysis. Now that you've independently pointed to him...well."

Yven looked just as perplexed as I felt. "Pateme," I said, "I...I don't understand why—"

"Why I've been sitting on my hands all this time?" he offered. "Why Inade is a free man, and I continue to send teams to pick off the lowest members of his organization? Why I allow him to torture and kill individuals in DPP and DOL custody?"

"All of the above, *yeah*," I snapped.

He sighed again, and I heard a chair creak as he sat. "We've accumulated a mountain of evidence about Silver's criminal enterprise. His lieutenants, *their* lieutenants, the brewers, the growers, the transportation links. I can point to ten people in DPP who take payment from him, and at least as many in Laws. He's paid for the portal attendants' assistance for decades. The problem is that Silver is *very* adept at distancing himself from his underlings. All of the evidence we've obtained only amounts to a circumstantial case against Inade—and given his wealth and prestige, circumstantial won't be enough to bring him down. We'll only have one shot at him, and it must strike true. For years, we've sought irrefutable proof of Silver's true identity. You're not the first farseer to touch this matter, but—"

"The blinding potion," I murmured, seeing where Pateme was going. "Farseers can't find him because he keeps himself protected. You would need someone with a blood connection to see through it..."

"Precisely. He could drink the blinding potion by the barrel, but he can't stop you. You're the key to his downfall, Rose. The question now is whether you're willing to help us."

Again, I looked to Yven, who squeezed my free hand and whispered, "However you want to play this, I'm here."

I held the phone against my shoulder and kissed his cheek, then turned my attention back to Pateme. "What do you need me to do?"

"Watch him and tell me what you see," Pateme replied. "I want his movements, his associates, anything that could be of use. If he's having meetings, if he mentions activity involving the portals—"

"I could do that," I interrupted. "But before I do *anything*, you're going to answer my questions."

After a brief silence, he said, "That…sounds fair. What do you want to know?"

"Well, for starters, what the hell is Project Floodtide?"

Pateme's chair creaked again as he shifted his weight. "A joint operation among DPP, DOL, and DOI that's been working since 1903 to monitor Silver."

"You're going to have to give me more than that."

He grunted but acquiesced. "To the beginning, then. In 1902, I was the chief deputy here. My director took notice of the influx of illegal product on the market. Interdiction had *massive* hauls, and they pressed sources for information. Eventually, people began whispering about a man called Silver who was running the operation…and then those people wound up dead. Fairly obvious pattern. My director studied the problem for a time, and the following year, he established Floodtide with his peers at Laws and Intelligence in order to combat the problem."

Intelligence. "Was the DOI director—"

"Diriem ti'Dana? Yes. He's had his fingers in this project from the beginning. Anyway, I was put in charge of DPP's sector and given leave to recruit anyone I trusted. I worked alone for two years, pursuing the leads we uncovered and reviewing the files. The more I saw and studied, the greater my suspicion became that Inade was involved."

"Why?" I asked.

"Because his wealth had exploded. We've been brothers-in-law since 1548—I have a fairly decent idea of my sister's family by now," he replied with a touch of reproach. "They were always rich, but never extravagantly so. That changed around the turn of the twentieth century. Suddenly, Inade was funding arts programs and throwing lavish parties left and right, and he wasn't sweating. His business has never foundered, but jewelry alone wouldn't have built his fortune like that." He let slip a soft sigh. "I'd suspected for a time that Inade had been working on both sides of the law. Heard rumors that he'd been bankrolling low-tier producers for the interest payments, but I could never prove it. So I took Liventi aside and asked her in confidence how they had come into so much money. She hedged, but she eventually confessed that she didn't think all of Inade's business dealings were legal. Begged me not to go after him."

My hand clenched around the phone. "So you gave him a pass because he was married to your sister?"

Pateme said nothing for a moment, and I thought we might have been disconnected until he murmured, "I gave him a pass because I love her, and I didn't want her to die like the others. She's in deeper than she's told me, I'm sure of it, but there's no spark left in that marriage. If I went after Inade and lost, I fear he'd turn on her."

After eavesdropping on Inade's breakfast, I had to concur.

"And she wouldn't be the first he's killed," Pateme continued. "I'd bet my life that he murdered his sister."

Yven's brow furrowed. "His sister, sir?"

"Venya. Lady ti'Cren's eldest child and the heir presumptive to the Hall. She drowned as a young woman under mysterious circumstances. The story goes that she became depressed when a young man rebuffed her, but the version *I've* heard for some time is that Inade drugged her and dropped her in a lake. This was more than a century before the Pact, and no charges have ever been brought against him, but…" He let the thought trail off, then said, "So yes, I held my tongue for Liventi's sake, and then I dug into the Silver problem, and…well, it coalesced."

"But you didn't go after him then, either," I pointed out.

"No. Again, my evidence was purely circumstantial. But in 1905, after I'd reached my conclusions, I decided to draft in an agent I trusted to check my work and see whether I was out of my mind." He paused, then quietly said, "There was no agent I trusted more than your grandfather. Fradin was among the best of the best."

"I'm sorry," Yven interjected, aghast, "but you asked him to investigate his own *father*?"

"Inade and Fradin were never close," said Pateme. "Teolm, Liliol, and Fradin were made of different stuff than their father. Jomin, the second-born, went into the family business, as did Otun and Kilch, but I think it's always bothered Inade that his eldest son decided to spend his life with plants. Liliol might have had a pass as a daughter, but then Fradin came along and went into public service, and that just *irked* Inade. Of course, considering what Inade's been up to, I can understand his displeasure," he said dryly. "But yes, ti'Ansha, I asked him to review my findings and tell me if he thought of a suspect. Within two years, we were both convinced of Silver's identity, and Fradin was absolutely disgusted."

"Did he confront Inade?" I asked.

"*No*. Not then," Pateme amended. "All of us involved in Floodtide were exceedingly careful to keep up appearances around him. I continued to be social with my sister's family—in fact, I visited more often, trying to make it apparent to Inade how much I cared about Liventi. I've been gambling that he won't do anything to her while I'm around for fear of an investigation…and judging by what you've said this morning, Rose, I think that was the wise wager. On the other hand, if I move prematurely and can't get a conviction, then I fear he'll have her killed. Maybe as dead weight, maybe out of paranoia…hell, maybe as a fuck-you to me."

"Your devotion to your sister is touching," said Yven, "but what about all the other people who've died because of Silver? What about the drugs? Gentle Breeze lost a cousin to Sweet Heat just last year—"

"I haven't sat on this information because of Liventi," Pateme protested. "Her hands aren't clean. If I could arrest him today *and* see him convicted, I would. Instead, I've been waiting for an opportunity like the one Rose has afforded us. If she can track him and give us leads to corroborate, then I think we stand a chance."

"You said Fradin didn't confront Inade *then*," I commented, pulling Pateme back to the information I sought. "When did they have it out?"

"Early in 1948," he replied. "Fradin had been with Floodtide all that time—he carried a full caseload in Regulatory, but he continued to work with us, hoping we'd find the necessary evidence to bring Inade down. But then he met Miranda in 1946, and he was smitten. Fradin's fire-haired beauty," he muttered. "Spunky little schoolteacher who took no one's nonsense. Do you know what she did when he came clean with her? Has Liliol ever told you?"

"No…"

He chuckled. "Miranda had Fradin over for dinner, and he said he needed to confess. Told her about the Pactlands and dropped his mask. Apparently, she stared at him for a *long* few minutes, and Fradin was about to get up and leave when she said, 'I don't care what you look like behind closed doors, but promise me you won't do that in public. I don't know what the principal would do if it came out that I'm going steady with an elf.'"

"*Seriously?*"

"I think she was more shocked than she let on," said Pateme, "but once your grandmother made up her mind, it was difficult to sway her. And she had made up her mind about Fradin. Anyway, I think he proposed in January 1948, and then he told his parents that he was marrying her and taking the draught. Liventi was distraught, obviously, but Inade was *furious*. He used every connection to the Forum he could find in an effort to keep the draught out of Fradin's hands."

"Not enough friends in high places?" I asked.

"That had nothing to do with it. The decision to take the draught was Fradin's alone. So once Inade realized he wouldn't be able to stop his son, he made the mistake of threatening Miranda. Fradin knew as well as anyone that Silver had no qualms about killing inconvenient people, so he went home, cornered Inade in his office, and told him he knew all about Inade's double life. Said he'd been holding that information in reserve for years, and if Inade didn't stand down and leave him and Miranda alone, he would go public with it—and if the two of them 'disappeared,' there was a backup plan in place." Pateme snorted. "Nothing of the sort, of course—that was a pure bluff—but Inade bought it. He settled for publicly disowning Fradin."

Suddenly, Inade's antagonism toward his son made *much* more sense. "It's not the fact that Fradin left that made Inade so angry," I mused. "It's the betrayal."

"Oh, it's both," Pateme quickly replied. "Inade has carefully cultivated his image, and it's a poor look for a lord's son to take the draught and run off."

"But Fradin gave you up, too?" Yven asked. "When he told his father—"

"Fortunately, no. He didn't bring my name into it, clever boy. Now, I suspect that Inade knows that I *also* know about his connection to Silver, but I've never mentioned it, and so here we sit. But Rose, you could change that. I know it's a lot to ask, but if you're willing…"

Yven met my eyes and nodded. "I mean it," he whispered. "Whatever you choose."

I held the phone closer and murmured, "Let's get the bastard. What do you want me to focus on first?"

"I'll leave that to your discretion," he said. "And thank you. Call this number and *only* this number unless I tell you otherwise."

"How long do you want me to spy?"

"I can't give you a firm date, but we need this case to be airtight. Can you give us a month?"

"A month?" I repeated, thinking of my locked-up studio in Richmond. "Uh...yeah, I can do that."

As if he'd been reading my thoughts, he said, "I understand this will cut into your work schedule, and I'll find a way to compensate you—"

"It's all right—"

"Not once you factor in travel costs," said Pateme. "You *cannot* go home. Not Richmond, not Charlottesville, and I sincerely hope you'd have sense enough not to ask Liliol to hide you. You need to find a place where Inade can't hunt you down. That's part of the reason why I've been so careful with you," he added. "I worried that Inade would hear about what you've done for us, put the pieces together, and realize the danger he's in from a farseer in his bloodline. Perhaps he isn't aware of what you can do to him. But what I *do* know is that you embarrassed him in front of his security detail and my team, and he's not going to forgive that. Or forget that—you outsmarted him in his own home. You're not safe anywhere that he can find you."

"That much was obvious from his breakfast meeting," I said.

Leaning toward the phone, Yven added, "I'm staying with her. Someone has to watch Rose's back."

"You have my full support," Pateme replied, "though I fear there's little I can do to help you at this time. Just find a place to hide, and tell *no one* where you are. Not even me. I will inform you when it's safe to return to Beukal. Got it?"

"We'll be in touch," I told him, and ended the call. Putting the phone aside, I sighed and shrugged. "Guess we're going to need to vacate, huh?"

"No great loss there," he replied, and pushed himself off the bed to begin packing. "Any idea of where we should go?"

"Actually, yeah."

Yven turned back to me, bemused, and I dug in my bag for the portal map my pen pal had sent along. "Only one state on the eastern seaboard has no portals at all. We're going to Maine."

CHAPTER 16

Late March wasn't exactly peak season in Maine. Sandwiched between deep winter and proper spring, it offered few of the perks that summer tourists and fall leaf peepers enjoyed, instead bringing forth an overabundance of mud as the still-thawing ground failed to absorb the early spring rains. My Internet investigation over breakfast offered warnings of seaside eateries shuttered until June and water activities unavailable until the lake ice melted. But the general lack of tourism meant that rates were at their lowest, which suited my budget nicely.

Searching for places off the beaten track, I found a small rental house in a tiny town down east, one of the many villages along Route 1. Given our travel timeframe, I called the landlady instead of waiting for an email, only to catch her snowbirding in Florida. I introduced us as a painter and her boyfriend, explaining that we were looking for a change of scenery and hoping to land in Maine for a month or so—prepaid. While the landlady initially seemed skeptical, I sent her to my online gallery as proof of my bona fides, which did the trick. By ten, I'd transferred the money, she'd sent me the access code to the key's lockbox, and she'd followed up with a list of local recommendations—most still closed for the season—and a plea to keep mud off the carpet.

Securing a place to stay hadn't been as difficult as I'd feared, but *getting* there was another matter. Our Pennsylvania hideaway was southwest of Harrisburg, while the house I'd found was barely more than an hour's drive from the Canadian border. We were looking at a solid twelve hours on the road in good traffic, and considering the rain falling all along the northeastern coast, we'd signed up for a slog.

But Yven didn't complain. Our Jeep's hidden hold was already carrying camping gear and the dry goods we'd taken from Toni's house, and Yven went shopping with me before we hit the road in order to stock up on things like trash bags and towels. We both left town with heavier coats and spare gloves, plus galoshes and sturdy umbrellas.

And then, thus provisioned, we made our long trek to the northeast, following I-81 through Pennsylvania, then picking up I-84 for the run to New York. We drove in two-hour shifts throughout the afternoon, chasing the early spring dusk and dodging showers. It was six and pouring by the time we hit the Connecticut line, and we still had a long night ahead of us. But the temperature was high enough to prevent icing, and Yven and I decided to press on. He extended his shift to three hours and might have gone longer had I not insisted that he share the wheel and take a nap, and though he swore he was fit to keep driving, he switched seats outside of Hartford.

While Yven dozed to the rhythmic sweep of the wipers, I navigated the network of highways across Connecticut and Massachusetts, eventually pulling off once we made I-95 and New Hampshire. From that point, it was just a matter of following the coast. I slept while Yven took us into Maine toward Portland, and when I awoke, he'd left the Interstate for Route 1, which snaked its way past coastal towns sleeping through the miserable night. The final push in the wee hours of Friday morning was mine—Yven surrendered the Jeep near Belfast, and I stuck to the speed limit, wondering if moose frequented the seashore.

Around two that morning, we pulled into Hitchens, a town that barely merited its blinking yellow light at the main intersection. Exhausted, I followed my phone's directions to the rental house, a two-bedroom cottage that allegedly had a sea view. Of more interest to us that night was the attached garage, which would both give us shelter from the elements and hide our vehicle, and when Yven jumped out to retrieve the key from the lockbox, he found the garage opener waiting for us as well. Finally, I parked the Jeep and dragged myself into the house, bleary-eyed with the hour and stiff from the drive. The bedrooms seemed adequate—a master with a queen-sized bed and a slightly smaller room with a pair of twins—and while I located the linen closet and made the bigger bed, Yven turned up the heat and began bringing in the luggage.

"Doesn't matter tonight," I told him on his third trip with food. "Come on, bed's ready."

He didn't need further encouragement. We found our nightclothes and collapsed, huddling beneath the quilt and a spare blanket as the heater fussed and clanked, and were asleep in minutes.

I awoke to gray daylight and the smell of woodsmoke. Finding Yven's half of the bed empty, I rolled over and spotted an analog clock on the nightstand.

Ten-fifteen?

Groaning, I pushed back the covers, shivered, and crept into the den, where I spotted Yven crouched in front of the fireplace, poking at the crackling logs. "Hey," I mumbled. "When did you get up?"

As per usual, he was already decently dressed—he'd even thrown on a navy cable knit sweater over his button-down and chinos—and he grinned at me as I loitered by the door. "Seven-ish. Couldn't sleep, the house was still cold, but I found some dry logs in the garage," he replied, and beckoned me closer. "You needn't freeze over there. I've got the smoke heading up the chimney again, so come warm up. Breakfast?"

My groggy mind considered the goods I recalled stowing in the Jeep: dried beans, bags of rice, pasta, yogurt-covered raisins to satisfy my odd craving. "Uh…*did* we pack breakfast?"

"Not to brag, I make a mean bowl of quick oats. Here, *sit*," he said, patting the brick hearth. "I'll do the honors."

Yven's idea of oatmeal was hot, thick, and heavy on the brown sugar, and I scraped the bowl clean between sips of coffee. Warm, fed, and with the world returning to focus, I took stock of our situation. We'd made it to Maine. There wasn't a portal within hours of us. And my job of stalking Inade was off to a late start already.

"I thought you might want to work in there," Yven called from the kitchen, where he'd resumed the previous night's aborted pantry-stocking. "The couch is a little saggy but comfortable. Or we could make up one of the beds in the other room if you'd prefer that sort of privacy."

"What about you?" I asked.

"Thought I'd get the lay of the land," he replied, slotting boxes of instant stuffing into a cabinet. "See what's to be seen…up east, was it?"

"Down east."

"Down east," he mumbled to himself. "Right. Down relative to *what*, exactly?"

The best I could offer him was a shrug. "I've never been up here. We always tended to vacation around the parts of the Atlantic that don't freeze."

"Fair. Anyway, I'll try to find a store with fresh food. We could use eggs and milk, meat and produce if they're available. Will you be all right for a few hours?"

"Sure," I said, and wiggled my thawed-out toes. "Toasty. And listen, I don't want you thinking you need to do all the cooking. If you can shop, I'll throw dinner together—"

Yven returned to the den, stooped, and kissed the top of my head. "Don't worry about that," he said, dropping into a squat. "You're the one on a mission. My job is to feed and protect you."

"I can help—"

"You focus on Inade," he said gently. "Let me handle the rest, yes?"

I sighed as he turned and settled onto the hearth beside me. "Yven, I…I am *so* sorry for getting you tangled up in this mess," I said, leaning against him when his arm snaked around my shoulders. "You just wanted a nice, quiet career in Regulatory, and now Inade's probably sending a hitman after us, and you're stuck up here with me in the middle of nowhere—"

"Come with me," he coaxed, pulling me to my feet, then led me to the back door.

We'd approached the house in the rainy darkness early that morning, and while the rain still endured as a weak drizzle, the cloud-diffuse sunlight revealed the place's view. Three steps down from the covered wooden porch was a gravel path through a tangle of marshy growth, which ended in a narrow pebble beach. Beyond that stretched the gray Atlantic, cold and forbidding in the gloom but close enough to scent the air with brine.

"Not bad," I said, huddling against his sweater as the wind chilled my bare legs.

"There's nowhere I'd rather be," he murmured.

"Oh, yeah," I teased, "you wouldn't prefer the Bahamas right about now?"

"I'm here with you," he replied, rubbing my arm. "No one knows where we are, and for now, no one can tell us what to do. So no, there's nowhere I'd rather be than by your side."

Looking up at him, I smirked. "*Smooth*, ti'Ansha."

"I mean it—"

I silenced his protestations with a kiss, and he held me close until the wet cold drove me back inside.

By nightfall, the day's sporadic rain had given way to sleet. Yven kept the fire stoked and cooked as I watched Inade go about his business—which, that Friday, was fairly innocuous. Having caught up with him in the late morning, I'd trailed him to his office at the shop, observed him take a turn about the showroom floor, and followed him to dinner at an upscale restaurant in Beukal with Jomin, Otun, and Kilch. I pulled myself away after their meal for a painkiller and a bowl of Yven's vegetable soup, then returned to Inade in time to catch him in his home office with the door locked, perusing a sheaf of reports that had nothing to do with the jewelry business. I sketched what I could, trying to copy the details of the reports on his desk, and managed to pull three names from the data. It wasn't a terribly impressive beginning, but at least I had something to offer Pateme.

I caught the director in his office late that evening, and he made me wait until he'd turned on the protective spell before saying more than "Hello."

"You're safe?" he asked.

"For now," I replied, and shared what I'd gleaned. "I'll take some photos of my sketches and send them momentarily. Anything we need to know?"

"Nothing new." He paused briefly, then said, "Liliol has asked about you. I've told her not to call, but if she does…"

"I won't tell her where we are."

"Good. Well, we should end—"

"Quick question," I interjected.

"Yes?"

"If this works out for you…that is, if I can give you enough to bring down Inade, uh…can you get me acknowledged?" I blurted. "*Please*? You know *he* won't do it."

Pateme hesitated before answering me. "I don't have that kind of power, and I can't make guarantees. But I promise you that if this succeeds, I'll take the matter to the Forum and see whether there's anything that can be done."

It wasn't a great offer, but I doubted I'd get anything

better that night. I thanked him and hung up, and with Yven's prodding, I collapsed into bed.

The weekend followed much the same pattern, though I managed to get going in time to catch Inade's breakfast conversations. On Saturday, he behaved himself, even having guests over for what appeared to be a purely social dinner. He smiled, laughed, and made a show of holding Liventi's hand until late in the evening, when the last of their company retired to guest rooms and he and his wife went their separate ways to bed. But the following morning, after seeing them off, Inade returned to his private club in the capital for lunch, where he received a briefing from another lieutenant, Nirene ti'Van. An attractive blonde with deep brown eyes and a natural pout, Nirene was deferential to a fault, and I could well imagine why. A ti'Van would have little inherent social clout, but with patronage from ti'Cren—or even subtle assistance, given their illicit business—Nirene might make something of herself. While Jona seemed to be Inade's right hand, Nirene had to be close behind him, and judging by their conversation, she specialized in transportation.

I passed the new intel to Pateme that night, and he grunted in approval. "The ti'Van woman is in the files," he said, "but we've never put her and Inade in the same room."

"She arrived at the club a full hour before he did and signed in under an alias," I explained, having glanced at the logbook at reception when Inade left. "And there's a big shipment of Sweet Heat coming in from Texas after midnight."

"Which portal?"

"Midland."

"Excellent," he purred. "I should make some calls."

Pateme must have been a busy boy that night, as Inade was in a foul mood when I caught him back at the club for breakfast with Jona on Monday morning. "Nirene said the portal attendants were on board," he griped as soon as the waiter had departed. "*What happened?*"

"An emergency schedule change, sir," said Jona, who hadn't dared to touch his food. "Or that's what our people are telling us. The orders came through late last night, and there was a delay in getting them to the people on shift. By that time, the Midland convoy was arriving, and it was searched."

"*All* of them?"

Jona nodded miserably. "Five seized. The drivers are in custody at DOL. No one's speaking yet, but we have eyes and ears on them in case they change their minds."

"And the product?"

"Documented and destroyed. Erenani is taking no chances on an evidence loss."

"Damn her," Inade muttered, and stabbed a sausage patty with his fork as I grinned. I didn't know DOL's director well, but she was highly competent at her job.

"How goes the search for the girl?" Inade asked. When Jona didn't immediately offer good tidings, Inade stared at him over the short flowers and scowled. "Tell me your people have found *something.*"

"They're crossing off places," Jona replied. "No sign of them in Charlottesville or Richmond. Her business remains locked, and the nearby shops don't have any information. Her mail was piling up at her residence. An old man emptied it yesterday, but he took it with him."

That had to be Mr. Eddie, my elderly neighbor. Our families had looked after each other's homes for years. I made a mental note to call him and feign an emergency involving a distant cousin.

"And we've seen nothing unusual around your daughter's town," Jona continued. "No strange vehicles since her return. The nursery is open, but she sleeps alone."

The thought of Inade's goons looking in on Aunt Lily while she slept sent a chill up my spine. I'd be leading my next call to Pateme with *that* nasty little nugget.

"They could be hiding in her greenhouse," Inade suggested.

But Jona shook his head. "We planted a bug in the woods, and she hasn't even been in that building for a week. No sign of life."

"Keep monitoring the place. I'd prefer that no harm come to Liliol, but...do what you must, understand?"

The sorcerer nodded. "We're listening at the portals as well, but as far as we can tell, they haven't returned to the Pactlands. Their vehicle—"

"Abandoned?"

"Tracker removed. There's no trace of it."

Inade softly swore. "They've had a week to go to ground—there's no telling where they are now. I need you to *find* her, Jona," he insisted. "Find her associates, her friends, anyone who might have knowledge of her whereabouts. She will have gone somewhere she feels safe. Where does she go when she's not at home?" He sipped his coffee, and his eyes widened as a thought occurred to him. "When did you and Nirene last take the blinding potion?"

Jona squinted at the ceiling. "End of December, I believe."

"Have it redone, both of you. *Today*."

"Yes, sir," he replied, frowning bemusedly. "I have a few meetings scheduled, but—"

"Cancel them. This is crucial." Lowering his voice, he explained, "The girl's a farseer. I'm protected, but if you're not..."

His lieutenant paled. "Last night's shipment. Could she have seen something?"

"I don't know, but we take no chances, understood?"

"Absolutely," said Jona, pushing back from the table. "If you'll excuse me, sir, I need to call Nirene."

Had I not been dealing with the anxiety attributable to the fact that my great-grandfather was trying to have me murdered, I would have thoroughly enjoyed his frustration that week.

Nothing seemed to work. Though Jona and Nirene were now invisible and inaudible to me during their meetings with Inade, I could still see and hear *him*, and half the conversation often provided enough information to let me throw wrenches into his schedule. Aunt Lily destroyed the bug on her property and closed up shop, deciding on an impromptu trip to sunny southern California. When Mr. Eddie was visited by a "concerned friend," he shared only that I'd left town to look in on my cousin, who'd just given birth to premature twins and needed help with the older kids. The imaginary cousin was out west—I'd been vague about that—but coupled with Aunt Lily's flight to Los Angeles, Inade directed the fruitless search for Yven and me to the portals west of the Rockies. And then there were his shipments. Having hastily scrawled notes about the contents of every piece of paper I saw him review, I had ample information to pass to Pateme, who managed to intercept six of the seven inbound deliveries that week.

"I let one slip through to give him a little hope," he explained. "But we have eyes on the delivery vehicle now, and we'll stop it on its next trip across the border."

What's more, the evidence I'd acquired was damning. I'd made drawings memorializing every meeting and conversation, and I'd taken careful notes of the information each encounter provided. As my leads continued to pay off, it was obvious to anyone with a shred of sense that Inade, though distanced from the day-to-day operations, was calling the shots. When I mentioned hearing particular names, Pateme asked me to focus on those people, and my observations added threads to the web of Inade's criminal enterprise.

And from what I'd seen, the three of his children who worked for him in the jewelry store were also involved in his crimes. Though Jomin never joined his father for breakfast at the club, he spent long hours with Inade in his office downtown, the topics of their meetings split between the family businesses. Jomin, in turn, gave orders to Otun and Kilch, each of whom had their own band of lieutenants. I never caught Liventi talking about Inade's dealings with him or their children, but he'd already admitted that she knew about the drug ring, and her silence marked her as a conspirator.

By Sunday evening's call, Pateme was positively gleeful at my offering, but he sobered long enough to ask, "Are you sure you're still safe?"

"Absolutely," I told him. Jona's searches in California and Oregon had turned up no trace of us, and no one in Hitchens seemed bothered by our presence. Having familiarized himself with the town, Yven had twice lured me from the house with the promise of doughnuts, and the clerk at the local bakery had greeted him with, if not warmth, at least familiarity. The locals couldn't quite fathom why we'd come up from Virginia during mud season for art, of all things, but they'd accepted us as a couple of harmless eccentrics and began telling Yven where to buy his lobsters. One of the town matriarchs, a solo force for Hitchens tourism, even stopped by with a basket of local goodies once she learned that we'd be around through April. I'd had better beer, but the maple syrup was unparalleled.

The start of the second week didn't provide me with any hints that Inade had changed his geographic search area, and I continued to trail him to the shop and take notes about his incoming shipments, pleased to watch his paranoia grow. His attempt at discussing a false lead in his office, which he feared was bugged, was painfully obvious, but Pateme sent a team to "intercept" the decoy just to mess with Inade. Confident that he'd found the source of the leaks, he held his next meeting with Jona in the security of the club…and then he raged on Wednesday morning when Jona had to confess that the shipment had been caught just past the portals by a waiting fleet of DOL agents. But while Inade ripped apart his office in the fruitless search for listening devices, I sat back and laughed, as he seemed utterly unaware that the weak point could be himself.

Thursday offered more of the usual, and I'd almost decided to make an early night of it and drive down the coast with Yven to a halfway decent seafood restaurant when I caught Inade in his car, speeding along a stretch of road I didn't recognize. The terrain was more of the usual for the Pactlands, gently rolling grass-covered hills dotted by stumpy trees, and I wondered where he was going until I saw the stone house in the distance.

I shouldn't have recognized the two-story house with the orange tile roof or its smattering of outbuildings, but they'd come from my own brush. I'd left them painted on the inside of my friend Maya's restaurant, a mural vaguely evocative of the Italian countryside. Yven was right—the trees in my version were far too tall when compared to their Pactlands counterparts—but otherwise, I'd accidentally produced a fair impression of Yven's family estate.

What the hell was *Inade* doing there? Ti'Ansha and ti'Cren ran in separate social circles, their only commonality being the fact that both Halls predated the Pact. While Yven's family had land, most of it was useless for growing anything more than grass. Their apple trees were located elsewhere, rented from a plot of agricultural land anchored to the outside world, and though Yven said their cider was well received, it didn't leave them rich.

Invisible, I rode with Inade until he parked in front of the house and disembarked. He scowled as he rang the bell, then stepped back and composed his features into a more neutral expression.

The brown-haired man who answered the door saw who was waiting on the patio and gaped, momentarily speechless. Coughing to disguise his shock, he managed,

"Lord ti'Cren? Good evening, I—"

"Tana ti'Ansha?" Inade interrupted.

The man nodded, and I noticed traces of Yven in his features—the large turquoise eyes, the angular chin, the dimples when he beamed back at Inade. "Yes, sir, that's me," he said, his words almost tripping over themselves as they hurried forth. "How can I help you? And please, come in," he added, stepping back and sweeping the door open.

Inade joined him in the foyer and made a casual survey of the room. If he had thoughts about the apparent lack of domestic staff, he kept them to himself. "You have a son, do you not?"

Tana chuckled as he closed the door. "Several. Our youngest is still just a boy, but we've sent nine others out to make something of themselves...oh, Runat," he called as a woman with Yven's white-blonde hair peeked into the room and gawped, "look who's come! Can we offer you a drink, sir?" he asked, turning back to Inade. "Tea? Or I've just received the first case of this year's cider, and it is *quite* smooth, if I do say so—"

"Thank you, no." Gesturing toward the blonde, he asked, "Runat ti'Comros, yes?"

"Yes," she squeaked, then cleared her throat and tried again. "Yes, sir. To what do we owe the pleasure?"

"Unfortunately," said Inade with a soft sigh, "my news should bring you no pleasure at all." He glanced again around the foyer, then asked, "Might we go somewhere private?"

Tana and Runat led him into a modest parlor and locked the door while Inade made himself comfortable in an armchair. Trading worried glances, the couple perched on the couch opposite him, awaiting the blow.

He didn't sugarcoat it. "Your son Yven works for Plants and Potions, correct?"

They nodded. "Is he hurt?" Runat asked, almost rising from her seat. "He's been so busy at work, we haven't seen him in two months…"

Inade held up a hand to halt her questions. "I'm terribly sorry to tell you this, but…" His mouth tightened, and he took a deep breath as if trying to center himself. "I have it on good information that your son has run away with a human girl."

Yven's parents stared back at him. Tana went slack-jawed, while Runat covered her mouth to muffle her horrified cry.

"I've not come here to unduly pain you," Inade continued. "And let me reassure you—as far as I know, your boy hasn't taken the draught. Yet."

That information seemed to calm the others, but only by a degree.

"I've been in your place. It's absolutely heartbreaking, and if someone had warned me while my son could still have been saved…"

"Thank you," Tana murmured, leaning forward as if he were preparing to launch himself at Inade in a bear hug. "*Thank you*, sir. Do you…can you tell us where he is?"

Inade grimaced. "Last I heard, they're outside the Pactlands. *But*," he added before they could despair, "my wife's brother is your son's boss. Surely Pateme would know where Yven has been. He could give you leads to search."

The couple looked at each other with fear in their eyes. "We don't have portal credentials," said Runat. "We can't just go out there and look for him—"

"Don't give up hope," Inade interjected with a grim smile. "Pateme is a reasonable man. Surely he could spare a few agents to save your boy." He consulted the clock in the corner, then rose. "Surprising him at home might not be the wisest course of action. Perhaps I could accompany you to DPP in the morning. Pateme *has* to see me," he said, dropping his voice to a conspiratorial murmur. "His sister wouldn't let him hear the end of it otherwise."

They thanked him profusely, and Inade took his leave.

I followed him until he headed through the portal back to Kelomb, then withdrew to find Yven sitting with his back to the crackling fire, reading one of the many old Westerns from the den's bookcase. Noticing me move, he put the book aside and smiled. "Anything interesting? Do you want some water?"

I sat up and rubbed my head. "Bad news. Inade just told your folks that you've run off with me."

"*What?*"

"Yeah. They're freaking out."

He groaned and joined me on the saggy couch. "Shit. What did he say?"

"Just that you've fled the Pactlands with a human girl. He pulled the Fradin sympathy card, and they're off to demand answers from Pateme in the morning. Maybe a search party."

"Too bad the director doesn't know where we are, then."

"I know, right?" Leaning against his shoulder, I sighed as he wrapped an arm around me. "Considering your parents' reaction to the news, I don't think I'm going to be invited for dinner anytime soon."

"They're messy affairs, anyway. Fifteen kids, spouses, the grandchildren…"

"I don't want to screw things up for you and your family," I mumbled.

In response, he pulled me closer.

Bright and early Friday morning, I watched in DPP's lobby as Yven's nervous parents huddled together and Inade informed the receptionist that he needed to speak with Pateme—not *the director*, not *Mr. ti'Tam*, but rather a casual drop of his first name as if the two were old chums. Within ten minutes, an escort took them up the elevator to the executive suite on the top floor, then showed them into Pateme's office. Professional as always with his formal robe and neatly trimmed hair, Pateme deployed a masterful poker face as his guests filed in. Gesturing toward his chairs, he said, "Inade, this is a surprise. What brings you here?"

It was all an act—I'd called Pateme late the previous evening to give him a heads-up—but he sold it.

Tana and Runat uneasily took adjacent seats, but Inade remained standing. "I'm sorry to interrupt your morning," he replied, "but I believe one of your agents is in grave danger. A young Regulatory agent, I believe. Have you had any interaction with Yven ti'Ansha?"

"I'm familiar with Agent ti'Ansha's work, yes. What seems to be the trouble?" he asked, leaning against his desk and folding his arms.

"Well," said Inade, "I've received rather...*distressing* information from an associate who knows the boy. Apparently, he's run away with a human."

Pateme frowned. "Who told you such?"

"My sources are my own. But seeing how you failed so badly when my son started down this path, I thought you might appreciate an opportunity to redeem yourself and save these poor people the heartache," he said, sweeping one hand toward the silent couple. "Do you know where the boy might be? His parents are sick with worry."

The tiniest look of triumph flickered in Inade's eyes and revealed itself in the twitch of his mouth.

"Regrettably, I do not," said Pateme, unruffled. "But I'd like to discuss the matter with them. Thank you for bringing them here, Inade," he said with a polite smile. "I'll let you get on with your morning."

"Kind of you, but I think I should stay and hear what you have to say about the boy. Perhaps I could be of use in locating him before he does something tragic—"

"Your concern is commendable," Pateme interrupted, "but I do not make a habit of discussing Pact business in front of the general public. You may go."

Inade stiffened at the dismissal. "Who are you to tell

me—"

"I am the director of this agency," said Pateme, his voice low and glacial, "and unless you would like to make a scene, I suggest you go about your day. I assure you that my security team is quite capable of returning you to your vehicle, should you have difficulty with your escort." A quick gesture opened the door, revealing the sorcerer waiting in the corridor. "Dup, if you'd please show Lord ti'Cren back to the lobby, I'd appreciate it."

Though Inade reddened with anger, he stalked out of the room before Pateme could call for a troll or two. Once his footsteps faded, Pateme manually closed and locked the door, then engaged the privacy spell around the room and pulled up a chair beside his remaining guests. "Let me put your minds at ease," he murmured. "Your son is alive and unharmed. I've spoken to him in the last week, and he sounds perfectly fine."

"Is it true?" Runat asked. "What Lord ti'Cren said about the girl…"

"That's what he called her? 'The girl'?" Leaning closer, he flashed a knowing smirk. "She's Fradin ti'Cren's granddaughter. Her name is Rose."

They regarded him bemusedly, and Tana took the lead. "Lord ti'Cren never said anything about—"

"Of course not. He didn't know she existed until last month, and I'm sure he'd prefer if she dropped off the edge of the world. But whatever Inade has told you, she's absolutely main-line ti'Cren, just unacknowledged."

Their mouths moved in silent *O*s of understanding.

"Rose is very talented," Pateme continued. "Not well trained, mind you, but the raw stuff's there. And she's a farseer. Yven found her on a case last year, and he tried to give her the basics. She's been gracious enough to assist DPP on a few matters." He paused, then added, "Saved your son's life, actually."

Judging by his parents' expressions, Yven hadn't told them the details of our December trip. "*How?* What happened?" Runat demanded. "He said his job is largely behind a desk!"

"Technically, it is, but he's been loaned to Interdiction in recent months," Pateme explained. "Long story short, their group was ambushed by a siren. Rose happened to be wearing earplugs at the time, and she woke Yven from the trance before they could be killed."

His mother's face drained of color. "So it *is* true," she murmured as Tana took her hand. "He's in love…"

Pateme nodded. "There's something real between them, despite my efforts to quash it. She's been adamant with him that he not take the draught, and for now, he's listened to her. I know she's holding out hope for acknowledgement, but…" He barely shrugged. "You've met Inade."

"I don't understand," said Tana. "Fradin ti'Cren took the draught, correct?"

"Yes."

"Then how would his…she's quarter-blooded, right?" He cocked his head in query. "How would his granddaughter have talent at all, let alone a *wild* talent?"

"The draught is not a particularly stable or well-studied potion," said Pateme, settling back in his chair. "Especially not after the second generation, and certainly not in a situation like Rose's. *Two* of her grandparents took it," he said slowly. "Neither of her parents ever exhibited talent, but both were half-blooded. And when they produced Rose…"

"Half-elven and talented," Runat finished.

He offered her a curious little smile. "You would think half, but it's not that simple. The parents were obviously half, and on average, you would anticipate seeing offspring from them with a similar mix, but it could swing either way if she more or less favored certain grandparents. Rose had bloodwork done at Laws in December, and I had the leftover sample analyzed to satisfy my own curiosity."

"And?" asked Runat.

"Ninety percent. She's elven in all but her looks."

Though surprised, I clung to the vision, telling myself I could digest that information later.

"Does Lord ti'Cren know?" Tana asked. "If she's that close, then perhaps—"

"My sister's husband is a proud man," said Pateme, shaking his head. "And her other grandparent's Hall isn't an option, either. It's...a difficult situation all around. But what I know to be true is that she loves your boy, and she knows damn well what the draught would do to him. They haven't run away together. She wouldn't risk his life like that."

I couldn't be certain—he had no way of knowing I was there—but I suspected that Pateme was addressing me.

"Rose is currently somewhere in western Canada," Pateme continued, lying through his teeth. "Not the best time of year for it, but that can't be helped. We're trying to track down a major brewer. Have you heard of Sweet Heat?"

They nodded.

"We think this operation is responsible for about a third of the product on the market. Rose's farsight has led us to targets before, but she works best in relative proximity to her subject. She agreed to go out there, and Yven went along to supervise the operation and keep her safe. He's not missing, he hasn't fled, and he's not carrying the draught. I'm in regular contact with them both. Now, I don't know where Inade came up with that information he gave you," he said, "as we make it a point not to discuss our agents' movements outside the organization in order to protect them and our cases. All I can tell you is that your son is alive and well, and while he may have feelings for Rose, he's far from stupid. I shouldn't have to tell either of you that."

They smiled with more warmth than I'd seen all morning.

"He's a credit to you and to this agency," Pateme

continued, "and we're fortunate to have him. I believe he has a long, promising career ahead. He's worked under both the Regulatory and Interdiction chiefs in the last year, and they speak highly of him."

"But what about Rose?" Runat asked. "Is there any chance of an acknowledgement?"

"That would make everyone's lives easier, but I'm not hopeful." He hesitated—a calculated move, I was sure—then asked, "Will you keep this information within the room? I know you wouldn't want to do anything to endanger Yven"—they vehemently shook their heads—"and the rest is of a somewhat personal nature."

"Of course," said Tana, and his wife nodded her agreement.

Pateme stood and headed for his computer, and after a moment of tapping, he said, "Join me, if you will."

I beat them around the desk and saw what he'd pulled up: a color photo of Yven and me, presumably the product of DPP's security system. Yven was dressed for work, while I was wearing sweats and carrying a bag, so the picture had to have come from one of my late-fall training sessions with Emarae's group in the agency's gym.

"A redhead," Tana remarked. "Like her grandmother, eh? You know, like in the song?"

"No," murmured Runat as Pateme zoomed in on my face. "A redheaded *farseer*..." Her voice drifted off, and she looked to Pateme in silent query.

He nodded. "As I said, her other grandparent's Hall is not an option...nor would I be inclined to try to force an acknowledgement there."

Tana, finally seeing what Runat had noticed, turned to the director with wide eyes. "*Ti'Dana*?" he whispered. "Are you saying she's—"

"She is in an unfortunate position," said Pateme. "But I trust she would not hurt your son." With that, he closed the photo and regarded Yven's stunned parents. "For Yven's sake, I do hope that this matter can remain—"

"Not a word," Runat interjected. "But if Lord ti'Cren asks, what should we tell him?"

He shrugged. "Tell him that Yven's doing fieldwork in service to the Pact and thank him for his concern. Occasionally, I have to remind Inade that he has no right to a detailed accounting of government affairs," he added, and picked up his phone. "I hope I've set your minds at ease. Let me call an escort."

While I did my job and spent the rest of the day tracking Inade, I couldn't get that meeting out of my mind, and I told Yven everything. I don't know what upset him more, that Inade had tried to strong-arm information out of Pateme by using his parents as pawns or that he hadn't been able to introduce me properly, but as we sat together by the dying fire that night, he murmured, "I meant what I said. I'll run with you, Rosie, and if the only option after that is the draught—"

"Don't even think it."

"We should be allowed to be happy. If your grandfathers' Halls and the damn Forum are going to insist that you're not enough, then to hell with them. They have no right—"

"Yven," I interjected as I turned on the couch to face him.

"*No right,*" he repeated, holding my gaze. "And if the director is going to sit there in his office while you do the work the rest of us can't, then say, 'Oh, well, such a pity, maybe someone will throw you scraps if you keep risking your own safety...'" He cupped my face in his palms and shook his head. "That's cruel and unfair. I don't need the Pactlands, and I don't plan to spend the rest of my life hoping that someone deems you worthy."

I stared back at him for a second longer, then pulled free of his gentle grip, darted forward, and kissed him. His breath caught with the surprise, but he quickly recovered and gave himself over to the moment.

The events that immediately followed were a hazy blur of movement. Somehow, as I continued to explore Yven's lips, he broke away to trail kisses down my neck and chest...which were bared in short order, as my shirt ended up tossed to the rug. His joined mine, another marker along the path between the couch and the bedroom, and our pants were discarded in a pile on the threshold. Yven didn't have Pars's linebacker build, but he was strong enough to hoist me, and I wrapped my legs around his waist for the final stretch before we hit the mattress.

As I reached around my back to unhook my bra, I came up for air long enough to tell him, "I'm on the pill."

He pulled away just enough to give me room to maneuver. "The what, now?"

"Birth control."

"Oh, great. So am I—"

I called a time-out with a hand to his chest. "Hang on, *what?*"

"It's a potion. I take it quarterly."

"Seriously?"

"It's the responsible thing to do. And just habit," he assured me. "I'm not involved with anyone else—"

"No, that's not what I meant. Y'all have actual male birth control? Beyond condoms?"

"Yeah..." he said, drawing out the word. "Don't you?"

"You know, we can talk about that later," I replied, and rose up to kiss him again.

When the last of our clothing reached the floor, Yven paused to drink me in as though he were seeing me for the first time—though to be fair, some of the territory was new to him. "Do you have any idea what you do to me?" he murmured, his voice husky with unaccustomed hunger.

I ran my fingers down one side of his face, then whispered, "Take it off. The mask," I clarified as his brow furrowed.

"Are you sure? I don't mind—"

"If this is the time we have, then I want to be with the real you."

With a single gesture, the mask disappeared—his dark eyes lightened to turquoise, his hair bleached to platinum, his cheekbones rose, his ears lengthened, and when he opened his mouth, I caught a glimpse of slightly sharper elven teeth. "Really, Rosie, I don't mind—"

"You don't know how much I want you," I interrupted, and pulled him down on top of me.

CHAPTER 17

On a cold, clear May morning thirty-nine days after our arrival in Hitchens, I lay on the couch in the predawn twilight and watched as Inade's world collapsed around him.

The coordinated strike, carried out by hand-selected agents from DOL and DPP, was codenamed Operation Midas. Pateme told me that many of those involved missed the reference, but he wasn't bothered. I'd come up with the name as an offhand joke, and apparently, enough people attached to Floodtide liked it to make the moniker stick.

By then, I wondered if the strike didn't come as a relief to Inade. At least eighty percent of his shipments had been seized over the last month, and teams had arrested three of his major brewers outside the Pactlands within the previous week. He was hemorrhaging in a dozen places and couldn't find the cause, and his mood had shifted from angry to paranoid, and then desperate. He'd limited his interactions to Jona, Nirene, and his three accomplice children, all of whom were unfailingly loyal, but the hits kept coming. He tore apart his store and home offices looking for bugs and bought new clothing in case something had been magically attached to one of his usual robes. He even eschewed his beloved club in the end, perhaps suspecting a waiter of listening in. Nothing helped. I didn't know if Inade was merely ignorant of the critical flaw in his blinding protection or if he knew but felt unduly confident that someone like me couldn't break through, but he never seemed to realize that the security breaches stemmed from a common point.

Pateme and I had planned the strike in detail for three days before it was executed. I knew Inade's schedule well enough to allow the agents to catch him at home, and while I couldn't directly follow his top lieutenants, I'd given Pateme sufficient information to have them tailed. Thus, when the arresting teams marched into seventeen homes and one unfortunate strip club at four-thirty that Tuesday morning, none of their targets slipped the net—or so Pateme said later. I had eyes only for Inade, who was awakened from sleep by a frightened servant and threw on his dressing gown to find five agents waiting in the corridor. I smiled to see among them Enva Orafer, the detective who headed the DOL team that liaised with DPP, and Gentle Breeze, who pinned Inade against the wall with one hand while he was cuffed and given an injection of the potion that would dampen his talent. The effect was only temporary—I'd seen it used on arrested suspects over the previous year—but it would prevent Inade from shaking off his restraints with magic. Once dosed, he was no match for Gentle Breeze, and the troll seemed to have left her kid gloves at home that morning as she manhandled him out of the mansion.

Within minutes of their arrival, the agents had loaded Inade, Liventi, Jomin, Otun, and Kilch into a transport van. I broke away briefly, then shifted my focus to Teolm and returned so that I could observe in the foyer as the servants and the rest of the family and spouses milled around, shocked and trying to process what had just transpired. Dania clung to her baby and railed against her poor, innocent Jomin's abuse, while Meala, Kilch's wife, stood blinking in a corner, muttering that she needed to call her principal and find a substitute. Mafora just leaned against the wall, shoulders slumped, refusing all suggestions that she sit down.

When Teolm walked away and locked himself in a

sitting room, I followed and watched as he pulled out his phone. "Good morning, Lily," he murmured, running one hand through his dark, bed-mussed hair. "Sorry to bother you so early, but, uh...Father and Mother were just removed from the house by armed agents, and I thought you might want to know." He paused, then said, "No, I don't know why. Have you spoken to Pateme lately? Maybe he—"

He fell silent for a long moment, and while I couldn't hear Aunt Lily's end of the conversation, I watched Teolm's eyes widen. "I'm sorry, wait," he finally interjected, "why would he try to have someone kill that painter? She—" Aunt Lily must have cut him off again, as Teolm was practically goggling ten seconds later when he got a word in. "Why didn't you tell me Fradin had a granddaughter?" he cried. "I would have...oh, that poor girl..." The phone squawked unintelligibly, and Teolm's jaw dropped. "She's a *what?*"

With that, I let my inner eyes close and returned to myself. Sighing, I sat up and found Yven waiting nearby, having stoked the fire and, by the smell of it, put a pan of biscuits in the oven. "And?" he asked. "Success?"

I smiled. "They got him. They actually cuffed Inade."

He stooped to kiss me, then lingered there with his eyes closed and his hand caressing my cheek. "I don't have to go back there today," he murmured.

"No," I concurred, and met his lips again. "They have far too much paperwork already. Better not add to the mess."

"They could be busy for some time."

"Maybe." I looked up at his true face—after our extended stay, he'd grown comfortable leaving the mask off at home, as we almost never saw another soul around our house—and partially rose from the couch to kiss him once more. "But whatever happens, we go together, got it? If they want one of us, they get both. If they kick me out, then they'll have to look at me when they do it. And this time, I *won't* go quietly."

Yven finally took a seat beside me and squeezed my hand. "They'll need you for the trial at some point. DOL wouldn't have moved on Inade without sufficient evidence, so we can assume this will go before a tribunal."

"How long will that take, do you suppose?"

He squinted at the ceiling as he considered the question. "Our laws demand speedy trials unless there's a massive need to slow things down, so assuming DOL already has its case mapped…a month, perhaps."

"That soon? I figured we'd have six months, at least…"

"Not unless something goes horribly wrong. Of course, seeing how witnesses against Silver have an unfortunate habit of dying in custody…" He grimaced. "Could be longer. But one thing's absolutely certain: you don't go back until your safety is guaranteed." The oven beeped, and as he jumped up to extract breakfast, he added, "Let's take the day, Rosie. You know you've earned it."

By early May, the last of the coastal snow had vanished, and we'd enjoyed enough dry days that week to make the mud more of an annoyance than a hazard. I had no desire to test the frigid Atlantic, but the sun rose to a cloudless sky, and the air quickly warmed into the low fifties. After breakfast, we threw on jackets against the wind and walked the beach for a time, sifting through the detritus for shells and sea glass as the birds swooped and dove for fish. We returned to the house with wind-pinked cheeks and pockets full of trifles plucked from the water's edge, and I filled the kitchen sink with soapy water to soak off the brine.

As I was carefully rinsing a small sand dollar, my phone began to ring, and Yven put the call on speaker. "She's right here, sir," he said, placing the phone out of my splash radius. "Any problems?"

"*Flawless*," said Pateme. "We grabbed every target. *All* of them," he stressed, sounding far too giddy for the director I'd come to know. "Neutralized, knocked out, and still being processed. The media have heard rumors, and they're salivating."

Once the story leaked, Hall ti'Cren's reputation would take a nosedive, and they weren't the only ones. "Have you talked to your mother?" I asked.

"Briefly," he said, sobering. "I told her Liventi's safe and that she made her own choices, and it's my job to follow the law. Mother's not happy, but she doesn't get a vote in this matter."

"*Is* Liventi safe?" I pressed, thinking of the ways in which a stay at DPP or DOL could go wrong.

"Barring the physical collapse of the Pactlands, I would say so. Kabno is taking no chances."

Kabno Erenani, the director of DOL, was a gnome who stood only a hair above three feet on a tall day, yet somehow, even the trolls within the organization had a healthy fear of her. I had no desire to see what her bad side looked like.

"She's hand-picked the guards," Pateme continued, "and she's using *particularly* secure cells."

"Better than the holding cells they used for Kritsa's group, I hope..." While those had seemed secure, most of the occupants had been murdered by a rogue guard, presumably one of the agency's employees on Silver's payroll.

"Oh, she's been busy," he replied, and chuckled. "If anyone breaks in without disarming the alarms—which can only be accomplished by authorized personnel—then incendiary devices within the cell walls will go off. Once Inade is permitted to wake, his guards will explain the situation. Unless he wants to roast alive, he'll need to be a good boy for Kabno."

"Heartbreaking, I'm sure."

"I'm devastated, truly," he deadpanned. "But even with Inade locked up, this place isn't safe for you yet. I need you to continue hiding elsewhere for the time being. Is that feasible? Do you need funds?"

I turned to Yven in time to catch his flash of relief. "We'll be fine," I assured Pateme, grinning at Yven. "Just let us know what you want us to do."

"For now, stay alive. I'll call once I have news. And Rose?"

"Sir?"

"Thank you," he said, and hung up.

As Yven returned my phone to my purse, I considered the shells remaining in the sink, then asked, "You want to do something crazy?"

"Like what?" he replied, coming up behind me to kiss my neck.

"It can't be more than a couple hours to Bangor. Want to go get dinner at a real restaurant?"

"Perhaps," said Yven, moving to the side to flash a teasing smirk. "You won't abandon me to stalk Inade halfway through the meal?"

"Oh, I think he's got enough eyes on him for now," I said, and scooped up a handful of shells to rinse. "We've earned some fun."

The month that followed was the closest Yven and I had come to just being a couple. Part of me had worried that once I wasn't following targets for fourteen hours a day—once we were actually spending quality time together in the remote cottage, watching northern New England warm up—we'd start to annoy each other, but aside from the odd bit of negotiation concerning the lone television in the house, we got on as though our three-month long-distance period had never transpired. We took walks and told each other embarrassing stories from our childhoods, tried new recipes and smoked up the kitchen, sat on an old stone wall near Hitchens's tiny harbor and watched the fishing boats come in.

But we didn't dare to plan for anything past the trial. Our extended stay in Maine was like a cross between a witness protection program and adult summer camp, and once the trial arrived…what then? Even if my work pulled Inade off the street, would that be enough to allow me to stay in the Pactlands? Legally, I had no right to be there— I'd been brought in either through off-the-books government arrangements or by subterfuge. Would the tribunal that considered Inade's case make an exception for me? Would this be the sort of mess that the Forum needed to consider? And even if I obtained some version of "resident alien" status, wouldn't I still be off-limits to Yven?

We tried not to talk about the what-ifs ahead, as neither of us wanted to spoil the time we had together. He'd promised me he wouldn't take the draught behind my back, and I reminded him of what Pateme had uncovered—since I was elven in all but appearance, we had a *long* time to figure out a way around the problem of my unacknowledged status. I knew he fretted that I'd be thrown out again and Pateme would find some reason to keep him chained to his desk, but there was nothing we could do about that other than ignore the problem and enjoy each other while we could. And since those days might be the last long stretch of time that we'd have together, we made the best of them.

That's not to say we ran wild, of course. Even with Inade, Jona, and Nirene locked away, I had no doubt that messages could slip out of the DPP building, and Yven and I kept a low profile in public. But to my great relief— I'd actually grown fond of the cottage—no one ever came for us. Our neighbors remained pleasant but distant, and if anything worse than the odd bout of public intoxication happened in Hitchens, I missed it.

Two days after the arrests, Pateme called with an update. The first of the trials had been set for early June— Inade's, in fact, as DOL's counsel had pressed to bring his case first. "Kabno has brought in two of her best as Pact counsel," he informed us. "Remari Houn and Cennis Paf.

Not a team I'd want to face, were I called to account for myself."

And judging by their names, neither was an elf, I noted. Kabno was no fool.

"Rose, you'll be called to testify, as so much of the last month's evidence came from your tips," Pateme continued. "Proven farseers can offer evidence of their visions. Your notes, drawings, memories, whatever you have can be presented. I'll let counsel discuss the specifics with you—I've passed on your number, so expect them to reach out in the next few days."

They did just that, *repeatedly*. Remari, per Yven, was a seasoned counselor as well as a descendant of one of the sorcerers who had built the Pactlands. She sounded middle-aged on the phone, which told me she was probably closing in on two hundred years old. While she was the stickler of the two, walking me in painful detail through everything I'd logged about Inade's activities, Cennis was warm and reassuring in our conversations. When I told Yven as much, however, he laughed—Cennis was a centaur, blonde and built like a Valkyrie, and had a reputation for making hostile witnesses cry. But she remained kind as she explained the trial process to me or gave me updates about their progress, and it was Cennis who called me on June 5 to announce that the time had come for me to return to the Pactlands.

"We'll begin on Monday morning," she said. "Since you'll be among our first witnesses, we'll need to have you here on Sunday evening to go through your testimony. Is that doable?"

"Of course," I replied, taking notes. "We could come sooner—"

"No, this will be a heavily orchestrated event. We're coordinating with the portal attendants to ensure that the queue is clear when you come through, and we'll have an escort waiting to take you straight to the office. Let's not take chances, eh?"

My pencil scratched across the paper as I hastily jotted that down. "Do you really think there's a risk at the portal?"

"I don't know," she replied, "but considering the number of attendants we've uncovered on Silver's payroll, we're playing this safe. I'll be in touch with your arrival time on Sunday morning." She paused to clear her throat. "I don't suppose you own a formal robe, do you?"

"Nothing even close, and most of my clothes here are casual—"

"Well, don't worry, we'll make do," said Cennis. "I'm sure we can borrow *something* appropriate. Oh, and tell your agent not to fret," she added. "The agent he listed as an emergency contact went to his apartment last night and found appropriate tribunal attire for him. He delivered it to us this morning."

I grinned. "Pars Mera?"

"Didn't catch his name. Big fellow, sparkly nail polish?"

"That's him." I wondered which of his daughters had insisted on giving him a manicure.

Cennis's assurances aside, I felt awkward about rolling up for a trial in leggings and an oversized sweater. Thus, we vacated our rental cabin a day early, said goodbye to Hitchens on Saturday morning, and made the four-hour trek south to Portland, which offered a decent mall. I promised Yven I'd be quick about it, but he was a good sport as I sorted through the racks at Macy's, and he eventually pulled up a chair outside the dressing rooms to critique my selections. After an hour and a bit of agonizing, I settled on a fitted charcoal pantsuit with an eggplant shell, then took the party to the shoe department to look for something quasi-professional. I found peep-toe pumps that gave me an extra inch in height—just enough to let me get away with not tailoring my new suit—and as I looked around for Yven, I spotted him considering a display atop one of the jewelry cases. "These would match, wouldn't they?" he asked, pointing to small silver hoops set with amethysts. "The shirt for your suit, I mean."

"They're pretty," I quietly replied, "but I was thinking of masking my earlobes." Having learned that pierced ears were only popular in the Pactlands among male fauns, I didn't want to scandalize the tribunal.

"You don't need to do that," Yven murmured. "You *shouldn't*. And you're right, they're pretty," he said, plucking a pair from the rack and holding them up to my ear.

"I don't want to make things difficult for Remari and Cennis…"

"You won't," he said, then kissed me. "And you have nothing to hide, Rosie."

I left the mall with those earrings tucked into my purse for safekeeping and Yven's fingers laced through mine.

We spent the night at a Hampton Inn outside the city center, quite a change after our two-month stay in the rental house. Back in the land of Interstates and necessary traffic lights, we found a pizzeria downtown and relaxed with local beer and garlic knots, then returned to our room to try to sleep. Curling up with Yven in the king-sized bed, tucking myself more tightly against him as he held me, I closed my eyes and tried not to think about the following night. We wouldn't be able to safely share a room in Beukal, much less a bed, and though I didn't want to sleep alone again, I wouldn't have a choice in the matter. From that point forward, Yven and I would need to keep our relationship a secret, as no matter how much I loved spooning with him, I preferred keeping him off of DOL's radar and away from the draught.

The last thing I remember before drifting off was his voice in my ear: "We'll find a way."

Shortly before six the following evening, and after a quick call to Pateme to figure out precisely where the New Hampshire portal was hidden, Yven drove down a rutted path through a thick forest of maples and pines. A boulder the size of a minivan seemed to mark the end of the trail, but Yven rammed it at twenty miles an hour and passed straight through—a useful bit of magic, albeit one that left me clutching the car door, bracing for impact. About fifty yards past the boulder was a grassy clearing, and there, Yven stopped, unmasked, and tapped a button on the Jeep's console.

A man responded in calm Pactish: "Name and location, please."

"Yven ti'Ansha," he replied. "Conway."

"Thank you," said the attendant. "The portal will open in two minutes. Prepare to stop for processing once you're across, and please have your identification ready."

Right on schedule, the portal opened directly in front of our vehicle, and we slowly drove through as a frightened doe bounded away. Yven pulled up to the booth for inspection, and the attendant leaned down to look at us. "Identification?" he asked.

Yven flashed his DPP badge, while I held up my driver's license and smiled hopefully.

The attendant nodded and stepped back. "Your escort is waiting outside the building. Maintain speed behind them, and the rest will fall in place. I've been asked to remind you to proceed directly to DOL."

"Understood," said Yven, and started forward as the wooden arm rose.

As we left the portal building, I saw three black Jeeps like ours pull out ahead of us and flash their headlights twice. Within ten seconds, another three had joined the pack, and the vehicles configured themselves into a tight formation around us while we sped through the city. The other Jeeps were equipped with strobing yellow lights, and the lead SUV turned on a siren, giving us a clear path downtown to the massive glass DOL tower. Once on the premises, we drove into the parking garage, where a squadron of agents waited. Some carried guns, but considering the percentage of sorcerers and elves in their company, the weapons seemed like an afterthought.

We pulled into a space and disembarked, but before I could grab more than my purse and the bag with my sketchpads, a familiar voice said, "Leave the rest of your things, Ms. Thorn. They'll be carried up for you."

Turning, I found Liogh Birrid standing in front of the security detail. The detective's black tactical clothing hung from their willowy form, and their pale green face shifted into a sly smile. "Don't tell me the hidden compartment is loaded down, eh?" they added.

I grinned at the nymph, and Yven's head bobbed in greeting as he joined us. "Just camping gear," I replied. "Shouldn't take more than two people to empty it."

They winced. "Oh, you haven't been *camping* all this time…"

"Far from it." I surprised Liogh with a brief hug, and they patted my back before we parted. "Good to see you again. How's Enva?"

"Resting for trial. Come, let's get you to counsel," they added, their blue braid swinging as they turned on their heel.

Our security detail rode with us in the elevator up twenty-three flights, and we stepped out into a corridor with abstract paintings and office carpet. Around a corner, down the hall, and past another quartet of agents, we paused in front of a door labeled as a conference room, and Liogh rapped twice. It opened to an agent who gave Yven and me a once-over, then beckoned us inside.

The waiting counselors smiled and stood, and I took in the scene: too many chairs for the people on hand, a scuffed wooden podium, a long table strewn with piles of paper, and a large coffeepot warming a dark brew on the sidebar. Remari, who wore her brown hair bobbed and streaked with gray, had chosen a ratty tunic and jeans for the evening's work, while Cennis—who did, in fact, look like she could work a breastplate and winged helmet—had opted for a long-sleeved T-shirt with the DOL logo on the front. Her blonde hair continued below the waist. While the few centaurs I'd met tended to eschew clothing on their lower halves, she'd donned hot pink leg warmers, and she made herself comfortable on a giant cushion on casters.

To my surprise, Pateme rounded out their number, and he nodded as Liogh closed the door behind us. "Welcome back. Uneventful drive, I hope."

"No complaints, sir," said Yven. "Are you, uh…"

"I'm not trying this case, if that's what you're asking," he replied with a smirk. "Assistance, if needed. I didn't want to abandon you to counsel."

Cennis snorted and motioned us closer to the table. "So nice to finally meet you two in person. Come on, pull up. We don't bite."

I was less unnerved by the counselors than by the evident fact that Pateme owned sweats. "Brought the originals," I said, hoisting my bag onto a clean spot. "And my notes. How do you want to do this?"

Remari tapped her computer, and a photo of one of my sketches from Pennsylvania flashed on a wall screen. "I thought we'd take them in order," she said. "The tribunal may want your originals, and we should tag them tonight for admission, but for walkthrough purposes, this will work." She rose and moved around the table, putting herself in my line of sight beside the screen. "What I'm going to do with you is a practice run of your testimony. We'll take this slowly, just to make sure you're comfortable and have your facts straight. When I finish, Cennis will take over with a cross-examination. If you don't know the answer to a question, say so—*please* don't try to make anything up."

Seeing Cennis flinch, I said, "I wasn't planning on lying…"

"Oh, no, I wasn't suggesting that," Remari hastily assured me. "You've not been under oath here, correct?"

I shook my head.

"There's a spell involved," she explained. "If you testify to things you believe to be truthful, then you have nothing to worry about. Even if you're wrong, if you *believe* it's the truth, then there's no problem. But if you knowingly lie, you'll experience discomfort—"

"It's usually a burning sensation in your hands," added Cennis, "but it can vary."

"Right. The longer the lie goes unremedied, the worse the pain becomes. Just be aware."

With that little delight looming over Monday's plans, I got to work with Remari, gradually relaxing as I acclimated to her questioning. Occasionally, Cennis or Pateme would interject with a suggestion, and I did my best to tailor my answers to the queries posed, giving Remari the information she wanted without babbling. "You're doing well," she insisted when we took a coffee break. "First-time nerves are common. Keep breathing, and if you start to look sick, I'll ask for a recess."

Around nine, Remari had questioned me to her satisfaction, and Cennis, who'd been cataloguing my stack of drawings, took her turn. "Don't be alarmed if this seems a little tough," she said with a grin. "We like to go hard in here so that the real thing will be easier by comparison."

She wasn't kidding. Her demeanor shifted in an instant as she slipped into her adversarial role, and she prodded at every facet of my previous testimony, looking for inconsistencies and challenging my visions. Perhaps I only *thought* I'd seen Inade. Perhaps I'd seen false visions—had I considered that? Or perhaps I had a motive for testifying against him.

"I doubt that defense counsel will bring up your ancestry," Cennis told me, "since it's safe to say their client doesn't want that coming out. But in case they go this route, we need to know how you would answer these questions, all right?"

So I told them the truth. I'd grown up with no family

but my parents and my great-aunt, and only the year before had I learned about my grandfathers. "Of course it hurts," I said in answer to one of Cennis's questions. "You like to think that your family would want you. Lord ti'Cren only came to me because he needed help, not because he wanted to get to know me. When he brought me over, he asked me to pretend to be someone else so that word of my existence wouldn't spread. I was just a tool, not a member of the family. So no, I'm not going to sit here and say that rejection doesn't sting," I continued, locking eyes with Pateme, "but I didn't go into this trying to frame the defendant. Director ti'Tam asked me to look for Silver— no suspected name, no possible photographs. That my farsight led me to Lord ti'Cren is unfortunate for him, but I didn't set out to ruin his life."

"If he had acknowledged you, would you be testifying here today?" Cennis asked.

I gave the question a moment's thought, then said, "Yes. I've seen firsthand what the defendant has done. I'm sure I'd feel conflicted, but acknowledgement wouldn't have bought my silence."

She wrapped up quickly after that, and Remari called another stop for caffeine. "I'll make a fresh pot of coffee," she offered, "and then we can look through your originals one more time to be sure they're in the correct order. After that, if you want to get some rest—"

A sharp knock at the door interrupted her, and she frowned as she crossed the room. "Yes?" she asked, opening the door, then glanced down, stiffened, and retreated a step. "Good evening, ma'am. What's…"

I recognized the DOL director when she walked in. Kabno was white-haired but childlike in her proportions, a youthful woman over three hundred years old. While she hadn't dressed quite as sloppily as her counsel had, she'd left her robe at home that night. "I'm sorry to interrupt, ladies," she began, and nodded to her DPP counterpart. "Pateme."

"Kabno," he replied, going to his feet. "Come to supervise the practice session?"

"Not exactly. I've brought guests."

She moved aside, and two men and two women in formal robes followed her into the conference room. The white-haired woman with the satchel on one shoulder and the bald man were evidently sorcerers, judging by their aged appearance. The other woman was a black-haired elf whose age was impossible for me to guess—she could have been my peer or as old as the sorcerers. The remaining man was another elf, almost as tall as Yven and of slim build. To me, his face suggested early thirties, which would have told me he was *quite* a bit older than that, even without the look of heaviness in his gray eyes. He wore his coppery hair long and loose over his shoulders, and he absently tucked a strand behind one ear as he surveyed our group.

From behind me, I heard Pateme ask, "Diriem? What brings you over here so late?"

CHAPTER 18

Diriem.

My gut clenched.

The redheaded man was my great-grandfather. The one who'd walked away from my mom once his son died, who had to have known of my existence but had never reached out.

At least Inade had the decency to look at me. Diriem was looking everywhere but in my direction.

"Thought I'd try to prevent disaster," he replied in soft Pactish, then turned to the counselors. "I have it on good information that you're planning to go to trial with an uncertified farseer."

Remari took the lead. "With all due respect, sir, her record speaks for itself. Her findings have been thoroughly corroborated—"

"I don't doubt that," he said, "but if you present her as your witness, defense counsel will eat you alive. Inade has hired an excellent legal team."

"I understand, but we only just got her out of hiding tonight. There hasn't been time for any sort of certification. If we explain that…"

He slowly blinked as her voice faded out. "Your judge is an old friend, but even I would be hard-pressed to convince him to accept uncertified testimony."

"Then what do we do?" Cennis asked. "Trial begins in the morning, and we're out of time."

"Which is precisely why I brought witnesses with me," said Diriem, nodding to his colleagues. "We can test her now."

I stiffened and tried to keep my face impassive as he finally turned to me, his expression unreadable. But he held my gaze as he neared, then paused perhaps two feet away and considered me in silence.

I took a deep breath, willing myself not to make a scene. "Lord ti'Dana."

One corner of his mouth twitched, and to my surprise, I realized that he, too, was struggling to maintain his façade of calm. It cracked then, ever so slightly, into a brief but warm smile as he murmured, "Hello, Rose Lea."

I froze. Only one person ever called me that.

My anonymous pen pal.

Yes, I'd flirted with the notion that Diriem might secretly have been writing to me, but I'd never truly *believed* it...and yet...

"You?" I whispered.

He nodded. "I told you in my last letter that I hoped I could put your mind at ease. Bear with me a little longer, won't you?"

My confusing upswelling of emotions left me grasping for words, but I managed, "Uh...sure."

"Thank you. Sit, please."

I collapsed into the nearest chair, and he pulled another up, facing me as he sat. "This should not be a painful process," he said. "Nor, I believe, will it be particularly challenging to you."

"All right," I mumbled, and swallowed hard.

"I left something in the corridor. Tell me what it is."

Nerves made me turn to the table, frantically looking for one of my familiar sketchpads, but I pulled myself together and closed my eyes. I'd been trailing Inade for more than a month straight—I could trigger my farsight without doodling my way down.

Choosing a focus was simple. I'd memorized Yven's face, his scent, the timbre of his voice, and within seconds, my inner eyes opened to find him standing awkwardly a few chairs away from me. His expression suggested that he didn't know what protocol dictated, and so, denied instructions, he remained on his feet. Glancing past him, I saw that Pateme had found his chair, and a Kabno-shaped white blob had hopped onto another while I was distracted. When I turned, I saw myself sitting in front of a blotch that resolved itself into Diriem with a bit of focus. He barely moved, but he leaned forward as if anticipating a revelation from my lips.

Passing the rest of the DOI delegation, all of them protected from my eyes, I slipped out the door and into the hall. The agents guarding us were insensate to my presence, and so no one stopped me when I squatted beside the wooden box tucked up against the baseboard. It was dark in color, maybe oak or maple, and about the size of a shoebox. Its lid was on hinges against one of the long sides, and Diriem had left it open for me.

"There's a box," I mumbled, remembering that the vocal cords in my distant body needed to engage if I wanted to be understood. "Wood. It's not very big. Looks like there's a keyhole, but I don't see a key anywhere."

The small part of me that was still conscious of my body's sensations picked up on auditory stimuli—Diriem's low voice. "Is there something in the box?"

"Yes," I said as I peered closer. I couldn't touch anything in my incorporeal form, but I could make out details as well as ever. "A red rosebud. It looks preserved—crinkly, not as vibrant as a fresh flower would be. And there's a letter, it looks like. Sealed."

"Can you describe the seal?"

"Yeah. A quatrefoil," I replied, using the familiar term instead of searching for its Pactish equivalent. "The rings are fully drawn and interlocking, and one of the areas of overlap appears to be shaded…or however you render that with a seal. Raised, I guess. If you inked the seal, that segment would pick it up."

"I understand," said Diriem. "The letter, is it

addressed?"

I had to get within inches of the box to make out the tiny, faint writing just above the seal: *To Rose, From Caradin.*

"It's for me," I reported. "From my granddad."

Suddenly recalling who was with me, I worried that Diriem would be upset by my familiarity with his son, but he didn't sound angry when he spoke. "Do you see anything else?"

"The box is lined in dark green velvet, I think…and that's all I see. The box, the flower, and the letter."

"You may return now."

I broke my focus and opened my real eyes to find Diriem watching me with a small, secret smile. "How was that?" I asked.

"Well, I can't say. I've never looked inside the box, and Fenna was kind enough to arrange it for me tonight," he replied, gesturing toward the female sorcerer, who held up the missing brass key, "but let's see how you fared. Fenna, would you do the honors?"

She stepped out and quickly returned with the box, which she passed to Diriem. Carefully, he placed the dried rosebud on the table, then examined the letter for himself. "This was my son's personal seal," he said, and passed the letter to me. "Go ahead. It's for you."

I looked at him uncertainly as I took the letter, but he nodded reassurance, and I carefully separated the wax from the lower flap. Unfolding the paper, I found two sheets covered in neat Elvish characters:

Dear Rosie,

I'm writing this to you on April 29, 1970. My dad will visit tomorrow, and I want him to have this before I go. I still don't know the date of my death, but I can feel it drawing near, and there are certain matters that must be addressed before the time comes.

If you're reading this, then it's safe to tell you what I couldn't say on the recordings I've been making. By now, I assume you've heard of Project Floodtide. I'm involved, as is Dad. As all evidence points to Inade ti'Cren as Silver, we're well aware of how dangerous he can be. It's because of him that Dad will need to walk away from Joss and stay out of your life...until your now, I suppose. (This gulf of time between us has never become easier to linguistically navigate, I'm afraid.)

I've told you about how future-oriented farseers can see visions of possibilities, and it's our responsibility to choose the path of least harm. Even before I met your grandmother, I saw two ways in which the future might play out. If Dad continued to visit Joss after my death, then Inade would learn of it, become curious, and discover Joss and Henry. If that happened, he would kill your parents, in part to end Fradin's line but also because their marriage will be (well, is) the first joining of our Halls, and the rules we've long had in place to prevent families from intermarrying too frequently would stop a "legitimate" main-line ti'Cren–ti'Dana union for at least a generation. (It's a concern—two notorious Halls died out before my time because they almost exclusively married each other, and things weren't pretty by the end. Think of the Habsburgs.) The alternative was the future you've lived. We looked at every possible permutation, Rosie. Several farseers at DOI are involved in Floodtide as well, and they tried to help us find a path forward that didn't end in either abandonment or murder. Unfortunately, there were no good options.

I know the silence has hurt you, little girl, and I wish we'd found a better way. But please, please understand that we did what we did to protect your parents and you.

And now, if my visions were true, you're being asked to speak against Inade. I don't pretend to know how you feel about this—whatever else the man is, he's your blood—but I hope the extent of his crimes has been made clear to you. I wish I could be there for moral support, but I suppose this letter will have to suffice.

And about this letter: before you can give effective

testimony as a farseer, you need to be certified. DOI handles it, and the requirements vary for future- and past-oriented candidates. Given your unique orientation, Dad and I discussed how you could be properly tested, and we came up with this. I bought the box at an antique shop in Charlottesville, and I'll lock it before giving it to Dad tomorrow. He doesn't know what I'm putting inside, and he's promised that he'll keep it intact and secure until it's time to test you.

Whatever happens next, Rosie, I am so proud of you. I love Grace and Joss more than pen can tell, and though you and I will never cross paths in life, I've loved you since I first saw you. My darling girl, I wish you every joy.

Granddad

One last thing—while it is never wise to give someone her future, let me just casually mention that I like that agent of yours, and we'll leave it at that.

My eyes were watering by the time I'd read the letter twice. Folding it neatly back together, I handed it to Diriem and asked, "Do you want to see what he said?"

He opened the letter and scanned the pages, reading in silence while I sniffled and tried to swallow the lump in my throat. When he looked up at me again, I noticed the sheen in his eyes. "That's my son's hand. And no, I never opened the box. Not until tonight."

"Is what he wrote true?"

"Every word," Diriem murmured, then cleared his throat and looked at the rest of the DOI delegation. "I believe she's proven her ability. Does anyone disagree?"

The others shook their heads, and Fenna reached into her satchel to extract a slim computer. "I'll need a moment for the paperwork," she explained, smiling at me, and settled in at the cluttered table.

"So…our farseer is certified, then?" Remari ventured.

"She will be," said Fenna, "once I put her in the registry. Hmm…we've never had one with present orientation…"

The female elf peered over her shoulder, and the two of them quickly worked out the kinks in their system. Satisfied, Fenna glanced up and asked, "Birthdate?"

"March 16, 1993," I replied.

Her thin eyebrows rose, but she kept her thoughts about my age to herself. "All right, now we need your full name…" Turning to Diriem, she said, "I don't mean to ask an insensitive question, sir, but she *is* partly elven, isn't she? Does she have a Hall?"

Before I could answer her, Diriem looked at me with a hopeful smile. "Ti'Dana. If you'll have us, that is."

I stared at him for a few seconds, at a loss for words, then managed to nod. As my tears finally began to spill, he pulled a handkerchief from his pocket and pressed it into my hand. "None of that, now, or I'll start, too," he teased, smiling as I chuckled and dabbed at my eyes. "And I'm an *ugly* crier."

I pulled myself together as Fenna finished, then braced myself and cautiously asked, "So, uh…does this mean I'm, um…acknowledged?"

Diriem slid his chair closer to mine and took my hands. "As far as I'm concerned, little one, you have always *been* acknowledged ti'Dana. I couldn't tell you before now, but—"

His seat rocked as I jumped up and threw my arms around him, and he laughed with surprise and squeezed me back. "I'm so sorry it's taken this long, Rosie," he murmured in my ear. "If you'll give me a chance, I'll try to make matters right."

My face was wet again when I released him, and so was his. With a gesture, he produced another handkerchief from thin air and dried his eyes, then stood, collected himself, and turned to Yven, who was still lurking down the table as if awaiting a bomb. "So," said Diriem, folding his arms, "you're the man my great-granddaughter loves."

Yven swallowed hard. "Yes, sir."

"Mm. Well," he replied, smiling again, "if she'll have you, then you'll hear no complaint from me. Now, more pressingly," he continued, pivoting to Kabno as Yven gaped, "where did you intend to house them this evening? I assume trial preparation will end at some point before dawn."

Kabno turned to the counselors, and Remari raised her hands as if warding off her director's reproach. "We've basically finished, ma'am. The security detail was going to put their belongings in one of our storage closets, and the lounge on our floor has a couple of decent couches—"

"And you were planning to go home, then?" Diriem asked her.

She nodded. "Just for a few hours, sir."

"Our analysts suggest that would be particularly unwise. Kabno, could you send a team to counsel's homes to retrieve their clothing?"

"Not a problem," said the director. "We do have emergency cots here."

"And an angry, desperate man in your basement. Perhaps your people could be convinced to accept DOI's hospitality for the night," he said. "And for the duration of the trial, naturally. You won't find more secure apartments in the city."

Kabno and Pateme agreed, and so the counselors, Yven, and I were hustled into a nondescript gray van in DOL's deck—one with the back two rows removed, giving Cennis room to sit in relative comfort. As a quartet of agents helped schlep our luggage into the vehicle, I peered out the open door, still somewhat stunned and disoriented. The DOI crew had disappeared in the rush to pack and move out, and when the rear doors slammed without so much as a glimpse of Diriem, I gave up and buckled in for the ride.

The DOL agent who chauffeured us half a mile

through the capital apparently learned to drive by watching NASCAR, but we arrived at the fortified structure without incident. Unlike the DOL tower with its soaring glass walls, DOI was housed in a windowless stone building that rose a mere ten stories over the street. The protective spells surrounding the complex stopped our van until a guard on the gate gave us passage, and another set of spells blocked access to the stairwell and elevators from the deck. By the time Yven and I had assembled our gear and the counselors had loaded up their bags of trial materials, an assistant had come down to collect us, and she smiled politely as we loaded into the larger of the elevators. "Welcome to the Division of Intelligence," she said as she flashed a bracelet at the elevator console and tapped the button for the ninth floor. "I'm Keyne Benanae. First time?"

"*Oh*, yeah," I mumbled.

She chuckled and gave my arm a quick pat, and it was only then, beneath the elevator lights, that I realized she was a nymph. Unlike Liogh, she could almost have passed for human with her light brown skin and short black hair—*almost*, as nymphs' long ears made elves' look understated. She wore an earpiece in her left, a black plastic bulb with a small blue light, and seemed entirely too perky for the late hour.

"Did they call you in to babysit us?" I asked.

"No, don't worry, I'm currently on the overnight shift. And since the most immediate threat on our boards comes from Inade ti'Cren, this is no trouble."

"Analyst?" Cennis enquired as we rumbled upward.

"Assistant to the farseers," Keyne replied. "There's a whole cadre of us. Counsel, yes?"

She nodded. "Cennis Paf. Our lead, Remari Houn," she continued, pointing to the other counselor, "and this would be our witness—"

"Oh, I know who *this* is," Keyne interrupted with a conspiratorial grin.

"You do?" I asked, surprised.

Her smile widened. "It's not only the directors who are attached to Floodtide. I've been involved with this matter for a *very* long time." Giving me a once-over, she added, "I see a lot of Caradin there. The director used to bring him in when he was a little boy, and he'd steal my candy. *Such* a scamp."

It was, I recalled, more challenging to tell a nymph's age than it was to discern their gender, and Keyne had to be older than anyone else in the elevator.

We disembarked on a floor that wouldn't have looked out of place at a nicer hotel, and Keyne led us down a carpeted hallway lined with doors. She paused beside one, then used her bracelet to unlock it and opened it wide. "Ms. Paf, this should be comfortable, but if not, please call me. The phone in the room has already been programmed to ring me directly."

Cennis squeezed past her and flipped on the lights, revealing a high-top table and a low bed big enough to sleep half a defensive line. But what really caught my attention was the wide window, through which I could see the lights of Beukal. "Uh…I thought the walls were solid," I said. "Where did that window come from?"

Keyne laughed. "It's only illusion. We use that throughout the facility—it's more secure without glass to consider, but since hiding out in a windowless building suits few of us, we have a workaround. This way, please."

The next room she opened looked more like a standard suite, and she assured Remari that the bathroom had been stocked with toiletries in case the team sent to her house forgot the essentials. With the counselors settled, Keyne selected a room halfway down the corridor, another comfortable suite. "I'd be happy to arrange a fourth room," she said, giving Yven and me a knowing smirk, "but the director suggested you two might feel safer in a shared space."

"This is lovely," I replied, and Yven nodded. "Thank

you."

"Of course. Again, call me if you need anything," she said, leaving Yven and me to haul our baggage inside.

Once we'd dropped our gear in the sitting area, I flopped onto the generous bed, and Yven joined me with a sigh. We lay there together for a moment, staring up at the ceiling light, until I murmured, "Did that actually just happen?"

"I think so, yeah." He sounded distant, almost dazed.

The silence stretched between us while we processed that information.

"So," said Yven, "Rose ti'Dana."

"Weird, isn't it?"

"*Different*, but not a bad thing."

"Does this mean we can go public now?"

I caught a slightly hysteric note in his laughter. "If you still want to be with someone like me—"

"*Yven*." I rolled over and glared at him until he met my eyes. "I love you. Nothing has changed about that. And I'm pretty confident that we got a go-ahead tonight, so...I mean, unless you think your parents would throw a fit..."

"If I brought home a main-line ti'Dana to meet my parents, the last thing they would do would be to throw a fit."

"Even one with an asterisk?"

He kissed me as we lay there on the borrowed bed. "What *asterisk*? Lord ti'Dana said you're in, and no one can take that away."

"I mean, I don't exactly look the part..."

"You say that, but when you stand next to him...even if your features are a little different, you have the Hall's coloration."

I grinned. "A *little* different?"

"The important bits are accounted for," he replied, and kissed me again. "And for what it's worth, I find the whole package very...*very*...sexy."

"Hmm. Just a random question, but how thick do you

suppose the walls are on this floor?"

"Probably thick enough, I'd say."

I slid closer and kissed him deeply, feeling his breath quicken in time with mine, but pulled away and rolled off the bed before his hands could migrate beneath my shirt. "Let me hang up my suit first," I said. "And since Pars went to the trouble of putting your robe in a garment bag, don't you think that should go in the closet, too?"

Yven sat up and folded his arms. "Rosie, do you recall that I've actually studied magic?"

"Yeah…"

"I can get the wrinkles out in the morning. Promise."

"Ooh. That *is* sexy," I murmured, and gestured at the light switch until the room went dark.

The assistant who took over for Keyne woke us with a call at six a.m., and though I wanted nothing more than to curl up under the covers with Yven, I dragged myself out of bed to take the first shower. As it was my fault we were there in the first place, I figured that was the least I could do.

By the time I emerged with my wet hair in a turban, Yven had called to investigate breakfast possibilities, and according to the assistant, a tray was on the way. "I'm beginning to rethink my career path," he joked as he fiddled with the coffeemaker. "DPP certainly doesn't do room service." Watching as I exchanged my second towel for my pajamas, he asked, "Do you want to fix your hair? Surely there's a hairdryer in here…"

"It's in the cabinet under the sink," I replied, "and I'll do it once you've showered. A little air drying won't hurt it." After kissing his cheek, I started prepping the pair of white ceramic mugs waiting for us on paper doilies. Whatever else could be said for DOI, their hospitality left no room for complaint. "Go wash away your stench. I'll have this ready when you come out."

"My stench?" he said, feigning hurt.

"Uh-huh," I replied, and kissed his neck. "Don't know how your poor orchids stand it."

My giggle broke the moment, and he turned to kiss me properly. "Might put extra wrinkles in your suit, just for that," he said.

"You wouldn't."

He pretended to consider it. "Yeah, you're right. Don't drink all the coffee before I come back, eh?"

The brew cycle finished as Yven's shower singing commenced, and I laughed to myself. The poor boy really couldn't carry a tune, and he knew it, so the only time I'd ever heard him sing was in the bathroom. He'd begun the off-key concerts in the last two weeks, and while I never brought them up, I took it as a sign that he was growing more comfortable with me as a roommate.

Or something more, now. I smiled as I poured the coffee. Yven's singing wasn't going to win him any prizes, but I found it endearing that he was jamming to Phil Collins while shampooing his hair.

When I heard a knock, I assumed breakfast had arrived and hurried to open the door. But instead of an assistant, I found Diriem standing in the hall, looking far more presentable than I did. "Uh…Lord ti'Dana," I said, stepping back from the threshold. "Hi. Is something wrong?"

"No, not at all," he hastily replied, then pointed toward the bathroom. "Bad time?"

"He'll be in there for a while. Want to come in?"

He accepted the invitation and took a seat at the little two-top table, and I glanced around the room for more drinkware. "I'd offer you coffee, but I don't know if I've got enough mugs…"

"Don't worry about it. And good morning, Rose."

I absently reached up and remembered that my towel turban was still in place. "Morning, sir. I do intend to dress up before leaving."

"I'd assumed as much," he replied with a curiously shy smile. "Will you join me?"

Snagging my coffee from the sidebar, I pulled out the other seat and tried to read him. If anything, he looked nervous. "Thank you for putting us up overnight. This place is great."

"My pleasure." He paused, listening, then chuckled as Yven inexpertly segued into "Sussudio." "Am I to understand that Agent ti'Ansha's strengths lie elsewhere?"

"Far, *far* elsewhere, but I didn't say that."

Diriem waited while I sipped my coffee, then cleared his throat. "Rose, I...I wanted to apologize. For everything. None of this has been fair to you, and it wasn't fair to your mother, and I—"

"I read the letter, I get it," I interjected. "You didn't have a better option."

"But that doesn't mean you haven't been harmed. You should have been educated here, trained properly...or at least made aware that someone besides Fradin's sister cares about you. And I do," he insisted, looking me in the eye. "Caradin wasn't the only one who watched you grow up long before you were born."

Unsure of how to answer that, I nodded.

He sighed softly. "But just because I know you doesn't mean the reverse is true, and in your mind, I'm probably the ass who walked out on Jocelyn. I deserve that. If you want nothing to do with me, I completely understand." As my brow scrunched, he added, "The acknowledgement remains, regardless. Like I said last night, I've always considered you part of the family. As I did your mother, though I did a poor job of showing it."

"Granddad said not to blame you for abandoning her."

"He was more forgiving than I deserve. I like to tell myself that if I could have brought Jocelyn to the Pactlands and publicly acknowledged her without cutting her life even shorter than it was, I'd have done so. But..." His voice trailed off.

"Would have been a scandal, right?" I said.

"That should never matter. She was a wonderful child…" He paused, his face twitching. "And she adored you. Your parents were so proud. I hope you know that."

I sipped my coffee as I willed my tears to dry before they could fall.

"Anyway," he continued, his voice husky, "you're acknowledged, Rose. No strings attached, as it were. But, um…if you'd be willing to give me a chance, I'd like to find a place in your life. On your terms."

When I reached out across the table, he took my hand. "I'd like that very much, Lord ti'Dana. Thank you."

He squeezed my hand before releasing me. "It's I who thank you, little one. And, uh…you needn't be so formal," he said, relaxing a degree. "If you'd prefer it, that's fine," he quickly added, "but you don't need to address me by my title."

I cocked my head as the shower turned off. "What should I call you, then?"

"Well…Diriem is my name, and you're welcome to use it, but, uh…" He hesitated, then quietly said, "Jocelyn always called me Pop. Perhaps it's far too soon for that to be up for consideration—"

"Pop," I murmured, and smiled at his anxious floundering. "Yeah, I could do that. And I'm Rosie."

"Are you certain? I won't take offense…"

I reached for him again, and his grip was tighter that time. "It's nice to finally meet you. And I know you didn't want to walk away from Mom. Granddad told me."

"Those tapes?"

"I listened to every minute of them," I said, then smirked. "He said you can't dance."

Diriem—*Pop*—made a face. "He's not wrong. I haven't exactly been practicing since Learil died, but…"

When his voice drifted off, I turned and found Yven dripping at the edge of the bathroom, a towel around his waist and his eyes huge. "Your coffee's ready, sweetie," I said as he flushed scarlet.

Before Yven could explain himself, Pop rose and said, "You probably won't be called for the first day of trial—I've seen my share of cases, and counsel should begin with the older evidence about Silver. Pateme will almost certainly be called, but I'd imagine they'll save you for tomorrow, at least. Rest here today, and phone for an assistant when you get hungry. Your breakfast should be up shortly."

"Can we not go watch?" I asked.

He shook his head. "The goal is for potential witnesses to come before the tribunal with no knowledge of what other witnesses have said. However..." He shrugged. "You're a farseer, are you not?"

I smiled.

"We'll have an escort sent for you when you're needed, and counsel will give warning to let you freshen up. I'll be in my office in case of emergency," he said as he turned to go, then paused at the door and glanced back at Yven, who clutched his towel as if his life depended on it. "Young man, before you come to the trial, might I suggest a robe?"

"Sir," he squeaked, and Pop saw himself out.

CHAPTER 19

After Yven recovered, the promised meal arrived, and we settled in for a long day of vegetation. Sightseeing was out of the question, the whole point in bringing us to DOI having been to keep us secure and alive, but the room came with a television and a decent selection of channels—including HBO. That an intelligence agency full of sorcerers and elves could find a way to help themselves to human networks didn't shock me, though I had to wonder what they were watching in their downtime.

We found a local news program, which devoted several minutes to discussing the trial. A naga identified as the program's legal analyst appeared for an interview on the steps of the Tribunal building, and as he fielded questions from the studio, he offered tidbits about the case as his serpentine tail coiled beneath him. "The charges leveled against Lord ti'Cren are *staggering*," he said at one point, "and while his innocence is, of course, presumed at this point, the tribunal has taken unusual precautions."

"How so?" asked the presenter. She remained seated behind the desk, but her impressive pair of curling horns marked her as a faun.

"Well, you know, we'd ordinarily be discussing the scheduled witnesses for a trial like this," he replied. "But the tribunal has refused to release any witness list, and what I'm hearing from defense counsel is that some witnesses have been identified to them only by title. We *do* know that Pateme ti'Tam and Kabno Erenani, the DPP and DOL directors, are scheduled to appear today, but plenty of other witnesses have been identified as, say, 'Agent 1,' 'Detective 2,' and so forth."

She frowned at the camera. "Why the secrecy?"

"We don't have a firm answer to that, Kym—no one involved has agreed to discuss the trial with us yet—but the pretrial filings present a strong case for a pattern of witness intimidation. The evidence suggests that people who agree to talk about the mysterious 'Silver' quickly turn up dead."

"Troubling information."

"Quite. Apparently," he added, "even the farseer on this case is anonymous at this point."

The program promised updates throughout the day, but I decided to go to the source. While Yven sat at the table with his long-neglected computer, looking over the many files he'd left untouched since March, I stretched out and focused on Inade.

The tribunal looked a bit different than the courtrooms I'd seen on TV, but the main parts were easy enough to identify. The room was fairly modern in design, a domed space with cream-colored walls and a handful of skylights. Just past the double doors were two banks of half a dozen curving benches, which were packed that morning. A balcony above offered similar seating and was likewise stuffed with the media, the families, and the merely curious. Proceeding toward the front, a delicate piece of stonework carved with a wooded motif separated the audience from the action. Two draped tables arced on either side of the room beyond the divider, the left for DOL and the right for Inade and his counsel, a pair of elves who regarded the DOL team with barely disguised contempt. Completing the inner circle was an elevated stone table—the forest theme continued in its design— behind which sat an elderly troll. After hearing him speak, I guessed he was male, though I couldn't be certain. His skin was so violet as to be nearly black, making his shock of white hair all the more startling, and he'd decorated the tips of his tusks with gold caps. His robe was deep blue and ornamented only by a line of gold braiding around the collar, a marked contrast to the elaborate robes the defense favored. To his right sat a sorcerer—an assistant, I gathered—while an empty chair remained at his left.

Peeking over a reporter's shoulder, I gleaned that the judge's name was The Scent of the Smoke of the Home Fire—or rather, that was the Pactish rendering of the Trollish, a language nearly impossible for anyone but a troll to pull off—but everyone seemed to refer to him simply as "Honored Smoke."

Inade seemed tenser than usual, much of which came through in the way he drummed his fingers on the tabletop. As for his opponents, Remari just smiled, while Cennis, whose black robe stretched over her tail and fell to about an inch above her hooves, watched the defense table in the same way that a lioness might consider a straggling baby zebra.

Scanning the audience, I didn't see Liventi or any of the ti'Cren siblings who had been charged—no surprise there—but I found Teolm up in the balcony, sitting beside Aunt Lily. On Pateme's instructions, I hadn't spoken to her since Charlottesville, and I wondered how many of the charges against her father came as a shock. She'd done her best to hide me from him—surely she knew that he could be dangerous—but had Fradin told her the truth about Inade before his death?

I didn't want to get DOL in trouble, so I limited myself to the occasional peek at the proceedings, no more than ten minutes or so at a time. That first day was a parade of agents and detectives, starting with Pateme, who laid out the history of Project Floodtide and what it had uncovered. Kabno and several of her detectives testified about DOL's involvement, building the case against Silver. But with every witness, Inade's counsel were able to pull forth a damning fact: they had no evidence directly tying Inade to Silver's misdeeds.

"We expected this," Cennis told us over dinner in Remari's room that evening. The ravenous counselors had exchanged their robes for pajamas before the late meal—in Cennis's case, a T-shirt and a ratty green bathrobe that left most of her equine half bare. "DOL and DPP have had a case against Silver for decades, and we wanted the history before the tribunal at the outset. The trick tomorrow will be making the connection to Inade," she continued, pointing her fork at me, "which is where you come in."

"Not nervous, are you?" Remari teased. "I'll be gentle, and defense counsel are more bluster than bite."

"They're feeling good after today," said Cennis. "That's the trick: let them think they're winning, then spring the trap."

"If you say so," I mumbled into my pasta. I didn't know why it was purple, and I didn't bother asking.

Around noon Tuesday, word came via DOI assistant that I'd be called to testify after lunch. Suddenly having lost my appetite, I dressed with care and came out of the bathroom to find Yven in a black robe, a conservative choice for the occasion. He had me do a slow spin as he checked for wrinkles, promising that he'd teach me the trick, then held my hand as an assistant escorted us down to the parking garage and the waiting DOL van.

Three more DOL agents met us at the Tribunal building and hustled us up to the top floor, then into a windowless room away from the crowd milling in the corridor. "Media," one of the agents explained with distaste. "Don't worry about them. We'll stay in here where it's safe until counsel needs you."

As it turned out, I was the second witness to be called after the midday break. When my entourage escorted me into the room, I almost froze in my tracks—even having seen the place with farsight, I was unaccustomed to finding the audience's eyes fixed on me—but Yven gave my hand a last squeeze and leaned close to whisper, "Just breathe. I'll be back here."

I hoped my smile didn't seem too queasy as he stepped out of the aisle. Taking a deep breath, I headed for the front of the room, tried not to look at Inade's reddening face, and paused with the agents before the stone divider.

"Your witness?" the judge asked the DOL table.

Remari stood and dipped her head in acknowledgement. "Honored Smoke, the Division of Laws presents our farseer—"

One of Inade's counsel leapt to his feet before she could finish. "Defense objects, sir! This woman is no farseer."

The judge's thick eyebrows rose. "Your basis, counselor?"

"I've been coming before tribunals for three hundred years, sir. I know every certified farseer on sight. *She* is not among their number. Whatever testimony she could offer in that capacity is therefore improper and should not be entertained."

He'd barely managed to smirk at Remari in triumph when I heard a voice behind me: "If I may approach, Honored Smoke?"

Turning, I saw Pop standing at the end of one of the benches, perfectly calm.

"I was wondering why you'd come today, old boy," the judge replied, smiling, and beckoned with two clawed fingers. "Please. The tribunal recognizes Lord ti'Dana in his...official capacity?"

"Precisely."

As Pop came down the aisle to join me, I was pleased to catch the first glimmer of uncertainty on the faces of Inade's counsel.

"This," said Pop, placing a hand on my shoulder, "is Rose. As of Sunday evening, she's certified by the Division of Intelligence. You would have found her in the registry," he added, glancing at the defense table, "had you bothered to look in the last two days."

The judge grunted as one of the counselors frantically reached for his computer. "Orientation?"

"Present. She's unique in that regard. Rose's farsight shows her current events."

"Mm. Let's give counsel a moment to check the registry, shall we?"

I could tell the instant they found me in DOI's database. The two counselors whispered to each other, while Inade, who had been nearly scarlet with indignation, began to pale.

"Is this some sort of joke?" the lead counselor finally managed to ask Pop. "The girl is listed as—"

"Rose ti'Dana? Yes."

"But *she*—"

"Is my great-granddaughter. And the defendant's," he added, then waited a moment for the susurrus of the crowd to subside. "Fradin ti'Cren had a son, Henry, after he took the draught," he said, a faint smile playing on his lips. "My son, Caradin, shared Fradin's fate"—the murmuring intensified again—"but he had a daughter, Jocelyn. She and Henry found each other, and Rose is their only child...and utterly unaffected by the draught."

The judge's brow furrowed. "Your son..."

"Fell for a human woman, yes. He hasn't been hiding in his room for the last seventy years. They were very happy in the time they had together, and the draught killed him far too soon."

Smoke's face softened at the news. "I'm so sorry. You never told me, Diriem..."

"I told almost no one. It's nothing personal," said Pop. "Farsight cautioned that if word of Jocelyn and Henry reached the wrong ears, they'd never live to see fifty, and neither would their daughter. I took the necessary precautions."

The judge's gaze slid toward Inade as he considered that. "So...a half-blooded ti'Dana, is she?"

"DOL's blood test says her elven inheritance is closer to ninety percent, but that's of no consequence. Rose is acknowledged and certified, and if memory serves, only the latter is necessary for the tribunal to hear her testimony."

"Honored Smoke," lead defense counsel began, but the judge held up a hand to cut his protest short.

"I'll hear what she has to say," he announced, and beckoned me past the stone divider. "Ms. ti'Dana, take the chair to my left."

Briefly, I locked eyes with Inade as I passed, but his impotent fury only buoyed my spirits. I came around the high bench and perched on the witness seat, and a sorcerer in a red robe approached me. "Do you swear to give truthful testimony?" she asked.

"Yes," I said.

"Then you have nothing to fear," she replied, and murmured. A bright blue light seemed to explode around me, and when it cleared, she smiled and whispered, "It's always a little disorienting the first time."

I smiled back at her, then cut my eyes to the balcony and found Aunt Lily, who was again sitting with her brother. While I couldn't clearly make out her expression from that distance, she didn't seem angry.

Remari's voice drew me back to the task at hand. "What is your name?"

"Rose ti'Dana," I said, bracing myself for pain that didn't come.

"Are you known by any other name?"

"Yes. Rose Lea Thorn."

"And what is the origin of that name?"

"'Thorn' is a decent variant of 'ti'Cren' in English," I explained. "It's what my grandfather used, and my dad after him, and my parents gave me that name."

"So you do claim kinship to Hall ti'Cren?" Remari asked.

"I do. Ti'Cren through one grandfather, ti'Dana

through the other."

Remari paused, giving the reporters in the room a chance to catch up. "And your grandmothers? What Halls?"

"None. They were human."

"Let's change topics," she continued. "Your certification as a farseer is for which orientation?"

"Present."

"And what does that mean?"

"That I can look outside myself, focus on other people, and see what they're doing in real time," I replied.

"Ms. ti'Dana, are you familiar with the blinding potion?"

"I've never used it," I said, "and I couldn't tell you how to brew it, but I've seen its effects."

Though I kept my focus on Remari, I noticed from the corner of my eye that defense counsel were tensing up.

"And what are the effects of the blinding potion? From your perspective, I mean."

"Well...if I want to find someone with farsight, I usually focus on their face. Something easy for me to recall. I'm an artist—visuals tend to stick with me," I explained. "When the focus clicks in, I see the person like I'm standing there. They can't sense me, but I can see and hear everything that's going on around them. But when they're protected by the blinding potion, I can't get to that focus point. When I concentrate, it's like I'm walking through a white-out blizzard."

"So you *have* tried to find someone who was protected?" Remari asked.

I nodded. "Yes. Last winter, DPP asked me to help locate a missing agent who turned out to be working for Silver. He had been embedded in a group of producers, all of whom were protected by the blinding potion...except for the human with them. I'm not sure how she got attached to the group, but she was wide open."

I glanced at Inade in time to catch his eye twitch.

"While I was able to see her, everyone around her who had been protected appeared as a white blotch. I couldn't hear or see any details, but I could tell that they were present, if you follow."

Remari looked down at her notes, but it was merely an act. We'd run this part of the script. "You said that the Division of Plants and Potions requested your assistance. Are you affiliated with DOI?"

"No."

"Then how did DPP come to you?"

"I'm from Richmond," I said, and glanced at the judge. "It's near the Oilville portal, if that helps."

"I'm aware," he rumbled.

Turning back to Remari, I continued, "I didn't know anything about the Pactlands until last year. My great-aunt was attacked and fled her nursery, and when I went out to keep an eye on the place, I crossed paths with DPP. She had thought that DPP would find a way to make me go home, but, uh...guess I'm stubborn," I said, shrugging. "It was explained to me in pretty short order that my great-aunt's an elf. I hadn't known that was an option."

"And your great-aunt is..."

"Lily ti'Cren. Liliol," I amended. "She never told me about any of this. Anyway, during the investigation, the agents realized that I'd been doodling locations in the Pactlands, and that's how I learned I was farsighted. When Aunt Lily came home, she told me about my ti'Dana connection, which...explains a lot, really."

"So DPP asked for your assistance after that?"

"Twice. The director offered me some basic training," I said, leaving out the part about Yven's unauthorized tutelage.

"Do you know why?"

"I have guesses," I admitted. "It's my understanding that farseers are rare, so maybe he thought my talent shouldn't go to waste. Maybe it had something to do with Floodtide. Or maybe he just felt bad that I'd never been taught anything—he was fond of my grandfather."

"And to be clear," said Remari, "are you related to Director ti'Tam?"

"Yes. He's my great-grandmother's brother."

She nodded and once again riffled through her papers for a few seconds, giving that information a chance to settle in. "Ms. ti'Dana, do you know if he takes the blinding potion?"

"He does. Or he has," I hastily added, unaware of how sensitive the spell on me might be. "I can't say when he last took it."

"Have you ever attempted to locate him with farsight?"

"Yes."

"How did that go?"

"Not well at first. I got the usual whiteout. But I followed another person into his office, and as I watched, I began to see through the director's protection. I thought maybe the spell was degrading."

"Is there any particular reason *why* you were spying on Director ti'Tam?"

We'd discussed this, and I knew the question had to be asked, but I still squirmed in my chair. "Because I was angry. He'd stopped my lessons and cut off my communication with my, um…dear friend, and I was hoping to study him in order to find a way to…have that undone."

Remari's mouth twitched. "Leverage, could we say?"

"Sure."

"Now, you weren't a certified farseer at the time, were you?"

"No."

"Have you had any formal training as a farseer?"

"No," I repeated. "Self-study, more or less."

"So…has anyone ever made clear to you the code of ethics that DOI employs?"

I shook my head. "It hasn't been spelled out for me, no. But look, I'm not proud of what I did," I said in a rush. "The director's protected for a reason. I was just...desperate."

Her voice softened. "Why did he stop your lessons?"

"Because one of his agents and I fell in love, and he didn't want a repeat of my grandfather," I murmured. "I wasn't formally acknowledged at the time, and so he thought having me around would be too much temptation."

"The agent in question would be the aforementioned 'dear friend,' then?" she asked.

"Yes."

The room rumbled again, and Remari waited for calm. "Putting aside questions of propriety for now, were you ever able to clearly see and hear Director ti'Tam via farsight?"

"Yes. I can work through the blinding protection on him pretty quickly now."

"And how is that possible?"

Barely shifting my gaze toward Inade, I replied, "Because blood connection is a weakness in the system. The blinding potion and spell work against almost anyone except farseers in the subject's family. As the director and I are kin, I can punch through."

Inade's jaw began to sag, and a look of horrified comprehension crossed his face.

"Ms. ti'Dana," asked Remari, "were you ever asked to use your talent to search for Silver?"

"Yes, back in late March."

"Did you locate anyone?"

"Defense objects," Inade's lead counsel protested, going to his feet. "The girl—"

"Is certified, and I *will* hear her," the judge snapped, then looked at me. "You may answer the question."

"I did locate someone," I told Remari. "I was offered nothing—no possible names, no descriptions, just 'Silver' and what I knew of his doings—but my farsight continued to lead me in only one direction."

"And to whom were you led?"

I pointed to the defense table. "To my great-grandfather. And although he also used blinding protection, it wasn't difficult for me to look through."

As the audience's rumbling reached a new pitch, Remari calmly lifted my stack of sketches and notes from a box beneath her table. "Ms. ti'Dana, I'd like to go through a few exhibits with you."

"Of course," I said, and looked at Inade, whose complexion was veering toward chalk. "That's fine by me."

Inade's trial ended late on Friday afternoon, its fifth day. Once I was excused from the witness seat, I'd spent much of the remainder of the trial hanging out on a bench with Yven—well, Yven and half a dozen armed DOL personnel—watching agent after agent confirm my findings and report on the drugs seized. Defense counsel had done their best, but the pile of evidence against Inade was tall and damning, and by the end, there was no reasonable doubt that he and Silver were the same man.

The judge sentenced him to three hundred years' incarceration—three centuries in a DOL facility with his talent dampened to uselessness. It would, said the judge, give Inade an opportunity to reflect upon his choices, and the physical labor he performed in an agricultural district far from Beukal would benefit the Pactlands as a whole. By then, Inade had slumped over the table, but the judge wasn't finished. "As you can no longer competently lead Hall ti'Cren," he said, staring down at Inade, "it's my obligation to pass the title to the next heir. Your eldest child is of age and competent, and so Teolm ti'Cren will assume the title and take possession of the Hall's resources."

Inade had barely been led from the room before a group of people in formal robes swarmed the barrier at the front of the room, vying for a word with the DOL team.

"Counsel for the codefendants, I believe," Pateme whispered to me. "No one has been eager to cooperate to this point, but with Inade convicted…"

"Do you think DOL will bargain?" I asked.

He made a face. "You know, Cennis seemed to enjoy herself entirely too much with Inade's witnesses, but I suspect they'll make an arrangement. All of those counselors are throwing themselves at DOL because they know what they're up against." He elbowed me in the side. "Well done, Rosie."

I grinned back at him. "Suppose I should apologize for stalking you, huh?"

"Just don't make a habit of it," he replied, rolling his eyes, then brushed a speck of lint off my suit jacket, which by then was in its fourth day of service. "We're going to need to find a robe for you eventually."

"Hey, I'm getting my money's worth from this suit. These things aren't cheap," I groused.

"Yes, but it does attract a certain degree of attention."

Pateme had a point. Half of Tuesday's trial coverage had devolved into stories about me, the *unfortunate* secret of two of the Pactlands' most prominent Halls. On DOL's strong suggestion, I gave no interviews, and I didn't so much as go to the bathroom in the Tribunal building without an escort. Still, I'd seen myself in print and on the next morning's news, and the local program had even brought in a so-called expert in human fashion to break down my ensemble. Considering that it was the only outfit in my closet even vaguely appropriate for the tribunal, I was thankful that Yven knew a magical alternative to dry cleaning.

The director's phone beeped, and he frowned as he read the message. "Come with me, if you would," he said, and Yven and I followed him toward a quiet end of the room. I didn't know what was going on until I spotted Aunt Lily and Teolm slip down the side aisle toward us.

I lifted a hand in greeting as they neared, hoping Aunt

Lily wasn't about to disown me, and called, "Hi. Uh…"

She said nothing until she'd wrapped me in one of her rib-breaking hugs, then murmured, "That's my girl."

I pulled back enough to see her unmasked face, which was slowly beginning to become familiar to me. "Did you know about Inade?"

She nodded, her mouth a tight line. "Fradin told me everything, even if this one wouldn't confirm it," she said, pointing to Pateme. "Common sense alone would have counseled me to keep you hidden, but knowing what my father's capable of…" She hugged me again. "Well, at least he won't be bothering anyone for a while."

When she released me, I looked over her shoulder at her brother, who stood awkwardly by in a brown robe that probably cost far more than my suit had. "Lord ti'Cren."

He grimaced. "Teolm, please," he muttered, and offered me a sad smile. "Wish you'd said something back at the house, Rose. I…greatly miss my brother."

"I'm sorry about all of, uh…" I flopped one hand lamely in the direction of the high bench. "This."

"As am I, but more disgusted than anything. And grateful that I didn't listen when Father tried to nag me into the family business."

"How's Mafora?" I hadn't seen her all week, nor any of the other siblings beside the two with us.

Teolm and Aunt Lily shared a look. "She's been better," he said. "Upset, though I'm afraid that's not because of what Father has done, but rather because of what's about to happen to the Hall's reputation. And having the circumstances of her marriage discussed before the tribunal isn't going to help her social life."

"Most of our siblings are whining," Aunt Lily added. "And they wonder why I stay away…"

I thought of Dania, Jomin's wife, who'd seemed quite content to sit around the mansion, enjoy the family's prominence, and badmouth her sister-in-law for running a greenhouse in Virginia. "What's going to happen to them?" I asked Teolm.

"I'm not throwing them into the street, if that's what you were thinking," he replied. "The ones who aren't facing incarceration, I mean. And for *those* three, I don't mind if their families stay. The mansion's far too large for one person. Now, if Lily wanted to move home—"

"Don't even think it," she said, albeit fondly.

"I know, I know." Turning back to me, he said, "Incidentally, I found what was left of your family portrait. Father locked the guest room after you left, and I assume he's the one who put a fist through the painting, but that was quite good."

I grinned. "Thanks. I'd be happy to redo your portion, if you want. Maybe with that giant anophala flower of yours in the background."

"I might take you up on that," he said with a soft chuckle, then sobered. "Look, I'm not going to lie to you—the mansion is probably not the place you want to be right now. That said, if you're going to be around, there are plenty of other locations where we might get acquainted."

"Would you tell me about Fradin?"

At that, Teolm flashed a brief but genuine smile. "Absolutely."

Aunt Lily walked out with him, promising to return to catch up with me, and I watched the crowd mill about as the reporters finished their notes and made quick calls. Leaning against a bench, I looked at Pateme and folded my arms. "By the way, I'm going to need you to keep my portal credentials intact."

One eyebrow rose. "Leaving so soon?"

"There's the *slight* issue of the business I've abandoned and a backlog of commissions I need to complete."

"Fair, I suppose." He hesitated, then asked, "Do you see yourself in Richmond in the long term? Ordinarily, taking up residence outside the Pactlands requires permission and oversight, but given your particular circumstances…"

"To be frank, I haven't really gotten that far," I replied.

He grunted. "What I was thinking is that if you were amenable to relocation, there could be a job opening at DPP."

At that, I traded looks with Yven, who shrugged. "Thought you didn't hire anyone under forty."

"Well, not *usually*, but we could bring you aboard now and have you up to speed by that time. You need tutoring, and I believe Agent ti'Mal would be willing to have you back. We could find someone else to work on the less physical side of magic, teach you to brew, acquaint you with greenhouse safety basics—"

"Or," said Pop, who'd worked his way across the room to join our trio, "there's the DOI route. Rosie is a farseer, after all," he told Pateme. "We do tend to attract them."

"And they have room service," Yven muttered.

I nudged him in the side. "You've got Maya's café on the ground floor, plus real windows. What are you complaining about?"

"Of course," Pop continued as Pateme looked for a counter-proposal, "DPP might not be a bad place to begin. I believe Rosie has proven that she could be an asset in the field."

"Very much so, yes," Pateme quickly replied.

"And she already knows people within the agency. That said," he added, holding my gaze, "if you want a spot at DOI, say the word. And whatever you choose, you *will* be training with an experienced farseer."

Faced with two expectant directors, I struggled for a response. "That's really nice of you both," I managed, "but I do still have my life in Richmond, and…you know…"

Pop patted my shoulder. "Breathe. This doesn't need to be decided today. Take care of your obligations, and after that…consider us, yes?"

"But we could start training now," Pateme suggested. "You didn't see what she did to Inade—"

"Oh, believe me, I've watched that play out for years," Pop replied with a smirk. "*Satisfying*. And Rosie, he's right. You've got a strong talent, and you've already lost a few months of work because *someone*"—he glared at Pateme—"overreacted. Would you be opposed to coming back for training?"

"I think I could make that happen," I said, "just as long as one of you secures my credentials."

"I've already handled it," said Pop. "And, uh, let me know when you're coming over, eh?" he added, passing me a slip of paper with his number scrawled across it. "If you're not too busy."

Smiling, I tucked it into my purse for safekeeping. "Any interest in seeing my place sometime?"

He brightened at the offer. "Absolutely. And you? My house isn't quite as opulent as the ti'Crens'," he cautioned, "but it would be amply large if you wanted a place to stay while exploring your options."

"I'd like that."

"Just say when," he replied, then nodded to Yven and slipped off before the eager reporter hustling our way could ask for a comment.

The week that followed was, in a word, *bizarre*.

After spending two months either on the run or in the Pactlands, just rummaging through my own closets felt weird. The refrigerator could have been worse—having learned my lesson, I'd chucked the most perishable items before leaving with Inade—but every surface was in desperate want of dusting, I needed two trips to retrieve my mail from Mr. Eddie, and I called my lawn service to beg for help with my weed-choked bushes.

And while it was lovely being back in my bed, I missed having Yven beside me. The house seemed huge, and it echoed, and I wasn't sleeping well. Yven had offered to stay when he drove me home and jumpstarted my neglected Subaru's battery, but we both knew he was long overdue for an appearance in the office, and I insisted that I'd be fine.

I was, really. I tidied and changed the sheets and bought groceries and actually *painted*, for a change of pace, and I told my friends in Carytown about my imaginary cousin's medical woes. I even went out for drinks on Wednesday, trying to slot myself back into my old social scene, though the exercise felt akin to attempting to perform a dance I'd half forgotten. When Yven texted that night and asked if he could come over and take me to dinner on Friday, I gladly cleared my calendar.

On the appointed evening, he showed up at my house wearing a sport coat, then hung out in the hallway as I hastily changed into a less casual dress. "Sorry," I called through the crack in the door, "you didn't tell me you want to go *out* out."

"I'm actually paying this time, and you're owed a nice meal on someone else's tab." He stepped back as I emerged, took in my go-to little black dress and green heels, and grinned. "Well, now *I'm* underdressed."

"Hardly." I looped my arm around his and let him lead me to his Mustang.

He'd found a lovely seafood restaurant, the sort of place with floating tea lights on the tables and black linen napkins, and insisted we have a proper date night. The wine was perfect, my scallops were amazing, and I realized as we talked and laughed how much I'd missed him after only a week apart. I told him about the portraits I'd finally finished, and he warned me that Pars would be calling to coax me into accepting the job at DPP. "Gentle Breeze says hello," he added, "and something tells me she'll be joining Pars's effort if it doesn't seem to be working, so lock your doors."

After dessert, Yven drove me home, and we lingered in his car in the driveway. "Do you want to come in?" I asked. "Coffee? Something more exciting? You weren't planning to drive back tonight, were you?"

"Would you mind if I stayed?"

"Of course not! And hey," I murmured, "play your cards right, and you could sleep in *my* room, for a change."

I started to get out, but he said, "Hold on, Rosie. Before we go inside…"

"Yeah?" I asked, closing the car door. "What's up?"

He waited until the dome light went out, then took a deep breath and slowly released it. "I love you."

"I love you, too," I said, cupping one hand against his cheek in the darkness, and leaned over to kiss him. "I've *missed* you."

"Likewise. Rosie…I realize that things are complicated with you right now," he said, picking up steam, "and you've got quite a bit going on, and this may be the absolute worst time to bring this up, and honestly, I don't know how I'm even daring to do this, but I love you, and I want to be with you, and if you would consider having me—"

"Yven," I interrupted, stunned, "are you trying to propose?"

"I'm sorry, I—"

"*Wait.* Are you?"

"Uh…" He nervously cleared his throat. "Yes?"

I laughed aloud, then kissed him again, long and deeply. "This isn't just a ploy to get me back to Beukal, is it?" I teased.

"If you want to stay here, I'll relocate. I'll figure something out—"

"First things first," I said, and opened my door to trigger the light again. "My answer is yes, silly boy. Now, do you want to take this party inside? Figure out how we're going to scandalize the Pactlands together? Make up for the absolute drought of the last week while the oysters are still working?"

His eyebrows rose. "I thought that was just a myth."

"Maybe, but play along, okay?"

He really did have the best dimples when he beamed, even masked. "Yes, ma'am," he replied, and stepped out into the night to walk me home.

ACKNOWLEDGEMENTS

Thank you so much for reading! While this is the final volume of *Hall of Thorns*, the story will continue in *The Wild Hunt*, an upcoming trilogy. I hope you'll come along for the next chapter! (And if you enjoyed this one, reviews are *very* helpful and always appreciated.)

Once again, I'm grateful to Adam Domby for his suggestions and to the Novel Chicks, who've read far too many of my drafts.

And yes, here's to you, Mom and Dad.

ABOUT THE AUTHOR

When not writing fiction, Ash Fitzsimmons is an appellate attorney and an unrepentant car singer.

Find her online:
www.ashfitzsimmons.com

www.ingramcontent.com/pod-product-compliance
Lightning Source LLC
Chambersburg PA
CBHW020249200626
46816CB00001BA/198